R D. Thomas had tl
Pacific Northwest; the land of
capped mountains. All of which ...... daily reminders that the
contrivances of man stood pale alongside the beauty of nature.

His college years did not lead him to a literary field. A degree in engineering and a career in the world of "ones" and "zeros" have been his means of support. The work has taken him to numerous countries on various continents and he has never been disappointed with any of his travels.

Yet as many of us know, ones path in life has many twists with different possibilities presented around every turn. A notion chanced upon while in youthful solitude, finally found its way to paper as a two paragraph synopses for a story. Further ruminations generated an index of ideas for a book which was eventually brought to fruition by way of one full chapter of prose. Those first attempts at writing were many months of frustrated typing as an engineering discipline does not readily lend itself to the craft of weaving words.

But persistence proved an excellent friend and after five years of effort a novel was completed. The manuscript was well received by family members - an audience who try their hardest not to hurt the feelings of a relative. The next group of unbiased readers was his good natured neighbors. They too, were extremely polite with their critiques and encouraged publishing as the next logical step. And so, Reiben finally found his way to print.

R. D. Thomas currently lives in Europe with his wife, two youngest children, and a dog that is full of silliness with a smidgen of canine sense.

Book 1

Reiben the Se:

Lost to Lands Unknown

R D Thomas

ISBN: 978-0-9570363-8-3

eBook ISBN: 978-0-9570363-6-9

Published by Brodie Books

Acknowledgements

There is tremendous joy writing a story, but no tale is completed by the efforts of the author alone; such works are always collaborations. This is especially true for the first-time novelist. In Reiben's case he was an idea, a shadow really, which weaved in and out of my thoughts with no impetus to begin. His journey and mine, started with my wife's gentle prodding. She believed that this little fellow was interesting enough to find his way to paper. A clumsy first chapter followed and Reiben's adventures had begun.

After the initial prose, a grass roots effort ensued with assistance from a diverse group of individuals. Their busy lives had little extra time to assist an indie writer, but help they all did. These talented friends from America, Britain, and Holland contributed greatly to the story and the text is most certainly better for the international critique. My heartfelt gratitude to the following people:

Catriona Thomas-Brodie - your unwavering support, knowledge of "the old ways", and Scottish tenacity have been Reiben's midwife and my compass to a new path in life.

To our children - I am the parent but you have been my teachers in all that is important in life. The story is woven with pieces from all of you.

Sue Pine - you received the cumbersome first draft and molded it on your editor's wheel. After considerable effort, a readable manuscript was returned.

Dr. Dave Kelly - you brought your extensive academic rigor to bear and improved the diction, cadence, and metaphoric message of the book.

Paige McCullife-Cadice - your keen Colorado eyes found grammatical errors and story irregularities the rest of us overlooked.

Fares Zoghlami – you are a student whose artistic gifts far exceed your years. The design of the book's cover, inside map, and compass are simply outstanding.

Dr. William Brittain – your steadfast integrity, experience, and technical prowess have been invaluable along the way. Thank you for bringing an Ice Age Reiben into the twenty-first century.

Map

Contents

1

A Child is Born

All was pleasant and peaceful, as it should be on the island of Rune, with one exception; Munsi and his wife Rissa were having their first child. The excited couple were older parents, but the extra time had not improved their preparation. Munsi had discovered that children come into this world following a schedule only they knew and no amount of fretting would hasten the arrival. Presently, the best the father-to-be could manage was to pace his modest home in anticipation.

For the past day and a half, the expectant parent had had very little sleep and even less to eat. He'd completed every household chore, mended the fishing nets, walked the island at a hurried pace (shaking the hand of all he met), worrying continuously and still there was no birth. Munsi's anxiety proved to be of no use to himself or his wife and his mind remained in a thick stew of apprehension.

After a time of walking to and fro, he found their cozy abode too confining and decided to venture outside once more. Munsi needed to pause and spend time in reflection. The Se people were known for their ability to compose themselves during times of stress and since this afternoon was particularly difficult, he chose the calming effect a sunset on the beach had to offer as his next destination.

The people who called the Se Atoll home were a distinctive group as each was quite similar in appearance: thin, of medium height, brown hair and smiling eyes which accented a comely face. Munsi was clean shaven and well versed in the use of his hands, as were all the men on the islands. Rissa, much the same as the other island women, was a village healer and keeper of the fields. Those on the isles would have said this couple fit in rather nicely. And in the manner of the other Se, Munsi and Rissa considered themselves fortunate to be

1

living on the isles as the world around them was far less civilized.

Viewed from the shores of the mainland, the atoll was not noted for its natural beauty. The isle of Rune was sandwiched among five islands aligned in an irregular circle; covered in well groomed farm fields and dotted by rustic villages. They were positioned close enough to the mainland to spark interest from the rest of the world but at a sufficient distance to discourage any visitors. This isolation allowed the Se to become the best healers, fisherman and farmers while perfecting their even tempered disposition. Though such Se perfection did not bode well with the distant neighbors and the island folk were viewed with jealousy and resentment. Fortunately, all that discontent was kept at bay by the deep waters which surrounded their homes.

Munsi had been seated for just a few moments in a comfortable section of the beach directly facing the sunset when a passerby called out, "No little one yet? Don't you worry Munsi, she'll be here sooner than you think."

"Oh, yes, I'm sure you're correct," replied the distracted father. The people of Rune always offered words of encouragement even at the most inopportune moments.

"I remember my first child as if it were yesterday," continued the birthing authority without hesitation. "She is a Uni, as you know and took the longest time to arrive. Two and a half sunrises; I was exhausted from all the waiting. I do believe the Uni take just a little while longer to join the community and of course, my wife did a splendid job. I could not have done it without her," said his fellow Se with complete sincerity.

Munsi continued gazing out over the water as he pondered the fact that he had very little to do with the birthing process at all. "Well, Munsi, I wish I could stay and offer you my support, but work on the fishing nets is calling. Don't you worry in the least, Se children always arrive when the time and tides are right." And off went the bearer of neighborly advice.

"Thank you for the words of support, I'll continue to do my best," replied Munsi, ever the consummate Se. This short exchange had placed a novel idea in Munsi's head. Could their child be a Uni?

2

He and Rissa had never given any consideration to the possibility of a Uni, even while preoccupied with wishful thinking.

The Se, as mentioned earlier, were the most advanced in the art of healing during the challenging times of antiquity. They had the longest life expectancy and the least number of aches and pains, a feat attributed to the islands' superior healers. Among the numerous skills of the atoll women was the ability to predict the gender of a newborn; with an accuracy that was near perfect.

The practitioners took into consideration a number of factors: the age of the mother, season of the year, phase of the moon, size of the harvest, how cold the previous winter had been and combined that information with a large dose of innate intuition. Every Se parent knew in advance whether they were going to have a girl or boy – except for those rare babies who did not follow the formula of the healers – the unique children or Uni. Rissa and Munsi had been assured, after careful consideration, that their child was definitely a girl.

As one can imagine, the child who did not follow this time proven way of deduction was regarded to be special. To the people of the isles they always appeared a bit wiser, more intuitive and creative, were prone to be natural leaders and gifted with a quick wit. Such excellent qualities were thought to bring good luck to the atoll and every family could remember at least one relative who was a Uni. But this excited couple was looking forward to a normal Se girl, with ten fingers and toes, a wonderful smile, brown hair and eyes and none of the attention or responsibility of a unique child. Munsi was quite sure their first born was to be a girl; she was just taking her time arriving.

After this slight detour into uninvited reverie, Munsi returned to the task of calming his thoughts. He had selected a fine afternoon to visit the beach as the sunset was especially impressive. A streak of long red sunlight reflected off the still water.

The tiny specks of Se soil lay at the midpoint of two extremes. Facing north, one saw the Land of Ice, where an imposing glacier loomed clearly visible from each island home. The top of the ice mountain was hidden in thick clouds and its massive weight crushed all in its path on the slow march towards the sea. To the south, a more moderate climate covered the land which allowed trees and vegetation of every sort to flourish in the favorable temperatures. For the Se, the effects of colliding temperatures from these regions proved a challenge.

The cold air of the north mixing with the warmer winds from the south created constantly changing weather on the isles. Strong gusts blew most days, snow fell every month except for two, long days of severe cold froze the surrounding water, and fog swirled so densely that one could only see as far as the end of his nose.

The atoll climate was far from predicable and the weather dictated that the Se had to be punctual - every community activity followed a strict schedule. Yet the island folk did not mind the rigors of their daily life as they considered these isles the best place on earth to live.

As no additional interruptions came his way, Munsi began to reminisce on his people's past. A Se made sure he remembered where he came from so as not to forget where he was going. The atoll had not always been home to the Se. Many years prior, the island folk had resided in the southern land of abundance and had so for generations – far too many to remember. As one would expect, the lands south offered an easier way of life but unfortunately, no protection from a resentful neighbor – the Malus.

The Se and Malus had lived alongside one another for eons but it had not been a peaceful co-existence. The two peoples were similar in appearance, spoke a common language, and were both nurtured by the endless bounty which surrounded them. But at each new dawn the groups woke with very different attitudes towards their place in the world – one was content and the other not. This odd fact was a riddle the Se could never solve.

In a word, the Malus were envious of their kind hearted neighbors and this envy produced strong feelings of dislike which worsened with each passing generation. Eventually, the antagonistic disposition of the Malus proved to be too much for the Se and the time came to depart the southern lands.

A carefully thought out strategy for evacuation was formulated by the Se leaders, one initiated in late summer, under the cover of a moonless night. With long canoes as transportation, the Se took only the most practical of possessions: tools, herbs for healing, seeds, livestock, and high expectations for their future. The passage to new ground was carried out to perfection and relocation to the islands was successful. There was no damage to either person or property.

On the following morning, did the malcontented Malus rejoice that the Se were no longer next door? Absolutely not. It did not take long before their spiteful nature turned to anger which in turn led them down the path of revenge. What strange characters these Malus were. They boiled with mistrust while within sight of their friendly neighbors, but when the Se moved away, they planned a war! The Se's decision to leave the southern lands had been a good one and completed none too soon.

With anger as a taskmaster, the Malus's plan for reprisal was completed in several months. When the weather turned bitterly cold and the waters surrounding the atoll were frozen thick in ice, the Malus began the advance. Midnight was the time for action, the light of a crescent moon was their compass. Arms and legs fueled by vengeance, pumping fast, was the means of transport. Surprise was surely on the side of the Malus.

But the Se were the benefactors of a good measure of common sense and the simplest of precautions proved quite useful. Small flocks of alert geese were strategically positioned around the islands and an effective early warning alarm was set in place. The element of surprise, hoped for by the Malus, was completely lost.

As the noisy geese honked the call to arms, the Se had bows drawn at the ready when the first Malus foot touched the shore. The aggressors were only men while the Se had both men and women defenders. If a male Se fell to injury, a woman quickly picked up his weapon – fighting just as effectively. The Se's superiority in numbers, determination, coordination and higher quality weaponry, ensured the battle was brief and the cost of life for the Malus extensive.

The conflict proved devastating for the invaders. The few surviving Malus abandoned their fallen colleagues and feelings of revenge on the blood soaked isles as they hastily retreated south. Abhorrence for the Se grew deeper with each step they took towards the mainland.

On the following spring, the riddle of the Malus continued; they packed up all their belongings and moved west. The people of anger crossed over the Foreboding Bluff and passed through the double mountains – permanently leaving the South Lands behind. What prompted this trek west only a Malus knew and no Se gave chase to ask why? Regrettably though, on rare occasions, the historical enemies still encountered each other in the southern lands.

Each summer the Se travelled to the Land of Plenty to collect herbs, seeds and supplies over a two week period. At irregular intervals, a Malus would lay in wait to kidnap a gatherer. During these chance meetings, one of either group's members never returned home. Should a Se happen to fall into the hands of a Malus, his future stayed hidden behind the Foreboding Bluff, a fate no Se wished to experience. Fortunately, these confrontations occurred infrequently and the abundance that the south lands offered was worth the necessary risks.

In stark contrast to the southern lands, the harsh cold was the only foe a Se experienced while visiting the land of ice. Viewed from the relative warmth of an island home, the aqua blue glacier was beautiful and the wall of ice processed an important resource for the community. The glacier's pulverizing power on its slow advance to the sea crushed large rocks into easily manageable ores.

Timing the collection of these raw materials was critical. Arriving too early, before the narrow strip of land surrounding the glacier melted, one risked frost bite or freezing to death. Too late an arrival and the edges on the huge glacier became unstable, breaking off into massive blocks of ice which crushed everything in its path as they fell and rolled.

The Se were surprised to discover that the numerous elements of natural danger present in the north did not frighten all, as there was an odd collection of people who called this frigid region home. These hardy residents were known among the island folks as Groullens. The northern men displayed a coarse resemblance to the Se; two large arms and legs, walked upright, wore tattered clothing, had barrel chests, bearded faces, a fierce demeanor and crude tools. A blunt rock tied to a sturdy stick was their favorite. The Groullens had yet to realize the benefit of bathing as dirt covered all exposed skin.

Another distinctive attribute of the burly Northerners, which demanded considerable respect from the Se, was the Groullen's enormous strength. On random occasions, without any prompting, a single Groullen would heft a large rock over his head and throw it a sizeable distance. (The same rock required four broad shouldered Se, straining with every muscle they had, to lift it a finger's width off the ground.) Each attempt was followed by a thunderous growl and much to the relief of the Se that was the extent of any Groullen aggression.

The Se could not determine if the large humanoids possessed a language. The only sounds they ever heard a Groullen give tongue to was a guttural grunt – hence the origin of their name.

Yet, for all the oddness in appearance and manners, the northern men proved an inquisitive lot. Each time the Se arrived, a crowd of the thick boned bipeds soon gathered to observe them. They shadowed the Se's every movement whilst in the land of ice, never tiring from their vigilance. Where the Groullen slept, what food they ate or any information about the family units remained a mystery to the island folk.

Once the boats were full of ore, the Se glanced in the Groullens direction, gave a quick nod goodbye and cast off. They returned home with a long list of Groullen stories for the children and a boat laden with raw material to smelt. Who or what the Groullen were was left to speculation but the Se were thankful for the fact that the harsh northern territories had not given the men of might a fierce temperament.

Munsi's reflection on his people's past had finally led him back to the present. The setting sun was now just touching the top of the double mountains – soon it would be dark. After nearly two days there was still no word of a birth and Munsi's nerves were on edge once more.

A neighbor hurried down the road and called out with an update. "Munsi, good news, Aunt Sufi has requested the assistance of my wife and several other women with the delivery of your baby. The child will be arriving soon," said the smiling messenger.

"Oh, yes, that certainly is good news," replied a confused Munsi. The weary Se realized he had no notion of a good or difficult birth or how one cared for a newborn or how trying it must be for his wife or even if he would be a good father. Munsi's bundle of nervous energy offered him little help in answering those questions and certainly none to his wife. He did manage the absent minded reply, "I suppose a proper house cleaning is in order if the baby is near at hand."

The neighbor quickly said, "Quite so Munsi, you don't want the new one arriving to a messy home. Rissa would not look too kindly on that." Munsi had cleaned the house three times over the past day and a half but there could be a few bits of dust he had overlooked. "Hurry home to set the house right Munsi, and keep a warm broth ready for Rissa," advised the friend.

While Munsi followed the shortest path for home in order to put his anxiety to good use, Rissa was struggling with her important task. At her side was the best healer on the island, Sufi, who was using her extensive practitioner's knowledge to aid this first time mother, but as yet the baby had not arrived. Rissa was exhausted and the little one was still reluctant to join those assembled. This posed a dilemma for the experienced healer.

During her years on the island, Sufi had brought many of the Rune babies into the world – never losing a mother or child in the process. Such a stellar achievement did not happen by chance. Sufi's own personal misfortune had led her to a life dedicated to the art of curing.

As a young woman, Sufi was happily married with a head full of countless possibilities on the horizon. She and her husband had just finished building their first home and were looking forward to starting a family. Life for the young couple was at its best but sadly, the Se atoll was not immune to the impartial hand of tragedy and the universe had a new path for Sufi to follow.

Her husband was fatally struck by a large falling ice shard while gathering ore in the north lands. The suffering widow found herself lost to overwhelming grief from her inability to comprehend such a mishap; she finally concluded that woes such as these could never be understood.

For a distraction, Sufi concentrated every waking moment to the art of healing. She focused on delivering new members to the island, mending broken limbs and battered spirits, and making various herbal tonics to aid the sick - always with a keen eye to understanding the Se people and their relationship to nature.

Days are long when one has a broken heart and Sufi used nearly every bit of them tending to the needs of those on the island. Her diligence benefitted all and though she never married again, each island resident considered Sufi part of their family. She was affectionately called "Aunt Sufi" by all she met.

Sufi's distressed patient had her undivided attention. She knew Rissa and the baby were at an impasse as the energy of both was spent; they could not continue alone. In a soothing voice, Sufi reassured the weary Rissa, telling her the birthing journey would end shortly, that she was mentally strong and the baby was fine. With the help of a few more women, the child would soon arrive.

More hot water was prepared and the request for additional women sent out. Sufi's demeanor kept the attending ladies calm and focused as they bathed Rissa's face and arms to keep her cool and distracted. A short time later, the extra women arrived and no formalities were necessary; each knew what had to be done. Sufi with the poise of an experienced healer positioned three women on either side of Rissa before she began.

Aunt Sufi stood at Rissa's head and collected her thoughts then said, "Rissa, you have seven of your sisters beside you, so all is safe. Their energy is your energy, their strength is your strength. Your child will come into this world in a few minutes surrounded by those gathered here and we shall rejoice."

Sufi closed her eyes and continued, "Sisters, let us begin by honoring the bond we have between Mother Earth and ourselves. All that is good in this world we embrace. We are respectful of its inhabitants. We listen for the knowledge Mother Earth wishes to share and pass it on to our fellow man. We model our lives after the harmony found in nature. At this time, our collective energy needs to be directed towards one of our sisters. She is a first time mother and requires our help bringing into this world another beautiful child of the Se – her child. Sisters, please place your hands on Rissa and let us call forth the child of she and Munsi."

Each Se present breathed in unison and joined in meditation while they laid their hands on the expectant mother. Rissa relaxed. She grasped her sisters' hands tightly and clenched her teeth for one last effort.

After a few moments, the sound of a weak baby's cry was heard. Two days of strenuous struggle was suddenly replaced with the joyful sound of a newborn child. The assembled women had tears of happiness in their eyes and were surprised to see that the child was not the expected girl but a boy – a Uni. The boy was tiny, half the size of most babies, with ten fingers and toes and a healthy voice to let you know he was here to stay.

While the other women attended to Rissa, Aunt Sufi cleaned the newborn and was his first introduction to those on the Isle of Rune. She said in a gentle voice, "My reluctant little Uni, I have never seen one so small take this long to arrive – a fact which gives me reason to stop and think. From my years of healing I've learned that everything in this world has a purpose and I believe you have a hint as to what your future will bring. But do not fear tiny one, you're joining a caring community which will support and protect you always. And if the path in front of you appears daunting, take comfort that the people of these islands will stand by your side daily. I should also say that you were born with the gifts of the Uni and fortune will constantly guide your steps. I would like to tell you more about the atoll but there is someone else who is anxious to see you. It is time for you to meet your mother."

A large pot of hot brew was prepared for the attending ladies. The strong drink calmed the nerves, mended the body and bonded lives together. It was an excellent tonic to sip while viewing a newborn child. The women gathered around Rissa while a sleeping Uni, wrapped in a warm blanket, was presented to his mother for the first time. This prompted another round of tears from the ladies.

Rissa was smiling from ear to ear as she held her precious son. So overcome was she by the beauty of her first child that she forgot Munsi had not been told. "Oh my, could someone please run and tell

Munsi of his son's arrival?" asked Rissa. A volunteer quickly headed to their home.

Munsi had finished the house cleaning and was standing outside pondering which new project should be started when the messenger arrived and said, "Munsi, your baby has finally arrived and it is a boy. Can you believe it, Munsi, a Uni for a first child? And Rissa is doing just fine." The new father quickly stood up straight and stared at the woman.

"A boy, we had not planned for a boy, what's the baby to wear?" asked the confused Munsi.

"Never mind about the clothes Munsi, just make sure the house is in order and there is a warm broth prepared for Rissa when she comes home," replied the messenger.

"Right, excellent idea, I'll ready the home straight away. Thank you for the wonderful news," said a perplexed Munsi. Shaking her head in amusement, the volunteer returned to the new mother.

A relieved Munsi began cleaning the house for a fifth time when the realization that his first child had finally arrived set in. Such an important event brought pause to the Se. It was not long before the father smiled and absorbed the warmth a newborn brings to a parent. Rissa and he had a son and their child was a Uni.

And so, on the second month of the growing season, several millenniums removed from life in the south lands, and forty thousand years from the present, Munsi stood a proud new father.

2

An Ordinary Boy

As with every first time mother, Rissa was eager to return home to the comfort of familiar surroundings; she did so after two days of rest escorted by Munsi and Aunt Sufi. Not much was said by the new parents but there were plenty of twinkling eyes and broad smiles shared between them. Sufi did most of the talking, "There is not a better couple on this island than you two. Your little Uni has a wonderful mother and father." Munsi and Rissa responded with wider smiles and excited nods.

"I hope you've kept the home in order during Rissa's absence," jested Sufi as they arrived at the couple's front door. Upon entering Sufi exclaimed, "Why Munsi, this house is spotless. You've done a wonderful job while Rissa has been gone."

The proud father beamed as he fetched three bowls of soup and exclaimed, "Oh, yes, I couldn't have Rissa and the little one coming home to a mess."

The finest healer on the Isle of Rune did much more than bring new Se into the world. Her expertise extended to a host of other vital skills - counselor, teacher, and friend — all of which kept the island community running smoothly. Munsi and Rissa were transitioning into parenthood and Sufi was there to guide them through an important first step, naming their child.

The people of the isles took a simple approach to a person's name - no surnames, middle initials or titles were necessary - just a single word. The Se also believed that each person's epithet should come from the circumstance surrounding their birth. No two births were the same, each name was unique.

After the soup was finished, Sufi began the naming process by saying, "I have brought into this world numerous babies and I can say on good authority that every child is special. It does not matter if they are big, small, boy, girl, first, last, Uni or not, they are all the same – special. And tonight, we're going to determine what is unique about your little one and give him a fitting name."

The trio collected their thoughts and began discussing the facts surrounding his birth. The tiny one was a Uni, first born, there had been a full moon, it was the second half of the growing season, they were first time parents and he had taken his time arriving. Not one name could be found among the possibilities on that list.

After a number of other details had been considered with no success, the three decided to take a break for another bowl of soup. They ate in silence and watched the sleeping baby. The tiny Uni looked so peaceful and appeared to be in thought as his fingers were placed against his cheek.

The insightful Sufi posed a question, "Do we have a little philosopher sleeping among us, one who thinks before he acts. One who gives pause before making a decision? What do you say, little one, are we moving in the right direction?" The new born yawned and stretched his arms in acknowledgement.

It was not long before Rissa suggested the name "Reiben" which meant "Reflective One" in Se and a short time later the tiny Uni had a permanent moniker.

Sufi said, "Reiben, your name has found you and I must say it suits you quite well. I have seen many babies over the years, but never a Uni so small or hesitant to join this world. Rissa, Munsi, I believe your little Reiben will need a clever mind and much determination on the path which is in front of him." Rissa and Munsi grinned with joy as they looked down at their sleeping son.

Aunt Sufi had a few words of advice for the couple and continued, "Now that this Uni has a proper name, Reiben is ready for an introduction to the community. As first time parents, every Se will offer you plenty of opinions on how to raise your son but may I be the first to put forth several suggestions of my own? The most important thing you need to remember to do each day is to give Reiben plenty of hugs and pecks on the cheek and all the positive words you can say. Everything else in his life will be easier to manage when viewed through the eyes of a well-loved child."

For one who'd never had any children of her own Sufi had keen insights for young parents. With those last few words, Sufi's work with Rissa and Munsi was completed for the day and she took her leave. The new parents sat quietly and marveled at how wonderful their little Uni was.

Reiben's introduction to the Se community came at the most inopportune time of the year, the summer festival. Every Se was preoccupied with preparations for the festivities and this little Uni was only given their cursory attention.

The summer celebration began three days before the summer solstice and continued for seven days; a week of Se fun. It brought the people from each island together to enjoy the variety of activities an atoll social event had to offer: eating, athletic competition, mingling of the young folks, storytelling by the elders, parents scrutinizing newborns from the different islands, archery and the most popular attraction of all, Sand Ball.

Teams of every age from each island competed in the Sand Ball tournaments with the overall champions having considerable bragging rights and the Se were not known to be boastful people. Each game was closely watched leaving little time for distractions. Munsi, Rissa and Reiben arrived at a critical moment – near the start of the tournament. Reiben's introduction was going to be brief.

Aunt Sufi gathered around her all the folks within earshot and began, "I know everyone is anxious to see the latest addition to our island and the beginning of the Sand Ball tournament so I'll keep my introduction to a minimum." The men had their ears toward Sufi and eyes ogling the field of play as they watched the athletes warm up. Sufi hurriedly continued, "Let each of us come forward to congratulate Rissa and Munsi. These first time parents have a new son who happens to be a Uni."

The men rushed forward to offer their congratulations and words of advice as quickly as possible, "A Uni for a first child how auspicious."

"If you want a son to become a fisherman hang a fishing net above his bed, it will be the first thing he sees in the morning and the last thing he sees at night."

"A good carpenter starts at an early age, give him a little hammer and let him whack a piece of wood a few minutes each day but make sure your wife is out of the house, the banging will push her towards an unfavorable mood."

"My that Uni is a little one, no bigger than a puppy, well I mean, boys do come in all sizes."

The men slapped Munsi on the back, shook his hand, politely excused themselves and ran to find a good viewing spot around the Sand Ball field.

The women were not far behind. Quick hugs and kisses were given to Rissa as they mouthed, "I'll drop by in a few days" and the ladies were off jockeying for a good vantage point by the field of play as well.

Munsi and Rissa found themselves standing all alone, smiling as they looked down at a sleeping Reiben. They were not the least bit concerned by Reiben's rushed introduction. However, the Sand Ball tournament was about to begin so they thought it best to find a spot near the field from which to enjoy the match.

Sand Ball, the game which brought forth every emotion known to the Se - elation, exasperation, anger and pleading - was not difficult to understand. Even the youngest on the atoll found the game easy to learn.

There were seven players on each side: two defenders, a setter, a right handed spiker called the riker; a left handed spiker call the liker; a right footed booter called the rooter; a left footed booter called the looter; the goals were circular, waist high and several arm widths across set ninety paces apart. A half circle was placed five steps in front of each goal with a second half circle fifteen paces from the first. The action took place on a well-groomed field of sand; there were six respected elder men who oversaw the match (one at each corner of the field and two at midfield one on either side); shorts, tattered shirts, bare feet and one almost round ball. The object of the game was to boot or spike the ball into the goal.

The rules were simple: Only one defender was allowed inside the first semi-circle at any time. After each shot on goal, he would switch places with the second defender. All scoring occurred in the area between the first and second semi-circles. The setter had to kick the ball to a spiker or booter for a goal to be valid. Each spiker or booter could only use the hand or foot for the position he was playing. If a ball was knocked out of play, the setter kicked or threw it back into play. In the event of a tie, each team's booter, spiker and setter standing between the two semi-circles, hit a ball as close to the opposing team's goal as possible. The distance from the goal would be measured for each ball and the team with the lowest total was declared the winner.

The six men who oversaw the matches were known by the Se word "Sedza" (it was an honorable title which came with considerable frustration) and they sat on stools at designated locations around the field. The Sedza were elderly men chosen from the five islands for their wisdom and integrity. Yet, poor eye sight and a short attention span more than offset their impeccable character and these deficiencies proved to be a constant source of irritation for the fans.

Sand Ball was a fast paced game which required snap decisions. Was a player in the hit zone or two large strides over the line? Did the second defender position himself across the first semi-circle to deflect a shot? Had the setter touched the ball before the spiker scored? These were rulings that weak eyes and sleepy minds found difficult to render quickly.

During the week of the summer festival, the normally even tempered Se embraced a different side of his personality; he changed into a fan with a strong allegiance for his team and was quick to voice his dissatisfaction over any questionable call. Quite often, a fan found his composure completely lost and yelled out in haste, "Sedza, open your eyes, both of the defenders are standing in front of the goal."

"Sedza, was that your grandson who just scored one step from the goal?"

"Sedza, take your nap at the break."

And on the rare occasion when a fan crossed the etiquette line completely and uttered the worst insult a Se could ever use; which of course, slandered the integrity of the elders and brought the game to an immediate halt, "Sedza, your mother is an old goat." Harsh words indeed.

The egregious heckler was quickly removed from the side lines and given a stern lecture on all the important values every Se adhered to. Competition was good, a well-mannered Se much better. Fortunately, these severe lapses in judgment were few and thankfully, far apart.

Yet, for all the shortcomings of the Sedzas, the most unpredictable aspect of the game was the ball. The benefit of advanced tools was not available to the Se. Each ball was handmade and no two balls were the same except for the fact that none were spherical. A non-spherical ball when set in motion does not always follow a straight line and appears to have a mind of its own.

When the player who accepted congratulations for his goal at the end of a match declared, "I was lucky to score today," he was telling the truth. Every conceivable shooting technique had little bearing on whether the ball entered the goal or not.

Still, for all the randomness of the balls and unpredictability of the Sedzas, there were Se islands which consistently won the Sand Ball tournament. The Rune team was not one of them. In fact, the island Reiben called home had not fielded a championship since before many of its residents were born, ten years prior, although this disappointing fact did not hinder the community's enthusiasm for the game.

As the host isle, Rune initiated tournament play against last year's champion and perennial winners, Vidlin. The Rune team was determined to make a good show or at least keep the score close. The squad, fueled by hope, was flying around the field and at the break the score was tied at zero.

The friendly betting began. The folks on the island of Rune were considered the best fisherman and healers among the atoll while the Se on Vidlin were superior carpenters and seamstresses. A large fishnet would be wagered against a new roof, one jar of refined herbs for a new coat. After a reasonable break and much haggling, all the bets were finalized.

The second half of the contest began and the outcome was much different. For the eleventh year in a row, fishing nets and herbs would be delivered to the island of Vidlin. Rune had lost nil to three. The exasperated fans of Rune swore they would never, ever bet again; eleven years of losing was just too much to endure. But never was a very long time and by the start of next year's festival, those resolutions would be readily forgotten.

Sand Ball, for all its showmanship, was not the center piece of the summer festival or the Se community. The people of the atoll valued intellect over brawn and since the Se were an intelligent group, inclined to abstract thinking, rash decisions were not in their nature.

An idea, borne out of the conflict with the Malus after the Se relocated to their atoll, was quite original for those primitive times and it maximized the Se's readiness to their harsh environment. The implementation of the novel idea did not involve protective forts, advanced weapons, clever military strategies or superior physical strength. It was much simpler but more effective; a comprehensive education for the children on the islands.

Each young Se girl was taught fishing, carpentry, and archery skills by the men in the community and the boys healing, herbal, and agricultural practices by the women. The community felt it was critical that every child had a basic understanding of the collective knowledge among its people.

The less enlightened inhabitants of the mainland viewed such training as a waste of time. Of what use was a male healer or female archer? Surely the Se had been isolated on those islands for far too long to embrace such nonsense. The Se, however, were not swayed by their neighbors' ignorance and continued to raise well rounded children year after year.

The Se children's education began at the age of three and continued until eight or nine. There was no rigid schedule for completion. The youngest students aged three and four, followed their teachers around, took naps, played, made a mess of every task and imposed upon the considerable patience of the instructors.

By the age of five, the students were contributing on a small scale and during the last years of instruction, the teacher and their pupil enjoyed each other's company immensely. The teacher did not wish to part with his student nor did the student care to leave the teacher.

This parting occurred on the last day of the summer festival in an official ceremony. Forming two parallel rows at a reasonable distance apart; the women stood with the young boys by their side and the men with the girls. The instructors had kind words of appreciation for their students and whispered to their charges," You are an excellent and capable student. We are so fortunate to have such a person as you on the islands. You are not only a bright child but kind, helpful, and charitable to others, just like your parents."

After the words of affection were spoken and everyone had a warm embrace, the students walked across the open space to the opposite line of parents. The enlightened young Se's were then presented with a flower from the Hawthorn tree; with the hope that they would always be as resilient as this tree. No adult Se had a dry eye when the ceremony was over. And for the final event of the summer festival, the community gathered on the beach to watch the sunset, thankful for another year on the atoll.

Three week old Reiben was wrapped in blankets throughout most of his first summer festival, but like the other Se, he benefited from the positive energy the gathering generated. With the festival over and everyone refreshed from the respite, there was considerable work to be completed before the cold reality of the Northlands blew south. Harvesting the crops and smoking fish, gathering herbs in the Southland and ore in the Northland, repairing homes and mending fishing nets, meant long hours of hard work for every Se.

After the summer and autumn activities were behind them, the next pause in Se daily life came at the coldest time of the year – midwinter. The frigid temperatures forced everyone inside, although, there were brief windows of play time for the children when the wind died down and the air was still. However, it was still extremely cold.

The men gathered the older children outside for sled races. Building parallel tracks down a hill, across the beach, and over the frozen water, the children had an opportunity to race their best friends. It was hard to determine who had more fun during the contests, the howling children as they bounced every which way while speeding down the track or the men laughing at the children hanging on to the sled for dear life. At the end of the day there were plenty of red faces and abundant stories to tell the mothers.

Once the arctic weather gave way and spring was near, planting and fishing were on everyone's mind. Promptness assured a good harvest so thawed fields were sown and open waters traversed on time. Then all too soon, midsummer was around the corner and the Se once again looked forward to another week of festivities in the cycle of atoll life.

Reiben's birthdays coincided with the final preparations for the summer celebration. He slept through his first festival, began to walk at his second, spoke intelligibly on his third and was ready to begin school after his fourth. Three years, passed quickly even for a small Uni. Reiben had the good fortune of the ever watchful Aunt Sufi as his primary instructor once his third birthday arrived. Though he was too young for the trip to the Southland, upon the boats' return, Reiben was given his first jar, a little sieve and a seat between his mother and Sufi. He was an industrious little lad and stayed busy filling up his jar and emptying it out.

At three Reiben was by far the smallest of his peers and none of the other Se ever mistook him for a Uni. Besides his lack of size, Reiben had a touch of shyness. He listened more than spoke, constantly observed those around him and smiled with his eyes rather than his mouth. This tiny Uni was easily overlooked in a crowd.

However, the discerning Aunt Sufi was not fooled by appearances. She had taught many boys during her years and viewed each from the inside as well as the out. Though Reiben's bearing did not catch a person's eye, Sufi felt there was considerably more to him than had yet been brought to light, though she was unsure of what Reiben's special trait might be.

The other women seated around the table, questioned the accuracy of Reiben being a Uni at all. One women, forgetting her Se manners entirely asked, "Aunt Sufi, were you sure Rissa's child was to be a girl. Was that prediction given a lot of thought?"

The doting Rissa was not the least bit upset by this line of questioning as she had no interest in Reiben's Uni status. She and Munsi had only ever wished for a healthy child. Whether a girl, boy or Uni it did not matter to them and Reiben's mother did not pay a bit of attention to such silly chatter whenever it came her way.

The clever Sufi, though, quickly took charge and tactfully ended the inane babble when she asked, "I hope, ladies, you have not lost faith in my abilities as a healer?"

This immediately elicited the chorus, "Oh no Aunt Sufi, there is no better a woman when it comes to understanding the Se's health. What I meant was how difficult is it to determine if a child is a boy or girl?" With Se civility restored, Sufi patiently explained the various factors used to determine a child's gender and Reiben's Uni status was not challenged openly again.

With each passing summer Reiben's knowledge continued to grow; he found the healing and herbal subjects the most interesting and tilling the land a distant last. Reiben took his studies seriously and easily grasped each new concept, but his taciturn demeanor did not reflect that.

The young Uni enjoyed the company of his instructors, especially Sufi and as was the practice for all Se students, he brought whatever flower was in season to his teachers as a show of appreciation. Reiben always added a Yew tree cutting to each of his flowers so the instructor knew who it was from.

Sufi once asked Reiben, "Why do you add the Yew tree with your flowers?"

Reiben responded, "The tree has healing properties and no matter the season, its red berries and green needles are pretty." Sufi's initial opinion of Reiben had not changed; he was a boy with a lot more on the inside than out.

While Reiben was a keen student, he found his athletic abilities were not on par with his intellect; they were marginal only on the best of days. The Uni was the last boy chosen for a Sand Ball team or the foot race relays and each of his friends wished to be his opponent during the sledding competitions at midwinter in order to achieve an easy win.

Though he lacked athletic prowess, Reiben was a fun and loyal friend to his companions and he was always included in every activity his peers were involved in. His calmness, overlooked by most of the adults, gave him a natural leadership quality and his opinion was not disregarded. When one asked Reiben what he thought they should do if presented with a difficult situation, his suggestions always proved correct.

And as for Reiben's parents, they could not have been happier with their only child. He was growing into a fine young Se, a person better than they had ever believed possible; while the rest of the adult Se community considered Reiben just an ordinary island child and most definitely not a Uni.

With each passing year, fewer Se spoke of Reiben as a Uni to his parents, until finally, it was never mentioned. The community still whispered candidly among themselves about the tiny one. In a hushed voice, after checking over their shoulders, one would say, "Don't embarrass Munsi and Rissa about their son. Aunt Sufi says that poor child is a Uni but I'm telling you I have my doubts."

On Reiben's ninth birthday, it came as no surprise to anyone on the island that Rissa kept her undersized son at school with the healers for one more year. Sufi had her own opinion of this Uni and it differed from her neighbors; she was pleased to have another year with her favorite student. The clever Sufi found it hard to hide her soft spot for Reiben. As the oldest boy in training, Reiben and his mother were selected to join the collection party soon to be heading to the Southland. It would be his first time away from the atoll. Reiben was so excited that his mind raced incessantly in the days leading up to the departure. What possibilities did the Southland offer? Surely this would be a trip to remember.

3

Over the Foreboding Bluff

Shortly after the summer festival, preparations for the voyage to the Southlands were completed. Three long boats from each island, fitted with large woven baskets and seats for twelve passengers, pointed their bows in a southerly direction and set off. If the wind was favorable, the trip passed by quickly, otherwise a full day on the sea was required.

The crew for each boat included two strong men, eight women with extensive herbal knowledge, and two excited boys who had not slept a wink the night prior. The first day was dedicated to travel and organizing the lodging.

Reiben sat by his mother the entire journey, his eyes smiling continuously during the morning sail. Once the flotilla was positioned a safe distance from the beach, the boats dropped anchor and a scouting party of the largest men sailed a single boat the remaining distance. If there was no sign of the Malus a fire was lit and the rest of the group came ashore. The Se had not seen any of their former neighbors for a number of years, hopefully, the Malus resolve for revenge had finally dissipated.

After every Se was safely on the white beach, they stood in awe of the beauty flourishing before them. Shoes quickly came off and excited toes were soon covered in warm sand. The boys raced down the shoreline while the adults walked slowly enjoying the huge plants and fragrant flowers. This was scenery not soon forgotten by those who visited.

A short hike inland and stands of fruit bearing trees, wild wheat, barley and herbs of every sort were found. The lush greenery swayed back and forth in the pleasant ocean breeze. The Se forefathers must have thought at length before they decided to leave this place of abundance as long hours of harvesting were not called work in this paradise.

After the initial enthusiasm for the landscape had subsided, the gathering party returned to the task at hand and prepared their sleeping quarters. There were semi-permanent huts at several paces from the beach that required repair after nearly a year of neglect and it was well past dark before the party finally slept.

The sun rose to find the Se had finished breakfast and were ready to start the day. The gathering followed a well-organized schedule and each day's tasks had to be completed before anyone went to bed. Fortunately, excitement for the novelty of such a land meant only a few hours of sleep was sufficient for the workers.

The most time consuming part of the daily jobs was separating the edible fruit from the plant. The baskets were filled with only usable produce. A piece of straw did not add a bit of nutritional value to a Se's loaf of bread.

Nonperishables were completed first. Women handled the herbs and the men harvested the wheat and barley. Perishables, fruit and vegetables, were gathered during the last two days and the boys lent a hand wherever needed. Working with a system developed over the ages, the group filled each basket with typical Se efficiency.

The long hours of harvesting did not exclude play at the end of the day. When evening arrived, the Se had plenty of energy left to build bonfires on the beach, play Sand Ball, wade in the warm water off shore and enjoy the natural beauty the moderate climate nurtured. Not one person looked forward to the end of their two week stay.

Yet, all too quickly, the last day was upon them and the party members were left with only a few hours of free time for themselves before the group returned to the atoll. Rissa and Reiben decided to collect peaches for Munsi and they strolled towards a stand of trees which grew a short distance from the huts. As mother and son walked, they reminisced about the activities over the past fortnight. They concluded that the only improvement to their stay would have been if their favorite head of household had been able to enjoy it with them. Once at the small orchard, Reiben climbed the trees and picked the ripest peaches to hand down to Rissa. Mother and son were lost to warm conversation.

Unnoticed, at a close distance and hidden from the island folk, were a pair of crouching Malus who could not believe their good fortune - two Se stood within easy reach. Containing their excitement as best they could the duo quietly separated; one positioned himself near the path to the beach, the other advanced slowly toward the peach trees. The joy of the past two weeks had dampened Rissa's intuitive sense as she and Reiben had never been happier. However as the Malus neared, the young mother's instincts told her to stop picking and survey her surroundings. Fate was to deal Rissa and Reiben a dreadful hand that day.

In an instance, Rissa yelled, "Quick Reiben, run to the beach." She remained at the orchard and focused on two angry eyes in the bushes, wishing that Reiben had enough speed to reach the others.

The first Malus raced towards his target with blade in hand while Reiben bolted towards the huts, looking over his shoulder as he ran. The second Malus caught the under sized Uni and easily dragged him in the opposite direction away from the path. Reiben never saw how courageous his mother was nor witnessed any of her conflict.

Rissa was intelligent and practical, and she knew her situation was dire. The dread on her face was not for herself but for those she would most likely leave behind – a loving husband and son. Rissa's mind raced through a long list of frightful questions in the few seconds before confronting her attacker; who could help raise Reiben to be a fine Se, how would Munsi manage without her, why did this terrible event have to befall her? Rissa never reached the bottom of that list before her fate stood squarely in front of her.

Unarmed but light on her feet, Rissa managed to evade the Malus longer than one would expect. Through the use of sand, sticks and agility, she kept the frustrated attacker off balance and confused. Her cries for help caused confusion among the Se on the beach and moments of uncertainty in her assailant. Rissa's escape was almost realized but her defenses wavered for just a moment as she quickly glanced to see if Reiben was still on the path. The sharp point of the Malus dagger found its mark. She fell hoping her valiant efforts had allowed her son to reach the beach.

The Se community experienced energy as a collective and Rissa's death was immediately felt by the members of the gathering party, the Se on the atoll, and Munsi fishing on his boat. (Only young Reiben, who was too distracted with his own struggle, was unaware his mother's time on the Isle of Rune had come to an end.)

"No, no, no, please, no," silently passed the lips of those from the atoll.

The gathering party wasted little time assembling near the laden boats – Rissa and Reiben were not among them. The women and children along with several men cast off and rafted up a short distance from shore while the bulk of the men stayed behind.

By the time the sun reached midday the search party discovered Rissa's body. They had also followed Reiben's trail, along with two additional sets of tracks, to a fast moving stream where no signs of the young Uni's fate were left on the bank.

A hurried discussion among the men ensued, where much anger, despair and frustration bounced back and forth between them; anger for the slain Se mother, despair for a young Se who was pulled to an unknown future, and frustration at the fact that they could do nothing to rectify the situation.

Exhausted from the emotional exchange, the men finally decided that Rissa would be buried at sea, as was the Se tradition, after which the collection party would quickly return home. A few of the men felt there was hope Reiben was still alive but agreed that to give chase could endanger the rest of the gathers. The sad group of Se reunited offshore with the other boats and set sail for the atoll.

When the Southlands appeared small on the horizon, Rissa was laid to rest in the deep waters. Few words were spoken as everyone was lost to disbelief. Once close to the atoll, a flotilla of fishing boats greeted the returning gathers. The nervous Se had feared the worst and grief overcame them when they discovered Rissa and Reiben were not in the boats. Munsi was inconsolable.

With the captor's arm firmly locked around Reiben's neck, he had no chance to yell and little air to breathe. Reiben and his abductor waited by the stream for the second Malus to appear then all quickly crossed the water. (On the other side, after a momentary pause to tie Reiben's hands to the end of a short rope, two heavy slaps were administered to his face and neck for no apparent reason and the trio set off running due west.) By the time Rissa's body was discovered, the three were a good distance from the Se camp.

Another stop, more slaps and a harsh warning, "There'll be no going home for you, Se and if you wish to stay alive, you'd better pay attention to everything we say."

The frightened young Se knew his captors were Malus. The stories the tiny Uni had heard while safely seated at home accurately described his abductors. In Reiben's nine years on the atoll, a heavy hand had never come his way from his parents or any other adult Se. The same was true for the other island children. The idea of physical discipline was a foreign concept to the Se. But continuous rough treatment was a Malus form of communication and Reiben received additional blows from his captors before they dragged him in the direction of the Foreboding Bluff. The abductors had a destination they wished to reach in a hurry.

Another hour at a fast pace and it was late afternoon. Trees gave way to scrub brush and soon the bluff was squarely before them. The trio felt gusts of cold air roll down the face of the steep hill. The Malus located two hidden packs and removed thicker coats for themselves, while Reiben remained shivering in his summer clothing. The front of the earthen slope stretched beyond the imagination of the little Uni and was covered with grass on the upper half. After several more blows for the prisoner the three ascended the face of the bluff at an arduous pace. The path was steep and narrow – Reiben's heart raced with fear.

At the top, a strong freezing wind greeted the tired climbers and Reiben placed his arms against his body for warmth. One of the Malus, as he pointed towards the water, said, "Se, look at those people of yours making their way home. The cowards did not even take time to search for you."

From their vantage point, Reiben could clearly see all the long boats navigating a straight line for the atoll. "Give them a wave Se, this is the last time you'll ever see any of your kind," laughed the second Malus.

For the first time in his life, Reiben felt the sharp pain of despair, an emotion so cutting, tears freely flowed down his cheeks. Why was his mother leaving him and why was he captured by people such as these he thought? Difficult questions to ponder for a Se of any age. The tiny Uni's tears brought a smile to his captors. The more Reiben cried the louder were the laughs from the Malus.

One of them taunted him and said, "Every Se is weak, but don't worry, we'll knock that blubbering out of you." After several hard tugs on the rope, the trio turned and found their way to the rear of the bluff.

Contrary to Se belief, the bluff was not at the front of two mountains. It was the end of a glacier which had cut a mountain range in half. On either side of the glacier, the faces of the mountains were vertical and appeared like two stone blocks holding a huge piece of ice.

The Malus carefully surveyed the thick ice and considered it far too treacherous to cross. The summer temperatures had melted the glacier and formed deep crevasses. The captors decided scaling the sheer mountain cliffs and traversing its ridge a better option.

The island folk were not known as mountaineers. Moderate swells in a boat or sledding down a gradual hill was the extent of their aerial feats. A vertical climb was for the goats, but motivated by continuous pummeling and tugs on his bound hands; Reiben finally reached the summit after two hours. Escape seemed futile when viewed from so high a point.

The three were tired, hungry, and needed to find shelter for the night but there was more ground to cover before resting. After travelling far too many steps to count along the mountain cliff, several huts came into view. The small hovels were well maintained and regularly occupied throughout the year. Obviously, Malus visited the Southland far more frequently than the Se had previously believed.

Reiben was freezing in his summer clothing and welcomed the warmth a lit fire offered. There were provisions in the hut and a hot meal was prepared by the abductors. The prisoner was allowed to scrape what little remained stuck to the pot for his supper. While he ate his meager meal, Reiben took several moments to observe his captors. Apart from their angry faces and inferior quality clothes, the

Malus did not appear much different from a Se.

Se children were taught that the Malus had been their sour minded neighbors in the Southland many generations ago, sharing a common language but little else. No island person knew when the two groups had come to the bountiful lands on the southern continent nor could one fathom why the Malus harbored such animosity for the fine collection of people they rarely came into contact with. But there sat his two kidnappers with their foul disposition and smirks on their faces, pleased that a tiny Se had become their prize.

When it was time to sleep, the Malus directed severe threats and open hands in Reiben's direction, discouraging any attempts at escape. His feet and hands were bound and the dirt floor near the fire was his bed. Reiben's first night away from the loving arms of his parents and the Se community was overwhelming. Tears silently flowed down his cheeks but he made not a sound for fear of waking his abductors.

In the morning, what little sleep Reiben did manage brought him no comfort and he awoke to the same Malus attitude - harsh words and rough treatment. Reiben's only source of food was several bits of grain before they exited the hut and headed away from the rising sun.

Now that the captors were certain there was no risk of a pursuit, their pace became less strenuous. Pressing further west, they did not share any details of the next stopping point with Reiben.

The Malus and their tiny prisoner had advanced a good distance by the mid-afternoon break. The fast pace kept Reiben moderately warm and the scenery distracted. On the atoll, Reiben had seen a limited number of trees and few wild animals. But this mountain range was home to tall trees of varying types, open plains of grass, and numerous species of mammal all of which captivated the imagination of the curious Se: Massive woolly rhinoceros, mammoths, horses, mountain rabbits and huge red deer roamed past. Reiben, fascinated by his surroundings, lost his balance each time a new sight appeared.

Now that Reiben was covered in bruises from all their "corporal communication", the Malus were satisfied he understood they were not to be trifled with nor would he attempt an escape. They finally removed the rope which bound his hands. Much to his relief, Reiben could use his hands to rub his arms and legs for warmth. The small prisoner had not spoken a word in the last day and a half which finally prompted a Malus to ask at the next stopping point, "Do you know how to use your tongue, Se?"

Reiben thought it best to respond and said, "Yes."

The Malus continued to question him as they gave him his largest portion of food yet.

"How old are you, Se?"

Reiben answered, "Nine."

The Malus's eye brows knitted and he said, "Don't lie to us Se, you're no older than six."

Reiben carefully answered, "All the Se are of the same opinion, but my parents still tell me I'm nine."

The Malus acknowledged his answer with a grunt and continued, "Tell me your name, Se, for this is the last time you will ever say it. You are among the Malus now and all prisoners are called by the same word, Erda."

Erda, meant "dirt" in the old language. The Malus viewed dirt as that which is under foot, something to be walked upon. The Se considered dirt the source of life. From dirt came forth all of the food they ate to sustain their existence. Reiben answered with no inflection in his voice, "I am called Reiben among the Se."

The Malus smiled to themselves whilst considering this worthless speck of Se. Tiny, no back bone, could barely talk or think, he wouldn't last two days among the Malus.

A captured Se was highly prized in the town of Malus and considerable status was accorded the captors. These Malus needed this sliver of a Se alive when they reached home as he was no good to them dead. They decided to improve his treatment a bit so he would remain healthy. The captors emptied several more spoons full of food into his hands and gave him an oversized shirt for warmth. The beatings would end for now. Reiben did not question their change of heart nor offered any gratitude but he gladly accepted what was given.

Running with free hands was much easier for the young Se. No more tumbles with each new animal on the horizon and the Malus grumbled that they had several more hours of travel before reaching the next hut. Unbound hands allowed Reiben to think about more important things than preventing a fall; how were his parents and how could he escape and return to them?

Not knowing the fate of his mother, Reiben assumed both parents were safe and that their only concern was for his wellbeing. This ignorance was to be an asset. Reiben day dreamed about the surprise his parents would have when he walked through the front door. They would be so proud of him to have outwitted the Malus. All his friends would want to hear every detail of his captors and Aunt Sufi would be pleased with her star student.

The clever Reiben began planning his return to the atoll, plotting a mental map of their route so far, looking for any weaknesses his captors might display and opportunities that this landscape offered to aid in his escape. Each landmark was carefully catalogued by the little Uni. It was far too early for an attempt at flight, especially with a Malus standing on either side of him, but over time, an opportunity would present itself and he would seize that moment. The naivety of youth was a comforting friend to Reiben.

The three joggers arrived at the next hovel well before dark. This cabin was larger, equipped with bows and arrows and situated at the edge of a large meadow. A Malus' hunting outpost was its main use. Living on grains and mushrooms for the past few days had put the captors in a fouler mood.

"I need some meat," complained one Malus. Both men decided on rabbit and selected bows for the hunt.

"Erda, you sit by the hut where we can see you and don't move a muscle or even breathe," admonished the Malus as they set off.

With rabbits hopping everywhere at close range, Reiben was sure the brash abductors would have the main course in no time. The Se were masters at the art of archery and Reiben was proficient with a bow but by no means the best. These two, however, were lucky they did not hurt themselves.

An Ice Age comedy unfolded before the prisoner. The rabbits did not feel threatened by a bow toting Malus and leisurely hopped aside each time an arrow whizzed by. The archers yelled and cursed after each miss, blaming the other for his poor accuracy. They finally decided the smell of the filthy Se was putting the rabbits on edge and

Reiben was sent inside the hut.

There followed an extended period of screaming and, in the end, two older rabbits lacking any sense of direction ran headlong into the arrows. Of course the Malus version of the hunt, relayed to a dubious Reiben, was highly embellished.

The trio had a proper meal for the evening. A rabbit stew was prepared and Reiben found the meat agreeable. Full bellies assured the three had a good night's rest although Reiben had not grown accustomed to bound hands and feet whilst sleeping.

The group had walked for days yet travelled but a fraction of the total distance to their destination. It was obvious to the young Se that the Malus had been busy during the preceding millenniums. Their spheres of influence reached dangerously close to the atoll, making the land mass of the five islands seem insignificant in comparison to the expanse of territory under Malus control.

Another two days and the path along the ridge ended. They headed down the rear of the mountain range and continued to follow a wide path until the grasses of the higher elevations gave way to a thick forest. Reiben found it harder to keep his bearings as they walked through the dense trees. Any hope of finding his way back to the Southlands was diminishing.

A few more days among the tall trees and the Malus took a detour from the well-worn path toward a quaint dingle, at the end of which stood a small house. Smoke rose from the chimney and two elderly Malus were sitting down to dinner when the trio entered. They were the parents of one and aunt to the other of Reiben's captors.

Smiles and a look of surprise were exchanged between the relatives. There was a teeny Se standing in the home. The cousins wasted little time to recount the evolving tale of their trek to the Southland and capture of the prized Se. The adventure was told over a dinner of mushroom soup.

The elders' eyes remained fixed on the tiny prisoner. The senior Malus had seen a Se on only a few occasions and never one up close or so small.

"Are you sure you didn't snatch him while he napped," asked the mother. "He is a bit small to be visiting the Southland."

The two kidnappers, boiling over with feelings of an exaggerated accomplishment, reiterated how they had defeated five strong Se men before capturing the little one.

"Well, being so small, I'm sure he wasn't too much trouble to travel with. Did you drop him along the way? He certainly has a lot of bruises," declared the elderly father.

The group of Malus agreed that a better future was near at hand for the family. This valuable Se was their token to an improved life. These four of the forest had eked out a meager existence, collecting mushrooms for sale in town. Once the Pravis, leader of the enemies of the Se, saw how brave the two cousins had been, a farm would surely be theirs. Perhaps the one their grandparents had owned before it was seized. The parents could not have been happier with their son and nephew or their future prospects. Very few Malus families had such caring children.

"We'd better make sure this Se is in good health before you present him to the Pravis. You don't want the leader thinking you found him lost among the trees," said the mother.

The now pampered Reiben ate mushrooms morning, noon and night during the following two weeks with the occasional piece of meat thrown in. He was looking forward to taking leave of this mushroom way of life. After too long a stay in the tiny house built for two, the cousins and Reiben set out for the town of Malus. As the travelers exited the door, the confident son proclaimed, "Next time you see us mother, we'll have a farm of our own again."

Back on the Island of Rune, Munsi's time alone without Rissa or Reiben by his side, was devastating. Aunt Sufi and the other Se had tried everything to console him but to no avail. Sufi had carried the same emotional burden when she lost her husband and knew the best way to proceed was to sit quietly and calmly reassure the widower whenever he voiced his grief. The Se were known for their ability to listen before speaking. Sufi remained attentive during Munsi's emotional ups and downs and interjected, at the appropriate time, a few words to help guide him down his path of sorrow. During the silent moments between conversations, Sufi sat in Munsi's darkened home, thinking.

Everyone on the island knew Rissa had been buried at sea and most believed Reiben was lying dead somewhere in the southlands, but Sufi did not accept that second notion. Reiben was very much alive in her mind. Aunt Sufi was confident in her talents as a healer and her keen sense of intuition. She had never lost a mother or child during birth nor had been wrong about the prediction of a Uni. Even though, Reiben was small, reserved, and did not exhibit any qualities which elevated him above his peers, he was a Uni. A Uni who was still walked this earth. On that fact she was certain.

During this terrible time of pain, Sufi finally realized what Reiben's unique gift was. The nine year old had yet to understand that he was on a great journey, one where he would have to walk softly and possess a nimble mind, a journey that no Se she had ever met could undertake. Reiben's ability to forgo anger, jealousy and resentment when such character flaws were directed his way was this Se's greatest attribute. He was a Uni who had always remained true to the tenets of his upbringing no matter how difficult the circumstance.

The cold hearted Malus would play their part in Reiben's travels, setting him on the path to his final destination but there would also be others as well before this Uni's journey came to an end. The purpose of his odyssey or the question of whether he would ever grace the Se Atoll again was left to the unknown.

Sufi also knew her insights could not be shared with the distraught Munsi or the other Se. It would only add to everyone's sorrow; she had to keep her beliefs close to the heart. Sufi decided to send her positive thoughts his way, wherever he was, hoping they would slip past those despicable Malus and find Reiben.

4

Town of Mlus

The three travelers were well rested and the cousins' spirits high as they headed for the town of Malus. Reiben's bruised coloring had given way to his normally light tint of pink and though the cousins had no new found empathy for their prisoner, they did treat him moderately better as he was their key to a different life. The journey to the town could not end quickly enough for the anxious mushroom harvesters.

Each day the group continued their descent down the back side of the mountain until finally, the last bit of decline was behind them. The path widened and farms lay as far as the horizon. An occasional seagull flew overhead indicating salt water was not far and the three met ever increasing numbers of Malus as they drew closer to town. Both cousins took every opportunity to retell their evolving story of how this hated enemy of the Malus had been captured.

In their best orator's voice, they declared, "The small Se of privilege was surrounded by five well-armed warriors before we plucked him from their protection. We're sure he is of noble birth." The crowd of fascinated Malus found the tale entertaining but hardly believable.

Another half day's walk and the large town was in sight; the trio had attracted a sizeable entourage when they crossed the city limits. All were curious to see how the Pravis would greet the latest arrivals. For effect, a rope was once again tied around Reiben's hands at the edge of the town and he was slowly paraded along the main street. Word traveled quickly and it was not long before a throng of excited Malus slowed the pace of the three toward the town center. The young Se was fraught with dismay. Two angry cousins were difficult enough to endure but a multitude of shouting town folk shook Reiben to his core.

At long last, the trio stopped near a large circular dais which stood chest high to the cousins. It was Reiben's final destination, the Erda platform; a home open to all the eyes in town with no shelter from the weather. The three slowly climbed the steps of the dais and Reiben was fettered to a pole at its center. The cousins strutted around the platform with hands held high, acknowledging the enthusiastic crowd. The captors were confident that mushroom gathering was no longer in their future.

Once those assembled became quiet, the cousins recounted their adventure in the Southlands with grandiose rhetoric and poor acting. The crowd was in a festive mood and enjoyed the antics of the hapless actors; yet there was one person in the audience who expressed no emotion to their tale – the Pravis. The town leader had positioned himself within earshot of the theatrics but out of sight of the story tellers. He did not wish his presence to influence the duo's fictional narrative.

The Pravis, undisputed leader of the town, was a solidly built man of medium height and midway through his third decade on this earth. The numerous conflicts he'd had during the rise to the leadership position were etched on his face. A flattened nose, scars on his eyebrows, cheeks, jaws, and forehead; each distinctive mark had a story. Determined black eyes dominated his face. One look at the Pravis and every Malus was quick to give him a wide berth. With the cousins' elaborate fable completed, the Pravis slowly walked through the parting crowd toward the dais. Once the two adventurers saw the leader their stage bravado quickly evaporated.

"Good day, brave Pravis, we are back from the Southland and have a gift for you, a Se," said one cousin. The Pravis' movements were fluid and deliberate as he acknowledged the nervous captors with his intense stare and a raised eyebrow.

"We could think of no better way to show our courage than to capture a Se, wise Pravis," said the second cousin.

The Pravis walked to the center of the dais, knelt on one knee in front of the prisoner, held Reiben's chin in his hand, and looked straight into the little Se's eyes. Though his heart was pounding, Reiben did not flinch. He simply stared back at this Malus leader without a hint of fear or contempt. The Pravis had peered into the eyes of captured Se before and each had the same composure, even when bodily harm was imminent. The leader thought how effective an army of Se would be, they could look danger in the face and not succumb to panic.

The cousins continued, "Brave Pravis, we thought this display of courage on our part is deserving of a plot of land. As you know courageous men make excellent farmers. Our grandparents' farm should be a fitting reward for our efforts."

The Pravis stood and walked around with his arms crossed and a hand on his chin in thought. The cousins' grandparents had owned a large piece of property close to town years ago. They fell out of favor with the previous Pravis and were removed from their land on questionable charges. The grandparents were never seen in town again and a close relative of the previous leader enjoyed the prosperity of its fields.

"You have captured a tiny Se, which does show some courage and is thus worthy of a small parcel of land. There is a recently vacated property not far from town that you may have," said the Pravis.

The cousins started to protest but were cut short when the Pravis looked in their direction. "Thank you, wise Pravis, you are too kind," said the cousins as they quickly left the dais. A one cow, two pig farm closer to town was far better than mushroom collecting. The successful cousins hurried home to collect their elderly parents.

The Pravis looked at the latest arrival for several more moments then left the dais. Reiben could not determine what the leader was thinking but he was sure the Pravis was curious about him.

The town's newest attraction, the tiny island boy, drew Malus from near and far and they were not impressed by what they saw. With his back firmly placed against the pole, Reiben sat quietly throughout the excitement. Occasionally, a Malus child threw a rock in his direction to force some movement but for the most part, only curious eyes and unkind words were directed his way.

Every Malus had an opinion about the Se and his cowardly community and they expressed themselves loudly enough for Reiben to hear.

"I know his mother is surely happy to be rid of such a small Se."

"There must not be much food on those islands. They are shrinking in size."

"The Malus should not waste another day and go invade those worthless islands."

After a long day of gawking, darkness finally arrived and Reiben found himself alone at the end of his first day in town. The tiny Uni at last had time for thoughts which offered him little comfort. A return to the Se Atoll did not seem possible nor did his future appear bright in this group of hostile people. It was an inauspicious beginning for a young Se amongst the Malus.

For several weeks the town's latest addition drew large numbers of curious town folk but after a time the crowds began to dwindle. By the beginning of the harvest season, few Malus ever looked Reiben's way as they walked through the town center.

The Uni found his daily routine simple and unchanging; food and water were offered twice a day along with a weekly bath in a glacial waterway. This simplicity afforded extended periods of uninterrupted time for Reiben to survey his new home.

The town of Malus was large, nearly the size of the Island of Rune. It was located near the ocean, the weather was temperate and a large stream ran through its center. The north of town ended in vertical cliffs and the south stopped at flat farm land. Off in the distance, a thick, dark forest marked the end of tillable soil.

The Malus had far more resources than the Islands of Se, yet all that wealth had little influence on their disposition. As a group, the Malus were a miserable lot. Parents constantly yelled or spanked their children, town folks were afraid of their leaders and everyone vied to get one up on his neighbor. This constant angst left most Malus with an unhealthy outlook on his place in life.

Reiben and the Se captured before him could not comprehend why the Malus had such a negative mindset. To an island person, their frenetic energy was unsettling and physically draining. How could anyone survive such a fragmented way of life?

For every Se who sat on the Erda dais in years past, their time in town was short. Neither escape nor accepting the Malus way of life was ever viewed an option. Once the prisoner understood the reality of his situation, they found peace with themselves and went to sleep never to rise again.

But fortunately for nine year old Reiben, he had two important advantages which his predecessors did not: the immense optimism of a Se youth and the fact that he was born a Uni. These two critical attributes ensured this tiny Uni would stay alive and well amongst these inimical Malus for the foreseeable future.

As the time slipped by, Reiben's presence was no longer a novelty and he was eventually rarely noticed. To those around him, he had become a permanent part of the Erda platform. And in all that time, not a single Malus had shown any interest in holding a civil conversation with the prisoner. One could say Reiben was the latest Se statue in town.

The Pravis found his way to the town center once a week to observe the condition of the island boy. He never said a word to the Erda but had an inquisitive look on his face; the leader was surprised to find the Se still healthy and alert as he watched the daily activities of the town.

Reiben, for his part, paid close attention to the leader whenever he passed the dais. He discovered the Pravis to be a busy man as a constant crowd surrounded him wherever he went; there was a long queue of requests for favors or pleas for justice. The leader would stop for a moment, contemplate the facts and render a decision and then continue on his walk. All his decisions were final. Reiben correctly surmised that the Pravis's rise to power had been accomplished through his use of brawn but he also felt that there might be an inquiring mind inside that scarred head. Reiben wisely chose not to find out and was content to sit quietly tethered to the Erda platform watching the hectic lives of the Malus.

Another month and considerable commotion came to the town center. The blacksmiths' building required renovations and a new forge was to be installed. The Erda platform offered Reiben a front row seat to the construction. In typical Malus fashion, the job began with an argument as the laborers had given little thought on how the project should proceed.

The first half of the day was dedicated to shouting and walking around the building in frustration, but in the end, it was decided that the structure should have all its contents removed before any repairs were begun.

"We don't want the items smashed while we are working," said the brightest worker.

"We'd better bring in the beasts to help with the heavy lifting," said a second worker. Reiben had heard the word "beast" used before while he had listened in on the various conversations but he had no idea what type of animal it could be. The Malus always spoke in a respectful tone when referring to these creatures.

The following day the workers returned and started the day with another heated disagreement before the work began. By mid-morning all the smaller items had been removed and at noon the beasts were to arrive for the heavier lifting.

After lunch, a horse drawn cart surrounded by large crowd of excited children, travelled down the main street. In the back sat two large workers. Reiben's youthful curiosity began to bubble over. For the first time since the dais had become his home, he stood up and walked as far as his tether would reach for a better view of the beasts – or as the Se referred to them – the Groullen.

They sat in the cart, each with his legs chained together, waiting for the handler to direct them. The Groullen's handler was an unfortunate Malus whose position in town was that of caretaker to the beasts. His title was "Pundir" and his social status was the lowest person in town.

The two beasts showed no interest in all the attention they received from the wide-eyed children and jumped from the cart when prompted by the Pundir. The Groullens were everything Reiben had ever imagined and more. Standing a short distance from the dais they paused waiting for further commands. This gave Reiben time to take in the stature of these huge workers.

The Groullen resembled the Se but at much larger proportions - big noses, eyebrows, cheek bones, arms, legs, chest, hands, and feet. The top of their heads reached well above the floor of the dais and the little Uni did not have to ponder for any length of time as to whether these beasts had considerable strength. Yet, for all their physical extremes, Reiben found it hard to believe these Groullens were animals. His intuition told him they were not.

The beasts had been brought to the blacksmiths to do a job and it was time to get started, their display of power was the reason the children were present. When the Pundir led the Groullen into the building and pointed to the heaviest items for removal; large stone anvils, one under each arm, and out the door they walked, a massive forge with a beast on either corner was easily carried from the building. Every piece of equipment removed elicited a "Wow" from the young audience and the Se had never seen such feats of strength on the atoll. The Groullens removed heavy equipment, knocked down walls and support beams faster than a horde of town folk could have done in a week. The demolition was completed well before supper and the Malus workers assured all watching that the beasts would return tomorrow. Heavy lifting was also required for the renovations.

At the end of the day's work, the Groullens jumped up in the cart and returned to wherever they lived. Reiben could not understand why such strong beasts did not break the chains which held him and fight his way to freedom. Surely, the Malus held some sort of power over these men of might.

To the delight of Reiben, the Groullen did return each day for two weeks and he continued to marvel at their strength. Watching them became the highlight of his day and he observed every nuance of these beasts. They sat to eat like a Se, appeared to be talking to one another like a Se, appeared to laugh on occasion, and stopped to watch the world around them for brief moments. They were not the least bit bothered by all the excited children who constantly followed their every move.

At the end of the fortnight, Reiben concluded that the Groullen were not animals as the Malus believed, but a group of extremely strong people who had the misfortune of being shackled in this town. It appeared that the Malus treated all their neighbors with contempt.

After two entertaining weeks of observing the Groullens feats of strength, the only resident on the Erda platform sat quietly once again watched the slow march of changing seasons. Cooler temperatures eventually arrived and told everyone in town the shortest days of the year would soon be here. It was not long before the Malus mood became jovial as their attention was now focused on the Winter Carnival.

The day arrived when the Pravis led a large group of men on horseback out of town. They headed south, past the farm lands and through the dark forest to the frontier of the Malus world. The riders' objective was to capture half of the entertainment for the carnival - Malus fugitives.

The Pravis's brother Slugan, a smaller, younger version of the leader whose diminutive size was more than offset by his aggressive temperament, found his mount and led another group of men north to trap the second half of the entertainment- fierce Ice Age animals. Such plans for a festival were foreign to Reiben and he had no idea what they could entail.

With the departure of the town leadership and the bulk of its able men, the more reserved Malus were no longer shy and freely strolled down the streets as they enjoyed a peaceful reprieve from the angrier members of the community. Reiben realized that not all Malus shared the same unfriendly temperament. Smiles could be seen, laughter could be heard, and for a brief few moments, Reiben could imagine he was back on the Isle of Rune.

During this merrier time in town, two children took the opportunity to have the first Malus conversation with the Se. Without any hesitation, a girl about the same age as Reiben and a boy slightly older, climbed the dais and sat beside him.

The girl was not the least bit bashful and asked, "What is your name?"

Speaking for the first time in five months, Reiben was slow to answer, "Reiben."

"My name is Fij'n and this is Sanft," exclaimed the girl. "Are the islands of Se much like Malus?"

"No," answered Reiben.

"Do you miss your mother?" asked the girl.

"Yes," replied Reiben.

"Do you want to become a Malus?" asked Fij'n.

"No," answered Reiben.

All the talking was done by the girl – Fij'n. Sanft said nothing but appeared to be a keen listener.

It did not take long before the civil young girl offered Reiben a brief history of her short life. The Pravis's youngest sibling was her mother, Drist, and her father had died when she was two whilst in the frontiers of the south. He had been a baker and an artist and was known for a fine sense of humor. Fij'n was an only child and her mother had no tolerance for the frolicsome nature she inherited from her father. Such an attitude was disapproved of by her Uncle Slugan and viewed as contrary to the Malus way of life.

Sanft and Fij'n were cousins. Sanft was Slugan's youngest son and his mother was the previous Pravis's daughter. Sanft did not talk much at all, in fact no one knew if he could, and he spent far too much time drawing pictures which, of course, his father Slugan had little patience for.

On most days, Fij'n and Sanft were to be found indoors as their parents did not want them to be an embarrassment in front of the other Malus. But now that the uncles were out of town, they could play outside.

"Reiben, do you have any brothers or sisters?" asked Fij'n.

"No, I'm an only child and I was allowed to draw at home," answered Reiben who found he still had a bit of his humor after so long a time away from the atoll.

Their pleasant conversation was cut short as Fij'n's mother appeared with an angry scowl. She admonished her daughter and exclaimed, "Fij'n, Sanft, why are you talking to that troublesome Se? If your uncle finds out, more than one stick will be broken across your backside."

"All right, mother, we're coming," answered Fij'n in a carefree tone. Before running off Fij'n said to the Se, "Don't worry, Reiben, we'll be back tomorrow and you can tell us more about the islands you were born to."

True to their word, both returned the following day and their conversations lasted until Drist took a break from her busy day to look for her curious daughter. Fij'n brought bakery treats and delicious meats for Reiben which he ate slowly savoring the unusual tastes.

It did not take long before Reiben felt comfortable speaking to his Malus peers and he told them every detail about the Se atoll, most of which, the two young cousins found hard to believe.

"Wait, you are telling me that girls are taught archery and boys are taught healing just so they can learn all the knowledge on the atoll? And you're absolutely truthful when you say that no Se child is ever spanked?" asked an incredulous Fij'n. "How is that ever possible?"

Reiben made up for his months of silence as he talked incessantly. He explained to them the game of Sand Ball, sled racing, bonfires on the beach, the Southland, fishing, and the happiness found in every Se. Reiben spoke so many words in such a short time, his voice became hoarse.

However, after two carefree weeks, Reiben the chatterbox was forced back to silence as his time with Fij'n and Sanft came to an abrupt end. The gathering parties had returned. The fortnight of secret conversations had passed far too quickly for the three young children.

The leaders had been successful during their expeditions. Twenty-five chained Malus were paraded through town before assembling in Reiben's neighborhood – the dais. The prisoners were tethered alongside Reiben, each with a forlorn face. Their ages ranged from young to old and they appeared in excellent physical and mental health.

Having escaped the town of Malus and finally in control of their own lives, these prisoners did not look upon Reiben with disdain. The new Erdas no longer viewed the Se as an enemy.

A large crowd surrounded the platform and voiced their delight at the predicament of the less fortunate prisoners and some of the theatrics surrounding the winter carnival were about to begin.

The Pravis, never the orator, left most public speaking to his fervent younger brother. Taking a position atop the dais, Slugan began his speech. He started by outlining the virtues of the Malus way of life and described how the Se and Malus had once been neighbors in the lands southeast of town.

Slugan continued his pontification, "The Se lost their way and made the erroneous decision, so many years ago, to abandon the Malus in the Southlands and isolate themselves on those small fragments of land in the water. For reasons known only to our forefathers, our ancestors chose to relocate to this present location, which has offered us an unlimited bounty ever since. Yet, even today our greatness and riches are not enough, as some of our citizens become disillusioned, abandoning the community for the frontiers. These twenty-five misguided Erdas shall feel the consequences for those actions during our winter celebration and the pathetic Se will remain in bondage as a constant reminder of the reckless decisions of his people."

The crowd erupted in a chorus of cheers and many in the audience were relieved that their dissatisfaction with the town had not propelled them to leave only to be returned in chains. There was only one way of thinking in the town of Malus and it was dangerous to voice opposition through words or with your feet.

The crowd now had an opportunity to view the twenty-five new prisoners up close and peppered the Erdas with unnerving comments.

One callous Malus yelled to the condemned, "This year, the wild beasts look extra ferocious for you runaways. The Pit of Strength is only a few days away. Make sure you eat well and get a lot of sleep."

Several prisoners eventually yielded to fear after a steady tirade of such taunts but most remained brave in the face of what was to come.

After the Malus had had their morbid fun with the prisoners and were off to their homes for the evening, an eager Erda asked Reiben, "Se, how long have you been sitting on this platform? "

"Five months," replied Reiben.

A second prisoner said, "I think I'd prefer my chances in the pit instead of a set of chains the rest of my life."

A third prisoner asked, "Do you have a pit on your islands, Se?"

A confused Reiben answered, "I don't even know what a pit is."

The eldest condemned Erda explained in painful detail the spectacle each prisoner was about to face.

The Pit of Strength. A contest which embodied the warped thinking of the Malus – placed two weak Erdas in close proximity to a strong beast in mortal combat for entertainment. The stage for the drama was an arena which abutted the cliffs at the north of the town. Caves in the cliff were the staging area for the participants, both Erdas and wild beasts. Under the guise of entertainment, the Pit of Strength served two purposes. First, to rid the territory of former town residents who had escaped the town and second, to scare those who remained into forgetting any thoughts about leaving. When the idea for the pit had been initially conceived no Malus could remember but it had been the highlight of the winter carnival for many a generation. There was but one objective in the arena, defeat the wild beast, and if an Erda did, the prisoner was a free Malus once more. As yet, no prisoner had ever walked through the pit gates to freedom.

The grand finale occurred on the last day when a Groullen who had outlived his usefulness to the town was sent into the pit. An aging beast was far stronger than any Malus and had no fear for the fierce animals. With a spear in hand and a zeal for conflict, the men of might amazed the audience with their abilities in combat. Yet there was also no memory of any Groullen who had survived in the arena.

Reiben found the Pit of Strength's description disconcerting. He assured his fellow prisoners that the Se had no such contests. Their most raucous event was an evenly matched game of Sand Ball. The Malus never ceased to amaze Reiben with their cruel practices and he did not understand what path they could have followed to embrace such a brutal mindset.

During the two weeks prior to the winter carnival, several more Malus lost heart due to the continuous gibes. These men cried and begged for a mercy which never came. The remaining prisoners were steadfast and resigned to their dismal fate.

Two days before the carnival began the twenty-five prisoners said their farewells to Reiben and wished him a better ending than theirs. They were loaded in wagons which slowly wound their way through the rowdy throng to the holding caves of the pit. Reiben sat alone on the platform once more.

After the frantic final preparations, the gates opened and every seat in the arena was soon occupied. Reiben found himself the lone person in the town center and he heard the cheers of the crowd each time the animals were triumphant. He counted twenty-eight celebrations before the last day. A few more citizens who were no longer welcome in Malus had been added to the list of fatalities. On the final day of the carnival, there were three thunderous cheers – the beasts had been culled in the pit.

The drama of the Pit of Strength was on everyone's tongue during the following week and quite disturbing for the young Reiben to overhear. Each gory detail was repeated a number of times by those who walked past the dais. The additional town folk added to the entertainment list had been citizens whom Slugan found offensive.

The town's second in command fancied himself occupying the position his brother currently filled and he appeared quite presumptuous with his authority. Slugan's ambition far exceeded his abilities and no Malus had any idea where his quest for power would take him.

Of the three Groullens who fell in the pit, one was the largest beast in the cave – their leader. The dynamics surrounding the selection of a new leader of the beasts unfolded a few days after the Winter Carnival. For reasons unknown to the Malus, the position of Pundir was particularly precarious during this time; the current one did not survive the week and the post of beast handler was now vacant.

It had been almost a half year since Reiben's departure from the Southland and his days of idleness in the hostile town were to end. The Malus leaders had selected the Se for a new job, a new home and a new title. Reiben was to be the latest Pundir.

On the following morning, three guards arrived at the town center and told a surprised Reiben, "Your time sitting on the Erda platform is over Se, you have an important job now, one with a title. You'll no longer be living off the sweat of the Malus."

A laughing guard untied the little Erda and led him through the streets towards the north of town.

"I doubt you'll last as long as the one you're replacing. The beasts will take one look at you and snap your neck like a twig," said another Malus with a chuckle.

In Reiben's mind, the Pundir position was the furthest from good fortune one could possibly wish for. Since his introduction to these people, Reiben had experienced nothing but hardship, yet he had little time for self-pity as his new job started immediately. Reiben said not a word as they walked to the cliffs or when the guards shoved him through the barred doors into the beasts' cave. He neither spoke nor dared move from where he stood once inside. At several paces from the frozen Se stood a group of Groullen, all eyes were trained on the tiny Pundir.

5

Servant to the Groullens

A prolonged staring standoff filled the space at the cave entrance. The Groullen had appeared large from the comfort of the dais but now standing two paces in front of the Se they were huge. Reiben could not detect any emotion in their bulky faces but he dared not move. Both Pundir and beast stood motionless for some time before the Groullens finally grunted and moved to the back of the cavern.

"There you have it Se, a proper beast introduction," said one the Malus from the safety of outside the cave.

"Now listen here you worthless Se, you need to do some cleaning up before you get too comfortable in there," ordered another guard. "There are bodies which have to be removed. You get the beasts' attention then point to the bodies and point to the cave door. They'll do the rest."

"Which bodies?" asked a nervous Reiben.

"The ones lying on the cave floor not moving, you dim witted Se," barked a guard in irritation.

It was a long few minutes before Reiben cautiously made his way to the back of his new home. After twenty paces the cave opened into a spacious, high ceiled area, devoid of any stalagmites or stalactites and a slight breeze could be felt moving towards the front gate. It took several moments for his eyes to adjust to the dim light but he found there was more than ample room for the twelve Groullen in the cavern.

Now able to see, Reiben walked with slow deliberate steps and looked for the deceased bodies. He found the previous Pundir with a broken neck and two Groullen displaying fatal wounds on the ground.

Reiben quickly returned to the front of the cave and told the Malus that he had found three bodies then asked if they had any suggestions on how he should get the Groullen's attention.

"I told you, you useless Se there should be four bodies and a loud whistle or hand clap will get their attention. Then just point to the body and point to the cave door and the beasts will do the rest. How many times am I going to have to tell you how to do your job, you inept Se?" yelled a Malus.

Reiben returned to the first body, whistled his loudest, pointed to the deceased and then pointed to the cave door. The closest Groullen grabbed a foot and dragged a lifeless Pundir to the door.

After the three deceased had been pulled out front, a Malus yelled, "There is one more in there and he's the biggest. You can't miss him. Find him and get him out here quick."

Feeling slightly more comfortable amongst the cave dwellers, Reiben hurried around the cavern looking for a Groullen larger than the rest. There were no more bodies on the ground but one lay on an elevated stand of rocks at the back of the cave.

Carefully Reiben approached him; he appeared to be sleeping. Reiben watched for breathing and tried to assess his overall physical condition. The Groullen was alive, dry blood on his temples indicated a severe bash to the head and he had a nasty broken leg. Reiben ran to the cave door to relay the information. "The biggest one is still alive."

"Is the beast awake?" asked a Malus.

"Yes and I don't think he is too happy," replied Reiben in a stoic tone.

"Just leave him alone, he'll not live long. Now keep those other beasts at the back of the cave while we get these bodies out of there," ordered an angry Malus.

"What do I do next," asked an inquisitive Reiben.

"Keep your scrawny neck away from the beasts' hands you bothersome Se and get back in there with your cave mates," laughed the Malus. Reiben returned to the large open space he now called home.

The Se had completed his first task as the new Pundir - removing the corpses. His second and most pressing issue was to attend to the large Groullen's wounds. With caution as his guide, Reiben carefully positioned himself by the huge patient for a more detailed physical examination. It did not take long for the inexperienced Pundir to deduce that this Groullen was the leader; he was massive and had his own bed of rocks. But he was incapacitated at the moment.

Reiben determined the leader had a deep cut on his forehead which resulted in a serious concussion and rest would mend that injury. His broken femur was a more challenging matter and far too difficult for the nine year old to manage on his own, it necessitated some assistance from the larger members in the cavern.

On that day, the inhabitants of the cave had their first basic lesson in healing. Deploying the same technique used to remove the bodies, Reiben whistled loudly and pointed to the leader. None of the Groullens moved. He whistled several more times which had the same results. No movement. Reiben was determined to administer a simple, corrective procedure to the leader even if it meant risking physical harm to himself. He made a bold decision and walked over to the nearest Groullen, grabbed his index finger (the Groullen hand was far too large for the young Reiben to hold) and pulled with all his strength towards the rock bed.

After a few moments of vigorous Se tugging, the Groullen followed Reiben. He positioned the Groullen near the leader's head and placed the leader's wrist in his newly appointed assistant's hand. He then said, "Stay right there." Three more helpers were also brought into service. One stationed at the other hand and at each foot.

Fortunately, the Groullens were familiar with the "pull" command. That is to say, the Groullens knew how to pull with their considerable might. Once directed, quite a scene unfolded. Four huge Groullen used their extraordinary strength to stretch a patient who had been thought to be near death. Between the yelling and flopping about, the not so dead leader's leg was easily set and the four assisting Groullen thankfully understood the word, "Stop."

Reiben, the mastermind behind this procedure, received the undivided attention from his furious patient. Shouting in a low growling voice, the Groullen leader brought all cave dwellers to a standstill. Reiben stood a safe distance from the patient and believed the leader was well on his way to a complete recovery. Though, he would wait some time before he placed a splint around the leg.

Having completed the two most important tasks for the day, Reiben now had time to survey the cave more thoroughly. In a word, his new home was - filthy. For too many years, the cave occupied by these servants to the Malus had not received the benefit of a broom. There was debris everywhere, limited cooking utensils, one medium sized pot and a fire pit without burning wood. No torches lined the walls and garbage was stacked high in the corners. This cave required a serious scrubbing. Reiben's next project was to collect all the debris and place it at the door. It was an hour before midday when Reiben began and not one of the other cave dwellers helped. They simply watched the new Pundir carry arms full of trash past them.

By early afternoon a large pile of rubbish sat by the bars. The guards, who had brought half cooked meat for lunch, were not happy with the collection of trash blocking the door.

An incredulous Malus barked, "What you doing you ignorant Se! Keep all that Groullen filth in the cave. Don't block the front gate with it."

The quick minded Reiben responded, "I think the garbage upsets the beasts and that's why they broke the last Pundir's neck. I wish to keep my neck as long as possible."

Irritated, the Malus replied, "We're not picking up beast refuse. We'll bring a wagon around tomorrow and you and your thick headed cave mates can load the rubbish into the wagons before you take them out to work." Reiben was more than satisfied with that solution.

After several more minutes of ranting about the inferior character of every Se, the guards presented a slab of under-cooked beef for the Groullen and a bowl of slop for Reiben; not a proper meal for either. Adequate food was another challenge Reiben would have to sort out in the near future.

The Groullens did not appear to be troubled by the quality of the beef and quickly devoured every bit. Their leader, deep in sleep, had no interest in food and his body had not moved on the rock bed since his leg had been set.

Lunch completed, the industrious Pundir continued the cave cleanup. Before dinner, the remaining cave refuse blocked all but a narrow path to the front door. There was more cursing by the Malus about the trash, more under cooked beef for the Groullen and another bowl of swill for the Pundir. Reiben's first day as the beast handler was nearly complete.

Shortly after dinner the cave grew dark. The Groullen wasted little time and lay down on the dirt floor near the leader's rock bed. Sleep soon followed for the cave dwellers with the Groullen snoring louder than a pack of howling wolves. Before Reiben found his own dirt bed he carefully set the splint on the leader's leg; gingerly placing two pieces of wood over the injury and wrapping them with an old hide, then he found his own spot. The novice Pundir found little sleep that night due to the loud snoring echoing off the cave walls.

True to their word, angry guard arrived with two wagons after breakfast, one for the Groullen and the other trash. There was so much rubbish it took two more full wagons to haul it all away. During the night, the pile of garbage had attracted scavengers, one of whom was a less fortunate member in the town of Malus, a runt puppy.

Dogs were not members of the community on the Se Atoll and Reiben had only seen them from afar on the Erda dais. Reiben and the tiny pup had a quick introduction. After a cursory inspection, Reiben could tell the poor animal had been abandoned by his mother and abused by the cruelest children in the town. Reiben immediately empathized with one so small and mistreated and brought him to the back of the cave. Would the Groullens view this tiny piece of fur as a snack? Reiben had little time to find out. Work in the town was calling. Thinking quickly, Reiben took a chance and placed the pup in the armpit of the Groullen leader, both needed plenty of rest to recuperate. Satisfied, Reiben ran to begin his second day as the Pundir.

The trash wagon was full and the second one was used to carry three of the Groullens. Reiben followed the wagon carrying the beasts. Today the work crew was travelling a short distance from town to fell trees. The Groullen wagon was once again a source of excitement for the youths; the little Se was just an afterthought to the group of children. For Reiben it was good to be outside, stretching his unshackled legs by walking and breathing in fresh air.

After walking a quick half hour from town, they arrived at the logging site. Growing between the abundant trees, Reiben discovered that much of the flora surrounding the town was the same healing plants found in the Southland. The Malus were obviously ignorant to all the useful herbs flourishing by their doorstep.

It was time for work to begin and the tasks were distributed as follows: The Malus men acted as the lumberjacks and chopped down the trees. They did not wish for a beast running around loose with an axe in his hand. The Groullens were the heavy machinery, carrying felled trees to the river for transport to the town and Reiben was the machine operator.

Once again, the Groullens' display of strength amazed all. Reiben was sure he would never grow tired of watching their power, but on this day, a new dimension was added to the work force's list of tools. Reiben was proficient in basic geometry and rudimentary mechanics which he brought to bear on this job. Logging was no longer dependent solely on brute strength to maneuver a log. Fulcrums, center of gravity, leverage, angles, and a good deal of Se common sense proved highly effective when applied to the task of hauling felled trees. Reiben directed the Groullens efficiently as they navigated each log towards the river.

Besides an understanding of basic math, Reiben possessed an additional quality which had never before been seen in a Pundir — synergy. The Se and beasts worked well together. The tiny Pundir and the huge Groullen became a competent team. This effective combination placed the work crew well ahead of schedule and the logging was completed in one day instead of two.

The new Pundir had another surprise for the Malus as he broke a long standing practice at the midday break. He ate alongside his fellow workers. During the afternoon meal, Reiben took time to evenly distribute the under cooked food among the Groullen, then promptly seated himself between two large beasts. The diminutive Se appeared so out of place beside the huge Groullens and no Pundir had ever eaten with the beasts before. With knitted brows and several grunts exchanged between them, the confused creatures stared at Reiben. Both Malus and Groullen were intrigued by this island boy's actions.

But the unassuming Pundir was not finished with his breach of protocol. When the day's work ended, all four of the cave dwellers went to the river and bathed. Reiben unshackled the Groullens' ankles and sat them in the water to soak off years of grime. The men of might were tentative at first but after much coaxing they sat in the cool water and splashed each other like playful children. The bathing experience appeared an enjoyable first for the Groullen; there was considerable growling among the beasts to complement their pushing and splashing but Reiben did not perceive any of it as anger.

After half an hour in the glacial waters, bath time was over. A tired Reiben loaded the three clean workers onto the wagon, along with a bundle of firewood and herbs he had collected. They returned to the cave earlier than expected and Reiben decided to leave the shackles off the Groullen, a decision the Malus guards, surprisingly, did not object to.

Back at the cave, Reiben quickly checked on the newest member – the pup. To his relief the runt was unharmed and still lay asleep in the armpit of the Groullen leader. Reiben picked up the tiny ball of fur and gave him a thorough inspection. He discovered malnutrition, matted fur and lacerations in every stage of healing but also a pair of smart, twinkling eyes staring back at him. The two runts formed an immediate kinship and the insightful Reiben was soon to realize the most important trait of his new found friend.

When a dog who has walked in the shadow of his own demise with no hope on the horizon, had a hand reach out to pluck him from his cruel path and gave him the simplest of creature comfort: food, a pat on the head, a few words of kindness and a warm place to sleep at his benefactor's feet, then that hand would receive the greatest love and loyalty in all the world. Such was the bond now formed between Reiben and the tiny wolf. Reiben whispered to the pup, "I don't have a name for you as of yet little one, but it will come, because every name finds its owner." Reiben placed the pup in his shirt for warmth and to let the runt hear the beat of his heart. It was not long before he slept again.

Dinner without a fire was no way to prepare a meal but the herbs collected that day added some flavor to the cold beef. When the late meal was served, all the cave dwellers sat in a circle (another Pundir first) with the pup in the middle. The runt excitedly ate the bits of meat each Groullen offered. As Reiben watched the interactions around the circle he was sure the Groullens possessed more Se qualities than those of a feral beast. Unlike other wild animals, they appeared to communicate with each other with growls and hand movements and found the company of the runt as pleasurable as he did.

After dinner it was early to bed for the tiny pup. The Groullen leader's armpit would remain the runt's bed for now. Reiben adjusted the splint on the leg of the leader under the watchful eyes of his cave mates and carefully completed the task without a single outburst from the patient. Night arrived early in a cave without lights and Reiben like the other cave dwellers welcomed the comfort of his dirt bed. He was too exhausted to wake from the thunderous Groullens snoring.

A belly full of food and a good night's sleep brought significant improvement to the bright eyed pup. While the Groullen leader continued to lie unmoving. Reiben began to think that the Malus may have been correct; the leader would succumb to his injuries. Though, it did not seem reasonable that a healthy Groullen with only a concussion and broken leg should wither away. Reiben had to get some nutrients inside the leader but the day's work outside the cave was calling.

Today, the crew had to dislodge several felled trees which were stuck on the river's bank. Reiben selected three different Groullen for the task and headed to the wagon.

By the noon break the logs had been safely floated to town and all four inhabitants of the cave ate then bathed in the river. These Groullens found the aquatics just as enjoyable as the others.

Reiben collected additional firewood and herbs on his return trip to the cave and upon arrival to his new home, found two visitors waiting for him - Fij'n and Sanft. Their conversation began when the excited Fij'n asked, "Reiben, have the beasts beaten you up yet?"

Reiben replied, "No, they have never seen a Se before so they don't know what to do with me".

A candid Fij'n said, "The town is talking about your treatment of the beasts, eating beside them and making them wash, what plans do you have for them next?"

A clever Reiben replied, "I am glad you asked as I was wondering if you could help me. As you know, the Pundirs are known for short life spans, but I think if I can keep the beasts well fed that might improve my chances. Can you two get me a few items?"

Fij'n cautiously replied, "Like what?"

Reiben answered rather matter of fact, "Simple things, like a few more pots, some bowls, a metal rod for a spit, and something to start a fire. Not much at all."

Fij'n said, "I can't get all of that, maybe a few items."

Reiben smiled and said, "Whatever you bring would be much appreciated."

Their conversation was cut short as several adult Malus walked by. Fij'n quickly feigned anger and shouted, "You're too easy on those beasts, Se. They're here for one reason, to work. This town needs more work out of them!" Then she added under her breath, "I'll see you later," and off she went with Sanft.

Reiben found the brief moments with Fij'n and Sanft hard. Several minutes of a civil conversation scattered across irregular intervals was difficult. But he did appreciate talking with someone who spoke intelligibly and did not grunt a collection of growls.

Reiben returned to the back of the cave and found that the health of his two patients was quite different. The runt was happy and full of energy while the Groullen leader continued to sleep and his breathing had slowed. Reiben risked a bold move and shook the leader; he did not stir. Reiben's limited resources left him rather frustrated. If his simplest appeals were answered, a fire to make a bowl of broth and the Groullen patient to drink the broth then this leader would recover. He was in a quandary as how to proceed and after dinner sleep came to him late.

Reiben woke early to find the items he had requested were neatly stacked by his dirt bed: a bowl for each member of the cave; three more pots of varying sizes; a ladle, one sharp knife, a metal spit with support hardware and a flint to start a fire. Reiben and the pup walked around the cave and looked for whoever could have brought these items. They found no one. Did Fij'n and Sanft steal into the cavern in the early morning? Reiben was anxious to find out and also to discover how they snuck past the guards an entered the cave.

His first task of the day was to start a fire and prepare a healthy soup. Reiben's skill with the flint was minimal but after numerous attempts, he finally had flames. Part of the morning breakfast beef was diced and placed into the pot, along with every herb collected by Reiben. By dinner, the Groullen would have a new entree on the menu.

Today's schedule of work was to collect large rocks on the opposite side of town. Reiben and a new group of Groullen set out to complete the task. The path to the work site went through the town center. Barely a week had passed since Reiben had left the prisoner platform and the dais already had several new occupants. Their faces were pitiful and it was evident that they were not long for this world. The Se was so distracted with his new position as Pundir, he had almost forgotten that for seven months the Erda platform had been his home. The position of Pundir was hard work but much better than being shackled to the dais.

At the work site, the effective combination of Se and Groullen was again placed in to motion. The Groullens' strength and Reiben's analytical mind meant another job was completed early. The work party, washed and hungry, returned to the cave and the delicious aroma of beef stew greeted them well before they reached the door. Their Malus guards declared, "Se, since you got rid of all that rubbish, the cave smells much better."

Reiben found a hungry group of Groullen awaiting his return and an excited runt jumping up and down on the leader's chest. The Se was soon to discover yet another one of the many talents of the dog.

Besides an acute sense of smell and excellent loyalty, the Ice Age dog possessed a number of innate qualities which were beneficial to the bipeds. The dog could read human emotions, detect human illness, recognize human mental shortcomings, and was eager to share this information with any person who stood nearby.

At present, the excited pup was desperately trying to

communicate with the Se. The runt feverishly licked the leader's face, nose and ears with the enthusiasm of a young pup with something to say and the intuitive Reiben had stopped to listen. He walked over and stood by his large patient.

After several minutes, a groggy leader moved his head from side to side and started to pat the runt. In a voice weakened by injury and malnutrition, the leader growled the word, "Grrick." Every cave dweller heard the word and they slowly gathered around the leader. Reiben was as curious as his cave mates to see what happened next. The leader repeated the word, "Grrick," several more times then opened his eyes.

The runt's effusive licking did not slow nor did the Groullen leader appear bothered by persistence of the little pup. He continued to gently stroke the dog as if in thought. All assembled held their breath and waited for what the leader might do next. Finally he picked up the runt in his massive hand and sat up.

Feeling light headed, it took him several moments to focus. The Groullen looked down at his splint and then at Reiben; he had no emotion in his eyes. Reiben seized the opportunity to fill a bowl of broth and present it to the leader. Still confused, the leader took some time before he accepted the soup and drank it. Reiben offered him additional bowls of soup; all were consumed. (The rest of the cave inhabitants would have to go with less broth tonight.) The Groullen leader sat holding the puppy for some time and then finally stood up. A collective, low growl could be heard from the other Groullen. It had always been believed impossible for a fallen Groullen to ever stand again.

The guards had not understated the size of this leader. Weighing more than two good sized Malus adult males, the leader stood a half a head taller than everyone in town. He was by far the largest beast in the cave. Steadying himself for a few moments, rocking slightly to his right and left, he took a halting first step. The energy level among the other Groullen was high as their leader had not been expected to live much less walk.

In Groullen society the complexities of a non-Groullen life did not exist. The strongest Groullen was always the leader. A cave was just fine as a home, the long spear was preferred to the bow, and a sharp stone was the knife of choice. Such an unsophisticated way of life made it appear that the Groullens were only a few rungs above the rest of the animal kingdom.

Another simplistic belief of these cave dwellers was that when a Groullen slept he was in the clouds with his forefathers and when he awoke and stood up, he was alive. This leader, with a broken leg, could not stand and every Groullen, including himself, assumed he remained in the clouds. Many a fallen Groullen was left for dead with just a minor break to his leg on the open plains during a hunt.

Unbeknownst to Reiben, the cave dwellers' view of their leader was now turned upside down and confused. How could a few pieces of wood wrapped around a leg allow the leader to walk again? Why would a non-Groullen, the Pundir, take the time to help a Groullen? Reiben was too busy preparing dinner and trying to convince the leader to remain seated to notice the puzzled looks on each of his cave mates' faces.

After frantically preparing the evening meal, it was again served in a circle that included an important new member. The pup had an additional hand feeding him pieces of meat. The growling and hand movements among the Groullen were livelier now that the leader had rejoined them. Reiben thought he detected a few smiles from these Beasts and knew each enjoyed the antics of the pup.

At bed time, Reiben was exhausted. The job of cooking, cleaning and caring for twelve Groullens with a rambunctious pup under foot was tiring for a nine year old boy but no words of complaint ever crossed this Se's lips. Reiben was using his mind and hands and was no longer fettered to a pole as a constant object of Malus amusement. Like a true Se, Reiben had made the best of a situation which was far from ideal.

Reiben held the runt before placing him with the leader for the night and declared, "Little one, you're a runt no longer. A proper name has found its way to you, "Grrick" and I must say it is quite unique. I also believe you're the most popular one in the cave. I hope that does not go to your head." Grrick excitedly licked Reiben's face. The pup understood every word the tiny Uni had said.

On the Se Atoll, the worst of winter had arrived and no one could be found outside. Munsi was still mired in his sadness. The widower's heart had not healed during the previous months nor had his despair subsided. Munsi was lost in the sea of his heavy burden.

Sufi, on the other hand, missed her little Uni but was convinced more than ever that Reiben was safe. There were many questions in this world that Sufi could not answer even with her extensive knowledge; why had her husband been plucked from her side so long ago and why had that chain of events occurred which placed Munsi, Rissa, and Reiben on a drastically different path in life?

Her eyes became teary from these heart wrenching thoughts. A good cry never solved the mysteries of the universe but did keep Sufi moving forward. After her eyes were dried and she had calmed herself Sufi said, "Well then, now that my tears have stopped, a strong cup of warm brew is in order to make things right."

With a cup in hand, Aunt Sufi sat by the warm fire and pondered some more about the one who was lost but still very much alive in this world, her favorite Uni. She said, "Ah, my tiny Se, I know you're out there, living in a place which no one knows where. I wish I could lend you a hand, but I can't. The best I can do is offer you my positive thoughts which, hopefully, will find their way past those ill mannered Malus. Please always remember that you're a Uni, so there is no reason to ever fret. Reiben, I know you'll choose the right path to follow and ...." Sufi's voice suddenly fell silent. Her well of tears was full once more.

6

Midnight Thieves

A new way of life, beneficial to those in the beast cave, had now been established. The cavern was cleaned regularly and healthy food served daily. The enticing aroma of soup filled the living space and most of the northern corner of town. Every Malus with an appetite was tempted to stop and ask for a bowl of delicious broth when they passed by. The Pundir and his cave mates, with the exception of the Groullen leader, enjoyed frequent baths; Reiben thought it best that the leader's leg completely heal before he took him outside. A warm fire was always lit and Grrick offered constant entertainment for those in the cave. The work crew's efficiency continued to improve and the Groullens had more free time as each daily task was finished early. As for the new Pundir, he found no idleness in his day. Reiben's time was spent perfecting his skill as the beast handler and assuring each town project was completed on time.

It had been four weeks since Reiben became the latest handler of beasts and the guards finally realized that the third Groullen from the pit should have died. That morning when they opened the bar door in their normal surly mood a Malus yelled. "Se, when are you going to bring that dead Groullen to the front door, we don't want his unsavory smell filling up the town."

Reiben walked to the bars and replied, "He's still alive."

Another Malus angrily yelled, "Listen here you ungrateful Se, no beast can last a month without food or water. You get those other slow wits to drag him to the front quick or I have a thick piece of leather that will fit nicely across your back if you don't."

Reiben walked back into the cave and returned with the leader. The guards and every Malus within eyeshot of the door stood gaping. No beast had ever survived the pit, yet there stood the Groullen looking healthier now than before his ordeal.

Reiben and the leader gazed back at the Malus; a pregnant silence filled the space between them. Finally a Malus guard asked, "What type of trickery are you up to, Se? That beast was sure as gone when he was carried to the cave the only thing left to do was bury him, now he's standing right in front of me."

A calm Reiben replied, "He was just knocked unconscious that is all, no trickery." The Malus did not believe Reiben but they could offer no other explanation for why this Groullen stood before him.

"I can assure you, Se, the Pravis is going to hear about this and he doesn't take kindly to any form of deception," exclaimed another of the perplexed guards.

A month of excellent service as the Pundir and what was Reiben's reward? Trouble. No good deed went unpunished in the town of Malus.

The following day, guards arrived at the cave to escort Reiben to a private audience with the Pravis. Word had reached every home in town that the Se had saved the beast and was now to meet with the leader in order to explain how he did so.

A large crowd, certain the Se's end was near, followed the Pundir on his route to the Pravis's home. The island boy was outwardly calm but feared this meeting would have an unpleasant outcome. When he reached the house, Reiben took one last deep breath before passing through the Pravis' front door.

It came as no surprise to Reiben that the leader's home was the largest and most lavish in town. A square structure with plenty of room to stand straight and stretch ones arms and it was filled with the latest furnishings. Bench chairs with cushions, a large hearth, pewter flagons, embossed cutlery, bunk beds covered in thick bear furs and shelves along the wall stocked with the finest food. A large elevated chair for the town's leader was the centerpiece of the home and four lowly stools stood in front of the seat of authority for use by nervous visitors.

When Reiben arrived, he found the town's elite had gathered to view this Se. The Pravis' wife and three daughters, Slugan, his wife and two eldest sons stood in the audience along with several broad shouldered men whilst two servants prepared food. Reiben positioned himself on one of the small stools and was now the focal point for all in the room.

After a few minutes of silence the Pravis began. "I hear so many stories from every corner of this town about the tiny Se. How is it that one so small can be that busy?" Reiben did not respond to the rhetorical question. "I would like you to begin by telling me about the islands of Se. My niece and nephew were quite impressed by what they heard," asked the Pravis in a voice which carried no emotion.

The cautious Reiben chose his words carefully. He was well aware of the mindset of his audience and much like Fij'n and Sanft, the assembled Malus found Reiben's account of life on the atoll hard to fathom.

The Se's view of the world was quite different to the way the Malus saw things. Slugan, the most vocal of those in the room, belittled the Se society and likened it to weakness. "While the Se raise their children without the aid of a sturdy stick and teach them useless knowledge, we Malus are expanding our reach and will soon be knocking on the islands front door. What will the Se do then?" The ever clever Reiben remained silent. The Pravis's temperament, however, was neither impetuous nor narrow minded like his rash sibling. The leader was not as hasty to discount the teachings of the Se based on a historical dislike for a people he rarely saw.

The Pravis had a keen mind as well as brawn and a genuine interest in understanding why the Se viewed the world so differently. The leader asked, "Of what use is a Se upbringing in a time of conflict? How could it withstand the strength of the Malus?"

Reiben's quick mind and diminutive size were to be an asset on this occasion as he responded. "I am but a child of nine, small in stature and far from the years of wisdom. Why the Se elders' choose such a path is beyond my understanding."

The impulsive Slugan responded with a barrage of unkind words, whilst the Pravis sat in thought. The leader felt sure Reiben was clever enough not to disrespect the Malus beliefs in front of the ones who controlled his future.

After some time in thought and still staring at the Se, the Pravis changed his line of questioning and asked, "I would like you to tell me how that beast is alive today after near death in the pit." Finally, a topic with which Reiben felt comfortable expounding on. He explained in detail what had transpired over the past four weeks concerning life among the Groullen. The cave cleaned, the improved diet, the need for proper beast bathing, and the addition of the pup; he did not mention the gifts which arrived during the night.

The Pravis continued, "Se, for one so young and small, your quality of care for the beasts is a surprise, but would you be so helpful to those who bind your hands and whip your back – a Malus?"

Reiben, with no hesitation answered, "Yes."

"And why?" asked the expressionless Pravis.

Reiben replied without condescension, "Because you would be in need of the help. As foolish as the Se may be, they do not heal a friend and abandon a foe. All amongst the Se are given aid." Again the Pravis found himself lost to his thoughts. The Se, indeed, had a profound view of the world.

Slugan, the first to offer an opinion on any topic, wasted little time assuring those in the room that he would never ask a Se for anything. In fact, if Slugan were in charge, every one of those filthy islanders would be shackled in the town of Malus.

After a few minutes of rumination, the Pravis concluded the meeting by saying, "I believe your Se education is well suited for the position of Pundir and the beasts are fortunate to have such an attentive handler. Guards return this Se to the beast cave." And with the simple flick of the leader's hand, Reiben was once again the Pundir. The crowd waiting outside was surprised to find the Se was led back to his cave without a scratch on his person.

Reiben's audience with the Pravis quickly brought a welcomed shift in attitude from the other members in town. The Se, sworn enemy of the Malus, had sat before the leader for an extended period of time and was returned to his position as Pundir unharmed. No one knew why and his treatment by the citizens immediately improved.

Each morning the guards continued to speak in a gruff voice to Reiben during the daily escort but it was for appearance sake only, "You lazy Se, time for you and those dim witted beasts to earn your keep. Get out here so the day's work can begin." There were no more threats of rough treatment and the guards allowed Reiben to collect all the herbs, firewood and any other natural item he found without protest. Everyone in the cave benefitted from this changed Malus attitude.

Grrick had enjoyed his new family for a month before Reiben decided it was time he became a well-mannered member of the cave. The intelligent Se had no prior experience with these four legged friends of man but his Uni intuition told him that they had quick minds and were anxious to follow a two legged leader. The runt required dog training. After some time in thought, Reiben chose the first two commands Grrick should learn: come when called and sit when told. The Groullens could at least say the word - Grrick.

The sobriquet of dog was a stretch for this pup as the wolf's time among the humans was still in its infancy. The bond between Malus and wolf had been formed a mere century and a half prior and there was considerable knowledge yet to be discovered between the two.

Grrick looked every bit the wolf pup he was. As the smallest, his mother had used her natural selection instincts to leave him behind when moving his siblings from one location to another, so he was left to fend for himself. The pup became an easy target for the least behaved children in town. But now, living in the safety of the cave and with death's door no longer squarely in front of him, Grrick was ready to learn where his place was in this new pack. The first session was to be simple and the lesson commenced before dinner.

The Pundir had two challenges to contend with during the initial instruction, teaching Grrick to come and sit and educating the Groullen in the value of a trained dog. The second task proved more difficult. The men of might considered the four legged creature an interactive toy rather than a contributing member of the cave and play was always on both of their minds.

The enthusiastic Se started the evening's class with a hungry and therefore motivated dog and a hand full of delicious bits of meat as reward. Grrick was focused and after several attempts with Reiben, the runt understood what was expected. Each Groullen was eager for his turn.

The Groullen leader was chosen next and Reiben positioned the dog a short distance in front of him. Before Grrick heard his name, the leader tossed him the treat. Reiben stopped the training and by means of animated sign language, tried to explain what the Groullen was to do. Another attempt at calling Grrick was made but as before the leader threw the treat to the hungry pup without hesitation.

The young Pundir was so absorbed in his role as lead trainer that he momentarily forgot who was in charge of the cave. He quickly exclaimed, "No, no, no" to the Groullen leader whilst he grabbed his massive arm and placed a piece of meat in his open palm. With two hands firmly around the leader's wrist, Reiben slowing pushed the palm forward to the standing dog and called, "Grrick .... come." The hungry pup ran to the leader and ate the treat from his hand. Reiben then said, "Very good, that is the way to do it."

All Groullen eyes were on Reiben as a tense moment filled the cavern, they were wary of what might ensue because of the presumptuous Se. The oblivious Reiben once more had Grrick stand a short distance away while he held the leader's forearm and said the pup's name; another tasty morsel was had by the clever pup. Reiben patted the Groullen's broad shoulders and said, "Good job, you're going to be a wonderful dog trainer." The small Se remained completely unaware of his total disregard for the authoritative hierarchy in the cave.

The leader for his part was not the least bit annoyed with the Pundir and may have had a slight smile run across his eyes. The Groullen allowed the Se a few liberties as Reiben was an unassuming lad and more importantly, he had brought him back from the clouds. The remaining Groullen, when it was their turn, followed their leader's lead and mimicked his exact movements with Grrick.

At the end of the first session, Reiben picked up Grrick and told him to thank his instructors. The Se walked Grrick past each Groullen as the pup excitedly licked them on the face. The men of might loudly growled their approval. Puppy licks completed, the runt then lay between Reiben and the leader while the group ate dinner uninterrupted. It was a good night of training for Grrick and the cave mates.

That evening Fij'n and Sanft could hardly wait to speak with

Reiben about his meeting with their uncles. Each uncle had an opposing view of Reiben. The Pravis found the Se view of the world interesting and Slugan believed no Se should be left on the atoll. The remaining Malus were divided in their opinions.

After the cave dweller's dinner, Fij'n and Sanft appeared at the bars. "Reiben, do you have a few moments for some friends?" called Fij'n. Reiben and Grrick promptly walked to the front of the cave. "I see your runt is looking quite healthy. Is he fitting in nicely?" asked Fij'n.

"Oh, yes, Grrick keeps us well entertained," replied Reiben.

"Well, Reiben, I must say you have made quite the impression with my uncles, one was favorable the other not, but I think you're safe for now," said Fij'n.

"I did not tell them about the items you'd brought me. How did you two get them into the cave unnoticed?" asked Reiben.

Fij'n looked at Sanft and said, "What items Sanft and how did you get them in the cave?" Sanft just pointed to the top of the mountain and raised his shoulder up and down.

"Can you bring a few more things Sanft? These beasts are always hungry." Sanft acknowledged the request with a positive nod.

The three talked about the beasts and how Reiben had managed to keep the leader alive; the cousins had a number of questions with regard to the Groullen. Were the beasts really wild animals? Did they look at Reiben and the runt as their next meal? Why had the beasts throttled the previous Pundir? Were they looking to break Reiben's neck any time soon?

The Se assured the cousins that the beast's ferocious reputation was not well founded and he felt safe amongst them. Reiben did not know why they had snapped the previous Pundir's neck and believed that he was much better off in the cave than chained to the dais. The position of Pundir was just fine for this Uni in the town of Malus.

This evening's conversation proved to be the longest since Reiben's arrival. The three talked without interruption for quite some time before a guard walked up and said, "You two finish up with the Se. Then off to home."

Reiben declared, "See, even the guards treat me better. No more threats of a heavy hand and we're allowed to talk at our leisure." With the fear of punishment no longer present, the friends decided to meet regularly in the evening to discuss the Se's view of the world.

The trio parted and Reiben returned to the back of the cave for bed. Grrick was placed beside the Groullen leader at bed time but always woke up next to Reiben. Sanft was once again busy during the early hours of morning and Reiben awoke to another set of pots and cooking utensils neatly stacked by his feet. How had Sanft entered the cave undetected? Or was it even him?

Simmering soup was now the norm in the cave. Pots were filled each evening with tasty ingredients which slowly cooked throughout the night and most of the next day. The delicious aroma filled every niche of Reiben's spacious dwelling and no Malus passed the cave bars without pausing to look inside and pat their hungry bellies. The guards arrived each morning with an empty bowl in hand and asked, "Se, can you spare a ladle of soup for a hungry Malus?" Reiben readily complied. Good food was the oil which kept the societal fabric running smoothly. Even the cold hearted Malus found it hard to look at the Se with scorn after a bowl of his delectable brew.

His culinary talents were quite popular and Reiben soon discovered each morning that the pots were slightly lower than expected. Was Sanft absconding with a midnight meal? During their regular evening conversations Reiben asked Sanft if he was sneaking in while all were sleeping and enjoying a bowl soup. Sanft shook his head to the negative. "Well then, can you bring me several more pots as I appear to be a little short each day?" asked Reiben.

Sanft was a prompt and reliable supplier and the items were at the foot of the Pundir's dirt bed the next morning. Six pots were in use now and Reiben found it vexing to keep the fires going twenty four hours a day with his worn out flint and firewood of limited quality. Yet even with the additional pots, Reiben still found each morning that the soup level was lower than expected. Surely someone was helping themselves to a meal while all were in slumber.

Reiben was determined to find out. After several failed attempts at sleeping lightly, Reiben finally awoke when the thieves appeared as silhouettes in his peripheral vision. Thin, nimble, quick and quiet, three child size figures ladled soup out of all six pots within seconds and then scurried down one of the corridors at the back of the cave. It was a fine display of pilferage. The young Reiben's curiosity was piqued. Who were these little people and where did they live? They obviously enjoyed his soup but why did they not come during the daylight hours?

That evening, during their nightly conversation, the topic was not about the Se Atoll. Reiben had pointed questions for his friend of no words. "Sanft, do you know of any little people who wander around these caves?" asked Reiben. The quiet Malus was caught off guard and took a few minutes before he slowly nodded a yes. "Do you know where they live or what they do?" asked Reiben. Sanft again responded in the affirmative. For one who had nothing to say, Sanft appeared to be a well-informed fellow. "Is there anything else you would like to share with us?" asked Reiben. Sanft simply raised his shoulders up and down. "Do you have any suggestions on how I should proceed with the little people?" asked Reiben. Again, Sanft's shoulder moved up and down. "I tell you Sanft, if you weren't such likable person, you'd be rather frustrating to be around," declared an irritated Reiben.

The little people were also news to Fij'n as well. "Sanft, are there any more surprises in these mountains or around the town?" asked his cousin. Sanft responded with a hesitant up and down movement of his shoulders.

"I'm taking that as a definitive yes!" exclaimed Reiben. "Well, can you bring me one more pot for these night time raiders? If they have their own soup pot, perhaps they won't take from the rest of us," said Reiben. Sanft responded with an emphatic nod and a wide grin.

The home of the lowest rung of Malus society, Pundir and Beasts, was now the epicenter of social activity in town. Unknown little people darted around it in the early hours of the morning and Malus arrived at the front door with empty bowls each day, all were eager for a taste of Se soup. The pots of delicious stew prepared daily kept those with an appetite satisfied. Reiben, the only cook, was a busy young man who did not utter one word of complaint because of all his additional work.

His day started well before sunrise and ended late at night. This Pundir was in constant motion: preparing the pots, maintaining the fires, working outside the cave, caring for twelve Groullen and training Grrick. And now one more task was added to Reiben's day as he attempted to satisfy a group of little people he had never met. The seventh pot of broth was placed in the corridor used by the tiny pilferers each night. The clever thieves picked up on Reiben's non-verbal cue and took only the contents of that pot. They were appreciative too as a well-scrubbed container was returned in the morning. And at the end of his long day, Reiben found his bed of dirt so comfortable for a short night's rest.

Reiben's regime continued without interruption for weeks on end and the young Se became one exhausted Pundir because of it. Yet for all his efforts, Reiben never received one word of gratitude; but accolades were not the driving motivation for this Uni. Reiben lived by a simple Se tenet; always perform a task well, no matter how difficult it might be. The Se filled the position of Pundir to perfection each day and unknown to him, his dedication was not overlooked by all. For those with a discerning eye, Reiben's character showed promise and it was time to place an object on the Pundir's path in life which could change him forever; if his heart was truly pure.

The most bothersome chore in Reiben's day was keeping the fires lit. His worn out flint was a reliable knuckle scraper not fire starter; so mundane a task, too arduous a tool. But one morning whilst lost in the land of dreams, Reiben woke with a start. Had someone just tapped him on the foot? In his hand was a small stick and by his side were the makings of a proper camp fire ready to be lit. Someone had been there and left a rather odd collection of items. Reiben looked around the cave and saw only snoring Groullen and Grrick wagging his tail. Had the little people left these gifts, the value of which was not yet apparent to the sleepy Se?

Once fully awake, Reiben examined the branchlet. The small piece of wood was more than a twig found on the ground or pulled from a tree. About as long as Reiben's forearm, it had been polished, was tapered, engraved and light to the touch. The branch came from the Hawthorne tree and it had the feel of importance. Even the tired Reiben knew there was a connection between this wand like twig and the stack of wood. Perhaps this twig offered an easier way to start a fire. Reiben took some time to think before he experimented.

Seating himself before the small pile of logs he began. First, Reiben rubbed the firewood with the wand. No fire. Then he poked the firewood with the twig. No fire. He waved the stick over the firewood. No fire. How many different ways can one strike a piece of firewood with a twig thought Reiben? The answer did not come to him that morning and any additional experimentation was cut short by hungry Groullen as they awoke. Reiben thought it was best to hide the twig before he began the day and he would have to wait until evening to continue his study.

The quiet time before sleep couldn't arrive soon enough for the excited Se but no new ideas regarding the wand had come to Reiben during the earlier part of the day. The twig still remained an enigma. Seated once again before the stack of logs with the small piece of Hawthorne firmly in his hand, the Pundir reviewed the various methods to start a fire; a poke, chop, rub, and stab at varying angles to the firewood, yet no flame materialized. Surely his understanding of this stick was not correct. Reiben finally decided to relax and clear his mind. Once in a calm state, perhaps a solution would present itself.

Growth was to find its way to Reiben and the validity of his Uni status would finally come to the forefront. Back on the Se Atoll everyone, save one person, held the belief that Reiben's extensive island education had made him a clever young boy before his abrupt departure from the isles. The astute Aunt Sufi agreed with her fellow Se that he was an intelligent lad and a diligent student but she also knew Reiben had an important attribute which stood by him each day. He was a Uni and as such, fortune constantly guided his steps. For the unique child such as Reiben, the universe on occasion, spoke softly to them with words that changed their view of the world, for those who chose to listen. On this night, the Uni was to have his first introduction to the power found in nature.

Reiben cleared his mind of all previous thoughts of a wand or a fire. Instead, he focused his minds eye on a detailed picture of a warm fire whilst he absent mindedly tapped the firewood twice with the wand - in an instant a fire was lit. The Uni suddenly became one very startled Se. What had just happened? Focus on a fire, tap twice with this wand and a flame would appear? An excited Reiben hurried to try again. Stacking wood under a pot, he thought of a fire and tap, tap with the wand – a prefect flame was lit. He repeated the scenario six more times each with the same result. What a splendid gift from the little people; it would save him so much effort during the day.

This powerful piece of wood could not be taken lightly. It required safe keeping to ensure it did not find its way into the hands of the devious Malus. Reiben decided the wand should remain on his person at all times.

He slept little that night and before the sun rose an excited Reiben was examining his new found mystery. The Se, ever the thinker, pondered at great length. How could such a small branchlet have so much power? Why had it been given to him? Was lighting a fire its only purpose? Though he gave these questions his best effort, no answers came to Reiben by the time the Groullen awoke and the day's responsibilities beckoned. Reiben hurriedly secured the decorative twig in his clothing and he remained deep in thought as bowls of soup were ladled for those around him.

On each new day, the wand proved reliable whenever Reiben called upon it. Just seconds to ignite, the fires he lit burned evenly throughout the day. Hours of tedious work were cut from Reiben's week.

With the added free time, Reiben's vigor was soon restored. He became a more efficient Pundir, dog trainer, herb collector, cook, and discerning friend. He also had ample time to examine the wand during the waning hours of the day. Reiben could not decide if his physical improvement was due to him having more rest or that the wand was close to him at all times. The perceptive Se leaned towards the wand. How could this small piece of wood improve his overall bearing?

Reiben's tenth birthday passed by unnoticed by him as did his first anniversary away from the Se Atoll. It was also his seventh month as a Pundir and the little Uni found himself at a welcomed impasse. Why was this power stick given to one with so low a status as his and where had this piece of wood come from? Could it offer him a way home? These were questions Reiben contemplated daily and though no answer presented itself, he was thankful that this enigma was in his possession.

Back on the Islands of Se, two others were lost in thought about the events of the previous year. Munsi, sat in his dimly lit house for long hours each day. It was the best he could manage. Despair occupied all of his time.

Aunt Sufi was more fortunate. She'd been distracted over the past twelve months, tending to the health needs of those who lived on the island. She did, however, find plenty of time to think about Reiben, especially on his birthday. Sufi's conviction that Reiben was still alive had not wavered. She knew over this past year he would have become a bit taller, wiser and was hopefully, coping well with the strain of his new living conditions. Her little Reiben was the consummate Se and this would give him a distinct advantage to handle all the negativity the Malus had to offer.

The Summer Festival had arrived on the atoll but no amount of persuasion could prompt Munsi to join the festivities. After the first day of the sand ball tournament, Sufi resolved never to wager another bet on Rune, they were the recipients of a two to one thrashing by Vidlin. Yet by the week's end, she decided the Rune team did show promise and who knew what next year's tournament might bring?

The journey to the Southlands was on every Se's mind with no one wishing to experience another incident like the previous trip. Extra men would travel with the collection party, tighter camp protocol was to be enforced and the stay in the land of plenty would be shortened by two days.

As the community stood on the beach and watched the sun fade into the west, the Se were grateful the sadness of the past year was behind them. The island folk were looking forward to a future that saw no Se lost to those terrible Malus.

7

Unexpected First Sergeant

It was a beautiful sunny morning the day Reiben realized his tenth birthday had come and gone. The foul tempered folks of Malus had not stopped to acknowledge that he had been under their control for nearly a year either. Reiben had endured much and been a busy young Se over the past year but it was not a time to rejoice - he was not walking through the door of his home on the Isle of Rune.

For the overworked Pundir, time passed quickly and change came to all in the town including him. Change on the inside as well as out. If an insightful Malus had taken stock of the little Se, he would have said Reiben's stature was larger than his measured height, his countenance that of an older child, and his resolve stronger than his years. But a Malus did not spend time reflecting on a maturing Se and the kind Reiben wasted little energy thinking about his predicament. His thoughts were for his parents as their grief for their only child must have been great.

The reality of a Pundir's life left Reiben no time to brood. The call of the guards could be heard at the front of the cave and it beckoned him to start his day in town, "Se, can you spare a bowl of soup for a hungry Malus." So began Reiben's second year away from the Se Atoll.

The best testament to a well-organized Pundir was the fact that the towns' projects were completed ahead of schedule and without incident. Such was the case with Reiben. Eight months as caretaker to the beasts and the town leaders could not have been happier. The Se's extensive education made Reiben an excellent beast handler and with this new level of efficiency at work, the Malus had more time for leisure. Unfortunately, the additional free hours were devoted to one of their favorite activities, stalking wayward Malus in the frontier. The hunting had been fruitful as the Erda platform was filled beyond capacity.

Four prisoners, selected for the precarious position of punching bags to aspiring Malus pugilists, were moved from the platform and put under the care of Reiben in the cave. The Se was ordered to nurse them back to health so their lives could once more be placed at risk in the Pit of Strength. Such reasoning was typical Malus logic, save a prisoner so he can die at a later date as entertainment. The four prisoners' regained consciousness as twelve massive Groullens, one well trained dog, and the undersized Pundir stood close by.

The Se's reputation, after so brief a time in the town, was well known among those in the frontier. The Erdas viewed the Pundir more favorably than the town folk and they were well aware of his kindness towards all before any introductions were exchanged. They were thankful to be under his watchful eye.

Reiben washed the dried blood off the prisoners' faces, arms and legs and then spoon fed them bowls of soup. Once the battered men had healed sufficiently to speak, an Erda said, "Se, you are much smaller than your sizeable reputation."

Reiben chuckled while he replied, "I should change my name to, "The Little One", as I'm called that so often. It appears every Malus has a distorted opinion of the island people." The prisoners managed weak smiles with their bruised lips.

A second apprehensive prisoner asked, "How is life among the beasts? A Malus knows he is not long for this world when confined in here with them."

Reiben replied, "They haven't collared me yet. The Groullens size and rough exterior belies a gentler side."

A third prisoner added, "Just the same, the four of us will keep our distance from those huge beasts."

No formalities had been exchanged between the prisoners and Reiben which prompted the Se to ask, "You know who I am but as yet I don't know your given names?"

One of the prisoners who appeared to be the leader answered, "When a Malus is captured for the pit, his family name is taken away and he becomes an Erda number. My number is seven, and his is two, there is three, and that is five. That is the order in which we were seized in the frontier. You can call us by our numbers."

Reiben thought for a while before he said, "Two, three, five, and seven are fortuitous numbers to have. They are significant to the Se and are important symbols in our world. The numeral two represents balance, the constant push between good and evil. The number three defines a plane, the points necessary to make the plane of knowledge. The figure five is the foundation of our number system; sprung from the five fingers on each hand. And the number seven embodies the essence of the universe and the seven ages of a Se's life. Hopefully, these fortuitous numbers will serve you well in the pit." Reiben's words were profound for one so young and not lost on the Malus prisoners but they did not respond. The Erdas considered the Se's favorable reputation well deserved.

By the second week under Reiben's care, the prisoners had overcome their fear of the larger members of the cave and were eating dinner in the circle. Grrick was quite the well trained dog now as he sat, stayed, rolled over, fetched, shook paws, jumped over a seated Reiben or Groullen and had dog licks for all in the circle.

The Erdas found it hard to believe that the beasts assisted in Grrick's training. Reiben jokingly said, "I'm beginning to think the beasts have more sense than a Malus." Which prompted a healthy laugh from the Erdas, however, the humor was lost on the thick browed Groullen.

Once completely healed, Reiben decided to bring the four Erda with him to the daily work sites. It was therapeutic to breathe fresh air, exercise the leg muscles and have the distraction of work. Taunts from the townsfolk had little effect on the new cave dwellers but an important date loomed in their future. In six weeks and it would be the winter carnival and the Erdas became distracted with their pending fate - the pit.

That evening after dinner, in the quiet time before sleep, prisoner Two asked, "Do the Se have anything like the pit?"

Reiben responded, "No".

After some time, prisoner Five asked, "Do the Se know how to handle crazed wild animals?"

Reiben paused before he responded with, "Yes." Reiben's

answer was not entirely true as there was no formal training in defense from attacking animals, but a Se education included details for the various techniques essential when confronting a wild beast. Reiben had the four prisoners' undivided attention and he added, "In six weeks' time, the necessary tactics could be mastered if each of you has the ability to think like a Se?" The rhetorical question brought a long moment of silence to the conversation before he added, "Because thinking like a Malus will be of little use to you in the pit."

The prisoners sat up straight with their eyes directed his way while Reiben outlined the four tenets deployed by each Se when faced with a difficult adversary. "To survive the pit, each of you must master four new concepts: control your fear, develop a strategy, understand the animals' energy core, and persevere towards whatever end awaits you," said the small teacher.

The prisoners did not move and remained focused as Reiben expounded on these ideas and said, "Fear is an emotion of great importance. It sharpens our senses to all that is around us, infuses us with tremendous strength for fight or flight and it keeps us focused on that which is in front of us. Fear is a friend not a foe but when left unchecked, this emotion leads one down a path to destruction. When you enter the pit, you will have fear but it will be your ally. Every predator can smell this emotion which in turn triggers an immediate attack response; however, you will have planned for such a reaction. The animal's feral impulses combined with the predator's exceptional size and strength are the only assets it has to overpower a prey. The impetuous beasts lack higher intelligence, a strategy, and the determination of a Malus, attributes each of you will deploy when your day in the arena arrives.

Your strategy, which you will have reviewed numerous times before you enter the arena, is critical. Upon entering the pit, you will not scamper about like frightened rabbits, running in circles towards your downfall. No, a focused head shall rest on your shoulders. Pit protocol dictates that two men enter the arena at a time. It is of utmost importance to always remember that disciplined warriors, working as a force of one, are much more effective an opponent than men flailing about with swords and shields. Each team will be synchronized, shields placed together in a phalanx with swords thrusting in unison, to counter every beast attack. If confronted with a woolly rhinoceros, the walls of the pit will serve to your advantage. With your backs firmly placed against the barrier and each man working together, the enraged beast's single horn will be no match against dual swords. The animal's feral impulse to charge will ultimately be its downfall.

All living creatures, Malus, plant, or animal have a source of energy at their core. Though a Malus can live without an appendage, he cannot survive a sword through his energy core. The same is true for the beasts of the pit. The focus of your attack will be directed at the animal's center of energy. Repeated assaults on their source of power will bring them to their knees.

Perseverance is the last tenet but by no means the least. Every predator that enters the arena has tremendous physical prowess and no Malus will leave the pit unscathed. You will be cut, bitten, have bones broken and be tossed about but each of you must not allow your injuries to distract you from the goal in the pit - survival. No matter how severe the pain, you must persevere and remain focused, standing strong alongside your determined teammate. Two, injured yet resolved men, will always defeat the untamed beast."

The Se lecture lasted but a few moments, yet it struck a clear chord with the Erdas. The idea that a man condemned to the pit was in control of the final outcome was a welcomed concept and this new possibility soon invigorated the prisoners. Reiben told his eager students that if they were willing, training would begin in earnest the following day.

The Pundir found four motivated prisoners awake before the others the following morning. Six weeks would pass quickly and they were determined to be prepared. Reiben assigned the prisoners to teams according to their height and ensured each set had a strong right and left handed swordsman. The shields had to remain locked together in a phalanx with the swords thrusting from the outer ends in unity. Reiben told the men they were to stay in the cave each day for the next six weeks and participate in rigorous training; strengthening the sword and shield arms, synchronizing the movement of shield with sword, developing stronger leg muscles to deflect an animals' frontal assault, and continually develop confidence in their skills as a team. Reiben would tell those in town that the prisoners were frightened and did not have the fortitude to leave the cave. A ruse each Malus would find humorous and readily believable.

That night Fij'n and Sanft arrived for their regular visit. Reiben asked Sanft if he could find shields and swords for the prisoners. Sanft acknowledged the request to the affirmative. Fij'n then asked, "What do they need shields for, no one ever survives the pit!"

Reiben replied, "I thought handling a sword and shield might improve their chances."

Fij'n then asked, "Why do you care for those who do not matter?"

Reiben hesitated a moment then replied, "The Se are viewed as worthless so I have something in common with them."

Fij'n's cheeks became flushed and she responded, "Aw, that is not what I meant."

Fij'n was preoccupied this evening and it took a while before she would say what was on her mind. "Reiben, do you think you can teach me how to shoot a bow?"

Reiben thought for a long time before he asked, "I know why Se girls are taught archery but why do you want to learn the ways of the bow?"

Fij'n replied, "I just do."

Reiben pressed her by saying, "To be like a boy?"

Fij'n replied, "NO!"

Reiben asked again, "To shoot someone in the village?"

Fij'n replied, "NO!"

Reiben finally asked, "To run away to the frontier?"

Fij'n emphatically answered, "NO!"

Reiben paused for several more moments then said, "I can teach you how to shoot a bow and arrow in one evening but if you want me to instruct you in the art of archery, you will have to come up with a better answer than, "I just do"." Fij'n sat, pulled her legs to her chest, wrapped her arms around her knees and was lost in thought. Reiben and Sanft also remained seated. None of them spoke.

Quiet time among friends was therapeutic. It cleared the mind and brought comfort to the heart. The three friends sat quietly for a long time before Fij'n finally spoke, "I want to learn archery for me, that's why, because everything Sanft and I do is for someone else. "Act this way, Fij'n," says my mother. "Don't do that, Fij'n," orders Slugan. We are forced to behave in a certain way so my mother and uncle appear the perfect parents in the eyes of the town. Nothing we are taught is for our benefit but theirs. Sanft, who says not a word, is a wonderful artist but his father uses every means possible to discourage him from his art, hefting a thick leather strap across his back each time a new drawing is found. Yet, Sanft has the courage to continue, because art is part of him. If his art were to go away, so would Sanft. I want something which is my own, a skill to learn, practice, develop and refine. I want to learn archery."

Fij'n sat still with her legs tucked in and chin on her knees. Reiben and Sanft looked at each other for a while before Reiben finally asked, "Sanft, can you also deliver a bow and some arrows with those swords and shields?" Smiling from ear to ear, Sanft nodded enthusiastically. Reiben continued, "I'll have to teach you the Se form of archery. This means there is to be no pouting, shouting or anger between instructor and student. But the most difficult part of the instruction, I'm afraid Fij'n, is that you will have to stop thinking like a Malus. That will be your greatest challenge; do you think you can manage to do that?" With a broad smile, Fij'n nodded an excited yes. There is no greater bond than the shared joy among friends. The three sat in silence, reveling in the friendship that had grown between them.

After a short time of quiet, Reiben decided a brief introduction in the art of archery was in order and he began. "Se girls begin archery lessons at the age of three. Elderly men place small bows and arrows in their eager hands and explain basic bow dynamics. The student tries her best to hit a target several paces away. After every attempt, the men tell their young charges how impressive their efforts were. For the next two years, the girls continue to familiarize themselves with the bow, always under the encouraging eyes of the elders. By the age of five, these students are capable archers. They would rival most of the Malus boys in town and at this point, just hitting a target is set aside as it is time to learn the art of archery."

"Archery is easy to explain but difficult to achieve. It can be summed up in two words – equilibrium and synergy. The archer must maintain equilibrium between her mind and body and synergy between her body and the bow when delivering an arrow. This requires every archer to continuously practice connecting her mind and body to the bow before releasing an arrow, a meditation the Malus would find difficult to master.

After several more years of developing this skill, a proficiency test is taken by the students. The archer runs to a designated spot where a bow and one arrow are tossed to her and she must hit the center of a randomly selected target, quite a distance away, within a count of five. Every Se girl passes this test by the age of eight or nine. The island people view archery as an art, an art which can have lethal consequences. There is great responsibility placed on the Se each time she draws the bow. Fij'n, you must embrace that responsibility as well as the art. "

Fij'n listened carefully to all that Reiben had to say and realized she had considerable work ahead of her. However, this did not dampen her eagerness for the task.

Reiben knew he could not leave the cave for these nightly lessons and no girl practiced the bow in the town of Malus, so logically, training had to be in the cave. The three friends decided that the last hours of each day would be the best time, while the rest of the town slept. The extra time Reiben saved by using his fire starting wand was now lost to training the Erdas and Fij'n, but he did not mind. Sanft was to purloin a bow, arrows and targets along with the shields and swords. Fij'n was to visit the cave two days hence for instruction. Reiben assured his skeptical student that she had no reason to fear the Groullen.

The cave continued as the daily hub of activity, by far the busiest place in town. There were the seven pots of soup to be filled, work detail outside the cave, training Grrick, perfecting sword and shield skills among the prisoners and finally, during the closing minutes of a tiring day, archery. These additional daily activities did not draw the attention of the town folk and the able Pundir had no free time once more.

To the surprise of Reiben, the Erdas' mastery of the phalanx strategy moved along more quickly than he expected but Fij'n's understanding of rudimentary bow and arrow mechanics was minimal and her frustration level high. In true Malus fashion, Fij'n blamed all her ineptitude on a small bow and arrow. Changing her Malus way of thinking was the greatest difficulty for Reiben to overcome.

Fij'n complained, "This bow and arrows are defective. I need proper equipment if I am to learn archery. I would like to see how well a three year old Se handled such a bow."

The ever patient Reiben waited for Fij'n to complete her lamenting before declaring, "A bow and arrow does not have a mind of its own and no amount of anger will send an arrow to the center of the target. It does not matter if you don't hit the target on the first attempt or second or the thousandth. What is most important is that your mind is clear and your body calm."

Repeated attempts by Fij'n only brought her more irritation. After too short a time in training, Reiben thought it best to end the first lesson. There was too much angst over the simplest of exercise. Reiben exclaimed, "Fij'n, you did fine today, come back tomorrow relaxed and don't fret about hitting the target."

Fij'n could not hide her annoyance with this introduction to the bow and only managed a curt, "Right, relaxed."

By the end of the first week, Fij'n's skill had improved little and her vexation continued to build and limit her understanding. With the Winter Carnival a month away and the prisoners' training of far greater importance, Reiben decided Fij'n should not shoot the bow until she became more familiar with it and the arrows. A more trivial exercise was to be practiced. "Fij'n, I think it best for you to find the center point of the bow and arrow by twirling it through your fingers. That will give you a better feel for each," suggested Reiben. Fij'n found the drill ridiculous as she wanted to learn archery not twirl arrows, but with Reiben's calm persuasion she agreed to try.

Sanft and Reiben sat watching Fij'n's numerous failed attempts but the Se continued to offer words of encouragement. Once again, her Malus way of thinking stood in the way of Fij'n's efforts and derailed the training. She complained, "I want to learn archery not become the town jester. This practice is of no use."

Reiben calmly answered, "Archery will come to you when you are ready and this drill helps prepare you for that time."

Fij'n, with her mind set on anger, decided the lesson was over and did not know whether she would return. Reiben reassuringly responded as Fij'n hurriedly left the cave, "That's alright. The bow will come to you when you're ready." She did not find her way back to the cavern on the following two days.

Sanft arrived each evening for a bowl of soup and to sit quietly amongst the cave dwellers. He found the atmosphere in the beasts' home soothing. On the third night Fij'n rejoined her friends and broad smiles welcomed her back. Reiben greeted her as if she had never missed a lesson and said, "The center point of the bow and arrow is where the equilibrium of mind and body connect. It is important for you to manage this point. I can see you are ready to begin tonight's session. " Fij'n stood twirling bow and arrow, dropping them only nineteen out of twenty times – there was improvement! Reiben reassured her and said, "See how much better you are?" Fij'n did not abruptly leave the cave in anger after his comment. Her aggravation was still there but it had ceased to control her feet.

With each subsequent evening, Fij'n showed slight progression or at least no regression but more importantly her attitude began to improve. There was no schedule for her to meet and she could advance at her own pace. Reiben told his frustrated student, "This is not a race to master the bow, it is an adventure. A journey, once completed, you will look back on with pride at your accomplishment." Fij'n was too annoyed with her performance to completely understand what he meant but she did not exit the cavern in exasperation.

8

The Pit of Strength

Erdas Two, Three, Five and Seven proved to be superb students; they had intellect, dedication, courage, and readily mastered the strategies of the Se. For Reiben, the effort put forth by these prisoners had changed his opinion of at least four adult Malus. Was it possible that a Malus could view the world as a Se? Perhaps there was hope.

The Winter Carnival was less than a week away and the prisoners found it hard to sleep. The outcome of their pit challenge weighed heavily on them. On their last evening in the beast cave, Erda Seven asked, "Se, are there any more words of advice you can offer?"

Reiben replied, "A clear mind and true heart always leads one to the path of honor and I believe the four of you have embraced those qualities. You shall be able to handle every eventuality in the pit."

And all too quickly, the six weeks of preparation came to an abrupt end and the holding cave by the pit became the Erdas new home. The prisoners were calm and they stood ready to meet their fate when guards led them away. The fettered men on the Erda platform were loaded onto wagons and accompanied by a large, boisterous entourage as they slowly wound their way through the streets. To the delight of the obdurate guards several Erdas cried out, begging for mercy. Their supplications received only laughter.

The wagon stopped a short distance from the large front gate where a guard, who was overcome with the festive mood of the town, exclaimed, "Erdas, blight of the Malus people, standing before you is the Pit of Strength. The pit has played host to many a criminal such as yourself, exacting a harsh judgment on all those who enter. If you are truly a Malus and survive all the rigors the pit has to offer, a free man you shall become. But pay heed Erdas, no prisoner has ever exited that opening once he has entered." The disheartened prisoners were enveloped by a thunderous cheer from the excited crowd and the wagons slowly continued through the front gates.

The Pit of Strength had not always been an arena so ominous. Shortly after the Malus left the Southland and relocated in the west, a winter festival of harmless games occupied the present location of the pit. The site was chosen because it required minimum effort; a large flat meadow located at the base of sheer cliffs.

The meadow's grass was tilled under and the grounds leveled. The manicured field was not large; a strong armed Malus could have thrown a rock nearly the entire length of the grounds and its pleasant appeal created many fond memories for the town folk. During those early days, it had been an arena of grandeur for games of fun.

The first Winter Carnival, commemorating the anniversary of their arrival to a new home, hosted innocuous contests of strength, speed and archery. The Malus of yesteryear was far happier and less cynical than those of today. They had left behind their foolish competition with the Se and the land's bounty was rich ensuring a good life was had by all. But a time came when the pit was renovated to accommodate very different contests.

The date at which unwelcomed leadership came to power has been lost to Malus memory but at one point the misguided town stewards found their heads filled with suspicion and fear; stringent laws were soon enacted. The confused people chafed under these new rules which were not based in rational thinking. Eventually, a life outside of town appeared a better option and a mass exodus to the frontier quickly followed.

After a few years of shrinking numbers, an iniquitous, yet ever so clever a Pravis conceived of a devious idea to halt the flight of Malus - fear and the morbid fascination of watching one's misfortune played out in a grotesque tragedy. Such terrible thoughts gave birth to the Pit of Strength. Malus society took a large step backwards on that day and the enlightened Malus was no more to be found. Brawn, power, and parochial thinking had ruled the town ever since.

The festival area was readily converted into the Pit of Strength. Wooden bars were installed on the cliff caves and the grounds were enlarged. A thick timber wall was installed around the arena perimeter with stadium seating placed on top. A prominent gate anchored the structure and came to symbolize the door to a horrific end.

The final theatrical props for this new drama consisted of captured Malus from the frontier and crazed, wild animals from the north. Like the actors from the first Pit of Strength played out so many generations ago, this year's prisoners entered the arena to a deafening cheer from the crowd. They were placed in the holding caves at the base of the cliffs within earshot of the roaring beasts.

Reiben and his four combatants had joined the other prisoners in the holding area. (The Pundir cared for those who entered the pit.) Through the bars, one had an excellent ground level view of the arena. The large gate at the opposite end was a beehive of activity as preparations for the carnival were still to be completed.

A guard standing near the Erda's holding area said laughingly, "Have a good look through that gate to the outside you miserable lot, because when you go through it again your eyes will be closed." The prisoners heard the menacing sounds from the confused wild animals in the adjoining holding areas. Despondency was thick in the Erda's cave and fear soon overwhelmed several more men.

No Se had ever witnessed such raw emotions and Reiben found it quite unsettling. But he soon discovered that the worst of conditions brought out the true character of a person. Erdas Two, Three, Five and Seven sat calmly, eyes closed and heads down in meditation. Ten year old Reiben followed their lead and attempted to clear his uneasy mind.

When dinner was served the guards peppered the Erdas with taunts but there was little interest in food among the prisoners. The last night before the start of the carnival brought little sleep to any in the cave.

On the first day of the Winter Carnival, the front gates were opened early in the morning and a host of Malus walked past the wild beast and then to the Erda holding area. The spectators directed numerous gibes through the bars towards the prisoners, "That one there will make an excellent saber-tooth meal."

"I don't see any who will last more than a few moments in the pit."

"Se, you'll be burying this lot by the end of the day."

Every one of the Erdas sat with their backs against the cave walls and looked straight ahead. The stadium filled slowly with the jovial fans, each anticipating the calamity which awaited the participants.

After every seat in the stadium was occupied, the Pravis and his brother assumed their positions at the arena's prominent midpoint. A hush came over the stadium as Slugan rose and said, "My fellow Malus, the Winter Carnival has finally arrived and the Pit of Strength is once more the stage for those Malus who have lost their way. As the Pit's rules dictate, two wayward Erdas shall enter the arena at a time. If they display the courage all Malus seated before me possess and defeat the challenges which await them behind those bars, then they shall leave this pit as free men, no longer an Erda. They'll walk through those front gates with head held high a true Malus. Though, I do not need to remind any of us that no Erda who ever entered this arena lived to tell the tale of his contest. But there is always that possibility for those today who now await their fate in this stadium. May the Pit of Strength begin."

A loud cheer arose from the crowd as six guards walked to the prisoners' holding area. Reiben opened the bar doors and the guards grabbed two random Erdas, dragging them out. The audience applauded the first two contestants. At the center of the arena stood two additional guards with shields and swords and once the terrified prisoners were positioned, the guards quickly jogged away leaving the frightened men to their doomed fate.

The eyes of the forlorn Erdas swept across the arena looking into the faces of the crowd. There was no empathy to be found staring back at them. However, the unfortunate prisoners had little time to wait before the contest began. A crazed beast was released into the arena.

Lacking a strategy nor any training, the prisoners scampered about the pit like frightened chickens. Their end was sealed in all too short a time and a rousing roar punctuated the prisoners' fall. For the wild beast, a saber-tooth tiger, victory was short lived. Malus bowmen ended any future contribution the tiger had for the Winter Carnival. The arena was cleared of the first contest's remains and a second pair of hapless combatants were readied.

Forty prisoners were to walk through the pit during this carnival or five contests per day. Reiben told his Erda trainees to wait for the final day before entering the arena as he believed the last of the wild beasts may not be as ferocious as the first.

Each pair of prisoners who entered displayed various fruitless tactics. Some fell to their knees begging for mercy, others stood awkwardly with shield and sword in hand and a few stood eyes closed with arms by their side inviting the final outcome to arrive quickly. Each contestant met the same horrific ending. Neither Reiben nor the remaining prisoners watched any of the matches. Days one and two of the carnival consisted of uninterrupted battles between man and beasts but on the third day there was an intermission from the bloodshed. The entertainment was to be archery.

The young men of the town between the ages of twelve and sixteen participated in the competition. The pit was scrubbed clean of the previous two day's activities and targets were positioned near the front gate. The boys entered the arena with much pomp and circumstance. Each Malus parent believed his child to be the best archer.

Slugan's middle son was to have a turn with the bow. At sixteen, this would be his last year of competition. As for Slugan's youngest son, Sanft would never be given the opportunity to demonstrate any skills he might have had before an audience. There was to be no embarrassment for the Slugan family.

The conniving Slugan placed a near-sighted judge by his son's target and to the surprise of no-one in the crowd, he was awarded first place. Second and third place went to sons of other prominent citizens in town. Once again proving that these wonderful leaders produced superior children as well as providing the town with excellent stewardship. Reiben found the Malus archers' bravado much greater than their bow skills.

After the champion archers were awarded their prizes, the prisoners were once again readied for their fate. The same scenarios played out in each contest during the third and fourth day until finally, only four prisoners remained - Reiben's trainees. These Erdas remained calm, focused and ready to face their destiny.

A nervous Reiben gathered his thoughts before he spoke to them. "Brave men of Malus, your time has arrived. Each of you has proved yourself to be a good man who has a strong heart and is on the path of honor and I must say that I find you to be very much like the people of the islands. There are just a few thoughts I wish to share before you walk through the cave doors. Enter the pit without the aid of the guards and walk to the pit center at your own pace for you are in control of your future. Once at the middle of the stadium, take your shield in one hand and sword in the other and salute the guards holding the handle of the sword at your stomach and placing the flat side of the sword against your nose. Turn and face the Pravis and salute him. You are honorable men even under the worst of circumstances and will remain so no matter the outcome today. Continue to be mindful of the fact that this crowd has no influence over your fate, each of you do, and don't forget that an Erda only enters the pit once, then he is a free men." After Reiben had finished his parting words he shook each Erda's hand and said, "Brave men let a clear mind be your guide."

When the guards arrived, the first pair of prisoners, Three and Five, stood and said to each other, "a clear mind will be our guide" as they walked past the guards to the middle of the arena. The Erdas walked shoulder to shoulder at an even pace. At the center, they took the shields and swords saluted the guards then turned and saluted the Pravis. Such a gesture was a first for the Pit of Strength and prompted a hush to fill the seats.

Both Erdas faced the cave holding the beasts and they did not cower. The door quickly flew open and a woolly rhinoceros bolted through the gate, angry and confused. The Ice Age rhinoceros was an animal not easily overlooked. It weighed more than many large stones, was as tall as a Malus, and half again longer. Thick fur and tough skin protected it from the frigid temperatures and it was a mammal of tremendous power. With a slight toss of its head, the rhinoceros could hurl any biped quite a distance.

Erda Three and Five showed no sign of fear and remained ready. After the large horned beast found its bearings he closed in on the two combatants.

The Erdas raced to the wall of the arena. They placed their backs against the thick timbers and locked shields together. The crowd rose to their feet as the enraged rhinoceros charged. The Erdas waited until the last moment before they separated. The large horned beast crashed into the wall and every spectator felt the power of its enormous strength ripple through the seating. Both men wasted little time and plunged their swords towards beast's energy core. This contest was not to be like the previous eighteen. A strategy was directed at the crazed beast and the battle between Erda and rhinoceros was not decided in the first few minutes.

As each minute passed, the superior size and power of the rhinoceros was held at bay by the elusive and determined men. Though the men were battered, gored, tossed about and trampled, they continuously worked in unison and never lost their nerve.

After a long half hour of savage to and fro between man and beast, the scales finally tipped in favor of the prisoners and the rhinoceros fell to its knees mortally wounded. The Erdas also fell to their knees exhausted, each thankful for his fellow teammate in arms.

It took several long moments for them to catch their breath, after which the combatants rose to their feet, saluted the spectators and slowly walked back to the prisoner holding cave. The crowd was stunned in silence. Not a word passed their lips and all eyes were on the Erdas who had achieved the impossible. Reiben and the other prisoners greeted the free men with words of praise. None of the combatants' injuries were life threatening and Reiben exclaimed, "There has never been such a display of courage in this town."

The final pair of Erdas, Two and Seven, were ready and stepped into the quiet arena before the rhinoceros had been removed. They walked to the center turning and faced each other, shook hands and exchanged, "a clear mind will be our guide." The confused guards hurriedly brought shields and swords to them. The Erda saluted the guards then the Pravis and faced the beast cave. The hush continued over the stadium.

The bar doors opened and released a large saber-tooth tiger who bolted into the arena. Far more agile than a woolly rhinoceros, these cats of the Realm of Ice had more weapons at their disposal than sharp claws and long fangs; they also possessed a cunning brain. The big cat was heavier than three large Malus and stood chest high to a man. A more sophisticated opponent faced the combatants.

The two prisoners locked their shields and stood knees bent awaiting the tiger's advance. The big cat surveyed the arena before it made a quick frontal attack, hitting the shields and knocking the men off balance. The long toothed cat escaped any jabs made by the men's swords. The combatants staggered but quickly found their feet again and moved to the arena wall to prevent the saber-tooth from knocking them backwards again. A game of wits ensued.

The tiger utilized his agility to strike with long claws at the men's legs, feet and arms and remain out of reach of the slower Erdas' swords. The cat's strategy of strike and retreat was effective and slowly wore down the combatants. The balance of power appeared on the tiger's side.

But the saber-tooth's feral instincts eventually blinded him to whatever plan he had and the urge to attack sieged the tiger's thoughts. The big cat lunged at the shields and separated the men, one of them falling. Erda Seven lay on the ground while the cat unleashed a fury of claws on his legs. Prisoner Two leaped forward and using his shield as a battering ram, knocked the tiger from his injured teammate. The nimble cat quickly maneuvered around the shield and sunk its two large fore teeth into the chest of prisoner Two. Down fell the combatant. The crowd was on their toes in anticipation of a deadly outcome.

For moments which seemed like hours, the future appeared lost for the men, but these combatants had been attentive students and adhered to all of the Se's training. Such an important detail was to be a critical fact which tipped the balance of the battle in their favor. For the combination of two disciplined and well trained fighters working as one and persevering through pain to whatever end the pit had for them, proved a far more effective force than the brute strength of the tiger.

Erda Seven quickly rose to his knees and drove his sword to the hilt through the neck of the saber-tooth. The tiger leapt spasmodically several times before falling to the ground. The last battle in the Pit of

Strength had been played out for that year.

Erda Seven crawled to his wounded teammate and implored him to stay alive. The severely injured combatant was breathing but faintly. Erda Seven did not have the strength to carry his teammate back to the cave by himself so he yelled, "SE .... HELP ME WITH OUR ERDA BROTHER."

Reiben ran from the cave to the wounded men. He took the feet of the semi-conscious man and Erda Seven grabbed his hands. The slow transport of Erda Two from the arena to the cave was the final encore to a new Pit of Strength drama. The efforts of a ten year old Se and a condemned Erda to save a fellow Malus evoked an emotion never before felt in the pit. The Pravis, Slugan, and the crowd did not make a sound as they watched. The guards ran to the aid of the trio.

The wounded combatant was laid in the cave. The three Erdas and the guards looked down at him as a Malus asked, "Se, do you think you can save this man?"

Reiben replied, "I believe he has already saved himself and he will survive his injuries. We need to get back to the beasts' cave so I can attend to him." Three Erdas and four Malus lifted Erda two and walked out in the arena towards the front gate, all eyes were on the group.

A brave guard yelled, "Open the gate for these free men." The gate was quickly unlocked and the group slowly stepped through it. No one else in the stadium moved. The Erdas had survived the pit in a courageous performance and their status as Malus men had been restored.

The Pravis, like the rest of the arena crowd, sat in silent thought. What had just happened before him? The leader was an astute man and he could not deny that he had witnessed a shift in the town which was a profound move away from the Malus norm. Was the Se the reason for this change? He did not know but as a man with a keen mind, the Pravis could not rule out that possibility.

After some time in thought, the Pravis finally stood and declared the Winter Carnival was over. There would be no fifth day of combat between Groullens and wild animals.

Slugan was enraged by the decision. He felt it showed weakness on the part of the leader. No Erda or Se should dictate how the Malus town was run but the Pravis was resolute.

The seed of contempt for this little Se continued to flourish in the mind of Slugan. He was confident that every aberration in the daily life of the Malus was caused by Reiben. Yet one person prevented Slugan from doing anything about it – his brother. Nurtured by a troubled mind and wicked heart, Slugan's disdain for Reiben was not to be stymied. The determined Slugan had to find a solution to this Se problem on his own.

The group of survivors returned to the Groullen cave where Reiben delivered healing attention to the combatants. Under the care of the Se, the health of men Two, Three, Five, and Seven was restored after a number of days. The freed men's celebrity status continued to grow during their convalescence as no one had ever survived the pit. But the former Erdas' modesty was far greater than their skill with the sword; they credited luck as the main reason for their success.

Once healed, the Pravis ordered the pit survivors to his home for their official decrees of freedom and to determine who they were and where they had come from. The street was crowded with Malus eager to see the victors as they left the Groullen's cave for their meeting. A throng of folks followed the group to the leader's home praising the brave combatants at every step.

Upon arrival, they found the home filled to capacity with the town's elite - the Pravis' family; Slugan and his family; several men who appeared familiar with the warrior's arms and other prominent members of town. There was little space available around the four small stools which awaited the freed Erdas.

The Pravis began once the men were seated and said, "I congratulate you, survivors of the pit, such skill with sword and shield has never before been seen in the arena. Did you develop this ability in the frontier?"

Malus Seven answered politely, "Pravis, we had some basic training in the frontier but we believe our success was due more to luck than skill."

The ever impulsive Slugan could not contain his troubled mind after hearing the words of modesty and he quickly jumped up and angrily exclaimed, "Do you mock those in this room by expecting the Pravis and I to believe you four survived the pit on luck?"

Malus Seven patiently replied, "Mocking is the furthest thought in our minds, Malus leaders, we believe skill was essential but luck tipped the outcome in our favor."

Slugan stood close to Malus Seven's face and asked, "And where did you receive such luck freed Erda, from that Se?"

Malus Seven calmly replied, "The Se is but a child and far too over worked caring for the beasts. He has little energy left each day to offer any luck." A slight smile came to the Pravis.

Slugan addressed the leaders assembled and said, "I tell you that the Se is behind all the odd happenings in this town. A beast surviving the pit, beasts working harder, these Erdas surviving the pit, none of this would have ever happened if that island boy had not come here." Slugan slowly strutted back to his chair.

With a touch of irritation in his voice, the Pravis then declared, "Slugan, do you consider a healthy, motivated beast to be a problem? Do you consider public works completed on time and without incident to be a problem? Do you believe a small boy who asks for nothing and works for nothing to be a problem? I, Slugan, do not." An awkward pause filled the room and it was several minutes before the Pravis collected his thoughts and addressed the Erdas, "No one in town has any recollection of you. What are your given names and where did you live in town?"

Malus Seven answered, "Steward of Malus, years ago we were young farmers living several miles northwest of town. During the reign of the last Pravis, a man far less gifted a leader than you, the bountiful farm we enjoyed was forcibly taken from us and our parents were led away in shackles. My three brothers and I with an older cousin were hidden in the fields shortly before this tragedy occurred. The brave cousin, distraught and fearful for our lives, led us on the long trek to the frontier to escape the wrath of the Pravis. She also believed that any remnant of the life we had among the Malus would hinder our future so she told us to leave the names given to us at birth behind and never utter them again. She gave us new names; epithets which are symbols of and constant reminders to a past broken into tiny pieces and cast to the wind by the people of this town. My name is North, beside me is South, beside him is East and finally West. We have no recollection of what our family names were."

The Pravis was lost to thought for a long while. He was well aware of the purges during the reign prior to his own and the room remained completely quiet. At last the Pravis said, "Your cousin was indeed brave, leading you four away from those times of trouble. But today you are free men with all the rights of a Malus. The people of this town will receive you warmly, especially after your exploits in the pit. Where do you plan to live?"

East cautiously answered, "We will go north of town to visit the farm of our parents and decide if tilling the land is still a calling for us."

The Pravis thought for a few moments then decreed the following, "Men from the frontier, you have earned your freedom in a most dramatic manner but the rule for a life outside our city still applies. If you choose to return to the lands south of here, the Pit of Strength awaits your return if captured again. May you find the town you left as boys a much better place as men. You are free Malus once more." And with the flick of the leader's hand, the four stood free men and exited the home.

A large crowd of town folk waited outside for the pit survivors and they greeted the four with a rousing cheer but the celebrities found such notoriety taxing. They were humble men who favored a quiet life away from an eager throng but they were surprised to find that these hostile Malus had a capacity for joy. Over the next few days, all the food, drink and song they could ever wish for was provided by the people in the town. The attention they garnered after a few days of freedom was stifling and the time came to finally take leave of the town once more.

Shortly after midnight the four found their way to the Groullen's cave. A tired Reiben had to wait a few more minutes before going to sleep. South whistled through the bars then said, "Se, do you have a few moments for those who hold you in high regard." Reiben hurried to the bars. North said, "We are taking leave of the town tonight but could not go without thanking our insightful teacher. Our survival in the pit rests squarely on your shoulders. We've also have come to ask you to join us".

The modest Reiben was slow to ask, "Are you heading back to the frontier?"

West then answered, "The frontier is far too dangerous a place and we have heard that the lands northwest of here are safer so we will follow the coast line to that new place, will you join us?"

Reiben replied, "I have thought everyday about leaving this town, dreamed about walking through my front door at home on the islands or escaping to the frontier or even heading north, but in the end I realize it is not yet time for me to leave and I don't know why."

North replied in a reassuring voice with words more astute than Reiben expected, "Young Se, you have wisdom beyond your years and we hope our paths will cross again. Your time among the Malus will come to an end and we know you will seize the moment when it does. Once you venture past the city limits, keep in mind the lands north of town as a possible destination. And always remember our helpful Pundir, let a clear mind be your guide."

A thoughtful Reiben replied, "Let a clear mind be your guide." All five shook hands, after which a heading due west towards the coast was set by the men into the night. The exhausted Reiben retired to bed and immediately fell to sleep. Hungry Groullens never slept late.

On the Islands of Se, the bite of winter was slowly melting into spring and two people still thought of Reiben every day – Munsi and Sufi. Munsi chose to remain seated in his home and never ventured outside; he had shrunk to a gaunt and pale Se. After almost two years, Munsi's broken heart continued to wither and his strength diminished.

Sufi still believed Reiben was alive and safe but feared he would never return home; held captive the rest of his days by those ill-mannered Malus. With a strong cup of hot brew in hand and seated in a warm spot by the fire, Aunt Sufi hoped her troubled thoughts with regard to Reiben's fate were only the result of the long cold winter.

9

Groullen Round Up

The pit survivors disappeared from town after three days of freedom and there was not a hint of them in any of the outlying areas. Why would free men leave a town where they were viewed in such a favorable light? No one could think of a logical reason. The brothers who filled the leadership position drew opposite conclusions from the recent departures.

The Pravis held his own counsel and shared his thoughts only with his wife, while Slugan could not hold back his fury and readily offered an opinion to all within earshot of his brother's home. Disgusted, he asked, "Am I the only one who has eyes for the strange happenings in this town? How did the four Erdas survive the pit and why would they leave after the town viewed them so favorably? I know why. It's that Se. This is his doing! That is why a Malus can never trust an island person. The Se continually tampers with the Malus way of thinking, trying to undermine our perfect view of the world. He should be dealt with immediately, in the harshest manner possible."

The Pravis thought briefly and declared, "Slugan, I see a town running far more efficiently since the arrival of the new Pundir. I see four Erdas who won their freedom yet are still under the illusion that the Malus way of life is not for them and I also see no reason to deal harshly with the Se. My over zealous brother, you may keep your eyes on every aspect of this town except one - the Se."

Slugan swallowed his loathing for Reiben and said no more. The younger brother's problem regarding this Se had reached an impasse but that did not deter him from his continued efforts to rid the town of the island boy.

Fij'n and Sanft were anxious to hear the latest from Reiben regarding the freed Erdas; what superior skills they possessed to defeat the wild beasts. The time normally allotted for archery was spent in conversation about the survivors. "Reiben, what do you think of those pit survivors? Their ability with sword and shield was extraordinary and no one in town knows who they are. Reiben, were they from the Se atoll," asked the inquisitive Fij'n?

Reiben responded, "I agree, they have excellent talent with the warriors' arms but assured me they were Malus not Se. As you saw, Fij'n, when a Malus controls his mind to a level not seen before in the pit, he walks through the arena's gate a free man. And you shall be just as impressive with the bow once the mindset from your upbringing is left behind."

Fij'n asked, "Did you talk to them like you speak with Sanft and I, explaining the ways of the Se?"

Reiben replied, "We spoke of many things including the ways of the Se. With the pit looming so near in their future, I think they listened. A Malus can change the way he thinks and the same is true for you. Fij'n, remember there is no schedule for mastering archery. Take your time and enjoy the journey and in the end, the skill of an accomplished archer awaits you."

Fij'n was buoyed by the prospects of her future success but she still pressed Reiben concerning the freed men and asked, "Do you think the Malus returned to the frontier? And why would they leave a town where everyone viewed them with such admiration?"

The ever cautious Reiben replied, "I don't know where they have gone but in their mind it was a far better place than the town of Malus. Even after so long an absence, I believe the four soon realized why they had left Malus the first time. In their eyes, the town has changed little during the interim." The three friends had no interest for the bow that night. A fascination with the four survivors occupied their time.

With each subsequent evening, Fij'n's proficiency with the bow and arrow improved slightly or at least it remained the same. Reiben found Fij'n to be a determined student which offset her lack of inherent ability in archery. Her diligence was indeed commendable but the intuitive Se did not understand why the bow had been placed on Fij'n's path in life when she had so little aptitude for it.

More importantly though, Fij'n's view of the world was shifting from the Malus way of thinking to that of a Se and her change in attitude continued to progress at a faster pace than her archery skill. Eventually, through her efforts with the bow, a new outlook on life would find its way to Fij'n but to what end, Reiben did not know.

Spring was in sight and the energy level in the Malus town was high. The town's heavy machinery had to be replenished at set intervals and this was the year for the Groullen round up. Every fourth vernal equinox, the Malus men mounted their horses and headed due north into the mountains; their destination was the Valley of the Caves, the heart of Groullen territory.

The reluctant symbiosis between Malus and Groullen began by happenstance shortly after the Malus arrived at their new home. The Groullen territory was far larger at that time and the two groups of people came in contact with each other at regular intervals. On a day with no particular significance, their unfortunate relationship began; a Malus farmer stumbled upon an orphaned Groullen child. The small toddler's mother had fallen victim to the cold reality of Ice Age life and the farmer brought the child home as a family pet. From their initial interaction, the Malus considered Groullens animals.

It was not long before the Groullen child bonded to his new family and proved an invaluable asset for those who tilled the land. The male Groullen's strength, at four to five times that of the average Malus and his gentle disposition, served the farmer well. Soon, every Malus tiller sought a Groullen to do the heavy work. Stealing young Groullen became a regular practice which forever created a rift between the Malus and their docile neighbors.

Within a few years, word of these powerful workers reached the Pravis, who felt the beasts could better serve the people locked in a cave under his strict supervision. No Malus was allowed to own a Groullen of his own any longer.

In less than two generations, the beasts vanished from the areas surrounding the town. The Groullen territory was pushed further north and this valuable asset was in a steep decline. It was not long before an intelligent yet vile Pravis decided that a Groullen round up would occur once every four years and the number taken were to be controlled. The beast was far too important a tool to lose all together. The same shameful Pravis also conceived of a terrible retirement for an aging Groullen. The beasts' dramatic last act was providing entertainment in the Pit of Strength, thus completing the arduous life cycle of a captured Groullen among the Malus.

The consummate hunter and gatherer, the Groullens had been one of the first bipeds to reach the Northlands. Following the wandering herds of larger herbivores in whichever direction they meandered, the Groullen arrived in the boreal region long before the freezing cold became the norm and thick ice covered the land. With abundant herds of large mammals available, the beasts found an easier way of life and their numbers flourished. They soon claimed this new expanse as Groullen land and made it their home.

To the casual observer, these men of muscle were never mistaken for a sophisticated group. A stout spear with a rudimentary point was the Groullens' preferred weapon, the bow and arrow was far too complicated for the thick armed bipeds. Crude clothing and a few carpentry skills was the extent of their technological expertise; all of which placed them well below the rest of those who walked on two feet.

Yet behind the Groullen's intellectual limitations and frightful countenance rested a gentle and caring nature; qualities lost to the Malus. The Groullen had strong family units and no ambition to rule any of their neighbors. When the Time of Ice did arrive, their thick bodies proved well suited for the cold and the natural refrigeration ensured caught game lasted a long time, there was plenty of food year round for every Groullen.

Soon their numbers increased, they were forced to find new homes throughout the entire boreal region. After a time every niche of the northland had an oversized footprint in it and the era of the Frozen Land saw the Groullen at the height of their reign.

During the millenniums leading up to the Age of Ice, different bipeds had followed the same routes as the Groullen and entered the land of temperate weather. The food supply was plentiful and the collection of people lived in harmony. Each viewed his neighbor in a positive light. Then, for reasons lost to the freezing winds, the Malus suddenly declared the Se their eternal enemy and the dynamics between the groups abruptly changed. The northlands' harmonious existence cracked as the snow began to fall and ice covered the land.

Leading the charge for a new social order were the Malus. Their hostilities towards others different to themselves bred mistrust and fear. The northern land quickly became fragmented into territories of varying sizes and each group fought for his own, with little regard for the health and wellbeing of his neighbor. Before long a period of discord permeated the Land of Ice and no one was spared its effects. The Malus quadrennial excursions north to capture innocent Groullen youth only perpetuated the friction among the peoples; on the morrow, another chapter in the Malus history of contempt for his neighbor was to begin.

Since the Se's arrival, four beasts had additional time added to their short lives and there were twelve Groullen still in the cave instead of eight. Yet the town leaders decided the round up was to continue as scheduled.

With much fanfare, the Malus men led by the Pravis and Slugan, pointed their steeds north and headed out of town early in the morning. It would take one month to reach the Valley of Caves by horseback, a week to capture eighteen Groullen and six weeks to return home.

The frightened captives would travel on foot for the return trip and not all Groullen completed the journey back to town. By the first anniversary of their arrival among the hostile people, only half of the young captives would be still alive. Failed escape attempts, despair or disease the cause for their demise.

The strategy for collecting the powerful beasts was simple: surprise and confusion. The Malus waited in hiding until the Groullen men left the valley. The men of might hunted migrating herds traveling from their winter range to the summer grazing areas. The most vulnerable segment of Groullen society, the elderly, women, and children were left to fend for themselves and from this group the young male beasts were seized.

For the captors, the roundup was a time of caution as close proximity to an angered female beast was fraught with danger. The

Groullen mother had a fierce maternal instinct and was twice as strong as the average Malus male. Coming between a beast and her child was a perilous proposition. On each expedition north, several Malus failed to return home but this possibility did not deter nor dampen the enthusiasm of the men.

The month long trip through the mountains ended without incident, the Malus arrived several days before the Groullen men departed for their hunt. Positioned on the cliffs above the valley, the Malus had an excellent vantage point from which to observe the caves. On the appointed morning, the Groullen hunting party departed in mass toward the routes used by the migrating herds leaving the rest of the community to manage on their own. The next day, the round up would commence.

In past expeditions, the following scenario always played out. Well before dawn, Malus riders were positioned out of sight on the valley floor. The horses' speed and size offered a superior advantage for the captors. From the cliffs, scouts waited until the women left the caves for their morning chores in the open valley. The young children always stood close by. When the Groullens were far enough away from the caves for the horses to easily overtake them, the capture cry was sent out and Malus riders quickly sped towards the confused beasts. Nets were thrown on Groullen children separated from the sprinting mothers and they were swiftly dragged away to waiting Malus on the ground. A few riders would fall to the defensive efforts of the protective beasts but the important prizes would have been captured. However, on this roundup a different set of sequences would unfold.

The strategy was carefully reviewed by the riders the night before the maneuver began. In the morning when the capture cry was sounded, galloping horses' and screaming Malus befuddled the Groullens as expected. This confusion initially worked to the riders' favor but at one point a new dynamic greeted the captors.

The riders deviated slightly from the strategy and failed to keep their spacing. The horses' superior speed ceased to be a tactical advantage as the mounts were bunched into a tight group. The captured youths were not quickly removed from the valley to waiting chains as in years past and the enraged mothers had time to rush in to defend their netted children. The powerful Groullens slammed into the horses, rider and horse were knocked to the ground and no Malus returned to his feet once throttled by an irate mother.

It did not take long before fear and bewilderment swept through the round-up party as the captors had not planned for this alternative scenario. The disoriented riders also made the disastrous decision not to sound the retreat. The dangerous consequence of confusion and lack of logical thinking, continued to control every movement of the Malus. In all too short a time, a number of riders found their backs on the ground with a strong pair of hands around their throat. When the retreat was finally called forth, four Groullens had been captured and ten Malus lay still on the valley floor.

Disheartened, the captors finally regrouped on safety of the cliffs. Once more, the Pravis and Slugan found themselves at opposite ends of deductive reasoning on how this disaster befell the Malus. The Pravis felt that the men were not properly trained and they made the costly decision to forgo a retreat when the plan unraveled. Slugan was sure this dreadful outcome was the direct result of the Se. Whichever the cause for failure, the Malus could not return home with only four Groullen.

Their strategy was thoroughly reviewed again and minor changes incorporated. The riders had to keep proper spacing when they raced through the valley so the captured youths could easily be hauled away. Also, the total number of Groullens to be taken was lowered. If the Malus managed to net ten beasts they would head south for home.

The Malus waited several days for the wary Groullen to venture a good distance from their caves. On the third day, a second raid began. Fear already had a prominent seat in the back of every riders mind and it was not long before panic gripped the captors again. The defending mothers were to rule the day once more. Six additional Malus would not return to town and just five Groullen had been captured.

As the riders galloped at a frantic pace away from the valley, they spotted a small beast just a few years removed from the age of a toddler. The lost child was racing as fast as his little legs would carry him to a hiding place he could not find. The riders quickly scooped up the baffled child and continued to the cliffs. Once the riders dismounted and the little Groullen's feet touched the ground, off the small beast ran. The youth's endearing antics were lost on the ill-tempered Malus.

The energetic youth quickly found himself stuffed into a sturdy sack and the nine other Groullens were tied to the fallen Malus's mounts. After three short days, the riders had captured only ten Groullen and lost any courage they had to enter the Valley of Caves again. The fearless Groullen mothers were more than the Malus could manage. The humiliated expedition gladly departed the heartland of the Groullen territory and headed for home.

Sixteen felled Malus for nine and a half Groullen. These beasts were certainly valuable. The Pravis was determined that every precaution was to be taken by the men so the captured Groullen survived the trip to town. The leader sent forth several orders to ensure the captives remained safe: There was to be no beating, starving, kicking or tormenting of any kind towards the beasts. The town needed these Groullens and all ten had to return home alive. The Pravis added another edict which was most unfavorable among the men: The beasts would be fed and watered first; the horses' needs were to be met second after which the gathering party could eat.

For riders whose confidence had been crushed in the Valley of Caves, these edicts were a reminder that the men were second class to the beasts. Slugan's volatile nature nearly erupted but he managed to just seethe at such preposterous orders. In the younger brother's mind, every beast whether two legged or four had to know who was in charge – the Malus. On previous expeditions, a thick stick hefted across the Groullen's back had been the first introduction he received from his captors. The health of a beast was never a consideration and if half the beasts survived this harsh treatment, so be it. The remaining Groullen knew who was in charge and to do what they were told. Now these beasts were to be fed and watered first without the least bit of discipline for their ignorant ways.

Was Slugan the only one who saw the effects of the Se? Why couldn't his brother understand the damaging influence the island boy had on the town? Slugan's rage had not yet boiled over but simmered just below the surface and it continued to fuel Slugan's desire to find a solution to the Se problem. If Slugan could not persuade the Pravis to see his point of view, then what was to be done with his brother?

Adding to the group's frustrations with the Pravis's orders were the antics of the Groullen youth. Each time he was removed from the sack and his toes touched the ground, off he raced. The Malus tried a number of strategies to calm the child but to no avail. The return trip home would take much longer if they had to chase this beast up and down the country side at every stop. Each Malus save one believed a good beating would knock proper manners into the toddler but the Pravis only exclaimed, "This is a young beast with a simple mind! What Malus can't handle one so small? Place a leash around his mid section and tether him to a mount. Let him walk behind a horse until he is exhausted."

Now everyone in the expedition had a mount except the toddler. The small one found his leash an irritation and never tired of pulling it. If a forgetful Malus happened to drop the rope, off ran the toddler and at night the child remained secured in a bag. If the toddler ever managed a head start while the others slept, they would never have found him. The men resented all of the energy expended on so worthless a beast and the level of vexation was high among the group.

The trek home was two days shy of nine weeks. Every Groullen arrived in town without a bruise and the gathering party was relieved they were no longer responsible for their care. Sixteen lost Malus was a heavy price for ten coddled Groullen and many a tear was shed by the relatives of the fallen.

After the long journey to town the captured Groullen were finally placed in the cave with Reiben. The nine adolescents quickly ran and stood behind the adult Groullen. The men of might were not bothered by the presence of ones so young.

The bag containing the toddler was thrown into the cave with a few disparaging words following it and the child babbled his discontent at such rough treatment. When Reiben opened the sack, off ran the toddler. He raced around the living area and down the various corridors before he finally stopped by the standing Reiben, threw his arms around the Se and cried out several times, "Brroud, Brroud, Brroud." The toddler had a tight grip on the Se and Reiben clearly understood the word the youngster said.

One of the adult Groullens growled a few sounds of his own and for the first time since Reiben's arrived, every Groullen burst into a thunderous guffaw. From the leader to the young adolescents, each Groullen enjoyed a belly laugh.

A confused Pundir wondered if that Groullen just told a joke? Did the massive men of the north have a sense of humor beneath those thick brows? And was Reiben the butt of the Groullen wit? Reiben had not understood a single growl uttered nor did he know if he was the topic of conversation but he found it hard not to join in the merriment after watching such joy flow from these huge men – in a short few minutes the Se had a big grin on his face.

When the Groullen saw the Pundir smiling, their laughter only got louder and his grin could not contain itself either. Soon pandemonium filled the cave. The Groullen fell to the ground and held their stomachs. Reiben found the display of amusement so infectious that his legs became wobbly from the expressed glee. All the cave mates ended up on the ground, rolling in hilarity. Any angst the new arrivals had had echoed off the cave walls and was lost into the laughter.

The Malus outside the cave did not know what to make of the raucous coming from the other side of the bars. The beasts were hooting and roaring over something and it did not appear good for the Pundir? However after a long period of mirth, peace returned to the cave.

The toddler was still holding on to Reiben's arm when the Pundir turned to him and said, "Brroud." Once again the Groullens were lost to a mountain of silliness. Reiben had no idea as to why the word, "Brroud" which he surmised to mean "Friend", could be so humorous but he had little time left for levity as dinner had to be prepared for the large group.

The young Groullen who now had the name of "Brroud", was Reiben's new shadow and both moved in unison around the cave. Whenever Reiben sat, walked or stood, the Groullen child did the same. The toddler did not interfere with any of Reiben's work but he was always just one step away.

The new arrivals also enjoyed the company of Grrick at dinner. Brroud selected a seat by Reiben and never tired of grabbing Grrick for a hug or a kiss and at bedtime, the smallest Groullen selected a spot close to Reiben while Grrick slept between them.

When Fij'n and Sanft arrived for the midnight archery lessons, Brroud woke and continued to mimic Reiben's every move. The young Groullen appeared to feel comfortable in his new environment and of course, Fij'n and Sanft found Brroud a welcome oddity. Reiben told his friends of the day's earlier antics and they were also at a loss as to what the laughter could have been about. Perhaps these beasts were not beasts after all if they talked to each other? And why would a small Groullen consider a Se to be his friend?

Reiben's daily routine had a new addition, Brroud, his constant shadow. The young Groullen was eager to help in any way; carrying wood, collecting herbs or filling pots with water. Brroud owned an excellent pair of helping hands and was eager to do his best. The Groullen also had plenty of toddler affection for Grrick. The Se did not consider Brroud's presence a nuisance and the adult Groullen still found plenty of humor when either Reiben or the toddler said the word, "Brroud" to the other.

Reiben arrived at the second anniversary of his capture, too distracted with his responsibilities as Pundir to pause and reflect on the significance of that fact. He also failed to notice the passing of his birthday; his eleventh in the time of antiquity. The hard working Se looked quite a bit different from when he had arrived. His lack of height was no longer a distinguishing feature; Reiben could have easily been mistaken for a boy of twelve. But physical size was never Reiben's most important attribute. In the whole of the Ice Age world, there was no wiser eleven year old Se than he. Yet this truth garnered no attention from those around him. And like those in the cave, not one person in the town of Malus stopped to acknowledge that Reiben was a year older.

Back on the Island of Rune, the second anniversary of that fateful day in the Southland fell heavily on two people – Munsi and

Sufi. Munsi's broken heart had not healed in the least. Distraught, he had come to the end of his ability to bear the loss of the two most precious people in his life.

On the evening of that unpropitious day, Munsi sat in his chair with an item in each hand. In his left hand was a toy he had made for Reiben when he was a small child and in his right lay a necklace presented to Rissa on their wedding day. After two years, Munsi's lake of tears was still full and they began to flow down his cheeks. He had never envisioned a life with so much misery.

But the universe was kind to Munsi that night, as his profound burden was finally removed. The heart broken Se went to sleep and did not rise from his chair in the morning. Aunt Sufi found Munsi in the afternoon of the following day. She too shed tears for the senseless loss of two wonderful people - Rissa and Munsi. Sufi knew Reiben was still alive somewhere in a world too large for her to fathom, fettered to a life so different from the one he had been taken from. Though, she found solace in the fact that Reiben had not seen his father's final days.

Later that afternoon, Munsi's body was placed in a long boat and accompanied by a flotilla of saddened Se, rowed due west towards the setting sun. At a good distance from the atoll, Munsi was laid to rest in the waters which held the body of his wife. Rissa and Munsi were finally together once more.

10

Service Through the Bars

A few weeks after the passing of Munsi, Reiben awoke with a startle before the sun rose. He realized that his eleventh birthday had slipped by unnoticed. Time passed quickly for the hard working Se. The young Pundir had spent one fifth of his life away from the nurturing Isle of Rune and Reiben pondered how different he must appear compared to the fateful day when he was captured in the southlands. Were he to walk through the door of his home now, would his parents see a Malus or a Se standing before them?

Living alongside his huge cave mates, the Pundir had not realized that he was a tiny Se no longer; he could easily have been mistaken for a boy older than his years. But at what age would Reiben's appearance make him unrecognizable to those he had left behind? And would the people of the isles welcome back a son who had spent so long a time under the influence of these dreadful Malus?

Reiben did not feel comfortable with the prospect of a life isolated in a cave alongside the Groullens, a dog, silhouettes of little people darting about each night, cooking, cleaning, and always at the beckoning call of a Malus. The weight of those thoughts suddenly became overwhelming and tears filled his eyes; the expectation of ever returning home appeared too remote a possibility.

But a moment of pause may be in order to remind ourselves of an important point which might have been overlooked. After two years on his new path in life, a unique trait had not been lost with regard to this overworked Pundir. Reiben was no ordinary boy - he was a Uni. The hostile town of Malus had not changed that fact in the least and quite to the contrary, Reiben's Uni character continued to grow right alongside his taller height. Fortune constantly guided his steps wherever he walked.

After Reiben had a good cry in the quiet before the dawn, he wiped the tears away and composed himself. The Uni sat up and proclaimed to the early morning light, "Well, if this is my lot in life, I'll make the best of it." So began Reiben's third year among the Malus.

The Pundir's daily routine continued at a smooth pace. The new additions settled in nicely and created little additional work for Reiben. The adolescent Groullens stayed close to the protective shoulders of the adults and the toddler, Brroud, was Reiben's constant companion. Reiben, the only island person in town, was still tolerated by all the Malus save one – Slugan, who spent every free moment racking his angry brain for a solution to his Se problem.

Sanft and Fij'n made their way to the cave each night for archery lessons and conversation. Fij'n was working hard at the bow even though she progressed ever so slowly, but more importantly she was steadily leaving her Malus thinking behind. For the eleven year old Pundir, he found his day busy but manageable. Yet, as this Uni had discovered at regular intervals in his short life, the universe was never static and change found its way to everyone with each dawn.

One night, in the earliest hours of a new day several months removed from the young Se's birthday, a voice called through the front gate. It was trembling and pleading for Reiben, "Se, Se, can you please come to the bars?" Reiben was deep in slumber but after persistent beckoning, he woke and made his way to the cave entrance. A young Malus mother stood before him holding a baby; her only child. The woman was visibly distraught. She had tears in her eyes, fear on her face and had not slept for many an hour.

The mother was from the least affluent side of town – the Paskar section. In Malus society, prosperity was not distributed equitably. At the top, a small segment of privileged Malus found life ideal in town and held sway over the vast majority who had only their basic needs met.

On the bottom rung of the social order were the Paskars. This downtrodden group had lost favor with the town's leadership and was banished to a life in the ramshackle segment of town. They survived on the scraps left by the rest and the unfortunate mother and child called this section home.

The woman began, "Se, I desperately need your help. My baby has a high fever and nothing I have done can bring it down. You have saved those beasts will you please help save my son?"

Without a moment's hesitation, the young Se said while reaching through the bars, "Let me feel the little one." The small boy was indeed dangerously hot. Lowering his fever quickly was critical to the child's survival.

Reiben asked, "Do you have a pot large enough to hold your baby?" The mother nodded a yes. Reiben continued, "First, you have to cool the child down. Go home and place him in lukewarm water. No matter how much he cries, he has to stay in the water until his fever is broken. I'll have a tonic prepared for you once he is not so hot."

The exhausted mother raced home to do as the Se had suggested. Reiben, though tired, busied himself with the preparation of a tonic. Shortly before dawn, the mother and a much cooler baby returned. Reiben with medicine in hand, instructed her on the proper use of the compound. The mother, whose concern for her child far outweighed the weariness of her body, thanked the Se and returned home before the town awoke.

Ten days later and once more in the earliest hours of the morning, the same mother with a bundle in her arms, tears in her eyes, and a trembling voice called for Reiben, "Se, Se, can you please come to the bars?" The woman's husband stood beside her. After a few minutes Reiben found his way to the gate. The women said, "Se, we are here to thank you for saving our child, he is healthy and free of fever. This baby is the most precious gift my husband and I have. The joy he brings to us makes our life worth living in Paskar and it saddens me to say that we have nothing of value to offer you for all your help."

Reiben looked into the weary faces of the parents. Their difficult lives had fostered an understanding that few other Malus possessed. Reiben replied with a smile, "There is no need for any tokens of appreciation, I am thankful for the opportunity to offer assistance." The grateful parents placed their arms through the bars and squeezed Reiben's hand.

The husband said, "Your kindness Se, will not be forgotten."

The Malus family then returned home as tears of gratitude streamed down both of their cheeks.

For the young Pundir, his daily routine soon changed; word of his skill at aiding the sick spread quickly among the Paskar residents. Reiben, the curative Se, now had little time for sleep as his services were in high demand each day. The least privileged Malus had a capable healer they could visit. In the early hours of morning, a line formed outside the bars of the cave. The worn out eleven year old, dispensed excellent health advice to all who asked but, if he were to continue, Reiben would need assistance as his exhaustion was exacting a toll.

During a brief quiet moment in his day Reiben formulated a solution; a plan which would ease his workload and still benefit the sick. That night at the end of the archery lesson, Reiben asked Fij'n and Sanft to arrange a meeting with their uncle, the Pravis. A request they were surprised to hear. Whatever could Reiben want from the town leader? Reiben assured the young cousins that they were part of a plan he had devised and they should be present when he met with the leader. The cousins told Reiben they would do as he asked and on the following day, presented the Se's request to the Pravis.

A few days later, an exhausted Reiben was granted an audience with the town's leader and once again, a small stool awaited him at the foot of the Pravis.

The large room had little free space as most of the Malus elite with the addition of Fij'n and Sanft filled the home. The curious Pravis wasted little time after all were quiet and asked, "What is so pressing, young Se, that you feel compelled to seek an audience with me?"

Reiben replied, "Pravis, I have a request which only you can grant."

The Pravis paused then asked with a raised eyebrow, "And what might that be?"

The ever cautious Reiben answered, "I wish to offer a healing service to the citizens of Malus and I need help in doing so."

The idea Reiben presented caught those assembled off guard and none knew what to think of such an offer. The Pravis again remained in thought for several moments before he asked, "An interesting proposition but why would a Se wish to offer comfort to a sick Malus?"

The ever quick minded Se replied, "Pravis, may I be so bold as to answer your question with a question?" Fij'n and Sanft were fidgeting in their chair; this was no way for a Se or Malus to speak to their uncle. Whatever Reiben had in mind it most certainly meant trouble for them if they were involved.

The Pravis after some consideration said, "Proceed."

Reiben cautiously continued, "And Pravis, may I also be so presumptuous to ask that for just a few moments, you, the leader of Malus, found himself to be a Se." A loud murmur was heard among those assembled. Fij'n and Sanft covered their faces with their hands at such a preposterous suggestion.

Slugan leaped to his feet and in three steps stared into the face of Reiben seething with rage and said, "How dare you insult the Pravis! To call a Malus a Se is the worst possible insult. The Se are nothing but dirt beneath our feet. Do you consider the Pravis to be dirt, Se?"

The calm Reiben replied, "Defender of Malus honor, in no way do I mean to insult the leader of the Malus. The Pravis is the pinnacle of all that is good in this town. I only pose this possibility to facilitate my request."

Slugan finished with, "At every turn, whether in deeds or words, this Se is a blight on the Malus people, his time among the Malus should come to a quick end."

The angered Malus returned to his chair, simmering with rage. The Pravis sat for several more minutes intensely staring at the Se then said, "Proceed."

Reiben took a deep breath and continued, "Thank you, Pravis. As a Se, you possess a wide range of healing knowledge, knowledge which could be beneficial to so many in need. On a day of no particular significance, a young Malus mother comes to your door in the middle of the night and her only child is deathly ill. Well aware that asking help from a Se is a capital offense, the young mother's love for her child is so great that she is willing to disobey her husband's order of not requesting aid from a sworn enemy. The mother standing before you has tears in her eyes and with a trembling voice asks, "Se, will you please help my baby." You look into the mother's face and see that her devotion to her child is far greater than any man made consequence. As that Se, most reflective Pravis, how would you answer the mother?" The assembled group was completely quiet. Not a muscle moved nor a breath was heard. Even the surly Slugan was at a loss for words and he, like all the others present, kept his eyes focused on his brother.

The Pravis sat and stared at Reiben but his mind soon left the room and was travelling back in time to when his life had taken a dramatic turn. The Pravis's father had recently fallen victim to the purges of a difficult period. Slugan was two and his sister only a few months old. This future Pravis was a shy, inquisitive and lonely boy who did not display any hint for his future position. A Malus would have found it hard to believe that this child of five could ever reach the chair of leadership.

In the summer of his sixth year, a Se was captured in the Southland and found himself tethered to the Erda platform. The island man was in his twenties and had been pulled from his caring community leaving behind no wife or children. The future Pravis' curiosity for this enemy of the Malus was so great that each morning he left his home well before dawn to visit the Erda. The shy boy never spoke a word to the prisoner and only peeked over the platform to view the man from the distant islands but the Se enjoyed the little Malus's company all the same.

Each day, the island man told the child about his life on the isles and the stories were of great fascination to one so young. The Se presented the tales as if this Malus youth was on the atoll and a welcome participant in all the activities. The wise Se also saw that the fatherless boy was in need of adult male guidance. At the end of each visit, the Erda offered him comforting words to sooth the young boy's fears for a life which had abruptly changed. The daily visits lasted for several months, until finally, the curious Malus came to the Erda platform and found the Se was in a somber mood but still glad to see his little Malus friend.

The Se began, "Oh, my faithful friend, I am so happy you are here. I want to say good bye before I leave." The young Pravis was surprised by this statement but as was always his manner he did not reply. The Se continued, "I also wish to say that I find you to be a courageous little Malus and that your courage will stay with you throughout your life. You're a smart lad who can think for himself and your insights will point you towards the best paths to follow as you mature. Between your courage and ability to think, I believe you will find the path of honor. I am glad to have known a young man such as you."

The next day, the young Malus raced to the dais to find the Se was no longer on the platform nor was he ever discovered in any of the outlying areas of the Malus territory. There was never another conversation between the two and curiosity always surrounded the Se's successful escape.

The young Malus did indeed grow into a courageous man who fought relentlessly to claim the position of Pravis. Along the way, he did not relay to any Malus details of his time with the Se nor did he lose the tiny soft spot he held for the island people which continually tempered all his decisions with regard to the young boy seated before him.

After a long period of strained silence for those in the room, the Pravis's thoughts brought him back to the present and he finally said, "Proceed."

Cautiously Reiben continued, "I wish to help the people of this town but I can't do so by myself. I need Fij'n and Sanft to work with me." Surprise flashed across the cousins' wide eyes as they sat up straight. A loud groan of disapproval filled the room from those assembled.

Slugan, who was already enraged, jumped to his feet screaming, "Never, never, never, will a Malus help a Se. This madness has got to stop. Fij'n and Sanft, you are going to answer to me after this meeting." The two cousins knew a punishment would be heading their way once Reiben's time with their uncle had come to an end.

The Pravis waited until the grumbling in the room ceased before he said, "Se, you have been bold this day, more so than I ever expected and your future in this town teeters on how well you answer this next question. Why should any Malus work with a Se?"

The young Se remained composed. He did not flinch or show any trepidation. Reiben believed in himself and his Se heritage. No matter how poorly the Malus treated him, Reiben had always been true to the Se way of thinking.

Reiben began, "I have been amongst the Malus for over two years. I find the people of this town to be like the Pravis, fearless, creative, smart, and wise; if presented with the possibility to learn valuable knowledge from a sworn enemy, I believe the Malus are wise enough to seize that opportunity. I know my time in this town is short and my knowledge useful, far too useful for a Malus to disregard. Fij'n and Sanft embody the highest qualities a Malus has to offer and they have quick minds. The skills they would learn could serve this town for many a year."

The room was quiet except for Slugan's muttering, "Never, never, never. This is only island folk treachery."

The Pravis after a short time in thought, answered in a slow and forceful manner, "Se, you have pushed the limits of the Malus' good nature, yet you have done so without arrogance or deceit. As Pravis, I must maintain law and order among the residents of this town and I do so in precise terms. I also know that the welfare of the citizens far outweighs any mistrust for a group of people we rarely come in contact with. Se, I cannot comprehend why you, our historical enemy, would offer aid to the Malus but as leader of this town the peoples' wellbeing must come first. Sanft and Fij'n will help you administer the healing knowledge of the Se and you two are to learn every nuance of said knowledge from the Pundir. Also, no person under my dominion shall interfere with your efforts to cure the sick of Malus. The three of you are to begin your work immediately." And with the flick of the Pravis's hand, so it was decreed.

After the three friends left the house, Slugan's anger boiled over. The Pravis was at the end of his patience with his younger brother and said, "Slugan, I suggest you think before your words lead you down a path with dire consequences. There will be no more discussion about this Se with me or any other person in this town.

This matter is over."

Once again, Slugan had to swallow his anger. Too much effort had been spent on the worthless Se. It was time for Slugan to act. The island boy was a problem only because his brother protected him. Slugan would have to deal with the Pravis first and the Se second. He had concocted a plan and all the necessary ingredients were secured. Slugan would wait for the most opportune time to initiate the solution to his dilemma.

Fij'n and Sanft could not believe what had just transpired in the presence of the Pravis. The Malus sick would come to a Se for help and the two cousins were to work with Reiben. Not in their wildest dreams had they ever considered such a scenario possible, but it was.

The friends were enthused to begin work. Some thought was needed on how to organize their efforts: such as finding the right space to accommodate more patients, preparation of the herbal compounds, and educating Sanft and Fij'n in the art of healing. But these issues seemed trivial to the excited practitioners. Reiben was thankful for the extra hours of sleep he would have and the cousins no longer had to sneak into the cave during the early morning hours. The front door to the Groullens' home was now wide open to them.

The friends did not take long to develop a new daily schedule: public works during the morning and early afternoon – Fij'n and Sanft would join the work group to gather herbs, followed by an early supper for the Groullens. The healers' corner of the cave would open after dinner and remain so until all patients were seen. The archery lessons would be before bed. Each night Sanft would be on call to help handle any nighttime emergency, sleeping on the cave floor with Reiben. The three's youthful naivety would aid them with such a rigorous undertaking.

Fij'n raced home to tell her mother the good news but her mother was not overjoyed by what she heard. Fear gripped Drist and she lectured her daughter, "Fij'n, no good can come from your association with a Se. No matter how much the people of Malus benefit, your Uncle Slugan is against any type of partnership with the island folk."

Fij'n replied, "But, mother, the Pravis said no one was to bother us".

Drist continued, "I am ashamed to call Slugan my brother. He is devious and cruel. I fear your dedication will be for naught. Slugan will have a plan to rid this town of the Se and any one sympathetic to the people of the islands."

Fij'n answered sheepishly, "Mother, it is already too late to change what has begun. The Pravis ordered, Sanft and I, to work with the Se."

Drist began to cry and said, "Oh, my dear child, I fear for what plans Slugan has for you three."

Fij'n answered evenly and without tears, "Mother, I believe I will be alright. My uncle's anger may affect my life but it will not bring me to an early end. I promise you, mother, I will always keep a clear mind and true heart so Uncle Slugan's wrath will not destroy me." Fij'n and her mother embraced. Her ten year old daughter was far more mature than she ever realized. That maturity, however, did not allay any of Drist's fears.

Under the official sanction of the Pravis, the young practitioners opened their doors to the town of Malus, their clinic located just inside the gate at the front of the Groullen cave. It took several visits before the patients were comfortable in such close proximity to the beasts but the Groullen paid little attention to any of the activities at their door. Benches were placed along the cliffs leading up to the cave to accommodate the numerous Malus in need of their services and it appeared that every resident required a visit to the young practitioners.

Sanft's and Fij'n's abilities were a pleasant surprise to Reiben. For all her shortcomings in archery, Fij'n's medical talents were exemplary. She had empathy, intuition and an analytical mind when presenting a patient to Reiben. And every Malus treated by Fij'n, gave her their heartfelt thanks before leaving.

The young man of no words, Sanft, worked out of the public's eye in the back of the cave. He displayed superior skill in developing herbal compounds and managed the tonics. Brroud, the able young Groullen, was never too far from the three practitioners and readily offered a helping hand when called upon. These four youths effectively oversaw the health needs of the town and the positive reception from the Malus was overwhelming. A critical need in town was now met.

The citizens' response to their leader's decision was a resounding "Thank you." When the Pravis made his way through town, he heard words of praise from every corner.

"Courageous Pravis, that clinic is the best idea …., er … what I mean is, one of the many wonderful ideas you have had."

"Who would have thought that you, Pravis, ever cared …. um … well, to put it another way, I've always told everyone you cared for the people of this town."

The Pravis, in his usual manner, did not display any emotion but did manage a slight nod in the direction of the speaker. If the town of Malus were to have chosen its leader by a show of hands, the current Pravis would have won by a landslide; their leader had never been so popular. Yet for all the good in the Malus world, there was a bit of bad which stood alongside it, Slugan.

This angry man had spent too many years on the wrong path in life to ever find his way back to goodness. Evil and Slugan were synonymous and only trouble could come from such an alignment.

The successful clinic continued to refine the quality of care it offered. Each month, the practitioners enhanced their level of skill and the town found itself the healthiest it had ever been. The healers did not consider themselves overworked as they found great satisfaction in aiding a fellow Malus. And while the friends' efforts continued to improve the town, Slugan concentrated his energy on a very different goal; one which would precipitate a negative outcome.

Two days before the start of the Winter Carnival, the Pravis's wife had her twenty-fifth birthday party. The town folk could think of no better way to acknowledge their leader's excellent stewardship than to knock on his door and present a small gift to his wife. The party proved the perfect venue for a devious Malus to launch his wicked plan. The distraction of the towns' groveling citizens offered excellent cover.

Slugan had limited understanding of the various plants in the forest, but he did know of a one which should never be ingested - hemlock. The innocuous looking flora brought low every man or beast that consumed it and was the preferred weapon for the cowardly assassin. Several months prior, Slugan had harvested the lethal plant from the meadows surrounding town and the toxic flower was dried and well ground before the party. To the casual observer the deadly powder appeared a spice - the desired disguise.

An nervous but focused Slugan arrived at the birthday celebration armed with his solution. After the normal civilities had been exchanged between family and guests, Slugan became unusually quiet. He found it difficult to hold a conversation while looking for the exact moment to initiate his plan.

An opportunity finally presented itself with the arrival of Fij'n and Sanft, the latest popular ones in the town. Most of the guests crowded around the two reluctant curiosities for word on their studies; what a stroke of genius from the Pravis to order the young Malus to learn as much as possible from that Se. The town would be forever indebted to Fij'n and Sanft for their courageous work with the Pundir.

Slugan found the space near the walls of the home the best vantage point to observe the Pravis and his bowl of soup. He strained to calm his shaking hands as the right moment was so near at hand. But what an excellent distraction these two Se colleagues proved to be as the Pravis paused for another Fij'n story and he set his bowl no more than two paces from his brother. The excited Slugan feigned interest and leaned forward to better hear his niece's tale. A sleight of hand was all that was needed and the Pravis's soup was seasoned with the plant of death.

Within half an hour, the leader's bowl was empty and Slugan waited a short while longer before he said his warm farewell. The merriment of his wife's birthday party kept the Pravis distracted while the hemlock's toxin worked its way through his body. Another hour of revelry flew by and suddenly the leader felt an acute pain in his stomach. He told the guests it was time for the celebration to end. The Pravis had a strong constitution and his wife found it odd he was sick. Once he became nauseous, she sent for Reiben.

An alert Se arrived at the leader's home after midnight. It was not long before Reiben realized the cause of the Pravis's sickness which prompted him to act quickly. The patient had to stay on his feet and continuously walk; there would to be no sleep for him that night. He also required large amounts of water and an herbal compound as an antidote.

The leader understood his condition was critical and asked the Se what his prognosis was. The young Se spoke frankly and told him if his legs went numb and he had difficulty breathing, that he should prepare his last words for his wife and children. But if he followed the Se's instructions exactly, there was a chance for recovery. Reiben assured the Pravis that he would walk every step with him along the road through this poison.

After a long night, a well hydrated leader finally lay down to sleep. The leaves of the hemlock no longer controlled his fate. The Pravis woke twelve hours later to find Reiben still by his side and he said to him, "The Se do have an excellent understanding of the power in a plant."

The astute Reiben quickly responded, "Fortunate Pravis, you have managed to navigate the worst of this poison, but it has sapped your strength. It will take six to seven days before you are back to normal. May I suggest that you recover in the comfortable surroundings of your home before challenging any possible threat to your authority? I have prepared a series of tonics for the next seven days and I will also relay to those in town any status you wish regarding your health."

The Pravis thought for a few minutes and said, "Tell the people my condition may be extremely contagious and all should remain cautious. Only the perpetrator of this crime will know otherwise. We shall watch my front door to see who comes for a visit."

The young Se did as the Pravis asked and he continued to spend long hours each day tending to the leader's health. Reiben found little sleep during the following week while his friends were overworked at health clinic.

Word of the Pravis's illness quickly spread through the town and surrounding area. As was the case with all news repeated by word of mouth, rumors were more prevalent than facts. The general consensus was that the Malus leader would never walk through town again.

And it came as a surprise for the few insightful Malus how quickly the ambitious Slugan assured those in town that he would assume his brother's position. Concern for the Pravis' health should have been paramount in everyone's minds especially from his sibling.

His first decree as interim leader was that the Winter Carnival was to proceed as planned in honor of the stricken leader. Slugan's devious thinking did not just focus on the Pravis. The Pit of Strength was also on his mind and he had a new arena protocol which guaranteed the carnival would not end like the previous one; the number of wild beasts the combatants faced was doubled.

The Winter Carnival began with a town in bewilderment; Reiben was still by the Pravis's side at his home while cruelty took center stage in the pit. The crowd watched in disbelief as those who entered the arena had no use for sword or shield; the combatants stood with arms by their side and invited a quick end against such insurmountable odds. For the spectators, this altered drama of Slugan's creation proved sickening.

Reiben spent not a moment at the pit as his time was dedicated to the Pravis but on the final day, he was called into service to lead the beasts to the holding area. The Groullen leader was among the three beasts selected and Slugan again assured the outcome was tilted against the men of might as three wild animals entered the arena for them.

The Pundir was saved the pain of watching his cave mates' tumble. For Reiben, the men of might were an honorable group and they faced their harsh service to the Malus without falter. The Groullen's courage did not waver before such formidable odds and their display of power and fortitude was a rare sight to witness. On that day, the people of Malus experienced a resounding first; they felt a bit of empathy for the Erdas and Groullen. No living creature deserved so horrible a death.

The Groullen leader was the last to fall and he was carted off to his cave with far too many injuries to ever stand again. Beside him lay his two fellow beasts, lifeless. Reiben eventually took leave of the Pravis and hurried to the cavern long after the Winter Carnival had finished. The Se's worse fears were realized and there was nothing to be done for the leader. It was a hard life among the Malus and at every turn, innocent lives were taken from the town. The eleven year old Se shed many a tear for the mortally wounded Groullen and the leader's face held no expression as he looked up at the weeping Pundir.

Yet, after a number of hours in deep sorrow, Reiben's tears became tinged with a new emotion – resolve. Resolve to do whatever a young Se could to protect the downtrodden people of this town from the fatal whims of the few. It was a resolution Reiben had little idea on how to achieve but such a conviction was the first step towards change.

The Pundir sat by the Groullen leader throughout the night grieving. As the first rays of a new day filled the cave, the leader departed the town of Malus for the clouds and joined his forefathers. A saddened Reiben returned to the home of his most important patient.

Slugan was one happy Malus. The Winter Carnival had been more successful than he ever hoped and the ill Pravis had not graced the town with his presence. Buoyed by this favorable turn of events, Slugan decide to visit his brother and relish the sight of his sibling's critical condition.

A light hearted Slugan entered the Pravis' home to find the leader seated at the table with the Se eating soup. The Pravis spoke first, "Slugan, my first visitor, how has the town been in my absence?"

The stunned Slugan's feigned happiness but could not disguise his surprise at the Pravis's restored health. He did manage to sputter, "Pravis, it is good to see you on your feet. I had feared the worst. The town is at a loss without your leadership."

The leader responded, "Slugan, I hope you did not find the position of Pravis too comfortable?"

Slugan quickly stammered, "I... I ... have no designs on your chair, my brother." The Pravis and Reiben knew otherwise.

11

Magic Revealed

Reiben returned to his position as Pundir a few days after the completion of the Winter Carnival and the spacious cavern was soon filled with his melancholy. The loss of three cave mates was a difficult pain to carry. The Pit of Strength epitomized all that was wrong in the town and the woeful Se had no idea how to rectify the injustices of the Malus. His knowledge from the islands offered him no answers either.

Reiben's resolution to protect the innocent residents from the whims of the few occupied his thoughts and they continuously revolved around the fact that he was only a Pundir locked in a cave. He had no authority over his own actions much less anyone else in town. Bleak did the prospects for change appear to the resolute Se.

However, lost to the contemplative Uni was the fact that the universe was never static. From the subtle maturing of a young Se to the tragic life ending contests in the Pit of Strength, the world was slightly different each day and no one knew what the future held for him.

For the past two years, Reiben had been shackled among the Malus with no hope of returning to the Se Atoll and in constant servitude to the town. Yet, Reiben's daunting life did not cause his character to waver as he remained an exemplary Se. This most important fact did not go unnoticed by all.

A powerful shift was set for the town and none of the inhabitants were the wiser; neither the town folk, the Groullen nor the Se saw it coming. The designated moment had been set by nature and the decorative stick was to play a key role. A moment of profound change was near at hand.

After a week and a half of convalescence, the Pravis walked out of his front door and down the main street of the town. A brisk salty breeze and bright sunlight were welcome sights after the confines of his home. The citizens were astonished to see their leader on his feet again. Rumors surrounding his condition had suggested that he would soon be lost to this world and that Slugan stood ready to fill the leadership chair. However, the Se's abilities to heal should never be underestimated.

In his usual reserved manner, the Pravis acknowledged the salutations of the delighted citizens with a slight nod and silence. His first destination was the new healing space in the Groullen's cave. The young practitioners were surprised to see the leader and eagerly showed him around their Ice Age place of curing. The deceased Groullens had been removed several hours prior and the cave was in fine order.

Fij'n was the docent for the tour and explained the system the friends had devised. The young Malus's enthusiasm for her work brought a slight smile to the Pravis. His niece and nephew clearly enjoyed their new positions and had worked diligently to learn the ways of the Se. After a short visit, the pleased Pravis said, "Well, I see the three of you have everything in proper order" and left the cave to continue his stroll around town.

Along the way, Slugan spotted his brother and ran to meet him. With nervous energy the younger sibling exclaimed, "Good to see your health is restored, Pravis. The town has sorely missed your stewardship." Keeping his eyes forward, the leader did not respond. He had given considerable thought to his younger brother during his long hours of recovery. The leader had been under the illusion that he enjoyed the complete support of his sibling. Slugan's attempted assassination was a poignant statement to the contrary and this act was not viewed with impunity. The Pravis had decided upon the appropriate punishment for the perpetrator. Slugan's days as a free Malus were numbered.

The loss of the Groullen leader resulted in a vacated position of authority among the beasts. Change was to come to the cave and the normally mild tempered men of might were on edge. A new leader was to be chosen and the outcome would not be decided by a consensus. Young Brroud was well aware of what was soon to unfold.

The Groullens had completed their public works for the day and shortly before dinner the air in the cave became thick with beast energy. Brroud motioned for Reiben to move from the center of the cavern but the Pundir was busy preparing dinner and oblivious to the seated combatants eyeing each other. He told Brroud there was to be no time for play as the evening meal was not ready.

Coming between battling Groullens was fatal as there was no regard for life or limb during combat. Three cave dwellers had decided it was their turn to lead the beasts and they were ready to put their strength to the test. The trio rose and faced each other at the center of the cave waiting for the right moment to attack.

Brroud, though only a Groullen child of eight, was already much stronger than Reiben and moments before the Groullens unleashed their prodigious strength, he pulled the Se and Grrick from their precarious positions. They placed their backs against the cave wall and Grrick hid behind Reiben's legs just as the battle began.

These competitions for leadership lasted varying lengths of time but the objective was all too simple – the last Groullen standing was the new leader. Punches, body slams and kicks were deployed during the conflicts and a good number of bones broken occurred by the contest's end. Reiben found his agility was pushed to its limit as he dodged the jousting Groullen.

After an extended display of brutal strength, one Groullen stood alone. It was easy to understand how the previous Pundir had met his end. Caught between these battling beasts, no one other than a fellow Groullen would have survived. Fortunately, the two vanquished combatants were still alive and all three had the same number of injuries and blood on their person.

Unlike the Malus, the men of might did not hold grudges for long and peace was soon restored once the leader position had been filled. The cave, however, had lost any semblance of order. After each fighter was cleaned, broken bones set and bandages applied it was cold meat and no soup for dinner. The raucous contest of strength left the town folk wary to visit the clinic that night and they hoped the able Se was still alive.

Fij'n and Sanft were spared the Groullen ritual; the safety of dinner at home occupied their time. Reiben with the aid of the helpful Brroud began the cave clean up without them. The pots were set aright and the few cave furnishing returned to their spot. Brroud's able hands were always at the ready and the young Groullen never tired of following Reiben around or throwing his energy into any project. Reiben could not find one fault with his enthusiastic shadow.

Before long seven pots had been filled with water, ingredients for soup added and fires lit anew. Reiben gave Brroud a large ladle to stir the mixture in each pot. After a bit of time the soups were simmering and Brroud continued to tend them with his usual zeal for work.

Reiben was lost in thought about the contest for leadership and had yet to secure the wand in his clothing; the polished piece of wood remained in his hand. The Se and wand were at a crucial junction in their relationship. At no point during his time among the Malus had Reiben's character vacillated. The Pundir continued to be an impeccable Se, a quality most fitting for this decorative stick. Reiben and the wand were about to follow a new path in life.

The young Groullen enjoyed his task of churning the pots and all seven received a vigorous swirl from Brroud's strong arms. During the Groullen's keenness to impress Reiben, he accidently pulled a boiling pot towards himself; third degree burns appeared to be imminent for Brroud's chest and legs.

Reiben had no time to think only react and with a command directed through the power stick, the Se sent energy Brroud's way; he thrust forth his hand and yelled, "Stop." To the amazed Reiben and to a lesser extent the Groullens, the soup pot stopped and Brroud stiffened. The two appeared to be frozen in those exact spots. Reiben looked down at the wand before walking around Brroud and the pot of hot soup.

Brroud's eyes were open and he had a smile on his face. He was breathing but not one of his muscles twitched and the pot with all its contents were but a finger's width away from Brroud's chest.

The Pundir quickly set the pot upright and removed the ladle from Brroud's hand but he was at a loss as to what to do next. He then heard Sanft and Fij'n near the front gate. With a move of instinctual reflex, Reiben thrust the wand forward again and said, "Go," just before Fij'n and Sanft entered the living area of the cave.

A confused Brroud looked around and found Reiben no longer on his left but on the right, his hand without a ladle and the two cousins walking towards him. Fij'n asked Reiben, "What's the matter with Brroud, he appears lost."

Reiben replied matter of fact, "I took his ladle from him and I think his feelings are hurt."

Brroud continued to look up, down and all around the cave. Since none of the friends understood a word the Groullen spoke, Brroud could not describe what had just transpired. Reiben discreetly secured the wand in his clothing and thought it best to keep the unexplainable event to himself. This wand would require further investigation before the Se offered his account to anyone.

Reiben shared the riveting details of the Groullens' battle for leadership with the cousins and he was thankful his friends had not been present for the contest. During Fij'n's archery lessons, Reiben's found his mind far from bows and arrows. Fij'n asked, "What is the matter, Reiben, you have little interest in archery tonight?"

Reiben replied, "The Groullen clash for leadership is on my mind. It was so dangerous to stand near but remarkable to watch."

Archery was finished early and the three discussed the next day's schedule. It was decided that a shortened night would be best and they retired to bed though sleep did not come to Reiben.

Reiben waited until the nightly chorus of snoring included Brroud and Sanft before he sat up. He removed the wand from his clothing and moved closer to the fire in order to carry out a more meticulous inspection. Reiben had used this ornate piece of wood for so long as a fire starter, he took it for granted. Now that the wand exhibited a new dimension, every bit of his free time would be spent exploring it.

But how was this insightful Se to begin? The wand was made from the hawthorn tree, resilient wood with healing properties. The branchlet had an intricate pattern on its thick end and four rows of characters were evenly spaced down the side towards the point. The characters were obviously significant to someone who understood them although Reiben was at a loss as to their meaning or origin.

Reiben was a clever Uni and he deduced that the rows of characters represented the four directions of the compass. The island people considered the compass more than an indicator of direction. They believed that it also reflected the seasons of the year and the four elements which made up their world: earth, air, fire, and water. Direction, season and elements all converged in each Se and every Se was his own compass through life. Whoever made this wand was well versed in this knowledge and if the wand maker thought like him, Reiben was sure he could unlock its purpose.

Reiben had become so engrossed in his study, he did not notice the three little people stood close by and watched him. The young Se had faithfully supplied these fast moving silhouettes with a pot of soup each night for months on end. Their previous movements about the cave were stealthy and quick, darting shadows against the cave walls. An accurate description of them had never been possible. But presently the little people stood quietly, eyes fixed on the Se, as he contemplated the wand.

Reiben felt their presence and looked up. No words were exchanged but he finally had an opportunity to observe them. At first glance the three men appeared to be but children about the age of six. They were slightly built with shoulder length hair and eyes which twinkled, yet even though they had no facial hair, he could tell they were men. Why did these little people suddenly stop to watch Reiben analyze a decorative stick they had given him? Were they here to take it away from him?

Reiben thought it best to find out so he tossed the wand towards the three and it landed a short distance from their feet. The men only stared at Reiben a few more moments then took off towards the back of the cave leaving the small piece of wood behind.

Reiben's analytical mind was in a swirl as he attempted to organize the facts of this evening, none of which made a bit of sense to him: The wand was far more than a stick to light a fire. By chance, he had tapped into its power to save a young Groullen from a disfiguring accident and then the elusive little people stopped for the first time to observe him as he studied its markings. And most puzzling of all, why was this conundrum placed beside him in the first place? The small piece of wood was indeed an important unknown and the facts surrounding it had not led him to any conclusions. Hopefully, Reiben's Se intuition would be an ally to unlocking its purpose.

He continued his examination and correctly surmised that this decorative stick was very powerful and constructed for a specific purpose. Its ingenious design captivated Reiben's creative nature and he realized the skill necessary to carve such detail was far superior to any that the inhabitants of the Se Atoll possessed. It seemed that every aspect of the wand held a mystery.

After an extended period in deep thought, the Uni in Reiben concluded that the wand was a key to a collection of knowledge, but the location to those ideas had yet to be discovered. The young Se became overwhelmed by the weight of so grave a gift that he found it difficult to catch his breath. Reiben was at the center of something much larger than himself and he could not fathom why so powerful a stick had been given to a boy with little to offer. The humble Uni felt quite insignificant by comparison to the wand in his hand. The hour was late and Reiben's overworked brain needed rest. His enthusiasm to understand this puzzle would have to wait until tomorrow.

As Reiben lay on his dirt bed, running through all the possibilities this piece of wood might offer, the joy of a youthful Se bubbled up. A smile crossed his face, the first heartfelt smile the young Reiben had experienced since his departure from the atoll. All the pain he had withstood over the last two years faded away as he grasped the depth of his good fortune. There was change coming to his world and life as the Pundir had suddenly became the perfect place to ready himself for it.

It was of utmost importance for the wand to remain a secret and any experimentation had to be discrete; never drawing the attention of the wary eyes around him. Reiben's long days of hard work were no longer a burden as he now looked forward to exploring the properties of the wand in and outside the cave.

Reiben woke early to prepare for his morning routine – feeding hungry Groullen. The combat of the past evening was clearly forgotten as the Groullen displayed no signs of aversion to their new leader. The Groullen's view of the world was not complicated. The men of might were satisfied with a dry place to sleep, a hot meal and wasted little time on anger towards his fellow Groullen. The Malus could learn from the people they called beasts.

After a hearty breakfast, it was off to public works. The Se exited the cave with a new agenda; he would tap into the power of his latest discovery when an injustice sat squarely before him. Reiben would still complete the town's projects on time but now he paid closer attention to the downtrodden people in Malus.

Reiben also decided that he would not use the wand to give objects - such as wealth, status or power - but rather change the way a mistreated Malus viewed his world. In keeping with the teachings of the Se - a clear mind should always be one's guide.

The three Groullen were loaded onto the wagons and the work party headed towards the Paskar side of town, home to the poorest Malus. A rock bridge severely damaged by flooding a number of years past was finally to be repaired. The least privileged Malus used the bridge to access the forest surrounding the town, collecting firewood and edible nuts for barter in the market square. The gatherers exchanged hours' worth of collecting for just a few scraps of meat. The bridge project required several days to complete and work had to be carried out on both sides of the river.

The larger members of the work party were not completely impervious to fear and sitting in a boat atop the water was their greatest. It took every bit of Reiben's persuasive powers to ferry the Groullen to the far side of the river but young Brroud, however, required little prompting to jump in the boat. The Pundir led his charges to the forest to haul the felled trees necessary for the new bridge spans.

Reiben walked past the town's outcasts; men, women and children who combed the fields and forest for every nut, firewood, squirrel or carrion which would keep them one step ahead of starvation. As with every aspect of Malus life, their eyes did not see the bounty which surrounded them. In this case, that which lay beneath their feet. A multitude of nutritious turnips, potatoes, beets and carrots, were covered by dirt several finger widths from their heels. But on this day, the lowest rung in Malus society was to discover new fruits the earth had to offer.

Reiben untied his wand and carefully concealed it in his hand. Looking for the right opportunity, the Se soon saw a child seated near a potato plant. A few silent words passed Reiben's lips and the wand was pointed in the direction of the child; oblong tubers were suddenly exposed.

The child's watchful mother who stood nearby exclaimed, "What have you gotten yourself into now?" She knelt down by the boy. "Now that is a plump root on that plant." The women called to her husband, "Come have a look at what your curious son just dug up."

Soon a crowd surrounded the newly discovered potato plant. "Put a knife through it and see what it has on the inside," suggested a hungry Malus and once halved, the potato looked inviting to the famished group.

"Here, give it to me, I'll give it a nibble to see how it tastes," offered a curious Malus. After which he said, "That's a mighty delicious root your boy just found."

The entire group of hungry Malus was eager for a taste. "Why, those plants are all over this field," cried a Malus as he glanced around. The crowd spread out and dug up as many potatoes as each could carry and a festive mood soon filled the gatherers. That night each Malus in Paskar would go to bed with a full stomach.

Over the next day and a half, the foraging Malus were surprised to discover turnips, carrots, and beets as well. How could they have overlooked so many vegetables in the past? There was enough food in these fields to keep all the residents of Paskar fed for a year. No longer would they be relegated to the towns' fringe begging for scraps.

As the Pundir and the work crew were about to leave the site, a humble man and wife with a child of two approached Reiben. "Se, you won't believe our good fortune. We have discovered food in the field and there is more than enough for everyone in Paskar and those in the cave. A basket will regularly come your way for you and the beasts." The young family had been Reiben's first patients.

"You are too kind. The hungry cave dwellers will appreciate all that is given", replied a smiling Reiben. He thanked the Malus couple once more and they exchanged heart felt handshakes before parting. Reiben's initial perception of the young couple had not been wrong; destitution had not destroyed their goodness.

Another day of work and the new bridge was completed. On the Island of Se this crew of workers would be considered excellent builders but the only acknowledgement they received from the Malus guards was, "Get a good night's sleep, Se. Tomorrow, you and the beasts will be at the quarry hauling rocks to the town center."

Working in the quarry was back breaking. During the time of ice, only the might of a Groullen and hand tools were used to complete the job and the rocks never got any lighter.

Reiben's project on the following day was to transport rocks from the quarry to the focal point of the town – the Erda platform. The dais required repairs and the job would finish their week.

During their time at the stone pit the men of might turned huge rocks in to small ones and then they hauled them to the town. The Groullens ability to work without tiring or complaint never ceased to amaze Reiben.

The following day, the Se returned to the first place he had called home - the Erda platform. It did not appear as intimidating to the maturing Reiben as when he arrived but it still held a lot of negative emotion for the Pundir. Reiben paused to think how long ago his first day in town seemed – it felt like a lifetime but in truth, it was only two and a half years. Would Reiben recognize the tiny Se he had been just a few years ago? What advice could he offer the young island lad tethered to the platform? Reiben's contemplation was suddenly interrupted by a gruff guard, "Se, can you sleep on your own time. I want you to finish this job so I can have my day off." The reality of Malus life offered Reiben little time for reflection.

The platform was weathered by the elements and constant use but the repairs would not be difficult and Reiben found the town center was still a whirl of daily activity. The town folk stopped to see the beasts close up and a crowd of young children followed the

Groullens every movement, hoping for displays of strength. They were never disappointed. The Groullens dismantled the heavy timber floor of the platform with ease leaving the sides intact. Cracks in the stone wall were to be patched and at several points reinforced. There was plenty of heavy lifting for the Groullens to the delight of the children.

The midday break arrived and Reiben prepared lunch for his fellow workers, they all sat together to eat. It was not long before the idle group of imps singled out a younger boy for torment. Reiben had a front row seat from which to observe their cruel efforts. The target was a thin boy of nine and the tormentors were five boys a few years older than their victim.

It did not take long before the young lad found his back pressed against a building and he was surrounded by the bigger boys. Escape was not an option. Reiben could feel the fear build in the smaller Malus. The ruffians teased and jabbed their prey incessantly and it would not be long before tears came to him. The young lad was all alone as none of the frightened bystanders came to his aid. Reiben was not far removed from his days as the recipient of such treatment and understood the fear swirling through the boy's head. But on this day the tormented lad had two unknown allies on his side – Reiben and the wand.

The tormentors continually jabbed their target as they attempted to knock the boy to the ground. Reiben carefully removed the power stick from his clothing and placed it in the palm of his hand. The nine year old would soon discover that he had more abilities with his hands than he ever believed possible.

The victim covered as much of his face and body his small arms allowed. Reiben discretely pointed the wand in the boy's direction and uttered a few words. Within an instance, the little punching bag found he had an effective pair of fists. From his defensive position, two well placed upper cuts struck the nose of the largest aggressor. One quick punch hit the throat of a second boy and two hard strikes found the midsection of assailants three and four. A thundering punch to the jaw of the last standing member of the group was the punctuated conclusion to the confrontation.

In the blink of an eye, the smaller lad was no longer surrounded. Startled, the boy looked down at his fists then to the bigger boys who were crawling away. The onlookers were wide eyed in disbelief. The boy stood still as he stared at those around him, his breathing was hurried and he did not say a word.

The battered tormentors took his silence as a sign of strength. "It wasn't my idea for the others to gang up on you. I told them to leave you alone," said the largest boy who was obviously the instigator. The young lad stared him straight in the eye. The instigator continued to back away and finally shouted, "Keep those fists away from me." Then he rose and quickly dashed down a side street. The other trouble makers also made a hasty retreat from the town center.

The crowd watched the vanquished until they disappeared then turned their attention towards the most unlikely victor. The small boy had earned a new found respect. The lad's future among the youth of town took a pleasant upturn; his days as a punching bag were over. The young boy's liberator Reiben, felt the warm glow of satisfaction. A tiny sliver of humanity had been changed forever when a few seconds of the wand's energy was directed his way.

During the next two days the platform repair was completed and several more undersized boys became acquainted with their latent boxing skills. The young ruffian crowd lost a bit of its swagger as the weaker boys now stood squarely on their own two feet. The Malus adults were oblivious to the subtle changes afoot.

A hungry mans' belly becoming full or a young tormentor knocked to his backside drew little attention from one concerned only with himself. It was no surprise to Reiben that the position of Pundir offered him total anonymity and his experiments with the wand passed unnoticed by every Malus who surrounded him. All the while the most vulnerable in town were finding life more enjoyable.

Each night after archery, Reiben continued to study the wand under the watchful eyes of the little people. No words were ever exchanged between them and once the weary Se had gone to bed, the little men took their pot of soup and scurried off. Over time Reiben memorized every symbol on the wand but his familiarity with the characters brought him no closer to understanding their meaning. Yet the young Se never tired of his nightly quandary over the purpose behind the wand.

In the poorest section of town, the new found bounty had a profound effect on its residents. With food no longer the main focus to their day, the bottom rung of Malus society had time to wash their faces, mend clothes, repair homes and enjoy each other's company. A smile finally returned to the face of Paskar.

After two months of a well-balanced diet, only the stigma of being a Paskar resident separated the ostracized few from the rest of the town in appearance. To an outsider like Reiben every Malus now appeared the same.

Slugan, to his credit, also noticed the improvement in the Paskar people and he was certain the Se had a hand in it. Slugan's dislike for Reiben had not diminished and his determination to rid the town of the island boy was still as fervent. With a plan for his enemy yet to be developed, Slugan used his free time to watch the young Se. Slugan felt sure he would eventually have the upper hand over this Se. Until then, he continuously trained his eyes on every movement of the Pundir.

On the Se Atoll, the home which Rissa, Munsi and Reiben once occupied was finally turned over to a recently married couple. They were thankful for an abode in such excellent condition. The people on the Isle of Rune had mourned the loss of the previous family long enough and it was time to move forward. Placing the young couple into the empty home brought closure to the unpleasant event. Rissa, Munsi and Reiben would not be forgotten by the Rune residents as the wonderful family's fate was a sad reminder of the dangerous consequences contact with the Malus could bring.

The wise Aunt Sufi kept her own counsel and knew it was important to the overall health of the island to let go of the past. Worrying about a little Se living amongst the Malus was not helpful to the community. As a healer, Sufi was well aware that sometimes the best advice was not the words you said but the ones you didn't say. She kept her opinion of Reiben to herself but not a day had passed that Sufi didn't hold onto the belief that Reiben was still alive.

Would Aunt Sufi ever see her little Uni again or could the young

Se resist becoming a Malus? The healer could only ponder those questions. No matter what Reiben's future brought, Sufi continued to send positive thoughts his way and she decided to place a small candle in her window each night, the flame a constant reminder of the beautiful spirit in the little Uni.

12

Communication Breakthrough

The home of the servants to the Malus remained a cave of constant activity. It rivaled the center of town for foot traffic which passed through its door each day. The clinic's efficiency garnered no negative attention from the town's leadership which was a testament to the abilities of the young healers and their able aide.

The friends did not find their hectic schedule too great a challenge. In fact, this period in their young lives was a happy one. Reiben's new area of study, the wand, offered him ample opportunity to challenge his keen intellect. Fijn found the art of healing fascinating and her abilities to mend a needy person far exceeded her proficiency with the bow. Her eagerness to master archery was still on display each evening but healing was her new passion. For the ever quiet Sanft, management of the herbal inventory and mixing the compounds offered an excellent outlet for his creative mind.

Brroud, the young Groullen assistant, never tired of walking in Reiben's shadow or failed to offer a hand in any task. The busy young adults did not shy away from the rigors of their daily lives and the town of Malus was a much better place because of their efforts.

The few moments of free time Reiben found during his day was at the break for the midday meal. When he was not directing the wand's energy towards those in need, the Pundir observed his fellow cave dwellers as they socialized. After several years amongst the men of might, the young Se was still at a loss for how to communicate with them. Reiben was sure the Groullen had a spoken language but the key to their growls had not yet been discovered.

The beasts were intelligent and quick to understand any command Reiben directed their way but as a non-Groullen, he comprehended only a few of the sounds they uttered. Reiben wondered who was the brighter group of people – Groullen or Malus?

The week began once more in the tall forest which surrounded the town. The difficult task of hauling felled trees to the river was their job. Once the strenuous day was completed, Reiben and the town's heavy machinery found the cool river water a welcome relief. Each beast knew to wash the dirt off their arms, legs, and face before they began play time. The Groullens enjoyed splashing each other immensely and Reiben found the aquatic antics of grown beasts all too humorous.

Brroud ran and jumped through the river while laughing with the same joyful abandonment as any other nine year old child. The young Groullen ran up to Reiben and shouted, "Trroat, purrllerr," before racing off. Reiben had heard the words, "Purrllerr" and "Trroat" before and was sure they meant water and run. The thick browed Groullens had at least two words he understood. With bath time over, it was back to the cave for supper and the rest of the evening's activities.

The overworked Reiben thought little more of the Groullen words after dinner as he started preparing soup for the following day. Brroud churned the pots while Reiben added the ingredients. The young Groullen randomly muttered, "Purrllerr," as he stirred the mixture and Reiben absent mindedly replied, "Purrllerr," in acknowledgement of Brroud's efforts. As the soups temperature increased, Brroud added a gesture when he said the word, "Purrllerr" and he pointed his hand upward. Reiben failed to realize this importance nuance in the beast's language and only replied, "I understand, Brroud, purrllerr means water." However, this young Brroud was not a Groullen easily discouraged and he continued to perform the one word lesson while the Pundir filled each pot with vegetables.

The adult Groullen enjoyed the exchange between the two cooks and laughed. The Pundir wondered why a Groullen would find it so humorous that he spoke one of their words. The persistent teacher and the hopelessly ignorant student continued their vocabulary lesson to a chorus of chuckles. Though Reiben indicated that he knew what the word meant, the young Groullen was not convinced but the lesson was finished for that evening after all the pots were simmering.

Each night for a week, the determined Brroud stirred the pots of soup and as the temperature rose, he would say, "Purrllerr," while pointing his hand upward. Reiben became frustrated with Brroud's fixation on a single Groullen word which he obviously understood the meaning of. But to the delight of the rest of the cave dwellers, this simplest of lessons was a new source of entertainment for them. Yet, Brroud was not disheartened by Reiben's lack of comprehension and he repeated the same word during the nightly soup preparation.

On a particularly trying day for the Pundir, one where he had more work to complete than hours available, Brroud once again began his "Purrllerr" lesson at the beginning of the soup preparation. The tired Reiben had no interest in vocabulary. At the cave door, the Malus family from Paskar delivered a basket of produce. Reiben went to thank them and collect the vegetables. Returning to the center of the cave, several pots were already simmering but the rest needed to be filled with water. Brroud resumed his single word mantra, "Purrllerr," as he pointed his hand upward.

The exhausted Se exclaimed with a tinge of exasperation, "I know, I know, I know, purrllerr is water, Brroud, can we please move on to a new word."

Brroud was not discouraged and on this night he was to display a stroke of Groullen genius. He walked over to Reiben who stood cutting vegetables into a pot of cold water, grabbed the Se's hand and placed it in the pot while he said, "Purrllerr," and pointed his hand downward. Brroud then turned and pointed to the boiling soups and said, "Purrllerr," and directed his hand upward.

The irritated Reiben said, "Yes, Brroud, this is water, I do understand the word." The adult Groullen laughed hysterically at the two trying to communicate.

Brroud was not deterred in the least by Reiben's ignorance and again he pushed the Se's hand into the cold water but this time, with a dramatic movement, bent at the waist and touched the ground with his hand and said, "Purrllerr." He turned towards the simmering pots, stood on his toes and raised his hand as high as it would go whilst repeating the word, "Purrllerr."

The other cave dwellers could not contain themselves and fell to the cave floor in laughter at Brroud's pantomime. A frustrated Reiben annoyingly said, "I know, Brroud, this is cold water and that is hot water, this is cold water and that is hot water, this is cold water and that ..." The young Se suddenly stopped in midsentence and Brroud smiled, for he knew his friend finally understood what he meant.

Reiben looked Brroud in the eyes as he placed his hands on his ever faithful companion's shoulder. An entry point into the Groullen world had finally opened for him. The Pundir now grasped a critical component of the Groullen language. Hand movement was part of their speech; an uttered sound plus the direction of the hand indicated the meaning of a word. "Purrllerr," water, hand down it was cold water, hand up it was hot water. These Groullen's animated movements were not acts of mental frustration but rather parts of his speech. And the beasts' massive necks and large larynx forced the rolling double "RR" sound in every one of the words they used.

The men of might were more than powerful beasts of burden with feeble minds as they commanded a language far more sophisticated than other members of the animal kingdom. Reiben could not believe his good fortune. He, or rather Brroud, had unlocked a door to the beast's world and a ready teacher was anxious to impart this new language to him – his constant shadow.

An enthusiastic Reiben wished for more hours in each day as he had so much to do and learn. He revised his daily schedule yet again; Groullen vocabulary lessons began during the work outside the cave. The Pundir could easily hide any form of teaching from the Malus guards.

At night the two practiced the language after archery lessons while the other cave dwellers were asleep and Reiben's study of the wand finished off his long day. For the young Se sleep was once again an afterthought. There were more important things to do than enjoy a good night's rest. The Pundir had returned to a routine which offered little time for dreams but he was thankful for all he had to learn.

There was no busier or more exhausted a person in the whole of the Malus territory than the Pundir but the thrill of understanding the Groullen way of communication kept him going. Brroud's positive attitude ensured that Reiben progressed well with the language. The young beast never tired of reiterating a lesson. Between the eager minded Reiben and the zeal of his teacher, the Se quickly mastered this new way to speak.

The Groullen language was deeply rooted in simplicity. Nouns and actions were spoken but the all important descriptors were indicated by hand movements. The Groullen word, "Trroat" meant, crawl, walk, or run depending on the position of the speaker's hand. The tense of a word was indicated by the direction of the speaker's thumb. The thumb pointed to the left of the speaker denoted in the past tense, no thumb present tense and the thumb to the right of the speaker, future tense.

Pronouns had limited use in the Groullen world and were denoted by the direction of the fingers. A thumb pointed towards the speaker meant "I or me." The index finger pointed away from a speaker was "you;" more than one finger pointing away from the speaker meant "them." The Groullen language had a spoken vocabulary of four to five thousand words but with the use of hand gestures the number or words jumped to over twenty thousand.

It did not take long before a rudimentary level of communication was established between teacher and student and Reiben started to probe Brroud for details about the Groullen world. His first question was what did the Groullens call themselves? "Naarrt" was the reply. A word well suited for the men of might. The word meant mountain when the hand was pointed up, hill when the hand was level and Groullen when the thumb was directed towards the speaker. No mountain, hill or Groullen could be moved by any other man. They had supreme strength over all bipeds.

The word "Brroud" was the Groullen word used for the male of their species. As there were no personal names among the men of might, every male Naarrt referred to his peer as a Brroud and the female Groullen responded to the epithet "Grres." A Naarrt always looked his fellow Groullen in the eye when speaking, thus there was no need for proper names.

Reiben was not surprised to learn that Groullen referred to non-Groullens as "Spurrv" - a bird - weak and fluttering about in constant chatter. The cave dwellers found it hilarious when the young Brroud, upon his arrival in the town, addressed Reiben as a "Brroud." In the eyes of these Groullen, the small Se was definitely a Spurrv.

The Pundir also discovered that the word "Grrick" stood for wolf in the Naarrt world. Groullens lived alongside these canines in the Valley of the Caves and they proved an important asset when tracking game. The Naarrt had domesticated the intelligent carnivores long before the Malus began kidnapping their children and the occasional wolf pup.

Each day, Reiben continued to query Brroud about the Groullen way of life and there were plenty of interesting facts to uncover. The Naarrts had a simple social structure with an extended family unit occupying a cave. Each cave had a male leader whose position was decided by strength and his wife became the dominant female. Like the other groups of bipeds during the Ice Age, the male Groullen leader was only a figurehead in the cave. The true leaders of the Groullen home were the female Naarrts and the Brrouds were wise enough not to challenge the authority of the Grres.

The spiritual world of the Naarrt was not sophisticated but it did exist. The Groullen God lived on earth and took the form of the woolly mammoth, the strongest animal in the Ice Age domain. The Groullen's relationship with his much larger neighbor was one of respect and aggression. The Naarrt revered the power of the woolly mammoth yet hunted the Ice Age creature to demonstrate that the Groullens were just as strong. When a Naarrt died, he believed he went to the Land of Dreams which each Groullen visited nightly during sleep. Once in the dream realm, the clouds above earth, a Naarrt was on an equal footing with the hairy mammoth and there was no longer a need for the hunt. The woolly mammoth and Groullen lived side by side in peace.

The Groullens' daily life allowed time for some leisure activities. They enjoyed the extremely dangerous game of "Girrgirr," a competition that only the bravest of non-Groullen would ever have ventured to try. Girrgirr was played on a large field with two parallel lines drawn at either end for goals. A heavy glacial rock, made smooth and round by millenniums of grinding under the crushing weight of a huge glacier, served as the ball.

The objective of the game: one team of Groullens held the rock and ran at full speed toward their opponent's end of the field while the second team also running at top speed in the direction of the rock carrier did everything in their power to prevent the ball from crossing the goal line. Tackling, collaring, tripping and a large scrum of punching Groullen were allowable defensive tactics. The rules for the game were quite similar to a head smashing brawl. The Naarrt's high tolerance for pain left many a player with multiple broken bones by the games end. Fortunately, the Groullen mended quickly.

Reiben was also surprised to learn that the Naarrt even had a crude ceremony for marriage. Each spring, Groullens of marrying age gathered in a communal area. A round robin of wrestling ensued and the eligible Brroud won his position to choose a mate by strength. The Grres had no say as to whom she would marry. Once the marriage order was determined, the Brroud selected his bride according to his position. The groom then left his family and moved into the cave of his bride. The matriarch of the cave supervised all child rearing by the new couple.

The uncomplicated life of a Groullen unfolded before Reiben as he improved his language skills and learned the ways of the Naarrt. It soon became apparent that a Groullen was an excellent friend to have; humble, honest, straight forward and willing to stand by a friend's side during a scuffle. Reiben was sure he wanted the Groullen standing next to him.

After a few months of lessons, Reiben had become reasonably fluent in Naarrt. The precocious Se listened in on the adult Groullen chatter and understood a good portion of what was said though he had yet to speak to any of the other cave mates. When Reiben finally felt confident in his Naarrt proficiency, he decided on the appropriate time to introduce himself to his fellow cave dwellers in their native tongue.

After dinner on the only day of rest, the young Se rose to address the Naarrts. Reiben began with the standard Groullen greeting, "You have the strength of a woolly mammoth." Every cave dweller sat quietly and stared incredulously at the Se. Never in the history of their service to the Malus had a Pundir uttered one sentence in Naarrt, yet here was a small Spurrv standing before them speaking in their tongue. "I am a Se male from the islands over the mountain in the waters by the ice." The Groullen men began to laugh. Reiben stopped speaking, confused.

One of the Groullen quickly spoke out and said, "You not Se male, you Se bird." The Groullen rolled on the ground in a heartfelt guffaw. The Malus outside the cave had not heard such thunderous laughter from the beasts and were certain a new Pundir would be required the following day.

Reiben was taken aback at the Groullens' light hearted response to his sincere attempt to communicate on their terms. The young Se decided a more commanding delivery would convince the Naartts that he was not a bird. Reiben stood straight and with as much conviction as a young Se could project declared, "I am a male Se just as you are a male Groullen."

This was met with the reply, "You are baby male bird." The humorous pandemonium that ensued was a sight to behold and it did not appear to be stopping anytime soon. It was not long before laughter overcame young Brroud and he rolled on the ground alongside his fellow Groullen.

Reiben's frustration with his cave mates soon dissolved and he found himself joining the hilarity; which only fueled the guffawing in the cavern. The Naarrts capacity for joy was far greater than their prodigious brawn and it was infectious. Reiben did not find fault with a group of men who had no malicious intent while making him the butt of their joke.

With Reiben's first two sentences of introduction, his nickname among the Naarrt had been established – Brroud bird. Not the name the young Se would have chosen for himself but he did look on the bright side of his new moniker, at least it was not – Grres bird.

After an extended period of incessant laughter, quiet returned and Reiben continued the tale of his life. The Groullen listened to Brroud Bird's saga of arriving at the town and life on the Se Atoll. The Naarrts asked insightful questions and to Reiben's surprise the Groullen were well versed in the character of the Se. The island folk had always been respectful of the Naarrts and never attempted to impose their will over the Groullen.

But these cave dwellers were not given to extended periods of idle chat and their conversation abruptly ended as they went to bed. Every Groullen required a full night of sleep. Young Brroud was also tired from the evening's activities and chose his spot on the cave floor instead of late night language lessons.

It had been an eventful day and Reiben was pleased that he had finally communicated with his cave mates. The young Se was certain the Groullen held much more knowledge about the Land of Ice than they offered tonight but he had plenty of time and the means to find out.

Once the Naarrts were sleeping soundly, Reiben removed his wand and continued his nightly pondering of the decorative twig under the watchful eyes of the little people. Reiben looked up and thought, "What stories of interest could you tell?" Their tales, however, would have to wait for another day.

The guards expected the worst for the Pundir after the night of boisterous laughter but the Se met them at the door when called for the day's work. "Why were the beasts hooting and hollering last night, Se?" asked the cautious guards.

Reiben shrewdly replied, "I'm not sure. I happened to utter a few sounds that they say and they were lost to laughter. I have no idea why the beasts found my words funny."

One of the guards said, "Se, you were lucky last night. One never knows when a beast will turn and snap your neck. Your time as a Pundir may be nearing its end." Reiben nodded his agreement. Contrary to the Malus perception, the Se's first day of communication with his cave mates had been well received – the Naarrt looked with favor on Brroud Bird.

Reiben did not wish the guards to know that he understood Groullen. The suspicious Malus would think only the worst and conclude that the Se was planning a beast revolt against the town. Reiben decided to speak openly with the Groullen only when the Malus were out of earshot. Outside the cave, all communication would take place in a Naarrt whisper.

The week's work began again in the quarry. The main bridge to town required repair. The necessary stones were to be hauled to the work site first before the repairs began. With Reiben's ability to whisper to his crew mates exactly what had to be done, the quarry work was completed even faster. The required number of rocks was mined in one day instead of two.

The following day the Groullen workers were joined by their leader. He was as big as the previous Naarrt leader but slightly more reticent. The repairs entailed lifting one side of the support beams for the bridge, replacing the damaged stones then securing the beams on the new stone pier, a task no Groullen would find difficult. The Groullen leader's was the obvious choice for the bridge jack because of his size and strength. His broad shoulders and height proved an excellent hoist for the cross beams while temporary supports were put in place and the leader did not find hefting the heavy timbers a challenge. The repairs went as planned until the leader accidently stepped on an algae covered rock, slipped, and fell into the deep river pool beneath the bridge.

Every physical attribute which made the Groullen the most dominant humanoid on land, failed him miserably in water and the leader quickly sank below the surface. Neither the Naarrts nor any Malus knew how to swim. No one moved to rescue the drowning leader. Fortunately, swimming was a skill every Se had to learn and Reiben dove into the clear, cold water without a moment's hesitation.

The Groullen was easily spotted on the river bed and he was not moving. Reiben quickly grasped the leader's large hand and with buoyancy as his aide, used all the strength his small muscles could muster to pull the Naarrt upward. Within a few seconds both reached the surface. Reiben struggled to tow the leader to shore where the waiting Malus and Groullen dragged the unconscious Groullen onto the river bank.

The quick thinking Se told the Malus to flip the leader onto his stomach and place his head to one side as Reiben commenced jumping up and down on the Naarrt's back. Water trickled from the Groullen's mouth and eventually he began to sputter. The cave's leadership position had, thankfully, not been vacated and the young

Se proved once again, in dramatic fashion, his usefulness to all in town.

Repair to the support beams ended early and the work crew returned to their cave. Reiben's aquatic abilities were soon relayed to the other Groullen. The opinion of Brroud Bird had moved up a notch among the Naarrt.

Once the bridge work was completed, the workers and guards were given their only day off. Reiben, again, looked forward to an uninterrupted conversation with his cave mates.

After dinner and during the lull before sleep, Reiben addressed the Groullen with the proper Naarrt greeting, "You have the strength of a woolly mammoth."

A Naarrt responded, "Brroud Bird can walk in water with a fish." The Groullens chuckled. The young Se realized his rescue efforts were viewed favorably by his cave mates. Though he had not been made an honorary Groullen for his heroics, the Naarrt had placed him squarely in their corner. The Se had earned his nickname of Brroud Bird in their eyes.

Reiben continued, "Every Naarrt in here was pulled from his cave as a boy. Do you have any memories the people left behind?" The Groullen's perspective of the Naarrt world was one through the eyes of a ten year old child; the age at which they had been captured in the Valley of Caves. Their stories about the life up north were not that dissimilar from the Se's.

Each Groullen missed their mother, father, siblings, and friends. They missed the return of the hunters whose broad shoulders bore freshly butchered meat and prompted a celebration of great feasting. They missed playing and watching the games of Girrgirr. They missed lying on the ground and watching the clouds (their heaven) pass by, imagining they spotted a recently deceased Groullen looking down on them. They missed walking as far as possible in any direction for half a day then turning around and returning home before dark.

These Groullen stories echoed the same sentiments Reiben held for his island home. There were a few more anecdotes about the Valley of Caves before the Groullen leader spoke and asked, "Brroud Bird, why do you carry a little tree under your animal skins?"

149

The Naarrts were more observant than Reiben had believed and he replied, "The little people of the night gave it to me. I use it to light the fires."

The leader then asked, "Why do you put it in your hand outside the cave?" Reiben found no reason to hide the truth from his cave mates. He untied the wand from his clothing, held it up for display and told the Naarrts all he knew about the small piece of Hawthorne. The Groullens had no interest in holding the wand or viewing any examples of its power. They listened to the Se's narrative in silence.

When Reiben finished recounting all he knew of the wand, the Groullen leader continued, "There was a time, when little trees were carried by many." The leader gave a brief historical account of much interest to Reiben but with few facts. Many generations ago a group of people walked the Groullen lands. The people were called, Brroud Wolf, among the Naarrts and were looked upon with favor by the Groullens. The Brroud Wolves carried a wand similar to Reiben's.

When the freezing cold came to the Valley of Caves and the glaciers began to grow, the Brroud Wolf was no longer to be found among the Naarrt. Sadly for the enthralled Se, the leader could add no more details to his short tale and as the hour was late, the Groullens retired to bed – the story with few details abruptly came to an end.

The curious Reiben was not ready for sleep and pondered the night's revelations as he held the wand. He had far more unanswered questions now than before the evening had begun and the little people who observed the Se's every movement during the closing moments of the day could not answer one of his questions.

The anxious Se reasoned that the wand was part of a much larger question but who had made it and why? The "who" and "why" would certainly unlock its power. The young Pundir took a deep breath and began his nightly examination of the decorative stick but was too distracted by the Groullen's revelation to concentrate. Reiben found his bed as well.

As Reiben lay and pondered the Groullen leader's enigmatic story, he suddenly realized that in a few weeks he would be twelve years old. Three years removed from the tiny atoll. His time among the Malus was passing by quickly. To a Se back on the islands, Reiben would have been considered tall for twelve and he favored his father's look with his mother's smile. Reiben, of course, had no point of reference for any of his physical attributes. Standing among the Naarrts, this Pundir appeared quite out of place and looked every bit the small bird they compared him to.

For the insightful Reiben, this birthday brought him no tears nor any hope of walking through the front door of his home any time soon. He missed his mother, father and friends but he had a new life now which was much different from theirs. He was still a Se, who just happened to live among the Malus. The Pundir had plenty of intellectual challenges to keep him distracted from the harsh reality of an island person held captive in a hostile town. After a time in thought, the Uni felt it best to go to sleep. Memories of the place he left behind only made him sad and a return home seemed more unlikely than ever.

On the Isle of Rune, Sufi also remembered Reiben's yearly milestone, his birthday was a fortnight hence and fell on a full moon. Aunt Sufi would soon be far too busy with the new arrivals in the community, Se babies, to pause and think of her little Uni. The healer lit a new candle for Reiben then finished the last of her hot brew while she sat by the fire. Her birthday gift this year for her favorite Uni was the same one she sent his way every year - positive thoughts. Aunt Sufi was still confident the son of Rissa and Munsi remained a true Se tethered to a land far from hers.

13

Art for the Ages

The Groullen's thick brows, guttural grunts and mass of muscles belied an exceptional sense of humor and the young Se found himself the butt of all their jokes. Reiben took no offense to any of their jocosity; the Naarrt's prodigious display of wit was worth the teasing. Reiben had not laughed so much at any point during his short life and for brief moments, he forgot that he was confined to a cave in constant servitude to the town of Malus. The power of laughter was indeed therapeutic.

Reiben's friends, Sanft and Fij'n, were also the happiest they had ever been. Learning the ways of the island folk and caring for the people of Malus brought tremendous joy to the cousins. It was an endeavor the two had never envisioned undertaking.

For the constant shadow of Reiben, it was hard to tell if Brroud ever experienced bouts of melancholy. His enthusiasm as the Se's unwavering companion had not waned and his capable hands were always at the ready. The ever shrewd Reiben continued to keep his Groullen language skills hidden away in his home, under the cliffs at the edge of town. He did not want the suspicious minded Malus imagining the worst about their capable Pundir – the Se leading a beast uprising against the town folk.

On a bright summer's day three years removed from his chance meeting with a different fate, Reiben once again marked another birthday away from home; his twelfth anniversary on this earth. Without any emotion, he acknowledged that his new life was now the best it had been since his abrupt departure from the comforting arms of the Se community. He cautiously gazed down his path in life at the beginning of another year among the Malus.

It had been some time since the Pravis had his unfortunate introduction to the deadly effects of Hemlock and the decision regarding the one who administered the poison had not changed. An unsuspecting Slugan found his confidence restored during the interim and harsh words born from his arrogance were once again heard in the town of Malus. The younger brother's dislike for the Se had not diminished either. With no outlet for this hatred, Slugan's seething anger continued to ferment and blinded him to rational thinking. Such animosity now controlled his every movement.

One evening after a normal day of long work, the cousins returned home for dinner. An infuriated Slugan sat glaring at the front door waiting for his youngest son. Sanft's passion for art had not ebbed and his father had found several detailed sketches hidden beneath his bed. The tyrannical head of household was enraged. Slugan had emphatically told his son never to draw again and tonight Sanft would feel the consequences for disobeying that order.

Upon entering the home, the young artist was grabbed by his father and a ferocious thrashing ensued. After numerous blows about the head and body, a semi-conscious Sanft was thrown on to his bed by the exhausted Slugan who yelled the admonishment, "If you ever draw again, boy, a worse beating awaits you." Slugan's words fell on deaf ears. In Sanft's condition, he barely comprehended that he was still alive.

The following morning, Sanft failed to appear at the clinic. The quiet one had never missed a day with his friends. Fij'n fearing that all was not well ran to Sanft's home to find the badly battered Sanft still lying in bed. A furious Slugan told Fij'n that no Se was to come to Sanft's aid and it was time this aspiring artist grew up and did what he was told.

Fij'n ran weeping to the Groullen cave and told Reiben of Sanft's condition. Reiben thought it best she notify the Pravis, so Fij'n raced to her uncle's home and described to him the state of his nephew. The Malus leader was visibly angered and quite finished with the brazen acts of his younger brother.

He collected several guards and marched to Slugan's home. Upon entering the house, a surprised Slugan rose from the table as a guard stood on either side of him. The Pravis wasted little time explaining the purpose of his visit and exclaimed, "Slugan, I ordered you not to interfere with the three clinicians of this town and you have taken it upon yourself to disregard my decree and inflict bodily harm on Sanft. Your actions are a direct affront to my authority and as such will be dealt with in the most severe terms. From this day hence, you shall remain fettered on the Erda platform until your future in this town is decided in the Pit of Strength."

Slugan convulsed with fear and disbelief as he fell to his knees, begging his brother to reconsider. The leader only motioned the nervous guards to lead Slugan away then turned on his heels and returned home. Distraught, Slugan was dragged towards the town center and a confused crowd of onlookers followed. This was a scene no Malus ever imagined possible.

By the time he reached his destination, all of Slugan's discordant speech and hubris were gone and he was unceremoniously tied to the Erda platform. Slugan suddenly appeared much smaller and inconsequential to those gathered. In a matter of minutes, this Malus had fallen from the second highest position in town to the very bottom. The town of Malus was changing and it appeared to be for the better. Despondent, Slugan sat alone trying to console himself. He covered his face with his hands to block out the pain of so high a fall.

Meanwhile, Fij'n quickly ran to the cave to gather Reiben. A fragile Sanft required immediate medical attention. The two arrived at a household distressed by the recent turn of events but they were thankful to be spared the random outbursts of anger from a patriarch lost to the delusions of hatred. Slugan's wife led Reiben to her youngest son.

Sanft had been cruelly disciplined and the bruises covering his body made his condition appear much worse but the injuries were not life threatening. He would recover in several weeks. As was always the manner of this young artist, he did not speak and only managed a slight smile at the attention Fij'n and Reiben directed his way. The silent one was in good hands.

Sanft's mother explained the particulars of her son's unfortunate punishment. The young Se said little and became lost to his thoughts; Fij'n did the talking for both of them.

After Sanft was attended to, he was given a dose of herbal tonic and Reiben politely bid his farewell and returned to the cave. Fij'n would spend the night at the side of her cousin. Once home, peace of mind did not come to Reiben and he continued to ponder the best course of action for his friend.

Within a week of convalescence a slow-walking Sanft made his way to the cave. It was smiles all around for the friends as the clinic had finally returned to normal. Even though Sanft was sore, he did not stand by idle, the herbal inventory needed to be replenished and he immediately set to work.

Reiben had thought in depth about his quiet friend over the previous week. Though Sanft spoke not a word, his actions were an excellent indicator of his character. The Malus of no words freely assisted those around him and never expected a bit of appreciation in return. He was kind, thoughtful, patient, enjoyed a good laugh and was the most loyal of friends; qualities often overlooked when one did not have a voice of his own. The one activity where Sanft displayed his uniqueness was art and he was forbidden to enjoy it for reasons only the cold hearted Slugan understood. Such a person of Sanft's caliber deserved much more than he currently received.

Within two days, the clinic was in proper order again and it was not long before Reiben found the right moment to relay his thoughts regarding his quiet friend. He began, "Sanft, how long do you think the Pravis will keep your father on the Erda platform?" Sanft shrugged his shoulder indicating that he did not know. The Se then asked, "Are you afraid that Slugan will have another fit of rage towards you if he leaves the dais and finds your art again?" Sanft sadly nodded the affirmative. Reiben continued, "Slugan never comes into the cave and no other Malus dares enter the living space. I think this would be the perfect cavern for your talents. With the walls of the living space as a canvas, you could paint anything you wish on a grand scale. Fij'n, Brroud and I could help you collect the necessary ingredients for paint and brushes and I'm sure the Groullens would appreciate some color added to the walls as well." The young artist, with tears of happiness on his cheeks, nodded his agreement. Reiben finished with, "Well then, the four of us will start tomorrow gathering all that you need." An excited Sanft slept little that night.

Reiben's plans for Sanft's art coincided nicely with the work detail scheduled the following day – gathering ore for smelting along a glacial river. One of the many run offs from the northern mountains of ice flowed through farm lands a short distance outside of town. Reiben had no idea what was required for the manufacture of Ice Age paint although, the fast running waters deposited large quantities of unrefined materials along its bank. That morning the guards, friends, and several oversized wagons led the Groullens to the waterway.

Set in the expanse of the glacial moraine was an abundant supply of colorful rocks for the Groullens to load into the wagons: copper, zinc, lead, gold and silver littered the river bank. The men of might found the task far easier than the quarry and shortly after lunch the wagons were full and readied for the trip back to town.

Sanft had several large bags which he distributed to Reiben, Fij'n and Brroud then pointed to colorful stones that lay on the river bank, iron oxide - ochre. The Malus had not yet found a use for so important an ingredient in paint. The ochre varied in color from yellow to red and the young artist easily found the necessary hues to create the different shades for his palette. Reiben asked, "Sanft, how do you know which rock is used in paint?" Sanft only shrugged his shoulders. The Se thought that there were many different sides to Sanft which few were privy to.

With the bags and wagon filled, it was time for a return trip to town. Back in the cave, Sanft set to work without haste. Using thick sea shells as crucibles, he ground the ochre to a fine powder then added oil from the aloe plant for consistency and powdered wood ash to create a variety of colors. He made paint brushes from horse hair attached to a smooth stick. Fij'n and Reiben were amazed at Sanft's proficiency with paint production.

It took several more weeks of nightly preparation before Sanft was ready to attempt his first painting. The subject chosen was a favorite of the Groullen, a small herd of woolly mammoths. Sanft and Reiben built makeshift scaffolding in front of a flat, smooth section of cave wall. No one had any idea what to expect from Sanft's first attempt at a large mural but it was not long before Reiben and Fij'n's realized the depth of Sanft's artistic abilities as a masterpiece developed before their eyes. The few who saw the young artist's work agreed – he was gifted with the brush – a prodigy.

In this young Malus resided a master and like all creative geniuses, once a painting was started Sanft lived for nothing but his art. The quiet one also followed a proven formula; he sketched the mural with charcoal before applying paint, adjusted the lighting with small fires around the scaffolding, and worked late into the night with meticulous patience. Sanft's art came before any other personal needs.

Sanft's masterpieces were not lost on the men of muscle for they too were admirers of art. The Naarrts sat for hours in front of the mural and stared at the illustration of mammoths. The two dimensional snap shot of life outside the cave harkened to a happier time. The paintings not only captured the imaginations of the Groullen but transported them back to their homes which they remembered fondly.

Reiben and Fij'n were in awe of Sanft's artistic aptitude. Though the young artist still had his day job in the clinic, the night was reserved for his passion. Sanft survived on little sleep and large quantities of inspiration. Reiben asked his friend, "Where did you learn so much about art? Did someone teach you?" Sanft looked at Reiben but he did not answer with his normal shoulder shrug. Sanft too had secrets he did not wish to share.

Not far from the cave gallery sat Slugan still tethered to the Erda platform. The Pravis had not given any consideration to an alternative punishment and with each passing day this Erda grew more sullen and resisted contact with his wife and sons, especially Sanft. Slugan cursed the Pravis, the Se, his son Sanft and his prospects in the Pit of Strength. With all the trappings of his former life removed and his future among the people of Malus appearing dim, Slugan's mindset hardened. He embraced more anger and discontent instead of finding fault in such thinking. Every bit of this Erda's energy was wasted on negative thoughts.

The town folk steered clear of the brooding Slugan as he stared down from the platform. Life was difficult enough for the Malus without an outburst from a deranged Erda who just a short time ago had held so much power. Slugan basted in his sour disposition and the Pit of Strength could not arrive quickly enough for him.

Sanft's creativity had been unleashed in the safety of the cave and his art supplies had to be replenished at regular intervals; the four friends collected the ochre every other week. And similar to the other important resource overlooked by the Malus, the ores for paint were abundant and in plain sight along every waterway which surrounded the town.

On this particular day the friends gathered the raw material at the edge of town as the Groullen work crew repaired an earthen dam. The dam directed drinking water to small channels which ran through the streets. The large stones and timbers required for the job offered plenty of entertainment for the town's children. The Groullen hoisted the heavy objects with ease and the friends collected the ochre which surrounded the waters.

At the midday meal, Reiben and Fij'n prepared the food while Sanft looked for a specific hue of ore. A number of children walked the banks of the river and everyone was preoccupied.

An unfortunate but not infrequent occurrence during the time of glaciers was the appearance of a rogue carnivore in the settlements of bipeds. Drawn to the village by hunger, due to old age or injury, these animals were always desperate and extremely dangerous. The normal plan of defense for the unlucky residents was to run at a frantic pace in every direction with each man responsible for only himself. The Malus who found himself at the end of the frenzied retreat inevitably fell victim to the powerful jaws of the predator.

On this day a large spotted hyena had found his way to the unsuspecting group and began to survey his options for a meal. Sanft and several smaller children stood alone a short distant up stream. Isolated from rest of the Malus, they became the target for the carnivore. Once the predator was spotted, the other Malus scattered at breakneck speed. Sanft remained stationary, determined not to leave the young children to fend for themselves and he huddled the little ones behind him.

Reiben and Fij'n had always known that Sanft had courage as he had the fortitude to risk a harsh punishment for practicing his art. On this afternoon, Sanft's bravery was again put to the test and placed on full display for the other Malus to witness.

Reiben quickly untied the wand and discreetly placed it in his hand. In a few moments the young artist would discover the effectiveness a stout club had when thwarting a hyena. The wand and Reiben's whispers were soon directed towards Sanft.

The artist selected a sturdy stick lying near the river bank and his demeanor remained calm as he held the club parallel to the ground in his outstretched arms. The hyena, lost to the pangs of hunger, wasted little time and lunged at the smaller Malus standing behind him. Each attempt was met with a powerful blow to the ear, jaw or forehead. Sanft finally directed a solid strike to the hyena's sensitive nose and the brief attack came to an end. Howling as he ran, the ravenous carnivore thought it best to look elsewhere for a meal.

Who would have thought that the one with no voice could be a hero? The overlooked son of Slugan, a child no Malus ever paid the least bit of attention to, was suddenly the bravest young man in the town. Sanft stood still as a group of Malus ran to him with their voices raised in praise. The artist stared at Reiben and in an instant Reiben knew Sanft understood that the wand had been deployed in his defense. At every turn, there was a lot more to this quiet Malus than he chose to share.

Reiben and Fij'n walked towards Sanft and joined in the congratulations. "I told you that Sanft was something special. Words don't make a person, deeds do," exclaimed a beaming Fij'n.

Reiben responded, "You're right, Fij'n, you're absolutely right."

The latest hero in town chose to remain in the Groullen cave and busy himself with painting. Celebrity status was of no interest to the well grounded artist.

Sanft occasionally found his way home for a change of clothes or a meal. His mother radiated pride for her courageous son while Sanft's brothers were more skeptical and full of envy for their younger sibling's heroics. But Sanft's time among his family was never long. For all practical purposes, he was the newest member in the Groullen cave. He slept, ate, and worked in the cavern. The young artist's roommates found him to be an acceptable addition. Sanft toiled for long hours on little sleep but the artist had never been happier and he expressed his joy through his murals and by whistling. He whistled to himself all the time.

Sanft's mother, filled with delight for her special son, could not wait to visit the malignant Slugan in order to relay the latest story about their youngest son. Not surprisingly the Erda was unimpressed and harangued, "If, Sanft is such a hero, why am I fettered to this platform? He can stop a starving Hyena but can't loosen the chains which bind me to this spot. Sanft is nothing more than a puppet to that disgusting Se and I am the only one in this town who sees it. And what is my reward for such a keen insight, a date in the Pit of Strength. I tell you this, that Se will be the downfall of the Malus and I shall not be here to witness it. I don't want you to mention Sanft's name in my presence again. He is no better than that Se."

Two months on the Erda platform had not softened Slugan's attitude. His heartbroken wife ran home in tears. Surely, her husband had become unbalanced. Fortunately, Slugan's youngest son was out of earshot of his father's tirade. Sanft did not need another reminder of how much his father disliked him.

Without any notice from those outside the cave, the young Se and Malus continued their late night routine – painting and study of the wand. Both were immensely satisfied with their endeavors and the artist showed no interest in the decorative stick caring only for his art.

During one such night Reiben chanced a question he was sure he already knew the answer to, "Sanft, do you know what this is?" Sanft nodded the affirmative. Reiben quickly posed a second question, "Do you know where the wand came from?" Again Sanft nodded to the positive. The Se sat up straight ready to learn more about the powerful piece of wood he held in his hand, "Please tell me what you know." Sanft reluctantly shook his head no. Reiben was incredulous and asked, "Sanft, you know how important this wand is to me. Please tell me what you know." Again, Sanft slowly shook his head no. Frustrated Reiben cried, "You and the Groullens both have knowledge of the wand but neither of you will share a bit of information. Sanft, do you realize how infuriating that is?" Sanft shrugged his shoulders and continued painting. The Se thought for a few more minutes and asked, "Sanft, do you think I'll ever understand this wand?" The artist nodded his head enthusiastically to the affirmative. After a brief time Reiben distractedly said to Sanft, "Surely there will be an end to my frustration."

The talented Sanft continued to add murals to the cavern walls and a world outside the town was slowly brought to life on the rock face. The current mural creation before the scaffolding was that of a large bull woolly rhinoceros. Each Groullen lost his tough countenance when seated before the art, the images brought out the child like wonder in them. To the Naartt, the murals were very real. They attempted to look behind the rock to see if the animals were embedded in the walls after which, they sat quietly in front of the paintings in silent admiration.

One evening during the cave dwellers single day of rest, a playful Reiben took advantage of the Groullen's fascination with the images. The Pundir decided to use a mural as a back drop to an Ice Age skit of his own making. Grrick, the well trained dog, was to be his understudy.

At the appropriate time, Reiben positioned himself in front of the Groullens favorite mural, the woolly mammoths and began his theatrical career as he exclaimed, "Oh, I am such a strong Brroud Bird walking in the fields. All know I'm the bravest Brroud Bird in all the land. But wait, what do I see on the horizon? A large hill stands before me which is moving and covered in thick hair." Reiben walked towards the woolly mammoths in the mural. "It is a woolly mammoth and surely he is afraid of such a strong Brroud Bird as I." The Se puffed out his chest and held up his arms and flexed the smallest muscles in the cave. The audience could not contain themselves and rolled on the ground in laughter. The young thespian had the most appreciative audience seated before him.

Reiben continued, "Woolly mammoth, do you see these wings of strength? You had better start running because this bird is stronger than you. Come on, get going." Reiben mimed the woolly mammoth stomping on his foot then kicking him below the waist line. He dropped to the cave floor and moaned, "Strong bird crawling away, strong bird crawling away." Reiben squirmed as he crept a short distance from the mural before finally standing. Thunderous guffaws could be heard half way into town. Sanft sat on his scaffolding, lost to the humorous talents of his good friend and thinking that Fij'n may have found such adolescent boyish humor mildly entertaining.

However, the clever Reiben was not finished as the heroes of the cave spoof had yet to arrive. He jumped in front of the mural once more and contorted his face into the best facial Groullen imitation he could manage, stuck out his chest, bent his knees with his hands hung low and walked slowly up to the mammoth exclaiming, "Woolly mammoth you are looking at a Naarrt, leave Brroud Bird alone or I'll punch you in the head." Grrick, the quick minded prop, played the part of the woolly mammoth and ran off on Reiben's command.

The raucous crowd could not contain themselves and they laughed until hoarse. The short performance was an immediate success and received the highest praise from the Naarrts. They demanded an encore and the young Se found himself an Ice Age star among the cave dwellers. Reiben repeated the exact same act a number of times that night to a continuum of joyful roars. These Groullen had hours of laughter in their huge bodies but as was the nature of the men of might, the Naarrts abruptly went to bed before it was too late. The larger patrons of the arts required long hours of sleep to refill their reservoirs of mirth.

For Brroud Bird, his acting skills never become stale to the Naarrts. Reiben found tremendous joy in the fact that Groullens reveled in the simplest of humor and the Se believed that many a biped could benefit from such a gift. As Sanft completed each new mural, Reiben added a different theatrical event to his repertoire. There was the woolly mammoth stamping on the Brroud Bird's foot, the woolly rhinoceros poking his long horn in the Brroud Bird's belly, the aurochs horns goring the bird's backside and the bison bopping the Brroud Bird on the head. Every skit was an Ice Age classic and the theme for each short play never changed. Reiben was the bumbling Brroud Bird while the heroes were the Groullen and Grrick; the clever four legged actor learned his parts to perfection.

Once a week, the Groullen Theatre presented a number of short plays and the Malus outside grew accustomed to the Naarrt's laughter. They believed that the Pundir must be working wonders with the beasts. For the cave dwellers, these simple pleasures provided them a short respite from their station among the Malus. A heart felt laugh kept one mentally grounded. Sanft, no longer under constant torment from his father, also flourished in his new life. With the supportive tutelage of the Se and the Groullens, the young artist's murals became an exceptional outlet for his prodigious creativity. Sanft was maturing into a Malus never before seen in the town. Fij'n could not be more proud of her cousin.

One evening before the start of the Groullen Theatre, Sanft had a surprise for his fellow cave dwellers – it was time to autograph the murals. The young artist selected a suitable spot on the cave wall and with a large paint brush made an outline of his hand. The Groullens found the handprint fascinating. Sanft motioned for Reiben to join him, took his wrist and made another outline of his friend's hand. The artist then brought each Groullen forward and repeated the process starting with the leader. Every cave dweller's handprint was grouped together in one spot on the wall; a symbol of the unique Ice Age fraternity they belonged to. The cave dwellers stared at the collection of signatures – it was a powerful image of who they were and a constant reminder that they had left their mark on the world. Reiben said to his friend, "Sanft, these handprints speak more clearly than any words we could say for ourselves." The artist smiled in agreement.

With a month to go before the Winter Carnival, the Pravis and a posse of men were headed to the frontier for the annual Erda round up. The cave had become covered in murals but there was one last spot which Sanft needed to fill. It would not take him long to find a subject.

After several days of thought and a few days of work, the painting was finished. It was an animal the Se had never seen before but it was obviously familiar to Sanft and the Groullens. The animal looked like a horse with a white body covered in brown and black spots. A single horn protruded from its head. The Groullens were very excited and they kept patting their head and arms. Reiben asked the leader what animal was this and he answered, "Morrln, makes the head and body warm." This horse could heal one's mind and body.

Reiben asked Sanft, "Where have you seen this animal?" Sanft motioned that it lived around the town. The Se said, "I have never seen such an animal. Have other Malus seen it?" Sanft responded with a shrug that maybe a few Malus had possibly seen the horse. Reiben quickly asked the artist, "Do you see this horse often?" Sanft nodded yes. The Se excitedly asked, "Sanft, do you think I will ever see this horse?" The artist nodded yes. Reiben's mind was racing and he asked out of the blue, "Does the animal have anything to do with the wand?" Sanft shrugged. Reiben took that answer as a most definite maybe.

The Se sat down alongside the Groullen and stared at the horse mural. He wondered how this animal could be connected to the wand. A horse with one horn and a wand did not make any sense; but since leaving his island community, very little in the world seemed to be logical. Reiben asked Sanft, "When will I see the horse?" The artist laughed and shrugged that he had no idea. Such meetings were always determined by the horse.

Everyone stayed up well past their bedtime as they continued to gaze upon the mural. This Morrln must be powerful indeed for the Groullen not to go to bed on time.

Reiben turned and saw the little people watching him. They appeared to have smiles on their faces. Perhaps these darting silhouettes of the night had met the horse too. He was the only person in the cave who had yet to have an introduction. Reiben took a deep breath and went to bed. His mind was far too full of questions for there to be any wand studying that night.

The heart of winter had a strong hold on the Se Atoll. To Aunt Sufi, the winter seemed colder this year; the ice was thicker around the islands and the snow deeper on the land. But it had been a year free of tragedy for the community. Sufi lit her candle for Reiben, added an extra log on the fire, made a stronger cup of hot brew and sat down to think about her little Uni. Sufi felt sure the positive thoughts she sent Reiben's way were helping – well, at least she hoped they were.

As Sufi sat thinking of Reiben, she experienced a sudden, yet ever so slight feeling, that change was coming his way. Not a harmful type of change nor a change which would see him return to the Isle of Rune but she felt certain that it was time for Reiben to move on. Sufi had a sigh followed by a sip of the calming brew; Reiben would soon walk further along his path in life. This little Uni was alive and still in need of her loving energy. After a time in thought, a sniffle and small tear came to Sufi as she was happy that her tiny Se would continue on his journey.

14

Surprise Introduction

The winter carnival was near at hand as the annual parade of prisoners from the frontier and wild beasts captured in the lands north had begun.

One prisoner had called the Erda platform home for several months, Slugan. The Pravis's younger brother was quite the curiosity for the new arrivals. All indications were that Slugan was still a participant in this year's Pit of Strength, but most Malus believed the Pravis would commute his brother's sentence at the last moment and he would watch the spectacle of man versus beast from the protected seats of privilege once more. Yet the condemned sibling remained tied to the platform and his possible demise only added to the excitement for the drama in the pit.

Had this distinguished prisoner used his time wisely on the dais of the doomed and reflected on the error in his thinking? No. A contrite heart did not beat in the chest of the town's most celebrated Erda. His conviction that every problem in the Malus world sprung from the efforts of a lone Se was still firmly rooted in Slugan's head. Reiben was the source of all the town's troubles.

Slugan's contempt for the Se was now permanently etched on his face. As each new prisoner was secured to the platform, they were greeted with an angry scowl and no words. Slugan's hatred for his station in life isolated him from the others. The Pit of Strength could not arrive soon enough for so wretched a person.

After three and a half years among the Malus, Reiben's reputation had spread far beyond the boundaries of town. Throughout the territories of Malus, unbeknownst to the hard working Pundir, his efforts were well known. Reiben was a young Se whose kindness knew no limits and he freely aided those in need without any expectation of gratitude. The talented Se was viewed with favor by every Erda on the dais save one.

On this day Reiben with the work crew found themselves walking through the center of town; the Pundir and Groullens were immediately recognized by those on the crowded platform. Every prisoners' eye was on the workers and one forlorn Erda called out to Reiben, "Se, do you have any words of advice for a Malus destined for the pit?"

Reiben stopped and looked at the collection of desperate faces peering down from the platform and said, "Let a clear mind be your guide men of courage."

The prisoner nervously replied, "A clear mind does not stop a wild beast."

Reiben calmly answered, "When two courageous men enter the pit, both with clear minds and superior intellect, a beast is at a distinct disadvantage against such a force. I believe all of you will find your way through the pit to freedom." The prisoner was not as confident in his abilities as the Se but he did not know how to respond. A weak nod was all he and his peers could manage.

Reiben was determined that this year's outcome in the arena would be much different from those of the past. These prisoners, whom chance brought to the front door of the pit, had an unknown ally - Reiben and his wand. They would find the strength and resolve not to succumb to the wicked spectacle of the Winter Carnival. As Reiben departed the town center he repeated, "Let clear minds be your guide men of courage."

Life in the cave was at its best. The Groullen appeared happier than ever and found Brroud Bird a constant source of entertainment. The cave walls were covered in Ice Age masterpieces and Sanft enjoyed his days as a free thinking artist. Fij'n was a healing practitioner whose archery skills inched along and the only Se in town was far too busy a young man for his mind to wander outside of Malus to the atoll. However, as was always the case during the ancient times of ice, change was just around the corner for the four friends.

In the first minutes of a new morning, a tired Reiben prepared for bed. Quite unexpectedly, three little people arrived and stood by a seated Sanft – all four were staring at the Se. Without any hesitation, the little people and Sanft motioned for Reiben to follow them and they raced down a cave corridor. A confused Reiben sat still for a brief moment before he followed. Reiben and his excited shadow found it difficult to keep up. The four fleet-footed guides lit a torch and led the pair through a maze of passageways and tunnels in the underbelly of the mountain before reaching its far side.

Reiben was out of breath when he finally emerged into a clearing illuminated by a waxing moon. The open area was surrounded by trees, manicured bushes, and winter flowers - his four guides promptly sat on the ground. Reiben and Brroud remained standing and took in the pleasant view offered by moonlight on vegetation that had been flawlessly groomed. Why had Sanft and the little people brought him to this place with a beautiful garden?

After a short wait, an old mare with a single horn in the center of her forehead walked slowly into the clearing. Reiben knew right away this was the animal from the cave murals – the horse the Groullens called Morrln. He quickly assumed from her condition that she required medical attention and that was the reason he had been brought to this spot.

Reiben walked cautiously up to the horse and found her to be dirty, haggard, under-nourished but had a gentle nature. He slowly walked around the unique animal and spoke soothingly while he evaluated her overall condition.

The horse had distinctive markings; a mottled coat of brown spots on white and her well worn single horn which was the length of Reiben's forearm. It was obvious the old mare had travelled this earth for many a year. Reiben patted her shoulder and neck whilst assuring her everything would be alright - she just needed a bit of attention.

He found her energy was warm and invigorating to the touch and to his surprise the collection of worries he had neatly tucked away in the back of his mind soon evaporated. After looking her over carefully, Reiben informed his five companions that the horse required a good cleaning and they were all needed if the job was to be done properly.

The able little people filled their empty stew pots with water, gathered soap and found childlike delight when they lathered up

Morrln and scrubbed away. They laughed and threw soap bubbles at each other while the horse stood patiently and paid little attention to their frolic. The months of dirt did not wash away in a single bath yet after several more washings Morrln finally appeared presentable.

The bath was followed by an extensive grooming and horn buff after which the horse of note was finally ready for her dose of herbal tonic. After the six had completed their work, Reiben assured Morrln that he would be back with additional grooming and tonics and within a fortnight she would feel much better. The old mare appeared to understand all the Se told her and at last a giddy Reiben, Sanft, and Brroud returned to their cave for a brief night's sleep.

Reiben woke without a single negative effect from his abbreviated rest. One could have said that his mind and body had never felt more refreshed. Working with the old mare had restored a bit of vigor to the young Se and Reiben's daily tasks passed quickly that day. Archery was over sooner than expected and the three little people along with Sanft stood by Reiben once more. They motioned for him to follow them. This time the mountain's labyrinth of tunnels was easier to traverse.

When the six arrived at the moonlit garden, they found several additional guests - more little people. Morrln's nightly visits were drawing a crowd. All sat on the ground and waited for the one horned animal. The old mare arrived on schedule and appeared healthier than the previous night and smiles on the collective faces greeted her. The Se spoke to the one horned, "You've improved Morrln and more of your friends have come to see you."

Reiben gave instructions to his companions and the additional little folks were anxious to lend a hand. There was no room around the horse when the bathing began and a shortage of brushes caused several to feel left out at grooming time.

To Reiben's surprise, he found his voice came easily to him when standing by the horse and he quietly told the old mare how well she was doing, what good energy she projected to those around her, how popular she had become with Sanft, Groullen and the little people and that she felt like an old friend to him after only two days. The old mare never made a response but appeared to listen to the Se. At the nights end Reiben said, "Well, Morrln you are improving quite well and I look forward to seeing you tomorrow. Your patience with my babblings is most appreciated." And with that, the three cave mates returned to their beds for another night of little sleep.

On each successive evening Reiben found a larger gathering of little people waiting on the far side of the mountain and they all jockeyed for their chance to bathe and brush Morrln. Unfortunately, the diminutive group did not have the civility of the Se as every one of them was well versed in pushing and shoving. The young Pundir wrestled with a language barrier and their poor manners but after considerable persistence, an orderly queue of helpers was formed. They all had a short turn at washing and brushing – thus ensuring Morrln's hair remained attached to her hide.

The old mare had the patience that many years on this earth brought and displayed no irritation at all the fuss made over her. In Morrln's presence Reiben found himself lost to his thoughts and continued to recount the highlights of his brief life which took longer to retell than a young boy of twelve might have thought: Born a Uni on the island of Rune, captured in the southlands by the Malus, the Pravis was a formidable man but may have a kind heart which belied his tough exterior, the Groullens with their massive strength had and even larger sense of humor and finally Sanft, Fij'n and Brroud, were the best friends a Se could ever wish for. Reiben felt calm and relaxed as he described the major events of his life and he surprised himself with his candor but the old mare still remained mute.

By the end of the fortnight, Morrln had grown quite youthful in appearance and the garden on the far side of the mountain was thronged with little people. Reiben was baffled by both facts. How and why did all these small people live under the mountain? How could the old mare's appearance have changed so drastically after two weeks of bathing and daily herbal supplements? The Se was at a loss for the answer.

After Morrln's last healing treatment, Reiben took a few moments to say a warm good bye to the horse and thanked her once again for her patience to his incessant rambling. He gave the horse a big hug and turned to leave.

Sanft, Brroud, and all the little people remained seated in a half circle around the horse. Reiben was perplexed and motioned for his friends to follow him. Sanft and Brroud only smiled back. As he stood confused, Morrln walked up to Reiben, tapped him on his arm with her horn and said, "My young Se, why are you leaving so soon? We have only just met." Reiben stared wide eyed at the horse but said not one word. The old mare continued to speak. "I must say, I have never felt better, Reiben. Thank you for tending to my weary body with so skillfully. I also enjoyed listening to the stories of your life - for one so young, you have experienced much."

Reiben remained silent and incredulous as he stared at the horse and tried to comprehend what was happening before him. Morrln declared, "Oh, but excuse me, a few words about me are in order as all the introductions have come from you so far. My given name is Gnos. But you can call me 'Morrln' as the Naarrt do. The Groullen vocabulary though simple in form is quite descriptive and they enjoy the use of an 'R' in every word. I am an animal born with only one horn and as you can hear, I have the gift of speech. My young Se, you should not be too surprised that a one horned horse can speak. After all you have discovered that the Naarrts have an extensive language as well. I have lived a long time on this earth, a fact you readily surmised and I travel the four corners of the world aiding those less fortunate. It is a considerable task as there is much need today but I do not find the work a burden. Among those I've helped are your friend Sanft, the Groullen, and the little ones assembled around you. I do know of the isolated people on the Se atoll but few have ever crossed my path and none has lived this long in the town of Malus. I find the Se to be a bright spot in the world and your actions since leaving those islands have not altered my opinion in the least. I think that is a short but accurate summary of who I am and what I do."

Gnos finished her speech and looked at the puzzled Se. After several minutes Reiben spoke, "Gnos, you are correct, I am surprised to meet a horse who can speak but I'm at more of a loss as to why you would wish to say anything to me."

The ever insightful Gnos responded, "I see my young Se is far wiser than his years. Your reputation Reiben, outside the town of

Malus has spread much further than you know. I decided to visit the boy who is kind to all regardless of whom that person might be and expects nothing in return. Reiben, do you have any insight as to why you have so pleasant an outlook toward others?"

Reiben felt Gnos was asking a question she already knew the answer to but he responded, "I am a Se and was raised to think no other way."

The Gnos replied, "Ah, the Se are undoubtedly a unique group of people and we are fortunate to have one amongst us. But it is late my young Reiben and you have much work to do during the day, all of which must be difficult on too little sleep. If you wish, we can continue our conversation tomorrow night." Reiben agreed with Gnos and bid her a warm good night.

Sanft, Brroud, and Reiben returned to the cave and Reiben's mind raced through the numerous questions he should ask Gnos. It was a long time before he slept.

The next evening could not arrive soon enough for Reiben. So many possibilities swirled around in his head. Once dinner was completed, Reiben told a surprised Fij'n there was no archery tonight as that he needed a good night's rest. Fij'n found this statement difficult to believe but she left the cave all the same.

The three cave dwellers immediately raced for the other side of the mountain and Gnos joined them shortly after their arrival. A skeptical Fij'n returned a short while later to a cave absent of her friends. So, what were those three up to?

The one horned began the conversation and said, "I can see, young Se, you had little sleep last night so I'm sure you have a number of questions for me."

Reiben replied, "Indeed I do, but I don't know where to begin. Gnos, you mentioned travelling the four corners of the world aiding the less fortunate, how do you offer help?"

Gnos replied, "Besides the gift of speech I do have a sensible mind and the wisdom that many years on this earth brings. I'm familiar with the ways of old and I strive to teach others how to look at their world through enlightened eyes; for many answers can be found when done so."

This explanation only generated more queries. Reiben continued and asked, "Gnos, with your years of experience, why do you think I was captured by the Malus?"

The old mare paused for a few minutes before she answered, "Like everyone in this world Reiben, you are on a journey and your travels have led you away from the security of the Se Atoll. In spite of the numerous hardships which have crossed your path, it has been a life few others could have endured. I know your parents told you that you were born with the gifts of a Uni. Yet that fact does not mean your path in life is an easy one. I ask you now, my helpful Se, as you stand before me do you find yourself a wiser person for all the challenges you have met each day?"

Gnos was certainly a horse with keen perception and Reiben was the one left pondering his thoughts for several minutes before he responded, "Gnos, your observations are correct and your words are filled with wisdom, they would be helpful to anyone in need. Besides the few people in Malus who have assisted me during times of need, my journey has been aided by a short piece of wood, a small branchlet, which was left at my feet whilst in sleep by one of those who surround us now. Sanft, the Groullen and the little people are aware of the wand but have offered few details about its purpose or from whence it came. Are you familiar with this wooden token?"

Reiben removed the wand from his clothing and showed it to the old mare. Gnos remained in thought for a long time. Reiben thought their conversation was over but the horse finally replied, "Yes, Reiben, that wand has found its way to you and I must say that you have used it as it was intended.

Many years ago, when the face of the earth looked much different, the wand you have and many like it were in the hands of men and women similar to you. They travelled to every niche of the known world, and like you, they used their wands for the good of those around them. But a time came when the stick of power could be used no longer. Snow began to fall and the ice accumulated. People were displaced. The world of harmonious existence became a far different place and the one horned horses have been encumbered with much work ever since." Reiben realized that Gnos's short history lesson was similar to the information gleaned from the Groullen's version.

Reiben continued the line of questioning around his real interest - what were the meanings of the wand's inscriptions and the reason for its power so he asked, "I have studied the characters inscribed on the wand for many a night and my understanding of them is no better today than when I first received it. Can you tell me what the markings mean?"

The old mare replied, "My quick minded Se, your thirst for knowledge is a pleasure to observe. The markings on the wand are very old, dating back long before history was even a thought. They are called 'Rune' which is from the ancient tongue of man and means 'root'. From the root springs all the beauty which fills the earth. The Rune characters were made for man and like the flowers, trees, and mountains which capture our imagination, these tiny symbols were designed to evoke a unique emotion in the eye of the reader. The Rune characters are man's way to express the same joy one feels when he views the wonder of nature.

The ancient ones believed they were one with the world not just observers of it and each person had a unique relationship with his surroundings and communicated that experience in the written Rune. With these marks of man, one can weave a tale as powerful as the first rays of a new day or a full moon setting atop a mountain range.

One of the many duties the one horned are tasked with is to keep the Rune alive and well. The writings from so distant a past offer great insight into how one should live his life today. The wand you hold young Se, reflects the thinking of those who made it and is a constant reminder of how one must carry himself as he moves through life.

To the ancient people, the four corners of the world were more than points of reference in this world; they reflected the makeup of man. The etchings on the small stick you hold summarize those beliefs from old: North – it symbolizes the earth from which all life has sprung; South - the fire which warms our homes and sparks creativity in man; East – the air we breathe which enables man to communicate with those around us; West – water which always finds its way; so too may man find his way to knowledge. And at the bottom of the wand the inscription reads, 'I will always remain true to the teachings passed down to me.' As you can see, Reiben, there are no finer words to guide a person through life."

The young Se was overcome with emotion. Every word Gnos spoke had struck a chord in him. Reiben's feelings swelled and it took him several minutes to calm down before he softly said, "I was born on the Island of Rune and I don't believe it was named such by chance."

Gnos replied, "Why yes, you were my young Se. An auspicious beginning for you I believe."

Reiben continued, "Gnos, everything you have said resonates with me and is reflected in the Se's way of life. The people who crafted the wand thought much like the island folk but a wand was never discussed on the atoll. Wise Gnos you have answered one question and generated so many more."

The enigmatic Gnos who always seemed to know more than she revealed answered, "My brave little Se, I believe in time all your questions will be answered."

Reiben, overwhelmed by all he had learned, decided to ask a question concerning those around him, "You mentioned helping Sanft and the little people. In what way did you offer them aid?"

Gnos replied, "My curious Se, you have all you need to ask them anything you wish. Just a tap of the wand on their shoulder, a simple command to communicate and you shall understand each other. You do not need me to answer that question."

Reiben looked at a smiling Sanft in disbelief. He did not waste another moment and moved quickly to Sanft and tapped him on the shoulder. Sanft hesitated a few seconds then said, "Thank you Reiben, for all you have done. I have no better friend than you." And with those few words, Reiben's and Sanft's friendship took on a new dimension.

Though Sanft's speech was impaired, his thoughts were clear to Reiben. The Se heard what the young artist was thinking. The excited Sanft began to tell Reiben the story of his brief life.

From an early age, the young artist knew he was not the son his father had wished for and his inability to speak only made life worse. To escape the harsh scrutiny of his father Sanft spent long hours by himself in the woods, soaking up the beauty of nature. One day after a dreadful thrashing at the hands of the cruel head of household, Sanft ran to the woods for solace. The one horned horse was waiting and introduced herself. It was not long before the quiet one had two bright spots in his life - Fij'n and Gnos. Neither judged him for his odd ways and both were always kind.

During each visit, Gnos told the young Sanft what a brave lad he was and not to be afraid. His day would come. Fij'n for her part, did all she could to shield Sanft from his father and risked her own safety in the process. The two cousins were inseparable and constantly stayed out of sight of Slugan. Finally the day came when a small Se arrived in Malus and his life improved once more.

During Sanft's tale, the half circle of little people continued to move towards the engrossed friends until their presence could no longer be ignored. These small ones did not let their size keep them from being in the middle of everything. Reiben finally tapped the shoulder of the one who appeared in charge and the Se could understand each and every word in his prolific talking.

The little people or Florians, the people of the flowers, did not have tiny voices nor lack for any words. Reiben found it hard to believe that from these diminutive bodies' flowed an endless stream of speech.

The Florians' leader, named Hirte, gave a lengthy narrative of his peoples' dealings with the one horn. He told Reiben that before the Age of Ice changed the landscape, the Florians had a wonderful life in the lush collection of vegetation which surrounded the mountains. When the frigid temperatures arrived and covered the expanse of small brush in ice, their habitat dwindled. They became easy prey for the wild beasts who roamed the Boreal lands and the number of Florians diminished.

The ever watchful Gnos led the little people to the mountain caves for their own safety. Life as cave dwellers was a trying adjustment for the active Florians. The people of the flowers could only make brief nightly excursions away from the alps; a silhouette's existence they found hard to endure. The Se's arrival offered an improved diet and comic relief from the doldrums of life in a cavern and Reiben's pranks with the Groullen kept their minds distracted with humor.

The talkative Florians would have rattled on all night but Gnos intervened and told Reiben it was getting far too late. There would be other nights for more questions. The friends retired to the caves with Reiben and Sanft's head swimming from all the revelations of the evening.

The following evening after dinner, Reiben, Sanft and Brroud raced each other to the far side of the mountain; Fij'n arrived for archery amidst a chorus of snoring Groullen with pointed questions for the absent three. Where had they gone to again? The wise Gnos was there to greet them and exclaimed, "I can see my inquisitive Se's head is brimming once more."

Reiben wasted little time and asked, "Gnos, why was the wand given to me? I am the least deserving of such a gift. And what am I supposed to use it for?"

Gnos chuckled and said, "A wand finds its owner no matter how insignificant that person thinks he is. The criterion for that selection was set forth by the people of old. Reiben, you have always used your gift for the good of others. The why is obvious to me and those around you."

Gnos's rhetoric did little to satisfy Reiben but he had another question which had been on his mind since his arrival in the town of Malus, "Gnos, will I ever leave the town of Malus and return home?" The old Mare felt the longing in Reiben's heart. Over a quarter of his time on this earth had been spent away from his island home. One's journey through life has many twists and turns and the outcome may not be to one's liking.

The Gnos said, "My resourceful Se that is a question I cannot answer. I do not see the future and sadly, to one so giving as you, I can offer you no answer."

As Gnos continued to explain to Reiben details of the important work the one horns had accomplished, an Ice Age blue adder entered the half circle of those assembled. This snake was a distant cousin to the adder of present and was a formidable reptile in the Time of Ice. At the length of several adult Malus, the snake's poisonous bite commanded a wide berth from all whose path it crossed.

Yet, there was more to this powerful snake than its venomous fangs. Its presence was an omen for those it slithered past; an omen of impending change. The large adder slid between Gnos and Reiben on his way to a destination only he knew. The significance of the snake's arrival was not lost on Gnos and she said, "My young Se, a portent has come your way. The snake who continuously sheds his skin, foretells change in the lives of those he passes. And from the size of this viper, your life will move in a new direction in the near future."

Reiben was startled at this prediction and asked, "What new direction is meant for me?"

Gnos reassuringly said, "Reiben, do not fear, change is not bad. I cannot predict the future so I don't know in which direction you will move. But if your new path leads you away from the town of Malus may I suggest you take those who are most vulnerable with you and head north along the coast to Foggerland. I only offer this advice because I feel you will find that which you are seeking in the north."

Reiben looked lost and did not know what to say but ventured a weak, "When should I leave?"

The Gnos calmly replied, "Do not fret, my brave Se, the time for change is close and you will know when to act. I too must leave this place and travel to those in need. I have enjoyed our time together, my friend from the islands and hope our paths will cross once more."

Reiben's time with Gnos was about to end as abruptly as it started and he was at a loss for what to say. As the full spectrum of emotions filled his young heart – admiration, sadness, apprehension, and adolescent indecision – Reiben's approached Gnos and wrapped his arms around her neck. Tears filled his eyes. He told her that he was so fortunate to call her a friend.

Reiben was sure the one horned had heard that many times before from all she had come into contact with. Then those assembled each had their chance to say a warm farewell. Finally Gnos, looking refreshed, quietly walked into the shadows of the night. A somber group returned to their cave. Reiben once again found it hard to sleep as his thoughts revolved around two notions - head north, when?

The winter solstice was less than two weeks away. As with every Se, Aunt Sufi used the winter months as a time for thoughtful reflection. Sufi was the only person on the Isle of Rune who thought of Reiben each day; he was on her mind now as she made a cup of hot brew. Unwavering in her conviction that Reiben was still alive, Sufi sat down to think about her little Uni. After three and a half years, Sufi managed the emotional pain of his disappearance without crying; although, her eyes became teary with grief when she thought of him.

Sufi was in tune to all the energy around her, a trait each Se woman of healing possessed. She felt Reiben was safe and that he had become the young man she'd always known he would grow into. Aunt Sufi also felt that this chapter in Reiben's life was nearing an end and he would move on to a new one. The wise woman found it difficult to sense from afar the struggles of one so dear to her and remained powerless to help. She could only send positive energy his way. Her favorite Uni had to continue down his new path alone.

15

The Pit of Confusion

After the latest revelations, the morning began with a tap of the wand on the young artist's shoulder, a few words uttered by Reiben to communicate and then a "Good morning" was exchanged – one verbal the other mute. Two broad smiles followed. It was such a joy that the friends could now talk. Words opened new doors to their friendship and Reiben had an opportunity for a civil conversation each morning with someone other than a Groullen. The Naarrts were one syllable growlers at sunrise and not given to idle chatter.

The friends' means of communication offered a distinct advantage outside the cave, no suspicion was drawn to themselves. Since not a word ever passed Sanft's lips and Reiben's mumblings were of little interest to the Malus, the two's incessant conversation went unnoticed by those around them.

With breakfast finished, the work crew started their daily routine – service to the town of Malus. Their task for the day was to ready the Pit of Strength for the carnival; repair several spots on the arena wall and reinforce the bars on the Erda holding cave. None of the renovations were difficult for the strong Groullen.

By midday the work was completed and the parade of prisoners had just reached the pit's gate; the largest crowd in memory surrounded the wagons. The Pravis's bother was still an Erda and he was this year's main attraction. No one in town wished to miss a moment of his horrific end.

Slugan sat in the lead cart and upon sighting Reiben and Sanft, directed his scowl their way. A sad hearted Sanft said to Reiben, "It is hard for me to believe so angry a man is my father. What could I ever say to soften such a heart?"

Reiben replied, "Do not burden yourself with his troubled mind my friend, only Slugan can change his way of thinking but his bitterness does play a part in our lives."

Slugan's wagon passed a short distance from the young friends but no words were exchanged. The high ranking Erda's threatening glare said it all. Reiben heard his name called from a number of the prisoners as they passed by, but the rumble of the crowd drowned out any questions they had for the Se.

Unknown to the prisoners, a capable ally stood ready to wield a powerful stick in their defense. Reiben was determined the Erdas' life would be spared this year. The ferocity of a wild beast was no match for the collective energy of the wand. The winter carnival started in three days' time and the work crew headed home after a short day at the arena.

As the work crew walked to the cave, the conversation turned to Fij'n. Reiben thought it best to tell her all that had happened over the past few weeks and asked Sanft, "How will Fij'n respond to learning that we've had an adventure without her?"

Sanft replied, "Fij'n will not mind because she's our friend." Shortly after dinner, Fij'n arrived for her archery lessons and her mind was not set on bows. She had direct questions for her friends.

Reiben and Sanft greeted her with boyish smirks and told Fij'n that there would be no archery this evening as Sanft and he had something important to tell her. It appeared the three friends and their constant companion, Brroud, had the same agenda.

Reiben began the conversation with, "As you know, over the past few weeks Sanft and I have been occupied during the early hours of the morning and now we wish to share with you all we have done." Reiben thought it best if he began at the beginning.

The Se told her of the wand given to him two years prior and how he accidently discovered its immense power which was now used for the good of the less fortunate in town; that the Beasts had a language which Brroud taught him to speak; that a one horned talking horse called Gnos, travelled the four corners of the known world to help those in need; a group of little people, the Florians, were forced to live in the mountains because the frigid climate of the north had destroyed their homes and the surrounding vegetation; and finally but most importantly, he described how with just a tap of the wand the thoughts of Sanft could be heard by her. After a lengthy account of the previous years, a smiling Reiben and Sanft sat beaming at all they had accomplished.

Fij'n had a pensive look on her face as Reiben asked her, "Don't you find this news exciting?"

Fij'n sat in thought and did not answer straight away. This refined young lady was gifted with a clever mind and had no inclination toward outbursts of anger or long bouts of sadness. She also did not find it difficult to express her thoughts concisely and was forthcoming when all did not appear right. Such was the case with the latest revelations. After considering her words carefully, Fij'n wasted little time in voicing her opinion to the smiling friends with regard to their escapades and pointedly exclaimed, "I want to make sure I understand you correctly. Am I to believe that my best friends waited two years to tell their best friend all the new discoveries they made without a bit of help from me? If that statement is true, how would you two feel if I had left you behind while I'm off on an adventure of my own? For as both of you know, I would have found the events of the past few weeks and years just as exciting had I tagged along. So in the future, my friends, an invitation to join your exploits would be greatly appreciated."

There was a long moment of silence as the smiles quickly disappeared from the boys' faces. The awkward pause came to an ended when Reiben continued, "I hope you don't remain vexed with us for too long Fij'n, as the Gnos added one more piece of information which we need your help with. The wise horse said my life would change direction in the short term and that I, along with others, are to leave the town and head north along the coast to a place called Foggerland. When this departure is to commence, Gnos did not say, but she did mention that I would realize the moment. I feel preparations should be made quickly by all of us for so important a journey as this."

Fij'n was overwhelmed with this added bit of information. As an only child, she had her mother to consider. She replied in a voice with a hint of heartache, "I don't see myself leaving Malus. My mother has only me and she will need my help in the future. I assume Sanft will be going with you?" Reiben thought it an appropriate time for Sanft to finally speak to his cousin. The Se moved toward Fij'n and tapped her shoulder with the wand.

Sanft then said his first words to Fij'n, "My courageous cousin, I have waited so long to thank you for all you have done for me. I would never be seated before you now without your constant help."

Any anger Fij'n felt toward her friends was washed away in tears. She was overjoyed to hear Sanft's thoughts. Sanft continued, "Fij'n, we did not bring you along because we feared for your safety. I could not stand the thought of anything happening to my dear cousin."

After a time, Fij'n dried her eyes and said with a weak smile, "I can not stay angry at you or Reiben for very long. You're the best friends a person could ever wish for." The three sat in silence for an extended period. Each hoping this bond of friendship would last forever and wondering how Gnos's latest revelation would affect it. Their lives were changing but they wished their friendship would not.

After a while Reiben said, "Fij'n, tomorrow I will introduce you to my cave mates and the elusive Florians but please do not take what the Groullen say seriously. They are far too mischievous a group and hold no ill will towards anyone. As for the Florians, you will be amazed that so many words are packed into their small bodies. They need to speak nonstop each day to feel healthy."

The day's disclosures were enough for one evening. The three friends said their good nights and went to bed as their heads swirled with thoughts of what the future would bring. Change was close at hand and the trio did not know what it would hold for them.

Two days before the Winter Carnival was to begin and the people of Malus were at a frenetic pitch. Everyone was eager to secure a seat and watch Slugan enter the pit. The town leaders had decided the upper tier of the arena should be reinforced and additional seating added to accommodate all.

The Pundir and his charges were busy once more in the arena. From the shadows of his cave, Slugan watched his nemesis, the Se. The other prisoners hoped Reiben would stop at their holding area to offer words of solace. However, the day's restorations did not afford that.

At the end of an unusually long day, the work crew returned home for dinner and Fij'n joined them shortly after they were finished. She normally arrived at the large cavern after the Groullen were asleep and the beasts paused when she walked into their living area.

Reiben waited until all were quiet, walked over and tapped Fij'n with the wand and said a few words before he proceeded to address the Groullen, "You have the strength of a woolly mammoth. Tonight Brroud Bird brings a Grres Bird to the cave. Grres Bird is a friend and works with Brroud Bird. Grres bird …"

Before Reiben finished his sentence a Groullen shouted out, "If Brroud Bird works with Grres Bird he is a Grres Bird." The Groullens' laughter bounced off the cave walls. At his friend's expense, young Brroud found the humor led him to uncontrollable laughter.

Fij'n was not prepared for the Groullens' flippant disregard for the nurturers of Malus society but Reiben was not deterred by the hilarity. Adding some theatrics to his delivery, Reiben continued, "I am Brroud Bird…."

Which was met with, "You Grres Bird with baby" and there was no chance for a reasonable conversation after that. The Groullens were rolling around on the ground holding their bellies. Fij'n's face was twisted with displeasure which only fueled their merriment.

Reiben said to Fij'n, "I think you have been well received. They'll continue laughing until it's time for bed."

After several minutes, the pandemonium rolling on the cave floor brought a chuckle from Fij'n. It was hard to keep a straight face with such heart felt laughter swirling around her even when she was the butt of their joke.

For a quite some time, the cave echoed with joviality but then, as if on cue, the Groullen stopped and lay down to sleep. There were never any late nights for the beasts. Reiben said, "That wasn't so bad Fij'n, you've had a proper Groullen introduction." Fij'n was undecided about how close a friend she and the Groullen would become.

The night was still young and the Florians had yet to be

introduced. With Sanft leading the way, the group traversed the belly of the mountain to the far side. The near full moon was sure to bring the Florians outside. To no one's surprise but Fij'n's, the garden area was teaming with Florians grooming the trees and brush. The little people raced to greet their guests.

Once more the wand was deployed so all could understand his neighbor and every Florian vied to be heard first. Reiben found the incessant babble of the little folk tiresome but his Se up bring taught him to remain patient and polite. Fij'n found their enthusiasm for conversation refreshing. They were a happy people despite their subterranean existence and had much to say.

The Florians' knowledge of plants, herbs, trees, and shrubs was unmatched in the Ice Age world. There was no genus of vegetation they were not familiar with and their willingness to share said understanding with the eager minds seated before them was a welcome surprise. Yet every bit of information came with a lengthy story and the ever polite Se did his best to not appear frustrated at the rambling accounts of the little folk.

To the contrary, Fij'n enjoyed each story behind a plant's history and found the tales a useful learning aid to remember which ailment they were used for. She too, quickly realized there were many and varied flowers which a person could rely on for healing.

Fij'n's first question for her diminutive teachers was how did the Florians discover that plants had healing properties at all? The little people were fortunate to not be shackled to a Malus way of thinking and their ears were open to a world full of whispers. They listened to nature for what advice a plant had to offer. The instructors readily gave an account of how their relationship with the flora began.

During the time before recorded history, when the world looked much different and the Florians walked cautiously upon the landscape, their expertise in herbology had not yet begun. A healthy Florian community was an idea the elders only aspired to. On a particular day lost to memory, a Florian of prominence became ill and the collective healing knowledge of the group was administered without success. After a long time in thought, the quick minded Florian asked himself, had every option been considered for this patient?

As a last resort, the Florians chanced on a bold assumption; listen to nature for a solution. If all living things were interconnected and dependent on one another, certainly within the bounty of nature a remedy could be found. Could a solution be revealed to the Florians from the bounty in their environment?

Chancing a different approach, the elder was placed on the open ground during the evening to see if solution would present itself and in the morning a single plant had sprouted close to where he lay. The plant proved to be the antidote for the Florian's aliment. A relationship between the little people and the flora was forged and it was the first of many such lessons nature provided to those who listened.

The enthusiastic teachers enjoyed such eager students but for all their knowledge in plants, the capable Florians had no sense of time. Fij'n found that the hours passed far too quickly. The young Malus could have listened the entire night but reason intervened and Reiben declared that the hour was late. There was always the following day. As the four returned to the town of Malus, Fij'n could not stop talking about the events of the night. It had been the most enlightening evening of her short life.

The last day before the Winter Carnival found Reiben busy transporting three Groullen to the pit holding areas and feeding the other condemned men. Slugan's foul disposition had not changed but his resolve to face his fate in the pit was quickly waning. Like all Malus who found comfort in the shadows, Slugan's courage disappeared when faced with real danger and his true character as a coward had started to work its way to the surface.

As Reiben fed and consoled the other Erda's, Slugan kept his eyes on the Pundir. He believed that the Se's arrival to town had marked the beginning of his decline. However, Reiben may yet prove the key to his restoration to power. Time was not to be wasted and Slugan's only hope was to remain fixated on every movement of the Se. The Pundir finished his tasks at the pit without incident and returned to his cave for dinner with the other Groullen.

After a quick meal, the four youths raced to the far side of the mountain and the Florians were awaiting their arrival. The little people greeted Fij'n like a long lost friend and she was excited to see them as well. The winter moon provided ample light for Fij'n to study every plant the Florians brought with them but tonight's lesson was suddenly cut short.

Hungry carnivores were on the prowl and their roars echoed off the mountain cliffs. The Florians raced to the protection of the underground; Reiben, Sanft, Brroud and Fij'n followed close behind.

Once under the alp, Sanft told his friends that this night would be like no other in the animal kingdom and that they should follow him. Cautiously venturing outside, Sanft quickly led them up the mountain to a secure ledge offering a panoramic view below. The full moon set in the cloudless sky illuminated the vista.

Each year at the winter solstice the carnivores' and herbivores' hunger was at its apex and the dance between predator and prey played out. There were no subtleties to be found in this waltz; the weakest animals, whose strength has been sapped by the effects of the cold or malnutrition, fell. Woolly mammoths, saber-tooth tigers, and giant hyenas used every bit of their skill to survive the night. The lack of edible vegetation swung the advantage in favor of the predators but with the coming spring abundant grasses would give the herbivores the upper hand.

From peaks on high sat the Ice Age Condors. These scavengers of old were as heavy as an adult Malus with huge wing spans and carefully watched the to and fro of battle from their eyrie. Any animal that tumbled off a cliff to a mountain shelf below became a meal for these birds of opportunity.

The sight and sounds were a wonder to Reiben, Brroud, and Fij'n. Fij'n asked Sanft, "How long have you been coming to this ledge?"

Answering with all the maturity a thirteen year could manage Sanft replied, "Five or six years. The combination of moonlight, animals, trees and mountains are so beautiful. I come here to watch and think. To capture such a scene with paint and brush is a dream of mine." It was a wonderful dream to aspire to.

The four sat in silence, reflecting on what lay ahead. They knew Gnos was correct, change was in their future. Sanft would follow Reiben wherever he went as the Se was more of a family to him than any other Malus save Fij'n. Reiben would head north to a destination as yet unknown and further from the Se atoll. Who would care for the Groullen once he was gone or continue his work in town? Reiben was torn by the prospect.

Fij'n planned to remain in the town without her two best friends and care for her mother. She couldn't help but feel that this was grossly unjust. Young Brroud's future was simple, he would never leave the side of the Se.

The friends found the time spent watching the dynamics of nature a fitting prelude to the Winter Carnival. After an hour on the ledge, they scaled back down the cliff face without speaking. Once in the cave, Fij'n embraced her friends, said good night and went home to bed. Tomorrow's spectacle in the pit was not an event any of them was looking forward to.

The morrow came early for Reiben. He rose in total darkness, fed the Groullen and was off to the pit where the waiting Erdas were desperate for reassurance from the Se. With his shadow in tow, the Pundir and Brroud arrived at the holding cave to find a group of agitated men pacing the small cave with despair etched on their faces. Reiben remained calm as he prepared their breakfast and paused to acknowledge their comments with a nod.

The concerns were the same from each Erda. How could anyone survive the pit and who would care for the loved ones left behind in the frontier? What guidance could one so young as the Se offer? Slugan said not a word but continued to watch Reiben.

After breakfast, Reiben stood in the middle of the distressed prisoners and began, "Brave men from the frontier, I believe several important facts have been forgotten during the ordeal of your capture and I wish to bring them to your attention at this time. As a Pundir who has met many captured Erdas, I can boldly state, that each of you has demonstrated bravery in the past by your very actions which have led you to this cave. I present to you the following examples as proof: How many of you seated before me now had the fortitude to leave the town of Malus and head to the unknown of the frontier? How many of you built a new life from this earth with only his bare hands? How many of you believe the man to your right and left are courageous and worthy of your support? And how many of you believe that the power of your brain is far superior to the might of a wild animal? I am but a boy of twelve and I see all of these qualities and many more in each one of you. Do not hold onto to your fear. Choose to grasp firmly the positives in your lives, for two men standing side by side with clear minds and strong hearts, will always prevail over the strength of a wild animal."

Calm returned to the holding cave as the Erdas sat quietly and were reassured at last. Such simple yet insightful words quelled their fears. The Se's demeanor was unassuming and truthful. The Erda's found him easy to understand and more importantly they believed what the young Se had said. Reiben continued, "I want you to see yourselves the way I see you. If each man can do that, then he will survive the pit. From now until you enter the arena, every man is to concentrate on his strengths, not his fears. Fear will no longer permeate your thoughts or this cave."

The Se's audience became focused. With the arena inches away from the prisoner, the Erdas had no choice but to follow Reiben's instructions. Slugan said nothing but he was impressed with the Se's ability to speak. Though his cold heart was not thawing he believed that Reiben's rhetorical gifts were surely a Se trick and he knew that he had little time to discover the technique.

Reiben continued, "When two men enter the pit, they will walk shoulder to shoulder, with backs straight and heads held high. At the center of the arena, the guards will give you sword and shield. Face the Pravis, with shield held at your side and arm bent across the front of you. Your sword hilt will be at your waist and the flat side of the blade inches from your nose, the proper salute of a courageous man. Salute the four corners of the arena in the same manner. Every person watching will know that brave men stand before them. Then face the entrance to the wild beasts' cave, unflinching. Whichever animal charges toward you, do not panic and remember two men working as one is a formidable force. I believe your last breaths will not come on the ground of this arena."

Every prisoner save one, Slugan, took to heart the words the Se spoke. They made peace with their fears and resolved to follow the instructions given them. Slugan rocked back and forth finding it hard to contain his anxiety while the rest of the energy in the cave was unified and steadfast. Each Erda was ready to face the challenge of the pit. Slugan was not.

The protocol for this years' carnival had changed slightly as the archery competition was to be the first event and the new order of events only heightened the crowd's anticipation. The outcome for this year's competition with the bow and arrow was the same as previous competitions; the children of the town leaders once again stood on the winners podiums. The crowd had little patience for so contrived an event and paid no attention to the matches. They were there for one reason only, to watch Slugan enter the arena.

After the midday meal the main event started. The Pravis, never one known for his public speaking ability, deferred to another town leader for the opening speech. The leader rose and declared, "Men and women of Malus, the much anticipated Winter Carnival has finally arrived. Each of us knows by heart the simple rules of the pit. Two men will enter to face the fiercest beasts known to the Malus. Should a contestant survive, and may I remind everyone seated here that only four men in the history of the Pit of Strength have ever felled the beasts, he will walk through those gates a free Malus. Without any more delay, bring out the first two men and may the contest begin."

A loud cheer rose from the crowd but the Erdas' spirit did not waver. Reiben grabbed the two tallest and told them that they would be the first to enter. He said, "Remember, to act like the brave men you are." Extending his hand Reiben said, "Let a clear mind be your guide." He shook their hands and the other Erdas followed suit with each other except for Slugan.

Two guards arrived at the cave entrance and motioned for the prisoners to come forth. The prisoners did exactly as the Se had told them. They walked shoulder to shoulder, straight and tall before they took the swords and shields and then saluted the Pravis and crowd. The crowd saw two brave men standing before them. Not a word could be heard in the arena, all eyes were on the combatants except two, Slugan's. His were focused on the Se.

The first beast entered the pit, a large bull woolly rhinoceros. The collective hearts of the crowd beat as one in anticipation. Slugan's did not. His fanatical persistence had finally paid off.

Slugan saw Reiben deftly untie the wand from his shirt and place it in his hand. The Pundir's attention was directed towards the two combatants and he did not notice as Slugan watched his every movement. Reiben uttered several words under his breath and the rhinoceros raced past the ready men towards the arena's sturdy gates. The wooden doors were no match for the force of the enraged beast. The gate flew open and the rhinoceros ran down the town's main street. In hot pursuit, every other carnival beast burst forth from their holding cave and followed the rhinoceros. The two combatants never flinched as the wild animals charged past. The long awaited Winter Carnival was over before the crowd had time to blink and the outcome was unprecedented.

Reiben slipped the wand back inside his clothing while the excited Slugan struggled to contain his glee. The two combatants stood straight once more, saluted the Pravis and crowd and remained at the center of the arena. The men were greeted by a thunderous cheer from everyone assembled, their courage acknowledged by the crowd.

Reiben and the other Erdas left the holding cave to join their companions. There was no more elated a prisoner than Slugan. He was free and had finally discovered the source of the Se's power.

Emboldened by the turn of events, Slugan was the first one to speak and yelled, "My brother, the wise Pravis, before you stand free men. Please, restore us to our rightful status as Malus with the entire town as your witness." The Pravis's countenance failed to belie any of his emotions but his loss for words indicated this outcome was not what he had expected.

The Pravis finally rose and said, "Slugan, today fortune has stood by you and the other Erdas. It has been a day like no other. These events will become part of our oral history - the Winter Carnival where the wild beasts took flight and every Erda won his freedom.

Each spectator here will tell his children's children at every Winter Carnival hence what happened before them today in this arena. As leader of the town I am bound by the rules of the pit and decree that every Erda before this crowd is a free Malus once he exits those gates. But if any man returns to the frontier or chooses to challenge my leadership of this town, an Erda he shall become again." The crowd roared its approval. The Pit of Strength was officially over.

Slugan smiled. He was determined not to squander his reprieve. The Se had revealed the source of his power, the small stick and Slugan's goal was to steal it before dealing with the Pravis again. What ploy was Slugan to use now that his freedom had been restored? He would appear a changed man - kind, helpful, and charming after so long a time on the Erda platform while his nefarious nature hatched a plan to obtain his prize – the wand.

Slugan struggled to contain his excitement. His unwavering belief had proven correct and hopefully soon he would be the new Pravis, but first, the guise of a reformed man. The plotting Slugan walked from the pit to his home, beaming all the way, his devious face now fixed with a crooked smile.

The town of Malus was in a festive mood. Never before had the Erdas, en masse, gained their freedom. Every home was opened to the free men and the streets were full of revelry. It was the happiest celebration the town could ever remember and was prompted without a drop of blood spilled in the arena.

The plotting Malus entered his home and embraced a relieved wife and three sons without uttering a harsh word; they had not been present at the arena. Slugan found his new role as reformed citizen easy to embrace when one had a goal. Gathering his family they all joined the merriment in the streets and for a few brief moments the coldhearted Slugan appreciated his time on the Erda platform. It had made him a more capable adversary.

The newly liberated Slugan went to bed that night with a head full of schemes. He was determined to learn every nuance of the town, shaking the hand of every Malus along the way if need be. At some point the Se would let down his guard and the wand would be his. He simply had to discover when that moment would be.

The following morning, Slugan rose and had a pleasant breakfast with his family. He decided that the best way to learn all the subtleties of town was to do it from the top down. A visit to the Pravis's home was the first item on his agenda.

The Pravis did not expect to see Slugan at his door so soon after his freedom had been restored but he offered his brother a seat at his table and a refreshing drink. The free man wasted no time as he outlined the benefit of his Erda life; time to think; time to bond with the other less fortunate prisoners; time to realize how well off his life was in the town of Malus. An impressive story without a doubt but the Pravis was not given to rash conclusions. He viewed Slugan's words with skepticism and would wait before deciding if his brother was a changed man.

The two parted on friendlier terms and Slugan left for another town leader's home. It would take time for the ex-Erda to visit all the people in town but the prize was worth the effort. The four young friends were completely unaware that Slugan had designs for the wand.

On the Se Atoll, Aunt Sufi prepared a hot brew – the elixir which mends physical and emotional ailments. As with everyone else on the islands, she felt that winter had dragged on long enough. She sat down to think about one of her favorite people, Reiben, when she heard a distinctive bird's song outside of her door. She rose to see which bird it might be.

Opening the door she saw a house wren singing on a tree nearby. The house wren was a tiny feathered creature only slightly larger than a Se's thumb. Its voice was far greater than its size and the wren's tenacious nature left many a larger bird fleeing in the opposite direction. It was a common sight in the Southland where the wrens fancied all the nooks and crannies offered by the huts of the Se as nesting sites. The bird's pleasant songs and appetite for bothersome bugs made them a welcome sight among the island folk. But no wren had ever ventured this far north to the Se Atoll. Yet, here it was.

Sufi could only withstand the winter cold for a few moments before she closed her door and returned to her cup and warm fire. She wondered at the odd set of sequences over the past few years:

The loss of Munsi and Rissa; Reiben hauled off to a destination unknown and now the arrival of the house Wren. There was a change coming to Sufi's world which she could not comprehend. What was an insightful healer to do? She decided to sip her drink, warm herself by the fire and continually send positive energy Reiben's way. This chain of events was beyond her understanding or control.

16

Abrupt Turn of Events

The theatrics of the Pit of Strength were brief with an unexpected outcome. Not a drop of blood was spilled by Erda or wild beast. Thirty-eight men walked through the arena's gate to freedom and the people of Malus were exceptionally festive. To the non-Malus observer, this was most certainly a peculiarity. The collective Malus psyche not rejoicing at the demise of one less fortunate? Something powerful was afoot in the town of Malus.

The remaining week of the Winter Carnival was filled with a celebration never before seen in the town. Every front door remained open, a continuous chorus of laughter was heard, delicious food was eaten, and each citizen took at least one turn dancing to the lively music. By week's end, the town folk were exhausted from all the revelry and it was difficult to believe that these cold hearted Malus could display so much joy.

The town's levity even distracted the Pravis from his thoughts regarding his brother. Yet after too short a time, the festivities concluded and the town's leader was left with a refreshed heart but uneasy mind. The Pravis was beginning to think that Slugan's words of atonement were only a deception. A changed heart did not beat in his sibling's chest but what was the younger brother planning? He was certain it involved the one who sat in the leader's chair. The Pravis resolved to remain vigilant and keep a focused eye on his brother. For the other freed men, it was time to return to the frontier but they had one final stop before leaving town.

In the early hours of a new morning, they gathered outside the Groullen cave. One man called, "Se, do have a few moments for some grateful men." After three and a half years without incident, the bar door to the cave was still locked each night. A Malus never trusted what a beast might do.

Reiben and his cave mates were not invited to the Winter Carnival but they did enjoy a week without strenuous service to the town. A refreshed Pundir came to the front of the cave and smiles could be found on all present. One of the men said, "Se, life in the cave serves you well, you don't look the least bit worn out."

Reiben replied, "The beasts are good company. No one in town realizes what excellent companions they make." A chuckle rippled through the men.

Another said, "Se, we have come to take you with us to the frontier. We believe you'll find life outside the town of Malus to be far more enjoyable." Reiben took stock of the collection of faces on the other side of the bars and he found no better group of fathers, uncles or sons staring back.

Reiben replied, "Brave men from the frontier, I would consider myself fortunate to join such men as you but my time in this town does not end tonight. I have a while yet in this place. When I do leave, I hope our paths will cross again under more favorable circumstances."

The early morning was fast approaching and the men needed to head south. Without a bit of hesitation each man placed his arm through the bars and shook the Se's hand as they said with a smile, "Let a clear mind be your guide." Then off they went at a quick paced trot towards the frontier.

The Pundir was left with only his thoughts as he looked through the bars at a beautiful moon. He wondered why so many difficult decisions rested on his young shoulders? Should he have gone to the lands south of town? Reiben was torn by the predicament to stay or leave.

Life as a Uni was overwhelming and every choice he made was on his own. When would he leave the town of Malus, how could a place further from the Isle of Rune be a better destination and by what means could he escape? The Se found it disheartening that the people of the atoll were no longer constantly on his mind and he hoped he would not forget them entirely.

The night sky and stillness of the town had a soothing effect on Reiben but it did not answer any of his questions. He stayed at the cave entrance until the first hint of morning touched the horizon. As with the beginning of every sunrise, the Groullens woke in unison and formed a queue by the pots of soup. A new day full of hard work left little time for the Pundir to contemplate his future.

The pardoned Slugan had been a busy man during the Winter Carnival. At every opportunity, he made certain that he spoke with each citizen he met and was quick to point out that the time spent on the Erda platform had opened his eyes to his errant way of thinking - he now believed the Se was a valuable asset to the community.

What words were these from so angry a Malus? Surely, they must only be the babblings of a man who had stood an eyelash away from his own end, thought the skeptical listener. For his part, the freed Slugan cared not for the opinion of the town folk. His goal was to steal the wand the Se carried and until that stick was in his hand, not a disparaging syllable would pass his lips.

The town of Malus was a bustling city with a large number of citizens. It would take several months before Slugan had met them all. However, undeterred he set out each morning to greet those who walked the streets, whilst keeping a mental ledger of Reiben's daily movements.

After a month of wandering the town, the day came when Slugan walked through the bars of the Groullen cave. It was his first visit to the home of the beasts. The clinic was busy and the "changed man" congenial. The trio were surprised by Slugan's arrival but had little time for idle chat. There were sick Malus who needed tending to.

Sanft's father took the opportunity to survey the living area of the cave. He showed no emotion while he viewed his son's masterpieces - Sanft's love for art would be dealt with at a later date. Slugan's primary interest was in Reiben's corner of the cave. There was no sign of a power stick anywhere but the Pundir's organizational skills were admirable. The stick must remain close to the Se's person speculated Slugan. Confronting Reiben in the cave within close proximity of the beasts and Sanft would be risky, too many of the Se's allies for him to overcome. He had to steal the wand outside in the open and a plan was already forming in his jealous mind.

Slugan walked to the front of the cave, smiled at all present, told the trio they were too busy for socializing and that he would return at some point in the future. With the veneer of a pleasant face, he set a course down the main street, hand extended in greeting. The friends looked at one another. None believed Slugan's positive outlook was genuine but what was he planning? Their discussion on the matter would have to wait until the end of the day.

The Florians had played host to their new friends each evening since the beginning of the Winter Carnival and Fij'n had had a wonderful time as a student of the little people. Their knowledge of the healing properties of so many different types of flora and their willingness to share these insights with others was unsurpassed. A well-documented history of curative plants had been introduced to the fertile minds of these capable students.

On this evening the first topic with the undersized teachers was not plants but Slugan's improved disposition. Brroud had no interest in Sanft's father but Reiben, Fij'n, and Sanft could not stop thinking about him. Reiben began the discussion with a question and asked, "Sanft, does Slugan still use the back of his hand when he becomes angry?"

The young artist responded, "My father has not uttered a harsh word since leaving the pit. No one in the family knows what to make of it."

The tactful Se then asked Sanft, "Do you think your father is a changed man?" The Malus children were far more perceptive than their reticent demeanor belied and these hard working healers were no exception.

Sanft replied, "I do not believe so. Sad as it is, my father cares little about me or those around him. He wishes only for power. I am still the son he never wanted." Reiben and Fij'n nodded their agreement and were acutely aware of the sting Sanft felt as a rejected child. There was no greater emotional pain than a father's disappointment in his son. The friends sat in silence.

Their pause in conversation was the cue for the Florians talkative leader, Hirte, to offer an opinion of his own, "We Florians have eyes for everything including the Malus. No detail escapes our attention. Slugan, father of Sanft, we have observed from afar for many a year.

No friend of the Florian is he. He has carried a heart of stone from his days as a young boy until the present. The position of Pravis fills his head and drives his actions. Slugan focuses only on the leader's chair. His cheerful words mask his true intentions to gain that which is out of his reach. My friends who live on the other side of the mountain, you are commendable students with keen minds but you must develop your ability to hear when the universe speaks. The answer you seek is not far from you, you must simply listen."

The friends thought for a long moment. What could Slugan want? The Se kept stumbling over the fact that he was from the Se atoll. After a time Reiben exclaimed, "Hirte, one wise in all matters, if the answer is found on the isle of Rune I do not see what it could be but I feel I'm looking in the wrong direction. The ways of the Se do not appear to be of any value to Slugan."

Hirte, like all Florians who found silence to be time lost to valuable words, quickly replied, "Island one, the answer to this question is for you alone to discover. We can offer you little guidance in its regard but the key to the Pravis chair is close by."

This was not the answer Reiben wished to hear and the question now became a heavy burden for one so young. He turned to Fij'n and Sanft and asked, "Surely my two friends have sound advice I could follow?"

Sanft answered first, "Hirte is wise, my father has eyes only for power and will stop at nothing to achieve it. Once he locates that which he desires, all his efforts will be directed towards his goal. My friend, we must keep Slugan off balance and make sure that his focus remains clouded."

Fij'n only echoed her cousin's suggestions and added, "Sanft and I will watch my uncle and keep a keen ear for all he says. None of us wish him to reach the Pravis chair."

The mood for the herbal lesson was dampened by the latest revelation. Every solstice brought a new challenge for the Se and the latest one was by far the most difficult. When the lesson had concluded, a somber Reiben bid the Florians and his friends good night. Little sleep came to him during the hours of darkness.

Spring was in sight and the town had a new routine of a smiling face which greeted all. Slugan walked the streets each day talking to his fellow Malus while he shadowed the movements of Reiben. Stone Heart remained true to his resolve, not a word of disparagement was spoken against the Pundir and his mind constantly evaluated different scenarios to acquire the piece of wood he desired.

For all his intellectual limitations, the Pravis's younger brother had one trait which would prove decisive; Slugan was a focused Malus once his mind was set on a goal. This trait of determination overcame his numerous mental and physical shortcomings. After months of following the Se, Stone Heart eventually refined his plan to steal the wand. The stratagem was simple with no use of weapons required but a good deal of chance would have to play in his favor for it to be successful.

The spring thaw was at its height and the Pundir, along with the work crew, once again found themselves across the river hefting felled trees. Access to the work site was a lone bridge on the south of the town. After two days of lifting and hauling, the job was completed and the tired group set out for home. The moment for execution of Slugan's scheme was to be when Reiben reached the center of the bridge.

Change was to come to Reiben on a beautiful Ice Age day. He walked home under clear blue skies filled with fluffy white clouds which left the Pundir a bit distracted to everything around him. Though, the devious Slugan found himself singularly focused.

Stone Heart had positioned himself at the appointed spot before the Se's feet touched the wooden span. The tired but always cautious Reiben moved towards the edge of the bridge to pass the standing Malus. Slugan was relaxed and his face set with a smile of anticipation.

Deploying the ruse of a walker who tripped, Slugan's shoulder hit Reiben as he stumbled to initiate the plan. The pull of gravity on a body which was off balance, sent Reiben to the swollen waters below. Two bags of tools were slung over the Pundir's shoulder ensuring he quickly sank to the bottom of the racing river.

The fast moving water taxed the submerged Se's strength and pushed his survival skills to a dangerous level. Between the thrashing of his hands and feet to pull himself to safety and the effects of buoyancy on wood, Reiben felt the protective energy of the wand leave his person. It reached the water's surface before he swam to the river bank. Reiben was exhausted but alive and the power stick bobbed further away from his side on the swift moving currents.

Stone Heart feigned panic and rushed to offer assistance. His sharp eyes spotted the wand and he followed the buoyant stick to where it finally rested near large rocks. Slugan quickly raced and grasped his prize some distance from the bridge, hiding it in his clothing. The fate of Slugan and Reiben had simultaneously turned and the town of Malus would no longer be the same.

The caring façade of a changed Slugan evaporated as he hastily left the waterway and relished the prospect of what he held. Once behind his front door, a delighted Slugan gave the power stick a cursory inspection. He had waited far too long for the Pravis's chair to waste time trying to decipher the scribbling on the side of the stick. Physical strength and sword superiority were all that mattered to Slugan. With the wand now in his possession, he would toil in earnest to achieve both.

The following morning, the friendly neighbor Slugan was no longer found wandering the streets of Malus. He was at home with power stick in one hand and sword in the other, thrusting blade and mumbling words. Stone Heart had one last chance to overthrow his brother and he was determined to be prepared.

The ordeal of surviving the river and the loss of the wand left Reiben's body and mind full of glum but he had to tell Fij'n and Sanft the latest news. After dinner the trio of friends fretted over the recent events. The cousins said they would keep eyes and ears open for any information and risk an adverse outcome to retrieve it. None of the friends were confident the wand would return to its rightful owner. Only five people knew of the latest twist in fate, four of whom feared for what lay ahead.

With heavy hearts, the four raced to the other side of the mountain to relay the news to the Florians. Without the wand, Reiben thought it impossible to speak with the little people but Hirte proved to be a far more resourceful a leader than the friends had previously thought. He was fluent in the tongue of the Se.

Reiben retold the story of the wand's loss and Hirte consoled the Se and said, "My friend from the islands, do not blame yourself. The wand has a mind of its own. Why it chose to leave its rightful owner to rest with Stone Heart is not for us to understand but it will not stay with him for long. You must look towards a new life and ready yourself for the moment when it presents itself. This is not a time for sadness; it is just a time of change."

Relieved, Reiben replied, "Wise Hirte, the astute Gnos was astute to introduce us to such a friend as you. Your words bring solace to a heart lost in a sea of unknowing. I shall follow your advice and ready myself for a future which presently appears daunting. Sadness will not be my guide."

A smiling Hirte, filled with numerous words in any language said, "Let us continue our study of the flora. A busy mind has no time for wistful thoughts." So the Florian, with the enthusiasm of an eager teacher who stood before clever minds, began the night's lesson. The friends were thankful for the distraction of learning.

With Slugan bolstered by the capture of the wand, his sour disposition and sharp tongue quickly returned and Sanft felt the brunt of his father's wrath once more. In less than a month of continuous practice, Slugan's proficiency with fist and sword far exceeded that of the Pravis. He was confident that leadership of the town was within his grasp. Stone Heart planned to catch the Pravis off guard away from the comfort of his home. Unaware of his role in his father's scheme, Sanft would once again be the catalyst for conflict between the two brothers.

Sanft arrived home a few weeks before the summer solstice and was greeted by an angry father. Slugan had seen the cave paintings and now decided the murals were a direct affront to his edict of no art. The punishment was the full measure of physical cruelty and the suffering Sanft found his condition far worse than the last time.

The next day, Fij'n became concerned when her cousin did not arrive at the clinic and all her fears were realized upon her visit to Sanft's home. The young artist was semi-conscious with a weak pulse. Slugan yelled, "My worthless son still has not learned to follow the rules of this household. No art means no art and if I find a single new sketch in this house or on the walls of the beast cave, the consequence will be more severe."

In tears Fij'n raced to the Pravis, a response Slugan had expected. Fij'n told the leader the condition of his nephew and the circumstances surrounding the beating.

The enraged Pravis collected several guards and made haste to his brother's home. A seated Slugan soon found the Pravis standing before him delivering a speech he had heard before. "Slugan, how quickly you have forgotten the lessons of the Erda platform but a return to it and the pit may bring a change of heart. Once again you will live the life of a prisoner."

The confident Slugan showed no emotion and responded curtly, "I think not brother. It is time for me to assume the position of town leader."

The struggle between brothers was short and the outcome quite different from the previous year as the wand gave Slugan an insurmountable advantage. The Pravis was on his back with a sword pointed at his throat. Slugan said in a slow, deliberate voice, "You are Pravis no longer, Ansu, and your new home will be the Erda platform. Your wife and daughters shall move to Paskar and I will fill the Pravis's chair."

No longer holding the title of Pravis, the leader had returned to his given name. Using the flat side of the sword, Slugan slapped his brother across the face and kicked him in the legs, Ansu was forced to crawl through the streets.

It took a long time on hand and knee for the former leader to reach the center of town and it was a vivid display of the change which had arrived in Malus. The subdued town folk watched the spectacle as Slugan continually struck Ansu about the body with the sword. No words of pleading could be heard from the prisoner.

Once on the Erda platform, Slugan's perverse theatrics continued and he exclaimed, "Erda, my brother, I welcome you to your new home, a fitting place for such a leader as you. People of Malus, it is time to rejoice as you have a new Pravis, one who will restore the values lost during my brother's reign. The town will be cleansed of those who embraced the views of Ansu and we shall return to the principles of yesteryear. Fear not true Malus, order will once again visit this town." Ansu was fettered to the platform and received a parting blow to his face. The first official task of the new Pravis had been carried out.

The new leader wasted little time in seizing the Pravis chair. Slugan spilled the blood of prominent Malus who had favored his brother, shut down the town clinic and relegated Ansu's family to the Paskar side of town. A frightened face once again returned to Malus.

Ansu sat on the Erda dais without the demeanor of a man fearful fear his future. He was resigned to his providence and like all honorable men, he looked the good and bad of life square in the face.

Each morning the citizens of Malus passed by the edge of the platform and whispered their sorrow for his current situation and support for his leadership. But there would be no uprising of the populace to restore Ansu to the Pravis chair. Their fear of Slugan was far too great to mobilize.

Though Ansu had little concern for himself, he felt the pangs of despair for his family. His wife, Eskal, and their three daughters now lived in Paskar – not the life he had planned for them. The people at the bottom of Malus society did not turn their backs on the latest arrivals. A dilapidated home and a hot meal greeted the new neighbors. Not one person in Paskar was there by choice.

It was a harsh adjustment for Eskal and her daughters – from the pinnacle of society to the bottom in one day and her husband the latest addition to the prisoner's platform. The four of them cried many a tear. Though Eskal did not lapse into misery, she allowed herself several days of mourning. Then it was back to the task of raising three daughters in a life much different than what they were accustomed to.

Eskal, like Ansu, had been born on a farm so her hands knew the value of hard work. A Pravis's wife was not a goal she had ever set for herself. When the two young adults married, they fully expected a future of tilling the land. But the follies of the Malus intervened and Ansu was forced onto a different path, one which led to the Pravis chair. Along the way, the couple's feelings for each other never faded nor did the joy for their three daughters. The position of power did not cloud their thinking as to what was most important in life. Now that the family was cast to the lowest rung in society, their perspective remained the same – make the best of that which comes your way.

Eskal's first order of business in her ramshackle neighborhood was to set her house in order. She worked to ensure the home had a roof free of holes, cleaned it from top to bottom, and decorated the interior with the few items they had left. The girl's found their new station in life demanding and all were exhausted at the end of each day from the hard work.

Under the new leadership, it did not take long before a new cadence filled the town. Hushed voices were the means of communication and trepidation filled every footstep with eyes cast downward, the mode of transport. No Malus wished for an errant word or an innocuous facial expression to bring a painful consequence their way.

Sanft was healing quickly under the capable care of Fij'n. His bruised face was once again seen in the cave after dinner alongside his three friends. In muted voices they discussed their concerns for the future. Reiben began, "Each of us must prepare to leave the town. Slugan will not spare any of us his fury. Fij'n, I am sorry to say that you'll have to travel with us for your own safety."

Fij'n was fraught with indecision, care for her mother was her first priority. The worried daughter declared, "Reiben, I have to think of more than myself. My mother has only me to help her, leaving Malus affects two people.

The compassionate Se replied, "You are right, Fij'n, but we still need to plan our departure in the event you do join the group. My thinking is that the four of us and all the Groullen will leave the town early one morning. We'll head north to the unknown territory of Foggerland on foot. However, once alerted, Slugan would follow on horseback. There is little chance we could evade capture. We need a plan to put as much time between ourselves and Slugan before departing."

The three friends fell silent, deep in thought. After a few minutes Reiben spoke again, "I believe we'll need help from other Malus to successfully execute our escape plan. I'll speak with several and continue to work out the details. Fij'n, please have a frank conversation with your mother. Your future is far more important to her than any risk to her own life. When you do speak to her, don't mention a word about heading north. Make passing remarks about the frontier. With the wand in Slugan's hands, she would have little chance of keeping any information from him."

The discussion came to an end. The forlorn trio said their good nights and slowly retired. Difficult as it was, they had to continue planning their trek north as all too soon, Slugan's attention would be directed towards them.

The following morning, Fij'n found the courage to discuss her future with her mother. Just the thought of Slugan as Pravis brought tears to Drist and she said, "My most precious Fij'n, I told you that any association with the Se would lead to trouble. Now my prediction has come to pass and your unstable uncle is finally the Pravis. I cannot protect you from one so full of anger. My dear daughter, I have slept little since Slugan sits in the Pravis chair. What am I to do? What am I to do?"

Both Fij'n and Drist cried and once their tears slowed, Fij'n said, "Mother, you were so right. A man who has no regard for his own son would not think twice about a niece. These are desperate times and decisive steps need to be taken if I am to survive. Sanft and I are going to head south to the frontier."

Fij'n's mother wailed loudly and sobbed at her daughter's words. Painful as they were, Drist knew her daughter's logic was correct and she replied, "My brave Fij'n, it pains me so to think of you leaving but it is far better a thought than having you gone from this world. You are the best child a mother could ever wish for. I shall find comfort knowing my most precious gift is alive somewhere in this world."

The two embraced and wept a stream of tears. Fij'n was too young for such a difficult decision. Adulthood was approaching quickly for the perceptive young lady. Time was short and hugs between them may soon not be an option.

Reiben had several Malus he needed to speak with, one of whom sat on the Erda platform. Risking an unescorted walk through town in the middle of the night, the Se arrived at the platform. Ansu watched him approach. Reiben stood at the dais with his head just above the platform and said, "Brave Pravis, I have come to bid you a good-bye. I will be leaving your town in the near future. Sanft, Fij'n, and all the beasts are to travel with me. Do not fear Pravis, I doubt your fate lies in the pit. Your cruel brother wishes you to suffer his ascension to the Pravis chair daily. Once we depart, I believe you'll assume the position of Pundir. If I may be so bold as to offer some words of advice regarding your new life in the cave. First, the group of beasts who will join you are not animals but people, like you and I. They have a language which is relatively easy to learn and a wonderful sense of humor. However I must stress one important point concerning your cave mates. Do not come between two Groullen when they are in battle. They have no regard for anyone around them while in combat and a misplaced blow to you would be fatal. Second, the Malus in Paskar will bring you extra food each week. I suggest you thank them for their kindness and respect them as an equal. Third, there are little people who live in the mountain and they'll expect a pot of soup each night. A daily meal is a small price to pay for all they can offer. Fourth, Slugan did not defeat you without help. He stole a wand from me which protects him and vastly improved his fighting skills. That stick will one day be his downfall. And finally, on a personal note, I have found you to be an honorable man Pravis, one who would fit in quite well on the Se Atoll. I have enjoyed my brief time in your presence and hope that one day our paths will cross again. And I shall take leave now with one more piece of advice - let a clear mind be your guide."

Ansu's eyes never left the Se while he spoke but he did not offer any words of his own. Though, he was curious how a Pundir could know so much more about the town than its leader. When the island boy had finished, he turned and hurried back to the Groullen cave.

The lone prisoner on the platform was left with a beautiful night sky and his thoughts. The farmer in him appreciated both. With his recently discovered clarity as the lowest person in town, Ansu now believed the Se was a good lad. A young man with intelligence, integrity, and manners; a son any Malus family would be proud to call one of their own. Such thoughts would never have entered his head while seated in the Pravis chair. How quickly the view from the Erda dais fostered a new outlook on life.

After a time, Ansu's thoughts led him on a wander. Beyond the city limits to the Se atoll, the frontier, the Groullen territory and whatever other unknown destination there might be in the realm of ice. He soon came to understand that this world of his was larger than he had ever realized and quiet different than what he was taught to believe. Ansu also concluded that the people of Malus were not the center of the universe and no amount of bravado on their part would make it so. Another first for a man who once sat at the pinnacle of power. The free-thinking prisoner found himself moving away from the Malus norm but he was uncertain as to the true order of his world. Ansu completed his mental walkabout with a question: where does the Se fit into all of this?

It was getting late and the Erda had one more pressing matter which needed immediate consideration; the position of beast handler? As the town leader, he had always proved himself an exemplary Malus. Yet, just one person had ever survived as Pundir – a little boy without a bit of brawn but rather a keen mind - a combination so foreign to the Malus way of thinking. Ansu had never backed away from any challenge he had ever faced but now he hoped his intellect was sharp enough to carry the title of Pundir.

The Summer Festival was a few days away and the new additions to the atoll, the house wren, raised the Se spirits. During their time on the isle, it was a first for the wren to venture this far north. The bird's morning warble evoked a hum or whistle from every Se who listened at his kitchen table. Surely this would be the best Summer Festival ever. As for Sand Ball, no amount of bird songs would improve the chances of Rune winning the tournament but it made the wagering less painful.

Reiben's most devoted supporter on the island, Aunt Sufi, saw a parallel between the tiny house wren and her little Uni. They both brought joy to other's lives. Was the wren a sign? Sufi did not know but there must be change coming somewhere across the waters from the atoll. Sufi's intuition told her it was so. Preparations for the

Summer Festival left little time for idle thought but Aunt Sufi was confident Reiben was walking a new road in life.

17

Travelling North

The busy Reiben had little time to stop and acknowledge his thirteenth birthday; he was preoccupied with planning a departure from the town of Malus. A full quarter of his short life had been spent away from his island home. The march of time did not slow for an overworked Uni.

Yet a movement of pause was in order to see how far this Uni had come. Were one to have placed a nine and thirteen year old version of Reiben side by side, they would have said there was only a slight resemblance between the two, perhaps in the eyes and mouth? But if one carefully scrutinized this Se's face, he would have concluded there was greater depth in the Uni's eyes; far more than that expected from a boy his age.

Reiben had accomplished much during his time among the Malus and his toil went unnoticed by all except a horse with a single horn in the middle of her forehead; she was pleased by what she saw in one so young.

Did his years of servitude in the hostile lands make him a better person? To the nonpartisan observer the answer was a definitive yes. Through his tireless efforts each day, Reiben's mental growth had far exceeded that of his peers on the atoll; he now stood unique among those born on the isolated islands.

But, to what end was this daily rigor to bring the Uni? The one horn had suggested Reiben head north to Foggerland for more detailed answers to his questions. Only time would reveal the reasons why.

Reiben had finished the particulars of their exit from Malus; Sanft and Fij'n were prepared to join the Se and the young Groullen would follow his three friends when the time came. Their plan was bold and by no means without danger. Walking down the main street in broad daylight with an entourage of beasts would attract attention and the timing of the escape was critical. One other person had to leave the town first before they traveled north; Slugan needed to head south.

With the aid of the Florians, the friends hid on the rear side of the mountain. The little people ensured the Groullen were well fed and after a days' time, there was not a single trace to be found of the four friends in town.

The start of the work week arrived when Malus guards shouted through the bars to begin the day. No sound came from the Se and nothing stirred within the cave. The guards called for Reiben again but he did not make his way to the entrance.

One guard said in a hushed voice, "Se, we are just as upset as you with the turn of events but all of us have to keep working. Would you please get moving and start the tasks for the day." No Pundir appeared.

A second, less tactful guard, yelled through the bars, "Se, the new Pravis already has a sharp sword waiting for you. If you don't leave this cave right now he may use it on you today." The guttural sounds of the Groullen were all that greeted the Malus at the door. The men found themselves in an unpleasant quandary. They had to find the Se but if unsuccessful none wished to tell the Pravis. Their decision regarding what to do next was soon made for them as Slugan came walking up the street towards them.

The Pravis arrived at the entrance with his sour temperament well intact and demanded, "Guards, why is that filthy Se not out serving the town of Malus?"

Timidly, one replied, "Most courageous Pravis, as yet we don't know why."

Slugan's temper rose in an instance and he ordered, "You, go into that cave, find the Se and drag him out here so that my fist may teach him some Malus discipline."

The nervous guard hesitated before he risked saying, "but Pravis, you do know there are beasts in there …." The man did not finish his sentence as he received a hard strike from the irate Slugan.

The Pravis shouted, "You get in there now or this sword will find your throat." A visibly shaken guard had little choice but to comply.

The door was unlocked and the slow moving Malus shuffled into the cave. The guard reached the large living area and observed that all was in neat order. The fires were lit under pots of simmering soup. The massive beasts were mulling around the cavern but there was no Pundir to be found. The guard made a hasty about face and raced to the cave door nervously declaring, "There is no live or dead Se among the Beasts." Slugan was not pleased.

Without a word he took his knitted brow down the main street toward his sister's home, the citizens of Malus jumped out of his way as he walked by. Fij'n's mother had dreaded this meeting. No matter the outcome, it would be painful.

Slugan burst through her door and without any greeting shouted, "Where is your irresponsible daughter?"

Fij'n's mother timidly replied, "Somewhere in town with your son?"

The Pravis quickly added, "I am going to ask you one more time. If your answer is evasive, I shall use every means I have to extract the truth. Now, where is Fij'n?"

The reply came slowly, "I don't know." That answer also did not satisfy Slugan. He discreetly removed the wand from his clothing, pointed it in the direction of his sister and muttered several words under his breath. Drist fell to the floor racked with pain. (The three spells Slugan had mastered - fists, sword, and torture - involved imparting bodily harm on an innocent person. Far from the original intent of the wand makers.)

After a brief few moments Drist could not withstand her agony any longer and Slugan had the information he'd come for. The three children, now enemies of the Malus, had departed for the frontier less than twenty four hours prior. Slugan left his sister nearly dead on the floor and the Paskar section of town had a new member that day. A posse would be needed to head south after these three Erdas.

Within an hour, Slugan had mobilized a large group of Malus. Every able male was given a horse and ordered to search for these outlaws. The posse set off at a fast gallop towards the frontier leaving

212

women, children and the citizens of Paskar behind. The father of Reiben's first Malus patient raced to the Groullen cave and signaled to waiting Florians the time to leave had arrived. Three young Florians ran to the far side of the mountain to alert their anxious friends.

After hasty farewells and a few teary eyes, the four friends with the Groullens and Grrick in tow walked through the bar doors into the midday sun. It was a sight never before seen in town. The Malus women and children on the proper side of town quickly ran to the security of their homes. So many beasts meandering unsupervised was surely trouble waiting to happen. Then at an even paced trot, the group of escapees headed due west from Malus.

The Groullens' adolescent nature could not contain itself at their new found freedom. The beasts pushed, pulled, and knocked one another around in the joy of open space. Reiben's admonishments to stay focused had little effect on their merriment but the group continued at a steady gait in a westerly direction.

At the first way point stood a man from Paskar. His sole purpose was to bid the travelers good luck and point them in the direction of their next leg. The runaways took an immediate right to due north.

After an hour on this new heading, a cold breeze from the massive glacier in the boreal region swept across the faces of the travelers. For the Groullen it was another reason to celebrate. It meant they were closer to the ice covered lands of their home. The frigid wind further distracted the Groullen but they managed to stay on course.

The last way point was reached after two more hours. A cold soaked sentry greeted the group and informed the travelers that beyond this spot, no Malus had ever ventured towards the northwest. From this point on, the four friends and Grrick would have to manage on their own.

It was also the location where the escapees would separate. Reiben was not looking forward to saying goodbye to his Groullen friends with the exception of Brroud. (The youngest Groullen, so long at the side of the Se, was not emotionally attached to his fellow Naarrt. Heading north to the Valley of Caves was never a consideration for him.) A small meal was prepared to strengthen the hungry travelers and delay the inevitable farewells. The Groullens sat in a half-circle joyful at the prospects of reaching home while Reiben stood quietly nibbling his food. Several more hours of good sunlight remained and the time finally came to move on.

Reiben had prepared parting remarks and cleared his throat to address the Groullen. In a reserved tone he said, "You have the strength of a woolly mammoth. I am saddened to leave my fellow cave mates ....."

Reiben's speech was interrupted by a Groullen saying, "Only Grres birds are sad, you must not be Brroud Bird." The already merry Groullen burst into thunderous laughter. The little Brroud Bird had offered so much entertainment to the Groullen in the cave and now, as they were about to separate, he was the butt of their jokes once more.

The Se shook his head while smiling and said, "I hope to see the Brrouds before I go to the clouds."

Another Groullen said, "You Brroud Bird, fly to our cave" a rousing guffaw once more.

Reiben walked among the Groullen and tapped his forearm on theirs – a gesture of hello or good bye for the Naarrt. Then the Groullen turned en mass and headed north, never looking back at the Se. True to the Naarrt way of thinking, they only lived in the present, not the past.

The friends thanked the Malus sentry and said goodbye. The young travelers watched him head south towards a much more familiar part of the world.

Navigating unknown territories was not a skill the group was familiar with but the friends turned their faces to the wind and headed northwest across a terrain which offered no path. It was a short time before the travelers discovered that weather around a glacier was unpredictable. Depending on the wind's direction sunny skies, rain, snow or fog could be experienced every day of the year. Fog and rain covered the four after an hour.

The one landmark they constantly referenced was the ocean. It was always to their left, but keeping track of the sea was the easy part of their trek. Blazing a new trail, managing the brush and fallen trees, scaling rocks and hills was more difficult and physically demanding. Their pace fell off considerably once this leg of the journey was underway. The four questioned their wisdom for not heading south to the frontier but that thought was only in passing.

As the daylight faded, the hikers had expended significantly more energy for a shorter distance travelled. It was time to find shelter and eat from their limited supplies. Trees in the northwest were massive and many had rotted hollows at their base which offered modest protection from the colder elements.

On the first night away from the town of Malus, it was early to bed for the tired group. Each lay in the dry mulch of a rotting tree trunk and Grrick curled up beside Reiben. The dog offered warmth and a soft pillow for the sleepy Se.

Slugan returned late to the town of Malus and was informed of the deception the three adolescents had successfully parlayed. The Erdas were gone, the beasts were gone and any credibility Slugan had had as a leader was lost. A thirteen year old Se had out-maneuvered the Pravis and his power stick. Slugan was livid and not one rational thought remained in his head. The Pravis's anger needed an outlet and Ansu was the target.

Late that night, Ansu found his sibling running towards the Erda platform with a club in hand. A crowd gathered around the dais as Slugan's wrath was directed upon his brother. He ranted continuously about Ansu's failure to deal with the Se which had led to all the town's problems. Ansu did not utter one word nor ask for mercy.

Those who witnessed the fit of rage felt a twinge of sickness in their stomach, but in the end, Ansu survived the beating and was ordered to be the new Pundir. Unconscious, he was carried from the platform to the empty Groullen cave. Once informed, Eskal and her daughters raced to the side of the battered man and a crowd of Malus joined them in the cave. Only limited medical attention could be offered now that the Se and Fij'n were gone. Many feared who would be next to experience such fury. It was a new low point for the town of Malus.

The following morning Slugan ordered another party of riders to assemble. They were heading north for a beast round up. Each one of Slugan's decisions was tainted with madness but no one dare disagree with his orders. For those Malus left behind it was a welcome respite from leadership gone awry.

Reiben and his fellow travelers awoke from a sound sleep with sore muscles and empty stomachs. The supplies were rationed and breakfast did not completely satisfy their hunger. The wind had shifted direction and frigid air filled with powdered snow pinched their faces as they headed in the direction of Foggerland. The soft flurry covered any tracks the friends left on the ground.

Grrick, who still had a bit of puppy in him, enjoyed racing through the light snow but the group's speed was further slowed by this change in weather. The various large landmarks, mountains, bluffs or valleys on the horizon did not appear any closer as they walked and the four remained frustrated by the difficulty of their trek.

At midday, Reiben looked back to estimate the distance they had travelled. It was not far. He suggested they head towards the ocean and see if the shoreline afforded easier passage.

Several difficult hours later, the party stood on a cliff that over looked the sea. The beach below consisted of coarse sand with few fallen trees and no brush and it offered an unobstructed path towards Foggerland. Climbing down the cliff was a challenge but once on the beach, the pace of the group picked up and Grrick raced back and forth through the waves with unbridled enthusiasm. They observed birds and sea otters cracking open shellfish and crabs. Reiben remembered from his days on the atoll the value of this food. In a short time they all had full stomachs of raw clams. The trek to Foggerland was improving.

By nightfall the group had covered a reasonable distance and was no longer hungry. They found a dry spot next to the cliff and built a crude lean-to from branches. The structure offered some protection but not enough to keep out the changing weather. The friends snuggled together and Reiben shared the warmth of Grrick with his companions.

The third day was the group's most productive yet traveled in the northwest region. Their muscles were no longer sore and the beach presented few obstacles. However, by mid-afternoon, they reached a large river which emptied into the ocean and it could not be forded. The river was wide and fast moving and was fed by the towering glacier which melted during the summer. They had no choice but to turn inland to find a safe location to cross. The detour would, once again, send the group through the demanding landscape.

The friends trekked for the rest of that day and never spotted a crossing point. The further up river they went the more irregular the climate became. Their night's sleep inland offered little rest because the weather changed on an hourly basis.

By morning an incessant rain and fog had settled in. The rain was not heavy only a soft spray which, over time soaked through their clothes chilling them to the bone and the fog made navigating difficult.

At last, a collection of rocks was spotted that traversed the river where the group could safely cross. There was no sure footing on the wet boulders and their speed was diminished as all were wary. Even four legged Grrick was cautious while he moved on the large boulders.

By late afternoon it was still raining, the fog had dwindled, the group was thoroughly chilled from the drenched clothing, but they were on the other side of the river. A warm place to dry out was more important than travelling any further that day.

The cliffs, which butted close to the river, appeared to offer the best opportunity for shelter and it was not long before the sharp eyed Fij'n sighted a cave. As the four approached, Grrick became hesitant and fell back. His ears were up and head down. Something was in the cave. The friends were on alert and stood at the entrance attempting to adjust their eyes to the darkness. Moving slowly they inched their way into the cavern.

In a flash a female saber-toothed tiger sprang from the shadows. She too was using the cavern to escape the constant rain and recover from wounds sustained in combat with hyenas. The large cat's physical prowess was compromised by her injuries.

Brroud, the passive youngest in the friendship chain lunged forward and grabbed the saber-tooth by the head holding her ears between his fingers. The young Groullen, even at the tender age of ten, was already much stronger than Reiben, Sanft, Fij'n and Grrick combined and his Naarrt instincts did not waver. He had no fear of any Ice Age animal.

Brroud spoke in the most commanding Groullen voice he could manage and said to the struggling cat, "I respect you, you respect us. We make you better." Whether it was her fear of Brroud or the saber-tooth understood the Groullen, it was difficult to say but the big cat settled down and only growled if Reiben, Sanft or Fij'n moved too close.

Brroud continued to speak to the cat as if she were his pet. Reiben declared, "My unselfish friend, we are fortunate to have you along. How quickly you can tame a wild beast." A carefree smile came to Brroud. In the Naarrt world there were no heroes, every Groullen was brave.

Brroud continued to stroke the cat's head to ensure Grrick was not her next meal while the other three lit a healthy fire, gathered food and prepared a salve for the saber-tooth's wounds. Brroud's expertise in controlling dangerous animals was needed to administer the salve. The friends thought it best to feed the hungry cat first before applying the ointment.

After a large meal of scavenged fish from the river banks was presented to the tiger, Brroud held the cat's head, told her everything would be fine and the healing balm was placed on her wounds. The saber-tooth struggled but Brroud prodigious strength held and no one was injured.

The travelers finally ate. The warmth of the fire made all in the cave sleepy and it was early to bed. Brroud had his own pillow for the night, the satiated tiger. To all in the cave's relief, he slept some distance from the other members. Grrick kept one eye open in case the big cat woke in the middle of the night in search of an early morning nibble.

At the morning meal, the friends decided it best to stay in the cave until the tiger's wounds had healed. Brroud had more time to enjoy his new friend and the group could use some rest before they headed on to Foggerland. The time passed quickly and the cave felt considerably smaller as the cat's strength returned. She paced the cavern testing the health of her wounds.

Eight days after they had found the cave, it was time to leave. The tiger did not growl at the cave mates as long as Brroud had a strong arm around her neck. All four friends stroked her before leaving. The healed saber-tooth was a powerful animal and her strong muscles could be felt beneath the thick fur. Grrick was the first to leave the cave and Brroud the last. The young Groullen hugged the big cat and whispered the parting words, "I meet you in the clouds." The group began the long trek back to the mouth of the river glad that the saber-tooth did not follow them.

At every turn in his Ice Age world a different wonder was presented to Reiben. Brroud, his constant companion, had never shown any signs of courage but when faced with tremendous danger the young Groullen stepped forward without hesitation. After which he returned to the docile Groullen. The people on the atoll taught their children to keep an open mind to the many possibilities around them. Reiben now understood why.

The trip down river was just as arduous as the one up but the four eventually reached the sea. Turning north they resumed their trek along the beach. The cliffs continued to tower over the coastline but proved too difficult an obstacle to scale.

At the end of the day, they were bedding by the ocean once more. When the moon rose, colder temperatures and a slight drizzle greeted the group but they enjoyed sleeping on the beach and all were in a good spirits. Come morning, the rested travelers woke to a light fog.

Continuing north, it was not long before the fog thickened and they were completely surrounded in white vapor. One could not see beyond the hand at the end of his arm. The fog added prudence to the group's steps and slowed their pace tremendously; they assumed their Foggerland destination was near at hand. What the group's eyes could not see, Grrick's sensitive nose and ears could detect and he continually looked in various directions along the beach. No one heard a sound but Grrick moved his head in a different direction at each new scent or sound.

Unbeknownst to the travelers, the land by the beach had

gradually changed to small rolling hills covered in trees. The trees were huge and centuries old. Large strands of moss covered each branch which was watered daily by the fog. The fog, trees, and moss offered ample hiding opportunity for one who did not wish to be seen. The young friends did not feel danger was imminent but felt something was following them. Their day ended as it had begun, in fog, and they had the distinct feeling they were no longer alone in the mist.

Each morning the group began their daily routine accompanied by the same weather – fog. Wake, walk, and eat then to bed in white clouds. The thick fog shrunk the travelers' world as they were placed at the center of a circle whose diameter was the length of their out-stretched arms. From the tip of their nose to the end of their fingers, was all they could see. The friends had to huddle together as they walked so as not to become separated from each other.

Life in white vapor disorients the mind and easily distracts one from the path he is on. The active imaginations of the four boiled with various possibilities as to who could be following them and what type of creature found comfort in a cloud? The travelers were on edge and lost but they could not turn back.

After two weeks of walking along the coast, making little headway, the friends decided to venture inland, hoping the fog was not as dense among the trees. Their thinking proved frustratingly inaccurate as the thick cloud did not lessen in the forest and the landmark of the ocean could no longer be heard. A return to the south was now completely lost.

Moss was not an edible food and their supplies were low. Fogged in and totally out of place among the large trees was a cause for concern but, fortunately, these travelers had rational heads and did not panic. In fact, Reiben did not find his current situation particularly hopeless. After so short a time in this new territory, the Se's intuitive sense was slowly awakening. The strangeness of the land did not frighten him but rather; quite to the contrary, it had the feel of the Isle of Rune. He pondered why an odd region such as this offered him comfort? Gnos's advice to head north appeared to be correct.

After a restless night of sleep, the friends decided that each time Grrick turned his head in the direction of a smell or sound – they would call out for help. They did not believe that whoever was following them had intentions for harm and this plan appeared their most reasonable option.

Starting the day with a small breakfast, the group randomly selected a pathway through the white clouds. Everyone had an eye on Grrick's head movements. It was not long before Reiben called out, "We are lost, need help and bring no harm." No one came their way. Undeterred, Reiben shouted the same words a number of times throughout the day with the same response.

By night fall, caution, not panic filled the group's mind and they went to sleep in the roots of the giant trees with the belief that tomorrow would be a better day.

The morning brought the same resolve to find help from whoever was following them. As they sat eating a meager meal, Reiben looked up and a man whose clothes were covered in moss, sat on a fallen tree with a dog seated at his feet. Grrick was lying on the ground with no interest in the visitor or his four legged companion. The man was neither old nor young and he had pleasant eyes above his thick black beard.

Reiben stood and introduced himself and his friends by saying, "My name is Reiben, I am a Se from the Isle of Rune. These are my friends Sanft, Fij'n who are Malus and Brroud a Naarrt. Our dog is friendly and called Grrick. We are from the lands south of here and on our way to Foggerland. As you can see and hear we are quite lost."

The man replied in a tongue familiar to each ear present, "You are in the land you seek. I am a Draich who lives among these trees; my name is Arwol and I know of the Se, Malus, and the Naarrt. What or whom do you seek in Foggerland?"

Reiben and his friends looked at one another in surprise before Reiben replied, "We don't know exactly where to go as Gnos, the one horned horse, just instructed us to head to Foggerland."

Arwol found the predicament of the young travelers amusing as his eyes twinkled a smile and he said, "Well, you have followed her instructions exactly, for you are squarely in the land she instructed you to find. Hopefully, she will send word as to where your destination is. I can offer you food and shelter until we determine your intended ending point." With that, Arwol stood up and motioned for the group to follow. The Se was surprised that Arwol spoke their tongue and knew of Gnos. Foggerland may not be as remote as he had originally thought.

Arwol was a tall, thin man, with moss carefully placed from head to toe; excellent camouflage for one tracking the movements of the four through the forest. His experienced legs easily traversed the large roots and fallen trees making it difficult for the friends to keep up.

It was not long before the party came to a stop before a huge tree. It was a Draich home and Arwol was the only resident. The hollowed out trunk and root was spacious and had more than enough room for all. The inside was clean and practical - tools were neatly organized along the walls. There was not a hint of a women's touch to be found in any of the decor. He brewed a strong tea whose taste had never before been sampled by the young friends and served a delicious stew – it was obvious this man of the woods understood which ingredients were best for a boiling pot of soup.

Reiben started the conversation and asked, "Arwol, are you the only Draich living in this forest?"

The woodsman answered, "No, there are many of my kind, most of whom are busy elsewhere throughout the forest."

The inquisitive Se asked a more direct question, "Arwol, I have not heard of the Draich nor have my friends, could you please give us a brief account of your people?"

Arwol found the Se curiosity endearing and he answered, "The Draich, like the Se, Malus and Groullen wandered this northern region before the beginning of myths and we finally found our spot in the land of tall trees. After spending so long a time surrounded by the forest, there is little about the woodlands we do not know. We dedicate ourselves to the plants you see around us and through our efforts with these giant trees we have developed a special bond to them. As each of you are aware, every person has a unique personality, different from the person who stands close by. So to, do the flora of the forest. The unique essence of one tree is quite different from the essence of the next tree growing right beside it. The Draich are the keepers of all the uniqueness in this forest."

The Se quickly asked, "Do the trees talk to you?"

Arwol answered, "Not in words, but in energy. My inquisitive Se, can you look at your friends and tell if they are happy or sad without uttering one syllable between you? How does one like you do that? By feeling the energy your friends are projecting. The same is true with plants, animals, and trees. They send energy to those around them and the Draich have learned to listen. The people of the trees can feel the mood of all that lives in the forest and we strive for harmony among these energies. If harmony is lost the energy will become fragmented and unravel. One can learn much from those who do not speak in words. "

The Se thought such a simple idea was profound. Reiben finally asked Arwol a question affecting all in the group and said, "Arwol, why has Gnos sent us to Foggerland?"

Arwol laughed and replied, "My young Se, Gnos walks this world and helps all who cross her path and every turn she makes has a purpose. Gnos's reasons for your trek to Foggerland are unknown to us. Though, you have been sent far from home so I believe your need must be great. There is much to learn in this land but first, we must determine where it is you are to go."

Arwol informed the group that their previous tromp through the trees had not been a proper tour of the forest. After breakfast, he was to be their personal guide and show them the important sights.

With the breakfast of oatcakes finished and dishes washed the group headed out the door to another beautiful foggy day. The fog seemed less intimidating with Arwol at the lead. As he walked, he spoke in a foreign tongue. It was a language as guttural in tone as the Naarrt; he was speaking to the trees.

Their first stop was beside the oldest living flora in the forest, a tree four millenniums in age with a great diameter at the base and its top was lost to the fog. Even the active imagination of a youth could not have envisioned a tree so enormous. Arwol patted the giant tree as if they were old friends and spoke in a kind voice. He told the travelers, "I must formally introduce you to my good friend." Arwol told the tree all he knew about the four and stood by each member of the group as he said their name.

Arwol placed his hand on the tree and stood silent for several minutes before he said, "This friend in the forest has rarely felt the energy from those in the lands south of here and at four thousand years old it continues to marvel at each new visitor. The tree indicated your energy is pure without a bit of malice, though each of you has experienced the worst in others. May your purity remain with you always. He believes you will discover what you seek in this land and feels that I should assist you in determining where your intended destination is. When our tour of the trees is completed, we shall find out where your journey should end."

After the visit with the large tree, Arwol was keen to show his young companions the many points of interest in this new land of wonder. Grrick was the only member of the group who easily kept up with him. Their day of botanical instruction came to an end long after the sunset had passed. The forest has many curiosities among the shadows cast by a full moon on tall trees.

The tour concluded at a large tree structure which butted up to a moss covered boulder. A community hall, filled with seated Draich eager to meet the visitors, greeted the travelers. Arwol positioned the friends before those assembled, introduced each one individually and told his fellow Draich what the wise tree had suggested. The Draich gathering nodded their acknowledgement.

Arwol turned to Reiben and said, "The Draich were presented a gift long before anyone here walked the forest. It is called the Grotto of Tears and the waters of the small cavern reveal the unknown events of one's past and future to those who enter. The images brought to light are powerful and always bring tears of joy or sadness to the viewer. Such pictures leave a permanent mark on a person's heart and not all are suited for the insights which can be painful. Young Se, there is no shame for those who do not wish to gaze into the grotto. Most of us are content not knowing every event which has shaped our lives. But it you choose to enter, it is important to understand completely, that the images presented will remain with you for the rest of your life. A decision to forego these revelations, I can guide you and your friends back to the beach and south from whence you came. Please, take time to ponder my words before answering."

Reiben discussed Arwol's warning with his friends. The group had come too far to not reach their final destination. Reiben turned toward the group assembled and declared, "Arwol, come what may, I shall risk the unknown."

At the front of those assembled was a green cloth which covered a rock wall. Arwol removed the covering and exposed a small grotto. The walls of the enclosure sparkled with the reflected light of many gems. A stone bench was positioned in front of a natural basin on the grotto floor. Arwol led Reiben to the bench and had him sit with his back to the basin. Arwol's stood before him and said, "To see the unknown of the past, one must place his back to the pool of water. Remain seated and wait for the water to stop flowing from the jewels in the walls into the basin. Once all is quiet, look up at the gems in the ceiling above you. They will sparkle in unison with images from your past. When the luster of the reflecting stones fades the events are over."

Reiben closed his eyes and listened to the soft purling as water flowed from the gems and filled the basin. It was not long before the grotto was quiet and he raised his eyes to the sparkling jewels above his head. An image eventually appeared of a nine year old Uni in the southland. A boy, far smaller than he remembered, was racing towards the beach away from his mother. The young boy could not see what events he had left behind but then Reiben's mother appeared. A defenseless Rissa was evading the thrusts of a Malus knife. Her courage and quickness frustrated the attacker but the sparring did not last long. The blade soon found a lethal spot which left young Rissa lifeless by a peach tree. A scenario Reiben never believed possible. He felt his stomach contract as if punched and his hands trembled from the raw emotion. Tears freely ran down his face but the gems were not finished.

The gems again illuminated a familiar sight, the front door to Reiben's home. On the inside, his gaunt father sat in the dark holding his wife's wedding necklace in one hand and a toy of Reiben's in the other. Munsi's burden in life was now too heavy to carry any longer. He kissed the necklace and toy one last time, closed his eyes, and never woke again. The jewels had no more scenes to reveal.

Reiben dropped his head and sobbed. No one in the room moved or said a word. The Draich closed their eyes, raised their hands and sent healing energy towards the stricken Se.

After a time, Reiben composed himself and looked to his guide through this emotional journey. Arwol said to Reiben, "The unknown of the past is for you alone. No one can change those events but as to what your future holds, I am here to point you towards the path you are to follow. Turn now and sit facing the water. When you see the images in the ceiling, describe the scene to those assembled."

An emotionally weary Reiben tuned to face the basin. Gazing into the sparkling gems, he saw a large circular structure of huge stones positioned on a gradual hill. The grounds surrounding the structure were well manicured. Four paths spaced at equal distances around the circle led to the stone structure. The image had a warm inviting energy. Reiben's troubled heart found solace by what he saw. The gems had no more images and Arwol told him to take a seat as Fij'n was next.

Fij'n followed Reiben's example and placed her back to the basin and waited for the sound of flowing water to end. The jewels above her head brought to light the dark forest of the frontier. Her father was slowly walking through the woods tracking a deer unaware that a second person was tracking him – Slugan. One man was armed with charcoal and parchment, the other a bow and arrow. Fij'n's father paused to sketch a deer as it ate and Slugan set his arrow and drew the bow. The artist's departure from this world was quick and Slugan's maniacal smile was proof of his diabolical nature. Fij'n was overcome by grief and she too lowered her head in sorrow. The gems had no more scenes to reveal. The Draich again directed their warm energy to one in need. She eventually composed herself and turned to see what lay ahead.

Looking to the future, Fij'n saw the image that Reiben had described. Their destination was the same place.

The two remaining members of the group declined their opportunity with the Grotto of Tears. Sanft's past was painful enough without any additional knowledge of his troubled childhood. He and Brroud's future were tied to their friend the Se.

Arwol told the travelers that he knew which path led to the destination they sought and believed a good night's sleep would ready them for the journey. The weary four returned to Arwol's home and a comfortable moss filled mattress. Two friends fell fast asleep and two others had more tears to weep.

A late morning arrived for the rested friends and Arwol had breakfast ready when they awoke. Reiben and Fij'n had little to say and Arwol did most of the talking. The helpful Draich told them that it was only a short hike to the trail which led to the stone structure and once on the path it was a two, possibly three day walk to reach their destination. Arwol did not tell them who or what was at the stone circle but they had no reason for fear. With breakfast finished they collected their belongings and set off on another brisk hike.

After walking for an hour Arwol stopped and indicated that it was time to part. He pointed at the ground to an indelible path. For so brief a stay amongst the men of the trees much emotion had spilled for Reiben and Fij'n. Arwol assured them they had completed the most difficult part of their journey. The final leg would not be such a challenge. Arwol was also sure that he would see the four again. And so, as quietly as the Draich had first appeared, he became a whisper once more, disappearing into the fog. The four friends looked at one another without speaking then down at the path. They turned and followed the trail towards the stone circle in silence.

Meanwhile, in a place all too familiar to the friends, Ansu had recovered from his beating and found the Groullen cave a far better residence than the Erda platform. He considered the murals on the cave a welcome addition and realized beneath his nephew's mute and compliant facade laid the mind of a gifted artist. Ansu also took to heart the parting advice the Se had given him - a pot of stew each night for the Florians and a heartfelt thank you to the Malus from Paskar for the vegetables they provided.

After eight weeks, Slugan returned to town with ten Groullen in tow, one quarter of the number who had begun the long trip back to Malus. The terrified Naarrts, who scurried into the cave, were small between four and six years of age. Their backs displayed evidence of Slugan's leadership.

The responsibility of family nurturer had never fallen on the shoulders of Ansu. As the town Pravis, his time was occupied with important decision for the people of Malus. But here he was, with frightened Groullen toddlers huddled around him looking for reassurance. Ansu's first task as the new Pundir was to give the little Naarrts a comforting pat on the head, then a warm bowl of soup. One could not say who would grow more in this cave, the Groullen or Ansu, but both would be maturing together.

18

Stone Circle

The trail to stone circle was level and kind to the legs but the pace of the travelers was still slowed by the fog and few words were exchanged between the four. The revelations of the Grotto of Tears gripped Reiben and Fij'n's thoughts and held their tongues; their emotions vacillated between sorrow and anger. They grappled with why innocent people filled with so much joy were stuck down long before their time? The two young hearts could find no reasonable explanation.

With Reiben's parents gone, the Se's strongest bond to the atoll was no longer there. He did not know if the islands were a place he could return to as an orphan.

Fij'n had few memories of her father, yet the grotto confirmed the description her mother had given of him. He was a man with a free spirit who did not follow what the Malus deemed to be proper. Fij'n worried her mother would also fall to Slugan's crazed thinking now that she was gone.

Few syllables passed Sanft's or Brroud's lips but that did not mean they were not capable of reflection. They reasoned that the stone circle must be a good place because the trail leading to it was an easy hike and the energy amongst the trees invigorating, a simple yet logical deduction.

The travelers walked for three days and camped along the path at night. On the morning of the fourth the fog finally lifted. Their eyes were sensitive to the bright sun light after weeks in the white vapor but their destination was finally in sight; standing on the horizon was the stone circle. After so long a trek, Reiben hoped this location would prove to be fruitful.

Though the visibility was excellent, the group's stride did not quicken as vigilance now controlled their steps. The landscape was deserted and Reiben had believed the people of the circle would have known they were coming. Why did they not show themselves?

After a short walk, the group stood before the structure and the circle's size dwarfed the travelers. The friends thought it best to inspect the edifice before knocking on a door.

The circle's stones were massive, taller than the height of all the friends standing on each other's shoulders. The blocks were as wide as the travelers outstretched arms, a half again as thick and they stood two long paces from the next pillar. A stone lintel connected each support to its neighbor and thick logs filled the gaps between the blocks. A roof made of timber rested on the pillars. The wood covering had a large hole in the center to let in light and vent smoke out. The structure was well built and clearly withstood any storm a glacial climate could muster. As in the image from the Grotto of Tears, there were four paths evenly spaced around the circle and each ended at a door.

They walked around the imposing rotunda inspecting it thoroughly before finally choosing an entrance. Reiben knocked. The person who greeted them was no stranger to the streets of Malus and his face was familiar to the Pundir. In a tongue understood by all the ears present the man said, "I see our visitors from the south have arrived. Please do come in."

Surprised, Reiben spoke first and said, "You were one of the four who survived the Pit of Strength. Forgive me, but I have forgotten which number and direction on the compass you were."

Their host answered, "Oh, what a clever Se you are. Indeed, I was in the Pit of Strength and with your helping hand, I was able to walk through its gates to freedom. I was Number Seven and West. You have entered the west door of the circle. My three companions are positioned at the north, south and east door and they are anxious to meet you and your friends. The door you selected tells us much about you, but that is for another time."

West's three companions approached the travelers with broad smiles and greeted them with handshakes while saying, "Let a clear mind be your guide." North said, "It is so good you decided to visit Foggerland. We can now reciprocate the hospitality shown to us in your cave. A midday meal is awaiting you."

The young friends found the inside of the structure more impressive than the outside. Twenty eight stone chairs grouped in clusters of seven were set along the wall of the circle on the axis of the compass. The diameter of the structure appeared larger on the inside and at the center was a big fire pit with a healthy blaze.

There were a number of people working inside, organizing hay which filled a good portion of the free space. They acknowledged the visitors with a nod and continued their work. No one appeared surprised to see them.

Once the visitors were in the stone circle, the doors were opened and additional people arrived carrying more hay. Reiben thought the interior appeared to be a ceremonial place of storage, the likes of which he had never seen before. Pots of soup lined the fire pit and filled the air with delicious aromas. The hungry visitors had choices for lunch and comfortable stools for seats.

After their bowls were filled and each found a warm spot to sit, North started the conversation. "Our adventurous travelers, now that you have arrived in the land of Toven, a proper introduction is in order. My name is Orden that is Ettel, there is Osten, and finally Lansi." Orden pointed to his friends who had previous been known as South, East and West. He continued, "We chose our former names as a ruse for the town of Malus. No need to give the Malus any hint as to where we were from. I can see by your inquisitive face you are asking yourself, why would four Toven risk a fate in the Pit of Strength - to visit you, young Reiben. Word had spread as far north as Foggerland that a captured Se displayed great kindness to those in the town of Malus. We decided to find out for ourselves who this person was. The Pit of Strength proved a greater challenge than we expected but thanks to your efforts we made it home. We are pleased you decided to leave Malus along with your companions and trek to the town of Toven."

Reiben's face was covered in confusion as he said, "I should first introduce my fellow travelers Sanft, Fij'n, Brroud, and Grrick. We departed Malus in haste and in fear for our lives. We were told to come to Foggerland by the one horned horse, Gnos, so that many of our questions could be answered, but since arriving I have more questions than when we left the lands south. The first is, why would you leave Foggerland to visit me?"

Orden answered, "The Se are isolated on their atoll, only travelling to the Southland for a few weeks each year and at irregular intervals they are captured by the Malus. It has been many years since a Se sat on the Erda platform and none was ever given the title of Pundir. The Se's reputation among the Toven is exemplary and our time spent with you did not sway that opinion to the contrary." The answer Orden gave did not satisfy Reiben's question completely but it would have to do. Orden continued, "After lunch we shall give you a tour of the town and show you to your small cottage." A home for the group, the Toven were certainly expecting these visitors.

After a delicious lunch the tour began. The centerpiece of the town was the stone circle. In neat rows of concentric circles around the rotunda were the homes of the town. As the tour proceeded through the manicured streets, all the inhabitants smiled and acknowledged their guests but only a few Tovens' offered any passing words of greeting. The group of newcomers found the Tovens' response to their arrival odd but they weren't uncomfortable.

The tour ended after a short hour of walking through a well laid out town when the group arrived at the home that had been designated for the travelers. The house was furnished with an ample supply of provisions. It was located in the first row of the concentric circles on the west side of the stone structure. The docents told the guests to organize the dwelling to their liking and at dinner that night they would be introduced to the other members of the town.

Once alone, the group discussed the wisdom of coming north. The Tovens were an amiable people but they did not appear to have the answers they were looking for. The four thought it best to wait several more days before they drew any conclusions.

Meanwhile, in a cave located far from Toven, Ansu's was finding his new job as Pundir full of frustration, mainly with himself. He did not understand a single Naarrt word nor could he make his point to those under his charge. The young Groullen were full of childish antics with no interest in following Ansu's hand gestures except when he tapped a ladle against the pot to indicate it was time to eat. Most of the work in the town proved to be far too difficult for these under sized Groullen and the wrath of Slugan towards his brother was a daily occurrence. A jab here and slap there, Ansu's body was one large bruise. Fortunately for this new Pundir, the helpful Florians were watching. Their keen eyes saw all the abuse Ansu endured and they were also aware of his lack of verbal skills with the other cave dwellers.

One evening after Ansu had fed the young Groullen and they had gone to bed in unison, Hirte appeared. It was the first time the Malus had seen a Florian and he was thankful the Se had told him of their existence. Hirte, the diminutive man known for his straightforward opinions, stood before Ansu and began, "Pravis, rightful leader of the Malus, I am Hirte, elder of the Florians and we have eyes for all that happens under the mountains. A state of disarray currently fills your living space. Though the Florians are small in height, we have many talents which overcome our lack of size - the art of healing, the art of protection and we are fluent in numerous languages. I believe such gifts would be of benefit to you? Tonight, I shall give you a collection of plants and herbs to aid in the healing of your injuries. I shall also give you a quartz stone which you are to keep on your person at all times. The quartz has the power to shield one if he is struck in anger. And finally, you will begin your first lesson in Naarrt. These young Groullen only follow a strong leader, one who speaks their language. Once you have a good command of their tongue, order in the cave will be restored."

Ansu could not believe what he was hearing. As leader of the Malus, all were under his control, yet he never received an offer of help unless it was ordered. Now as a Pundir, the lowest Malus, he asked for nothing but was offered much. Ansu responded, "Hirte, you are a Florian whose generosity only adds to your stature. A Pravis I once was, but never such an insightful leader as you. Your offer of aid I readily accept and I look forward to the day when I may return so gracious a kindness."

Hirte, as was his nature, wasted little time. He gave Ansu an herbal tonic, a smooth quartz stone to tie into his clothing and began his first Naarrt vocabulary lesson. As Pundir, Ansu had plenty of time to reflect on the generosity of the Florians and master the Groullen language.

There was little room left in the stone circle for dinner. The whole of Toven had arrived to see the visitors and eat. The twenty eight chairs which lined the stone circle walls remained empty but the ground offered plenty of comfortable seating.

After dinner Orden stood to address the crowd, "My fellow Toven, the guests who we heard were travelling our way have arrived, one Se, two Malus, one Naartt and their dog. They informed me that Gnos had directed them to our town so that their questions may be answered. As yet, I do not know what those questions are. I shall introduce our guests so that each of you may know their proper names." Orden then stood by the travelers, pronounced his name and continued, "I think at this juncture, I shall have the Se tell their tale of how they arrived in Foggerland."

Reiben stood and with poise far greater than his years, told their saga of the past four years. As he spoke, it felt as if a burden was slowly being removed from his shoulders. He explained in as much detail as he could remember, all that he had experienced since joining the community of Malus. His narrative took longer than he ever expected to complete and he was tired from its telling.

The Toven listened patiently to his compelling story and did not interrupt. When Reiben completed the tale he added the closing remarks, "The reason we came to Foggerland was to understand why each of us was pulled from our homes and why I was given a wand. But now that we have arrived, I don't know if a group of people so far removed from the life we left behind can offer us any answers to our questions."

Those gathered remained silent for some time before Orden stood and said, "I believe everyone in Toven agrees, the path the four of you have followed has been touched by unpleasant events but you are still pure in heart with an insatiable desire for knowledge. And though the land of the Toven appears far from the rest of the world there may be a few answers to be found in Foggerland. But first, the Tovens would like to meet each of you in person."

Every Toven rose with a smile on their face, hand extended in greeting, and formed a queue to introduce themselves to the travelers. The reserved Toven of earlier was no more. They welcomed the newcomers as a friend.

By the end of the evening, after each Toven had their moment with the group, the four found themselves exhausted. It was time for a comfortable bed and their small home was the perfect place for a good night's rest. Orden and his fellow door keepers walked with the friends to their cottage. He told the travelers that tomorrow would be an excellent day to see what answers the town of Toven might reveal.

Reiben and his companions slept all night and half of the following morning before Grrick's persistent licking told Reiben it was time to rise. The travelers could not remember a deeper slumber or one they ever enjoyed more. After breakfast, they ventured outside and the keepers of the door greeted them. Reiben told his hosts the town of Toven offered such a peaceful rest and Orden replied, "Foggerland has invigorated many a weary body and we are fortunate to call this land home. I can see your inquisitive minds are refreshed and ready for new ideas. Where should we begin; the arts, healing, written language, archery or the power stick?"

The group was excited at the list of possibilities and Reiben said, "There is so much to choose from but our first question concerns the four of you – what is a door keeper?"

Lansi spoke up and said, "Young Se, the one who follows the path of knowledge, what a superb question to begin your second day in Toven. The door keepers are selected to their post by the people in town. It is a ceremonial position today, far different than in yesteryear. We are the town guardians responsible for the needs of Tovens in the north, south, east, and west sections of the town. But in bygone times, the four directions of the compass were more important and reflected the essence of the people in this region. North – the one who embraces our earth from which all life has sprung; South – the one who is full of fire which warms our homes and sparks creativity; East – the one who is filled with the air we breathe, that which is required for communication to the world around him; and finally, West – the one who flows like water to the source of knowledge. All of you chose the west door to enter – you are in search of answers to the unknown and like water which always finds its way to the sea, you found your way to the stone circle on your own.

In former times, long before the ice came to the northern lands, the door keepers roamed the known parts of the world searching for young minds, such as yours, who aligned their thinking to one of the four directions of the compass. Those clever children were invited to study in Toven and learn the collected knowledge offered by the lands around us.

But a time of change came to our world, snow fell the ice increased, and the door keepers no longer wandered the region in search of inquisitive minds. They remained in Toven, standing at their positions on the compass as a constant reminder of the ways lost to the people. But now, after many an eon, four curious youths decide to venture out on their own, travel a great distance to Foggerland, knock on one of the doors of the stone circle, and ask for the knowledge which resides within. As door keepers and Tovens, we gladly offer you all we know." Any doubts that trekking north was a wise decision was cast asunder for the four. Lansi's words made their decision seem rational.

After a few minutes the west door keeper continued, "As door keepers, it is our responsibility to teach in a judicious manner. Your education is of the utmost importance to us. Therefore, you'll be instructed as every other young Toven is; in reading, writing, art, healing, and archery before there is a bit of talk about the wand. The stick of power must have a solid foundation of knowledge to rest upon before it can ever be understood. Your days will be filled with these subjects and you'll be happy to know that there is plenty of time to learn in Toven. It is also important that the teachings of this land come to each of you at your own pace. So, if the capable minds standing before us will follow me, your studies will begin today."

The door keepers led the young friends to the stone circle. Inside were the children of Toven seated in small groups on the ground. Each group had three instructors. Since none of the travelers had had any formal schooling, the visitors were placed with the youngest children for their first subject. The four and five year olds were excited that the new arrivals had joined them to learn the Rune. The youngsters snickered when the latest reading mates struggled with an alphabet they had no idea about, but were eager to lend a helping hand. As for the newest additions to the group, it was knowledge first and pride second; everyone must start at the beginning.

After reading the four progressed to writing and once again, laughing four year olds greeted the members. For art, medicine and archery the visitors were placed in a higher section – the six and seven year olds. The Se and his friends did have a bit of knowledge for those subjects.

To Reiben's surprise, Brroud proved as capable a student as he and the Malus. Though he could not speak the Toven language because of his thick neck and large larynx, the Groullen readily learned the Rune and the Toven taught Brroud in the same manner as the others. They did not find the Groullen's distinctive facial features an indicator of inferior mental capability and he was not bothered in the least by the snickering of his four year old classmates. By the end of the first day of school, four tired and sheepish students were ready for dinner and bed. The friends had discovered that educating one's mind all day was exhausting.

Lessons were not the only task a Toven child had to fulfill during their week. Everyone participated in the various daily chores necessary to keep the town running smoothly. From farming to smelting, each person lent a hand in some way. The new students adjusted nicely to the rigor of a Toven routine as none of them considered their schedule a burden. One could readily say it was the happiest time in the lives of the four.

After a number of months at an invigorating cadence, the visitors were elevated to the same groups as their peers. They were not the top students but with continued effort, they would eventually be on par with their classmates.

The group also found the weather in Foggerland to be different than one would expect so far north. The combination of moderate air streaming inland from the ocean and the large barrier of mountains acting as a buffer from the glacier's frigid winds set the weather of Toven squarely in the temperate zone. There were days the town saw snow and freezing rains but nothing as severe as those experienced on the Se Atoll or the rest of the northern region. The moderate temperatures allowed the students plenty of time to enjoy the outdoors year round.

On the winter solstice, the four woke to another excellent day and a town full of excitement. The one horned horses had arrived. The people of Foggerland always seemed to have another surprise for the four with each passing month. Gnos was among the group of visitors. The friends were glad to see their favorite one horn but they had to stand in a long queue before greeting her. The other Tovens enjoyed Gnos's company as much as they.

After a long wait that only heightened the excitement, they finally met their horned friend. The four hugged Gnos's neck, patted her flanks and scratched behind her ears as Reiben said, "Gnos, it is so good to see you again. All that you predicted has come true and we are much better off because of it. We do not know how to thank you."

The ever delightful Gnos replied, "It is good to see the four of you in Toven; this is a much better place than Malus. You safe arrival is all the thanks I need. It has been many a solstice since I have travelled to this part of the world but I wanted to see for myself how you were getting on in the town. I am not surprised to find that you fit in nicely." Gnos' words always made the listener feel so appreciated. As there were others standing behind the friends waiting their turn, the four would have to talk with Gnos at a later time.

The bitter cold of a glacial world was hard on all including the one horns. The grinding effect of limited food and freezing temperatures had forced the specials horses to find shelter amongst the Tovens. Of the many functions the stone circle offered, none was more important than the storage of hay for the horned horses during the winter. For two weeks Gnos and her kin were pampered, bathed, brushed and fed. Once their spirits and bodies were revived, the special horses ventured back out in the harsh cold to continue their work throughout the land.

The four finally had their turn at brushing Gnos and she said, "I hear your efforts in daily life and studies are proceeding well. You will find the knowledge of this land a benefit in whatever you are searching for."

Reiben replied, "Gnos, all our question are being answered and more. There are no better teachers than the Toven. Every new day offers us so much wonder."

Gnos had some news about the town of Malus for the friends. Slugan proved to be the ineffective and cruel leader they all knew he would be. Ansu had been spared the Pit of Strength and was given the position of Pundir. The former Pravis was diligently studying the Naartt language, was respectful of the Florians and Paskar residents, and he did not shirk from his duties as the lowest Malus in town. Fij'n's mother was managing without her daughter and the frenetic pace of Malus life continued on quite well without any help from the four friends.

After two brief weeks among the Toven, it was time for the one horns to move on. Gnos saved a few parting moments for the friends and said, "The life of a one horned can be a challenge. There is so much this world needs and only a few of us to carry out the tasks. I do take comfort knowing the four of you are doing well here." And like the other town members, the friends' parting hugs were a little tighter and longer than when Gnos arrived. They were going to miss her warmth and wisdom.

With the departure of the one horns, the residents were preoccupied with the thoughts of the special horses. The door keepers told the children their idle time was better spent outside playing games than sitting around sulking. Running in the fresh air relaxed their young minds and distracted them from the departure of the one horns.

To Reiben's surprise, the people of Foggerland enjoyed a game familiar to the Se – Sand Ball. The Tovens called it Grass Ball as it was played on grass and their passion for the game rivaled that of the Se. Reiben's skill at Grass Ball were minimal and still at the level of an undersized, nine year old boy.

Sanft, Fij'n and Brroud had never played the game and looked hopelessly lost on the field. Yet none of the four let their deficiencies prevent them from participating in every match possible. The Toven children were polite and did not tease the friends for their quality of play, but the latest participants knew where they ranked among the other players as they were always picked last when the teams were selected. Over time and with a lot of practice, improvement came to the new arrivals.

Besides learning the basics of Grass Ball, a player has to find the position which suits his abilities. As a Groullen, Brroud was not known for his speed but rather his power. The young Naarrt had long arms, big hands and superior upper body strength.

Reiben found that he was much faster at thirteen than nine and he favored his right side. Sanft was thin and quick favoring his left side. And Fij'n, who was never considered the least bit athletic by anyone in the town of Malus or by her three companions, had a keen eye for attacking an opponent's weaknesses.

With time the four gravitated to their natural positions on the field; Sanft was a looter – left footed kicker; Reiben was a rooter – right footed kicker; Brroud was a riker – a right handed hitter; Fij'n was a setter – directing the ball to the player with the highest probability of scoring.

Another important element of Grass Ball was synergy – each player understanding the nuances of his teammates. It did not take long before, with one look, Reiben, Brroud, Sanft, and Fij'n knew what the others were thinking and the day finally arrived when their skill rose to a high level of proficiency. Between team work and ability, the four became a winning force on the field.

There was no player in the land of Toven with more power than Brroud and the Groullen's capacity to focus ensured he scored a number of goals each game. He was soon the first player selected by every team followed closely behind by Reiben, Fij'n and Sanft. The four proved to be quite popular among their peers and they remained true to the Toven teachings. The newcomers were team players first and scorers second. Every teammate felt appreciated during a game.

School, work, games - after nearly a year, the visitors were no longer new arrivals - they had become completely integrated into Toven society. The four never forgot who they were a Se, Malus and Groullen, but they now found themselves thinking like the people of Foggerland. As the summer solstice approached, the friends did not look back on the Se Atoll or the town of Malus with any sadness. Life among the Toven's was far better than they had ever expected.

In the town of Malus, the Pundir was now fluent in Naarrt and order in the cave of the beasts was restored. For the former leader, the job of Pundir, nurturer, teacher, and the only cook in the cave proved to be far more difficult than the position of Pravis but unexpectedly rewarding. In fact, it came as a surprise to the others in town that the lowest Malus among them led a life much different than theirs. One which did not go unnoticed by those around him.

Whenever working in the streets of the town, Ansu never failed to stop and help a fellow Malus regardless of that person's status in the community. He risked a severe beating from Slugan by doing so. The bruises Ansu displayed were a constant reminder to the people that he was a man of courage and true leader of the town. Fortunately though, the Pundir's black and blue marks were not as severe as they appeared. The protective properties of the quartz the Florians had given him shielded him from serious injury.

It did not take long, with the Pundir at the lead, before an ever so slight shift came to the norm of the town. Ansu's exemplary behavior caused the Malus to pause and think about someone other than himself. A new idea began to slowly creep into the minds of the cold hearted citizens - should a person be kind to those he meets?

On many a late night, a frightened Malus would find his way to the beast cave because earlier that day, Ansu had provoked the wrath of his brother by aiding the worried visitor. The distressed person would call into the cave, "Pravis, do you have a few moments for a grateful Malus." Ansu always made his way to the gate and heard the same concerns he had heard from each Malus he met at the bars in the early hours of the morning, "Pravis, I am ashamed of myself. I did not stand up for you when your brother directed his anger your way because of me. I am a Malus without courage."

Looking into the eyes of the anxious visitor, Ansu would say in a kind voice, "My fellow Malus, I believe you are far too critical of yourself. For you are standing before me now, in the middle of the night, with empathy for the lowest man in town. That act alone is the essence of courage. Cast your thoughts of self-doubt away and I'm sure you'll find a very different person inside." The relieved visitor would thank Ansu and shake his hand before returning home a better Malus.

The lowly title of Pundir was a difficult moniker to wear but it did foster a different perspective on life. Ansu was surprised to find that his views of the world were being turned upside down. For he had chanced on a rather peculiar idea that had never appeared possible while seated in the chair of leadership: a person, having no other worldly possessions than the clothes on his back and a pure heart, could change all whom he met by his example. Ansu also mulled over the mystery as to why he had begun thinking like a Se?

The summer solstice was three weeks away and the one horned mares returned to Toven. It was birthing season for the special horses and Gnos again found her way to the town though she was not carrying a foal. The town's excitement was heightened and only the most experienced women of healing were allowed into the stone circle. There was to be no unsettling behavior around the expectant horses by the town folk.

After a week of isolation, mare and foal exited the stone circle to meet the Tovens. Only a small number of one horned gave birth, making each new arrival that much more important. The Tovens viewed the foals from afar, minimizing any risk to their health.

By the second week, Gnos eventually found a quiet moment to speak with her four friends from the south and said, "Though the one horned has many powerful gifts to aid others, few foals are ever born to them. Each new arrival is so precious."

The four gave Gnos a big hug before Reiben said, "It is good to see you, Gnos. There is no better place for birthing than the stone circle. The Toven have skilled hands in the art of healing. We also wish to thank you again for directing us to Foggerland. Every day, so much is given to us besides knowledge."

Gnos replied, "My young travelers, I know you will put to good use what you learn here and the door keepers are pleased with your progress." The special horse who roamed great distances could not offer them the latest news from Malus but she was sure the town was still the same.

242

After two weeks, the time came for Gnos and her kind to leave. The people of Toven formed two lines and the new foals and mares were paraded past them back from whence they had come.

The summer solstice arrived and there was a pause in the towns' daily routine for a celebration. The Tovens' once again surprised the Se as they had a summer festival also. It was a time to celebrate the birth of the new one horns, introduce the latest Toven additions to town, and hold a Grass Ball tournament and archery contest.

Reiben felt a slight pang for home as his memories of the Se festival were still vivid. He doubted few Se remembered him now. However, the intelligent Reiben did find himself in a quandary. How could two different groups of people at opposite ends of the Ice Age world, have the same celebration? It was another question for the door keepers.

A fourteenth birthday had also passed by Reiben without notice. Gnos and the arrival of the foals had captured his attention and the summer festival offered too much fun to think of anything else.

The Grass Ball tournament pitted the four areas around the stone circle against each other. The west region, with the addition of its four new players, found its way to the championship. There was no jealousy among the Toven and Reiben, Fij'n, Sanft and Brroud received heartfelt congratulations from all the town folks. Every spectator agreed the most dominant player in the tournament was Brroud – the powerful riker. No defender could possibly stop every ball Brroud drove towards the goal. In true Groullen fashion, Brroud had no interest in his celebrity status and down played all his accomplishments.

Fij'n had spent her year among the Toven diligently perfecting her archery skills. She was pleased with her excellent score in the five and under age group. Healing then archery were her main interests as she continued her studies.

At the end of the Summer Festival, the door keepers took a few moments to acknowledge, before the entire Toven community, what excellent additions the four travelers from the south were to the town. The ever insightful Gnos had been correct in sending them to Foggerland.

With the festival over, the four looked forward to their second year in the land of Toven. All their diligence in art, reading, writing, medicine and archery proved successful – they were becoming excellent students. Reiben's dedication to school distracted him from any interest in the wand, as the Toven knowledge was too captivating for a discussion about the power stick.

Time loses all relevance for a mind set on learning and the months and seasons passed quickly for the busy friends again; the second year flew by more rapidly than the first. At each winter and summer solstice Gnos returned to the town. She kept the four apprised of any news from Malus and offered words of encouragement to the excellent young adults. Gnos's biannual visits were the highlights of the year for all in town especially for the friends.

At the conclusion of their second summer festival, the four sat smiling as they looked west into the sunset, each thankful for a life among the Toven. As the friend's third year in Foggerland began, any interest in the wand had quietly faded into the recesses of their minds.

19

Forgotten by All But the Rune

Under the latest Pravis, one did not find a leader walking the streets of Malus accessing the overall wellbeing of its citizens. Slugan spent long hours in the seat of power relishing the position he had won and he was sure his joy for the chair would never fade.

The wand had given Slugan unbridled power, none of which he used for anyone else but himself. His position as leader was secure and never challenged and the people of Malus only spoke when spoken to. The Pravis was satisfied that his town was well run.

Yet the small piece of wood had a negative side effect in the hands of so a devious Malus. Each of his psychoses were soon manifest; greed, narcissism and aberrant thinking. For a troubled mind, the last thing it needed was a powerful wand.

With absolute authority at his fingertips, it didn't take long before Slugan fancied himself a great leader and the town he currently reigned over was far too small a place for a talented Pravis such as he. A Malus of his caliber could do much more.

After an extended period of musing in the chair of authority, Slugan's grandiose thoughts began to roam. His thinking eventually led him to the lands outside the city limits, to the frontier, a region where little was known other than the fact that it was as a haven for Erdas. Why had no previous Pravis brought the frontier under his domain? It was because those leaders did not have the wand by their side.

In his fractured view of the world, Slugan considered himself a unique person indeed. He had the power stick and the determination to handle any troubles the frontier might offer. It was time this leader marched into that uncharted territory and become Pravis to those wayward Malus. Slugan's vision of the future was replete with grand possibilities.

He worked at length before a plan to subjugate those in the frontier materialized. When preparations were finally completed, Slugan and a large group of reluctant Malus headed south well before the start of the Winter Carnival. Slugan's ambition was to be a catalyst for change in the Malus realm but the new order it would bring, most certainly, would not be to his liking.

The friends found the beginning of their third year as fulfilling as the previous two – the students' interest was always piqued by the knowledge Toven had to offer. As the four studied one evening in their comfortable cottage a knock was heard at the door. The door keepers entered. The Toven leaders were pleased to see the four busy with their lessons but they were not there to talk about schoolwork. They wished to speak to the friends inside the stone circle.

The four were taken aback by the request but gladly followed the door keepers to the circular structure. Upon entering, they found the area full of Toven. The door keepers led each friend to the seven stone chairs which marked the west axis.

Orden waited for the other Tovens to find a spot on the ground before he began, "Our four friends from the south, you have been exemplary additions to this town and diligent in all the ways of the Toven. As door keepers, we could not have wished for better youths or minds. When you arrived, each of you had a number of questions, most of which has been answered by the teachings of the Toven. But there is one point of interest which has never been addressed – the wand - the power stick which found its way to the Se.

For those who've had an introduction to the stick of power, its essence always appears to be within sight, yet impossible to grasp. Its purpose and scope rests in a haze of uncertainty and cannot be easily explained in a few sentences or during an hour of lecture. The wand is a topic that does not fit neatly in any form of explanation; it is the most elusive of subjects to teach.

Eons ago, the Tovens were entrusted with a book, an account which chronicles every event surrounding the wand. Though the pages are many, it is not a manuscript which is to be read in leisure. To browse just part of the book and not the whole does nothing more than clouds the understanding of the power stick. With an analytical mind, one must read the entire text, first word to last, before the true purpose of the wand becomes clear.

I also wish to point out, that no Toven has ever viewed this historical document. We were given the charge to care for the book, remain mindful of its importance, and present the volume to the persons for whom it was intended.

Besides the Toven's vigilant care of the manuscript, the one horned horses were assigned the duty of searching far and wide for those whose eyes were to grace its pages. The wise Gnos has finally determined the designated readers – you four. I must stress before we go any further that each of you must read the book as a group since no one is allowed as an individual. Gnos was very specific on that point.

As the book's caretakers, our first question to you is this – do you wish to accept such an undertaking? Keeping in mind that great responsibility comes with the knowledge of the wand and not everyone wishes for such a burden, while fewer still are suited for so grave an obligation. Declining to read the document shows as much courage as agreeing to view its pages. A person must understand himself completely before taking on the enormous power a wand has to offer. As door keepers, we realize the import of this task and do not wish to rush you in any way. Your answers cannot be given without serious consideration. The four of you may take as much time as you deem necessary to decide."

A dumbfounded Reiben, Sanft, Fijn and Broud could hardly blink much less think after what they had just heard. Reiben finally spoke, "We'll need some time to reflect on so important an obligation." Though the evening was still young, the wide eyed students returned to their cottage for the night. Sleep did not come early to the friends.

On the following day Reiben suggested the four consider the door keepers' proposal individually before discussing it among themselves. Their minds were racing with the different facets of what was presented and it took several days before they had calmed down enough to think clearly about the proposal. A decision did not come quickly.

More than a week passed before they discussed the book as a group. Fifteen was far too young an age to weigh so heavy a decision but decide they finally did. The eternal optimism of youth bested the rational fear of this great responsibility. The friends eventually informed the door keepers they would read the book collectively.

It was critical the four were each resolute in their decision. The door keepers asked the friends individually if they agreed to the undertaking. One after the other they nodded their heads to the affirmative. Broud, who spoke only Groullen could read and write Rune and understood the spoken language of the Toven. His interest in the book was equal to the other three.

One week hence, after the decision which would change everything, the four returned to the stone circle and the structure was full of Tovens once more. The friends assumed their seats on the stone chairs lining the west wall. The door keepers waited until all were quiet before they presented the readers with a thick book wrapped in a green cloth then joined the others on the ground. No one from the town of Toven had any idea what to expect once the book was opened.

The readers said not a word as they sat listening to their hearts beat. Each took a deep breath then Reiben removed the manuscript from the cloth. Written in Rune across the leather cover were the words, "The Book of What Was." It was an enigmatic title to events in the past. And so, on a day no different than any other during the Time of Ice, each reader placed a hand on the cover and opened it to the pages of an unknown future.

idea: videogame - sell to Forecastle
offer free copies to teachers/classroom
start Yautube/blog about process of
   writing which you can promote
           book through

38383457R00144

Made in the USA
San Bernardino, CA
10 June 2019

MARRIED

for a PURPOSE

52 WEEKLY DEVOTIONS FOR COUPLES
WITH GREG & JULIE GORMAN

BroadStreet
PUBLISHING

BroadStreet Publishing® Group, LLC
Racine, Wisconsin, USA
BroadStreetPublishing.com

MARRIED FOR A PURPOSE:
NEW HABITS OF THINKING FOR A HIGHER WAY OF LIVING

Cover by Jeremiah Yancy at jeremiahyancy.com
Interior by Katherine Lloyd at theDESKonline.com

Printed in China
18 19 20 21 22 5 4 3 2 1

Introduction

Do you desire to connect and grow with your spouse? If so, we invite you to lean in and embrace each weekly devotional designed to help you create new habits of thinking to enjoy a higher way of living for your marriage.

As small business owners, certified life coaches, and most of all parents of two teenagers and a now twenty-something-year-old, like you, we understand the everyday challenges of life. When we first married, we allowed those challenges to divide us. We lived into our problems instead of God's purpose. When we made a conscious decision to pursue God's purpose for our marriage, it changed everything! In saying that, we also understand that living purpose-focused doesn't just happen. It takes intentionality and discipline. Yet, discipline in and of itself isn't enough; oneness in marriage takes inspired discipline. So rather than providing you with another have-to-do list, our hope is to provide you with insights that help you uncover God's vision for your marriage, which in turn produces inspired discipline.

As you read through the following weekly devotionals, you'll uncover ways to help you create new habits of thought in your relationship, thought-provoking questions to enrich your communication, along with a passage from God's Word to nurture and welcome God's specific purpose for your marriage. Take time to embrace each application and pray together. Our hope is to inspire you to live the life God intended.

He created you and your spouse to live *Married for a Purpose*!

CONCENTRATE YOUR *Attention* ON GOD'S *Intention*

Concentrate Your Attention on God's Intention

*E*ver get tired of to-do lists? If so, you'll love this simple truth: God's purpose for your marriage isn't another thing you need to *do*; it's a celebration of *who* you are. God created every one of us on purpose and for a purpose, and the same holds true for our marriages. But in order for us to live God's purpose, we need to create godly habits that foster life and welcome His purpose into our everyday living.

Part of welcoming God's purpose means that we stop focusing on our problems and concentrate our *attention* on God's *intention*. We experience a higher way of living when we choose to look past our hardships and instead look forward and upward to live God's design, a practice George Washington Carver embraced.

George Washington Carver, a man born into slavery, certainly faced a lot of hardships. But he didn't allow those hardships to stop him from using his gifts as a botanist and inventor. Instead, Carver went into his private time of study and lifting a peanut toward heaven, prayed, "Lord, we have so many of these. Help me discover the purpose for this peanut."

And guess what? God did.

God revealed three hundred purposes for the peanut. Wow. Think about it. If God can reveal three hundred purposes for something as seemingly insignificant as a peanut, surely He holds a purpose for your marriage.

This Week's Scripture

For we are God's masterpiece.
He has created us anew in Christ Jesus,
so we can do the good things he planned for us long ago.
EPHESIANS 2:10 NLT

This Week's Application

- Each day this week, read Ephesians 2:10 together.

- Discuss how it applies to you as a couple. Ask each another: What do we care about? Who do we care about? How can we use our gifts and talents together for God's purpose?

- Pray and ask God to reveal His purpose for your marriage.

This Week's Prayer

Father, reveal your purpose for our marriage. Show us how we can serve you and each other, right where we are, every day.

MAKE *God* KNOWN

Make God Known

*A*s a couple, the highest compliment we experience occurs when our children say, "We see Jesus in you." Or, "I feel His love when I'm with you." Wow. What a feeling.

As a spouse (or parent), one of the best ways to cultivate new habits of thinking so we experience a higher way of living is by daily asking, "How can we make God known (most naturally) in our home?" After all, the greatest opportunity to make God known begins within our family relationships.

True, God calls us to make Him known through our random acts of kindness, by extending encouragement or benevolence to outsiders, or even by offering gentle responses to people we encounter day to day. But those same habits of extending God's love should first be extended to each other. We welcome a higher way of living for our marriage when we daily purpose to make God known in our words and actions to each other in the privacy of our own homes.

Can you imagine how much our relationships would thrive if we as a couple determined one way each day to concentrate on making Him known within the four walls of our home? Can you imagine how much we could impact our culture and future generations if every morning before our feet hit the floor, we invited God to reveal one way we could make Him known to our spouse and to our children?

This Week's Scripture

"You are the light of the world. A town built on a hill
cannot be hidden. Neither do people light a lamp and
put it under a bowl. Instead they put it on its stand, and it gives
light to everyone in the house. In the same way, let your light
shine before others, that they may see your good deeds
and glorify your Father in heaven."

MATTHEW 5:14–16

This Week's Application

° Discuss how Matthew 5:14–16 applies to you as a couple.

° Discuss a few ways you can add value to each other and to
your children this week. Then do it!

° When you wake up each morning this week, say a short
prayer, asking the Lord how He wants you to make God
known through your words and actions to each other and
your children.

This Week's Prayer

*Father, remind us to make you known in the way we respond, in
the actions we take, and in the way we treat each other. We want
to live full-on into your purpose, in a way that pleases you both
practically and spiritually.*

BRING *God* PLEASURE

Bring God Pleasure

*S*everal years ago, our middle child struggled between two decisions. She vacillated and wondered in which activities she should participate. Heavy-hearted and shoulders slumped, she asked, "Which do you want me to do, cheerleading or dance?" Without hesitation, we responded, "Which would you enjoy the most?"

As you take steps toward living God's purpose for your marriage, we encourage you to ask yourself the same question. Don't overcomplicate your marriage purpose. When we align our passions with our service to God, it brings Him pleasure. Just as we desire our children to fully enjoy life, God desires for us to enjoy life to its fullest. Our joint passions combined with our spouse's reveals His design and purpose for us as a couple. We bring Him pleasure when we use our gifts, talents, and passions to honor Him.

Eric Liddell, a famous Scottish athlete, understood this truth. In the movie *Chariots of Fire*, he was quoted as saying, "I believe God made me for a purpose, but he also made me fast! And when I run I feel His pleasure."

Simplify your thoughts and center them on this central truth: God created you and your spouse to bring Him pleasure together. When you submit your gifts, talents, and passions back to Him for His use, you bring Him pleasure.

This Week's Scripture

For from him and through him and for him are all things.
To him be the glory forever!

ROMANS 11:36

This Week's Application

- Make a list of the things you love to do (each spouse should make his or her own list). Compare lists. What activities, interests, or passions do you have in common? What do you enjoy doing together?

- Make a list of the gifts and talents you recognize in your spouse. Share what you wrote with the other. Use statements like, "I love how you _____ because that's a weakness of mine." Or, "You are so amazing at _____ ."

- Consider how you can combine your gifts to bring God pleasure in and through your marriage, and then pray together, asking God how you can use your gifts to bring Him pleasure.

This Week's Prayer

Father, we want our marriage to bring you pleasure. Cause us to live our life for you by simply being who you already created us to be. Inspire us to recognize each other's gifts and talents and to encourage each other in them. We desire to honor each other and bring you pleasure in the process.

DEMONSTRATE
GOD'S
Unconditional
LOVE

Demonstrate God's Unconditional Love

*N*either of us lived a squeaky-clean life. Even after our conversion, we made huge blunders. One time, in the midst of a really dark season, God showed up in a bar and lovingly impressed on me this single thought: *There's nowhere you can run that my grace won't find you.* Wow. Talk about unconditional love. God didn't condemn or pay back what I deserved. He demonstrated forgiveness and stirred repentance through His unending grace and unconditional love.

When you think of unconditional love, what comes to mind? Do you immediately envision someone who loved and served you selflessly? Better yet, how has God revealed His absolute, unrestricted, and unmerited love toward you?

For years, we've centered on this central truth: God's love is more tender than a mother's, more faithful than a brother's, and more intimate than a lover's. Jesus overlooked all of our indifference and pride, and willingly offered up His life. He nailed the weight of our sin to its final death on the cross.

Yet understanding and receiving God's love commissions us to reciprocate and extend His love. Jesus told the disciples, "A new commandment I give you: Love one another. As I have loved you, so also you must love one another" (John 13:34). So how did Jesus demonstrate God's love, leaving a model for us to follow? And how can we best model and demonstrate His love to each other in our marriage relationship?

This Week's Scripture

But God proves His love for us in this:
While we were still sinners, Christ died for us.

Romans 5:8

This Week's Application

○ Talk about Romans 5:8. Share how God has lavished you with His love, even when undeserved, and discuss any other thoughts or people that come to mind when you think about unconditional love.

○ Plan your intention for the week. Remember, developing new habits always requires more strategy in the beginning, so take time individually to write down the ways you'll demonstrate unconditional love to each other (and to the other members of your household). How will you live as an example of His unconditional love to each other?

○ As you start each day this week, meditate on how you will purposefully and intentionally demonstrate God's unconditional love in your home.

○ When you see your spouse demonstrating God's unconditional love, say something to let them know how much their love means to you.

This Week's Prayer

Father, at times it's hard to give love unconditionally because of our own needs and desires. Remind us to remain silent when we want to retaliate, to serve instead of always expecting to be served, and to love—even when it isn't convenient or doesn't feel warranted. Empower us to love each other as you love us.

REMEMBER,
Your Outcome
BEGINS IN
Your Mind-set

Remember, Your Outcome Begins in Your Mind-set

*E*ver glance off at a pretty sunset only to feel your car tires jarring along the roadside? Truth is, if we focus exclusively on driving between the yellow lines, we avoid veering. We can apply this principle to our life and marriage as well.

Napoleon Hill once wrote, "Every man is what he is, because of the dominating thoughts which he permits to occupy his mind."* He's not alone in his thinking. Thought leaders throughout time agree that our outcome begins in our mind-set. We find what we look for. We become what we think about. Their wisdom suggests that when we focus on fixing our issues, we unwittingly perpetuate our problems. However, when we focus on our desired outcome, aligning our thoughts with God's purpose, we reap the benefits of living His design for our marriage.

As a couple, what do you tend to talk about? Where do your thoughts most naturally gravitate?

If you want to live a higher way of living—God's way of living—in your marriage, create new habits of thinking. Instead of thinking and talking about your obstacles, consider God's purpose. Instead of focusing on the problems in your relationship, consider what you both agree on and desire as an end result. Instead of pondering what you want to change about your spouse, consider how your differences make you stronger. Envision your desired outcome and welcome God's perfect plan for your marriage, knowing your outcome begins in your mind-set.

---

* Napoleon Hill, *Think and Grow Rich* (Radford, VA: Wilder Publications, 2007), 43.

This Week's Scripture

For as he thinks in his heart, so is he.

PROVERBS 23:7 AMP

This Week's Application

o   Answer the following questions together: What is our desired outcome in our marriage? How is God calling us to shift our mind-set? What is His vision for us as a couple? How will we align our thinking with God's to better celebrate each other and welcome His design for our marriage?

o   Each day, make a conscious effort to focus your thoughts, energy, and prayers specifically on your desired outcome—especially when you're tempted to think otherwise.

o   Pray together daily, asking God to help you look past the obstacles and instead see His vision for your marriage.

This Week's Prayer

Father, empower us to see your vision instead of our obstacles. We want to celebrate your unique purpose for our marriage and see the beauty in our individual design.

Take Comfort ...
GOD
MEASURES
Success
THROUGH
Obedience

Take Comfort ... God Measures Success through Obedience

*D*r. John C. Maxwell wrote, "Once you taste significance, success will never satisfy."[*] And yet we often measure our significance by standards of success. Think about it. Do you ever feel like a failure because you evaluate your success by the world's standards?

Several years ago, God called us to step out of our comfort zone to pursue His purpose. It wasn't easy! We literally lived in three different states within eleven months. We went three years without a paycheck and watched our 401K vanish.

During that season, we questioned everything. We wondered if we misheard God. Somehow, we thought our faithfulness precluded us from trials, as if our obedience mandated God's blessings. Truthfully, we hoped God would grant us immediate success. Instead, God whittled at our pride and taught us to never adopt the world's standards of success (defined by dollars and results). After all, God isn't impressed by accomplishments. He values obedience.

How about you? What is God calling you to believe for as a couple? What steps does He desire for you to take together in faith? Has a fear of not succeeding stopped you from stepping toward God's purpose?

---

[*] John C. Maxwell, *Intentional Living* (New York: Center Street Hachette Book Group, 2015), 259.

This Week's Scripture

"These are the ones I look on with favor: those who are humble
and contrite in spirit, and who tremble at my word."

Isaiah 66:2

This Week's Application

o   Share ideas regarding the following: Since God measures
    success through obedience, how can we simply follow His
    lead and entrust our outcome to Him? What practical steps
    can we take to begin embracing God's marriage purpose,
    while releasing our outcome to Him? How can we better
    serve God and each other today?

o   Re-read Isaiah 66:2 a number of times this week—together
    and individually.

o   Be aware of your emotions this week. If you feel stressed or
    anxious, pray, *Lord, we release our outcome to you.*

This Week's Prayer

*Father, encourage us to live obediently. Empower us to tune into
your direction and respond to your prompting rather than dismiss
them. Inspire us to follow you, never measuring our success by
the world's standards, and to live passionately for your approval
alone.*

IMPROVE YOURSELF ...
Not Your Spouse

Improve Yourself …
Not Your Spouse

*E*ver try to change your spouse?

We spent the first few years of our marriage frustrated, seeing each other's differences as opportunities to change the other. At one point, God convicted us: *Quit being each other's Holy Spirit. Allow me to change in you what needs changing. And entrust [your spouse] to me. Allow me to change in [your spouse] the things I desire to change.* Whew. Talk about a new habit of thought to a higher way of living.

Johann von Goethe said, "Treat a man as he is, and he will remain as he is. Treat a man as he can and should be, and he will become as he can and should be."

In marriage, if we aren't careful, we slip into patterns of thinking that our way is superior, instead of remembering God designed our differences for His higher purpose. If we want our marriage to thrive, we must shift our thoughts from trying to improve our spouse and focus on how we can improve ourselves. We need to create the habit of growing personally, rather than imposing our ideas of how our spouse needs to grow. We need to allow God to change in us the things that need to be changed and entrust our spouse to Him.

Instead of trying to change each other, God desires us to ask: How do our differences better equip us to fulfill His purpose for our marriage? He wants us to personally reflect by asking: How can I be a better, more supportive spouse?

This Week's Scripture

If a house is divided against itself,
that house cannot stand.

Mark 3:24–25

This Week's Application

- ° Share ideas regarding the following: How can we better welcome our differences and even celebrate them? What do we admire most about each other? What practical ways can we better demonstrate love and respect for each other?

- ° This week, practice surrendering your thoughts and habits of speech, especially when you're tempted to try to change your spouse.

- ° Each day, write down one quality you admire about the other and share them aloud together.

This Week's Prayer

Father, change in each one of us the things you want changed. Energize us to truly celebrate each other and welcome each other's differences and perspectives in our marriage. Enable us to view each other through your lens of grace. Build in us a unified, purpose-focused marriage.

LIVE
Purpose-
FOCUSED

Live Purpose-Focused

*W*hether in business partnerships, interpersonal friendships, or in our marriage relationship, we govern our actions with a simple checkpoint: Do we want to be right or do we want to unite?

The most effective organizations welcome differences as assets, not competition. They build upon core values and move toward the desired outcome, rather than meandering in all the details of the issue or problem. The same applies to our relationships. If we want a healthy marriage, we need to welcome our differences and stop focusing on our issues. We need to shift from thinking about our problems and instead focus on our desired outcome.

How? By consistently asking each other: What do we both desire? What do we want our outcome to look like in this particular situation? When we do that, we align our lives, our differences, and our attitudes to welcome that end result.

For us, parenting offers the greatest opportunity for division. If we aren't careful, we believe our way of parenting is the right way and become critical of the other's style. We start focusing on our differences and forget that our desired result is to raise successful kids who embrace God's specific design. That outcome demands both encouragement and excellence.

So how do we invite God's higher way of living? By staying unified in purpose. Regardless of our individual parental expressions, our children need encouragement and accountability to live lives of excellence.

This Week's Scripture

Make my joy complete by being of the same mind,
maintaining the same love, united in spirit,
intent on one purpose.

PHILIPPIANS 2:2 NASB

This Week's Application

- To live more united, focus on what you agree on. Ask each other: In our potentially divisive areas, what do we agree on?

- Discuss how you can live unified in your parenting, finances, spirituality, and sexual intimacy.

- Each day, choose one of these areas of life (beginning with the least controversial) and begin celebrating the small successes of living purpose-focused in each area.

This Week's Prayer

Father, support us as we strive to live your perfect vision in every area of our relationship. Assist us in recognizing what we have in common. Sometimes it's difficult for us to unify completely in every domain of our marriage. Help us to truly grasp your perfect vision for our relationship and to live purpose-focused lives.

Believe the Best
ABOUT
EACH OTHER

Believe the Best About Each Other

*R*alph Waldo Emerson said, "Every man is entitled to be valued by his best moments."* Wow. What a thought.

When we first dated, believing the best about each other came easy. We were enamored. We sought to find the good in each other. We put our best foot forward and lived to please. Julie believed Greg was Superman. Greg constantly said Julie was the girl of his dreams.

Fast-forward two years into our marriage and it didn't take much to recognize something had changed. Somewhere between our sleepless nights of tending newborns, worrying about our mounting bills, and a whole lot of unmet expectations, our minds shifted from believing the best to speculating how we kept getting the short end of the stick. The more we drifted from serving and celebrating each other, the more neither one of us measured up.

Ever been there? Ever get sidetracked into thinking you're getting the short end of the stick? If so, it's time to commit to a new habit of thought. Reflect on the characteristics you admire most about your spouse. Remember, you find what you are looking for, so look for and find the best in each other. Truthfully, the more we intentionally look for the good in our spouse, the more we draw out their best.

---

* Ralph Waldo Emerson, *Selected Writings of Ralph Waldo Emerson* (Toronto: W. J. Gage & Co., 1888), 160.

This Week's Scripture

Love is patient, love is kind. It does not envy, it does not boast, it is not proud. It does not dishonor others, it is not self-seeking, it is not easily angered, it keeps no record of wrongs. Love does not delight in evil but rejoices with the truth. It always protects, always trusts, always hopes, always perseveres. Love never fails.

1 Corinthians 13:4–8

This Week's Application

○ Individually, write a quick note (no more than three sentences) expressing what you admire most about your spouse. Highlight and celebrate their greatest qualities.

○ Schedule times during the week to sit down together and re-read what you've written about each other.

○ Each day, look for examples of your spouse's good qualities in action and affirm your spouse for them.

This Week's Prayer

Father, thank you for our marriage. Thank you for all the gifts and talents you've created in us. Empower us to develop the habit of honoring each other by continually recognizing and voicing our admiration and respect. Encourage us to always believe the best about each other.

Inspire
THE BEST

Inspire the Best

I knew you could do it. Your answers are always so brilliant. You truly are an amazing person." After twenty years, Dr. Berl Best's words still echo in our minds and impact our marriage relationship.

As a college professor, Dr. Best always possessed a way of speaking confidence into his students. He certainly mastered the art of praise and constantly inspired the best in them and their abilities. Students who typically struggled finished his class with grades higher than anticipated. His praise and genuine belief that each student held value impacted their actions and produced a positive outcome.

Dr. John C. Maxwell wrote, "When a person feels encouraged, he can face the impossible and overcome incredible adversity."* As couples, we hold a powerful weapon to inspire the best in each other. Together, we can overcome incredible adversity and enjoy marriage as God intended. Though our actions begin in the meditations of our thoughts, our speech holds the power to bring forth life.

Reclaiming territory and creating positive habits takes a lot of work. Yet every week, when you and your spouse show up and commit to building new habits, you position your marriage to live God's purpose. Your God-given purpose is a celebration of who God already created you to be, and the habits you implement enforce God's best in you and your spouse.

---

* Maxwell, *Becoming a Person of Influence: How to Positively Impact the Lives of Others* (Nashville: Thomas Nelson, 1997), 47.

This Week's Scripture

The tongue has the power of life and death.

PROVERBS 18:21

This Week's Application

- ° Consider ways you can daily spur each other on to good works. Intentionally catch each other doing something right and share your appreciation for each other as often as possible.

- ° Inspire each other with your words. Make it a practice to look for one unique way you can inspire the best in each other every day.

- ° Share ideas how the two of you can inspire and speak life to your family and others you care about.

This Week's Prayer

Father, fill us with a genuine respect for each other and help us to more naturally speak praise over each other. Assist us to inspire the best in each other.

SURRENDER
Your Rights
FOR GOD'S
Ultimate Purpose

Surrender Your Rights for God's Ultimate Purpose

S urrender. What does that mean? And how does it apply to marriage?

From time to time, every couple fights the battle to surrender. Instead of surrendering, we fight to be heard. We fight for our rights. We fight for how we think things should operate. We even fight to change our spouse. Catch the common theme? We fight—at least until we understand that our surrender stops the fight.

Surrender means to give yourself up into the power of another. (In this case, God.) The truth is, we don't need to face a tragedy to give in to the power of another. We can choose surrender. After all, there's only one person we can change—ourselves. God invites us to work on ourselves and surrender our spouse to Him. Let's face it. God changes people better than we do anyway.

A. W. Tozer wrote, "The reason why many are still troubled, still seeking, still making little forward progress is because they haven't yet come to the end of themselves."

If we desire to experience the most in our relationship, we need to cultivate the habit of surrendering our rights for God's ultimate purpose. Rather than resisting change or demanding our way, we need to look for opportunities to serve each other and welcome God into every aspect of our marriage. Our surrender invites His unlimited power.

Jesus, the ultimate example of surrender, willingly gave up His rights and surrendered to God's purpose.

This Week's Scripture

[Jesus] Who, being in very nature God, did not consider
equality with God something to be used to his own advantage;
rather, he made himself nothing by taking the very nature
of a servant, being made in human likeness. And being found
in appearance as a man, he humbled himself by
becoming obedient to death—even death on a cross!

PHILIPPIANS 2:6–8

This Week's Application

○ Talk together about the ways you can model your life after
Christ. How can you best invite God's unlimited power and
purpose in your marriage?

○ Together, journal these ideas.

○ Share answers to the following questions (focusing on your
part, not your spouse's): How is God calling me to surrender
my control? What changes do I need to make to be a better
spouse? How does God want me to grow so I can better welcome His purpose for my life and for our marriage?

This Week's Prayer

*Father, we surrender our marriage to you. Cause us to serve each
other and create habits of thought that honor each other so we can
faithfully serve you together.*

Prefer
EACH OTHER'S
Needs OVER
YOUR OWN

Prefer Each Other's Needs Over Your Own

$\mathcal{F}$or a few years of our marriage, we thought we'd do marriage the tough way. We insisted on our rights. We demanded to be understood. We sought to explain why our way was the best way. A few hundred arguments and a ton of harsh words later, we stumbled across a verse packed full of wisdom: "If you bite and devour each other, watch out or you will be destroyed by each other" (Galatians 5:15).

And we thought, *Hmm. Maybe we should try something new.* Seriously. We had developed a habit of allowing our emotions to carry us and cut each other down to size. What kind of love does that? None. We realized we needed a new habit—a habit of preferring each other's needs over our own.

It wasn't always easy, and we certainly didn't do it perfectly. But we decided to throw out the scorecard and stop making each other our opponent and start being each other's partner. We practiced empathy. And we genuinely committed to rediscover each other.

So think about it. How can you begin to practically prefer each other's needs over your own?

This Week's Scripture

Do nothing out of selfish ambition or vain conceit.
Rather, in humility value others above yourselves.

PHILIPPIANS 2:3

This Week's Application

° Together, share your thoughts to the following questions (remember to prefer your spouse's needs over your own, seek to understand, and speak positively to and about them): How do you describe humility? Who do you know that consistently demonstrates humility?

° Take a moment to ask each other: What makes you feel the most valued?

° Share some of the ways you value each other.

This Week's Prayer

Father, enable us to demonstrate the same attitude as Jesus. Motivate us to serve. Prompt us to love. Cause us to prefer each other's needs over our own. We know you will empower us. Speak to us and encourage us to do the same for each other.

CELEBRATE
YOUR
Differences

Celebrate
Your Differences

*A*ndrew Carnegie said, "It marks a big step in your development when you come to realize that other people can help you do a better job than you can do alone."9

Think about this quote with regard to your marriage. Our marital differences aren't a matter of being right or wrong. Instead, our spousal differences offer diversity. When we welcome those differences, they expand our perspective, grant us strength, and further our wisdom. Just as one piece of iron sharpens another, our differences provide the necessary friction to sharpen us and empower us to accomplish more.

We further our impact when we celebrate each other's differences. In parenting, Julie offers encouragement effortlessly. Greg fosters excellence easily. Our difference in parenting used to invite spirited conversations. Today, we recognize the blending of our differences maximizes our parenting together. Likewise, God designed you and your spouse distinctly, purposed all of your differences, and then positioned you and your spouse together, on purpose, for His purpose.

Since God foresaw you and your spouse's differences and loves you both, consider how you can better leverage your differences together for a shared positive impact, and better welcome each other's perspectives.

This Week's Scripture

But in fact, God has placed the parts in the body, every one of them, just as he wanted them to be.

1 CORINTHIANS 12:18

This Week's Application

- ○ Ask yourself: Do I position my spouse as my partner or my opponent? Tell each other: I am committed to working together with you, unified in effort and vision.

- ○ Identify how your differences add dimension to each other. How do your different perspectives add wisdom and depth to your relationship?

- ○ Individually, spend some time analyzing how you can learn from your spouse's strengths. Then practice expressing praise over those strengths throughout the week.

This Week's Prayer

Father, we know that you designed us for a unique purpose and hold a distinct plan for our marriage. Reveal your plan and show us how to celebrate each other's differences to fully embrace all you've destined for us. Remind us to welcome each other's design and to embrace how we're stronger together because of them.

TAME
Your
TONGUE

Tame Your Tongue

*H*ave you ever noticed how the familiarity of your marriage leads you to say things to each other that you would never speak to others?

Several years ago, Julie worked for a man who constantly stole credit for her ideas and hard work. He made himself superior in conversations. At times, he absolutely infuriated her. He often failed to follow through on his promises and communicated more demands than praise. On one particular day, the Holy Spirit challenged Julie with these words:

Every day, you honor your boss because of his position. You don't feel the need to challenge every way he wrongs you. You extend him grace. You only speak about him positively to coworkers and never point out his flaws. You practice believing the best about him, even when it's unwarranted. If you can extend respect to a man who holds no bearing on your life except employment, how much more should you extend respect to the man you made a vow before me to love until death do you part?

Needless to say, a new habit of thinking began to form on that day. We took inventory of how we spoke *to* each other. We took inventory of how we spoke *about* each other and what thoughts preoccupied our minds about each other.

The truth is, no one can hide what's in their heart forever. Eventually, our private contemplations spill forth from our lips. Thus, if we want to tame our tongue, we need to tame our heart by taking every thought captive to Christ and surrendering our thoughts and emotions to God.

This Week's Scripture

For out of the abundance of the heart the mouth speaks.
A good man out of the good treasure of his heart brings forth
good things, and an evil man out of the evil treasure brings forth
evil things. But I say to you that for every idle word men
may speak, they will give account of it in the day of judgment.

Matthew 12:34–37 NKJV

This Week's Application

○   Remember, if we want to tame our tongue, we need to tame
    our heart; if we want to tame our heart, we need to control
    our thoughts. This week, only entertain positive thoughts
    about your spouse.

○   Commit to the habit of remaining silent when you want to
    retaliate.

○   Speak gratitude instead of complaint. Verbalize what you
    love about each other, not what is lacking.

This Week's Prayer

*Father, remind us to think and believe the best about each other.
Help our inner thoughts to cultivate admiration, gentleness, and
respect. Quicken us to honor each other in our words both publicly
and privately.*

PRACTICE
Praise

Practice Praise

*A*s kids, we played a funny little game called Mad Libs. (Mad Libs consists of pages of paragraphs with sporadic places to fill in the blanks with an adjective, verb, color, noun, etc.) We laughed hilariously as strange twists produced unexpected outcomes. Sometimes cows flew, other times a next-door neighbor danced with a purple flamingo. You could never tell what details would unfold, but one thing you could expect was laughter. The game was designed for silliness.

In marriage, we can ensure success by lacing our conversations with praise. In the last devotional, you read about the importance of taming your tongue, but taming your tongue isn't merely keeping it *from* saying something; it's training it *to* say something. In other words, controlling our speech isn't just keeping ourselves from saying something bad but consistently creating the habit to praise our spouse.

After all, people rise to the words we speak over them. If we point out how the other selfishly lacks empathy and never _____, we'll probably get that. But if we choose to shower each other with words of affirmation, we enjoy greater intimacy. Praising and believing the best about each other helps to heal our relationship and bring out the best in each other.

It may take a lot of discipline at first, but remember that perfect practice makes perfect, and practicing this habit is well worth our effort. What are some positive adjectives, verbs, and nouns you can provide to praise your spouse?

This Week's Scripture

Let your conversation be always full of grace, seasoned with salt,
so that you may know how to answer everyone.

COLOSSIANS 4:6

This Week's Application

- List seven or more reasons you love and respect your spouse.

- Express at least one of these thoughts—each day, every day—to let them know why you admire them.

- Be creative. Express your respect in ways they will most effectively hear you. Then commit to practicing the habit of praise. You will be amazed at the results.

This Week's Prayer

Father, motivate us to genuinely love and respect each other and then to openly express our admiration for each other. Help every blank we fill in about our spouse to be positive.

REMEMBER ...
YOU *Find*
WHAT YOU'RE
Looking For

Remember ... You Find What You're Looking For

A few years back, we decided to sell our home. Ironically, the next morning we noticed other houses all around our neighborhood with for-sale signs in their yard. Coincidence? Not likely. A similar thing happened when we purchased our Acura MDX SUV. Suddenly, we noticed the same make and model all along the highway. Why did it seem like everyone else decided to drive a similar vehicle? Was there a deviant plot for people to replicate our lives? Of course not. Instead, a great mystery was at play: we find what we're looking for.

In marriage, we can learn new habits to implement powerful truths by finding and searching out the good. After all, if we are to truly find what we are looking for, we need to look for what is good and worthy in each other.

Recently, we noticed that we felt irritated and a little short-fused. Our grace cup for each other certainly seemed lacking. Why? Truthfully, we were smack dab in the middle of a lot of deadlines and started to feel the crunch. We inadvertently kept a scorecard of all the ways we served and forgot to recognize each other's sacrifices. Ever been guilty?

The moment we remembered that we find what we're looking for, we acknowledged the ways we each served each other. Our appreciation grew. We felt like a team as we tackled the to-do list together. Our shift in thinking changed everything as we searched and found the good in each other daily.

This Week's Scripture

Be completely humble and gentle; be patient,
bearing with one another in love.

EPHESIANS 4:2

This Week's Application

- ° Individually, take inventory of the attitudes of your heart. Do you need to shift your thinking?

- ° Take mental notes of all the ways your spouse serves you. Remember, you find what you're looking for, so look for the best in each other.

- ° Search for opportunities to surprise each other with love; to be completely humble, gentle, and patient; and to bear with each other in love.

This Week's Prayer

Father, spur us to love each other, accept each other, and forgive each other. Let our marriage demonstrate your unconditional love, forgiveness, and grace. Help us to find the good in each other and to constantly seek to find the best in each other.

WHEN YOU
Can't Change
HOW YOU FEEL,
Change THE WAY
YOU *Think*

When You Can't Change How You Feel, Change the Way You Think

*E*ver run into an obstacle between *want to* and *how to*? Between *want to* and *follow through*? If so, you aren't alone.

The largest gap in life resides between knowing and doing. We may want to lose weight, but we just don't *feel* like working out. We want to forgive as Christ forgave but *feel* overwhelmed by hurt. We often know what to do but may not know how to put it into practice.

So how do we forgive when every emotion fights to hold us back? How do we make steps toward our desired outcome, together, when our feelings of fear or inferiority hold us back from the risks?

Truth be told, sometimes we can't immediately change the way we feel. In those moments, we need to create a new habit of understanding. When we can't change how we feel, we need to change the way we think. Every day, our decisions move us closer or further from our desired outcome. Our victory begins in the battlefield of our mind.

If we want to change how we feel, we need to change how we think by feeding the right thoughts. Remember, what you feed grows and what you starve dies.

This Week's Scripture

Do not conform to the pattern of this world,
but be transformed by the renewing of your mind.
Then you will be able to test and approve what God's will is—
his good, pleasing and perfect will.

ROMANS 12:2

This Week's Application

○ Take a moment to choose one way you want to grow as a couple.

○ How can the two of you partner together to feed the thoughts that will affect how you feel about each other?

○ Choose two or three ways you will daily renew your minds together, and then make room for those activities in your schedule.

This Week's Prayer

Father, teach us to be mindful of our thoughts. Empower us to embrace your thoughts and to see as you see. Give us more grace for each other. Cause us to recognize the good and the truth, especially when we need it the most. We are thankful for each other, Lord, and we choose to let go of offenses or irritations and recognize the traits we love about each other. Thank you, Lord.

Remember
EACH OTHER'S
Value

Remember
Each Other's Value

*W*hat's that?" Sheri asked, pointing at the small lapel pin we both wore.

We smiled and responded, "It's a JMT [John Maxwell Team] heart pin. It reminds us to add value to everyone we meet. It's a symbol of bringing transformation to your country."

Sheri's eyes widened. Like a little kid at Christmas, she peered at the small trinket and whispered, "I want one."

Each of Sheri's coworkers quickly chimed in, "Me too. I want one too."

Watching their enthusiasm inspired ours. One by one, each of our team members removed their lapel pin and put it on our new friends in Paraguay. Our eyes glistened as we reflected; what seemed like a mere trinket to us meant the world to them. What we took for granted, they held in great value. Isn't it funny how familiarity can rob us of our exhilaration and desensitize our appreciation?

Every day families visit Florida to appreciate a vacation at the beach. And though we intentionally keep the beach a part of our life, sometimes we may not visit it for an entire month. We get sidetracked and forget to delight in its beauty or soak up its majesty.

Think about how this applies to marriage. Sometimes we get so comfortable around each other, we forget to appreciate each other. We get sidetracked and forget to put our best foot forward to impress each other.

This Week's Scripture

Be devoted to one another in love.
Honor one another above yourselves.
Romans 12:10

This Week's Application

- The *Berean Study Bible* interprets Romans 12:10 to read, "Outdo one another in showing honor." This week, spend time considering how you can outdo one another in showing honor.

- Look at each other like you did when you first met. What is one thing you each can do this week to rekindle some of those feelings?

- Periodically throughout the week, express the things you most appreciate about each other.

This Week's Prayer

Father, remind us to never take each other for granted. Reveal ways we can celebrate each other, and enable us to see each other with fresh eyes of admiration.

SURPRISE
Your Spouse

Surprise Your Spouse

$\mathcal{N}$o one likes to be surprised by a broken appliance, a flat tire, or an unexpected bill in the mail. But a *wanted* surprise? Well, that's a completely different story.

When we first dated, Julie was as broke as a joke. She worked two jobs, drove an unreliable vehicle, and though she loves pasta, she ate more ramen noodles than she cares to remember. So when Greg surprised her by purchasing her favorite CD, Julie giggled out loud in gratitude. At Christmas, when he surprised her with a painting she'd wanted for more than six months, she cried. Not having a lot of money, Julie wanted to surprise Greg too. So she sold all of her jewelry and bought him a bronze statue of the *Trail of Tears* that he'd admired.

Other surprises came in the form of hidden notes, letters in travel bags, and special unexpected date nights including dinner at a favorite restaurant. Some surprises seemed big. Some surprises were small. The success of the surprises hinged on the heart behind them and the pre-planning and forethought put into them. We couldn't wait to thoughtfully supply each other with wanted surprises.

If we're looking for it, God surprises us every day. He lavishes our marriage with love. He grants us provision for our needs. He surprises us with gifts, talents, and opportunities, and He loves when we use them together for His glory. Scripture says, "For the LORD God is a sun and shield; the LORD bestows favor and honor; no good thing does he withhold from those whose walk is blameless" (Psalm 84:11). As a couple, God calls us to not withhold from each other when it is within our power to act.

This Week's Scripture

Do not withhold good from those to whom it is due,
when it is in your power to act.

PROVERBS 3:27

This Week's Application

° Spend time considering ways you can provide each other
  with wanted surprises. What are some favorite date nights,
  activities, or places your spouse might like to visit?

° Get creative. We've done silly things with each other and
  our kids, like declaring it *National [insert a name]'s Day* and
  then made it their special day—just because.

° Notes with flirty messages always make us smile. Or something as simple as surprising each other with a favorite candy
  or food. The key is to pay attention and be both a good gift
  giver and receiver.

This Week's Prayer

*Father, help us to be observant and then bless each other as much
as possible every day. Enable us to demonstrate our love through
the element of gifting each other with wanted surprises.*

SCHEDULE
Thoughtfulness

Schedule Thoughtfulness

*S*ometimes, especially in difficult situations or during seasons of prolonged struggle, it's easy to fall into a rut of the status quo. One way to break free is by intentionally scheduling thoughtfulness. At first, it may sound strange to schedule thoughtfulness, but if we really want to cultivate habits toward living unified and purpose-focused, we need to use every means possible to live intentionally.

Early on, during a particularly busy season of our marriage, Greg realized we lacked spontaneity. We told each other we loved each other, but our actions didn't always display our best intentions. He decided he needed to change some things, so in his day planner, he randomly peppered reminders to express love to Julie. He blanketed the year with little notes to remind him to demonstrate that Julie was top priority. It worked like a charm. Greg's intentionality paid off.

Fast-forward a few years. Julie realized the element of surprise was missing. What we once mastered now seemed deflated. Instead of sitting back and wondering why Greg hadn't surprised her, she decided to take matters into her own hands. Throughout the week, she listened for clues from Greg and then planned activities in the calendar to spice up their date night.

Individually, begin to strategize and schedule thoughtfulness this week. As you plan activities, keep your spouse in mind.

This Week's Scripture

My beloved spoke and said to me, "Arise, my darling,
my beautiful one, come with me."

Song of Songs 2:10

This Week's Application

° Ask each other: What one task would you like for me to complete? If we went on a day or weekend trip together, where would you want to go?

° Write down three thoughtful ideas or things you'd love to have—maybe a dinner at a certain restaurant, a new fishing rod, or perfume.

° Together, share ideas of what makes you feel most loved. What helps you feel connected? Share your desires, needs, and wishes positively. As the other shares, take notes for the immediate future.

This Week's Prayer

Father, thank you for our marriage. Thank you for all we are learning. Empower us to live in such a way that we constantly demonstrate thoughtfulness and kindness to each other.

Date
YOUR
SPOUSE

Date Your Spouse

*I*f you scroll through our text messages, you'd find sporadic messages like, *Hey, babe, whatcha doing tonight? Wanna sneak away together?* Or, *Hey, sexy, I miss you. What are you doing later?* We constantly send flirty notes causing us both to chuckle. We flirt in the kitchen. We flirt over our morning cup of coffee. When our kids bust us flirting, they roll their eyes— but they are the first to suggest a date night if they sense we're frustrated or fatigued.

For us, dating is a bit interesting. After all, we're together all the time. Does a couple who are together twenty-four hours a day, seven days a week really need a date night? Absolutely.

So, what constitutes a date and what important factors need to be included?

Dating prioritizes and makes room for personal connection. It includes the opportunity for a little one-on-one time to dream together. Dating involves flirting, dressing to impress, and an attitude of seeking common ground for compatibility and friendship. It involves intentionally putting one's best foot forward, yet relaxing enough to enjoy each other's company. The date should appeal to both, even if it's specifically designed with one spouse's interest in mind.

This Week's Scripture

Come, my beloved, let us go to the countryside,
let us spend the night in the villages.

SONG OF SONGS 7:11

This Week's Application

○ Individually, write out three fun, feasible things to do on your date night. (Sometimes finances call for even more creativity, but dates don't need to be expensive. Some of our greatest dates don't cost us anything; we love sitting by the water talking about the future and our dreams.) What are some cost-free dates you'd love to do?

○ Consider some of your most fun dates. What made them so special? What elements of the date caused such fond memories? Look for ways to implement those same qualities in future dates.

○ On your date night, strategize fun questions to ask each other: What are you dreaming about? What are you most excited about? You may also change up conversations by sharing what most attracted you to each other when you first met and what attracts you to your spouse now.

This Week's Prayer

Father, motivate us to love each other and to affectionately pursue each other. Inspire us to discover qualities we have in common and activities we love to do together. Remind us to flirt as much as possible every day.

PURSUE *Intimacy,* NOT JUST SEX

Pursue Intimacy, Not Just Sex

S ociety surrounds us with sexual messages all the time. If we're not careful, we forget God's intent. Love and connection through sexual intimacy is vital for a healthy, thriving marriage.

Our intimacy in the bedroom exposes our intimacy in life. A husband and wife are never more vulnerable. How we treat each other, accept each other, and respond to each other reveals our overall health, spiritually and emotionally. So how do we pursue healthy habits in the bedroom? How do we train our minds to best celebrate marriage as God intended?

Our dear friend and author Shaunti Feldhahn writes, "97 percent of men said 'getting enough sex' wasn't by itself, enough—they wanted to feel wanted."[*] Wives feel the same. Knowing that truth should inspire us to welcome God's intention in the bedroom.

God never intended our sexual relationship to be reduced to thoughts of duty or obligation, or for a mere physical release. Instead, God designed sex to provide belonging, exclusively between a husband and a wife. He designed sex for pleasure, for comfort, and for connection in the marriage relationship.

On the next page, look at the tender exchange between the bride and her bridegroom found in Song of Solomon.

---

[*] Shaunti Feldhahn, *For Women Only: What You Need to Know About the Inner Lives of Men* (Colorado Springs: Multnomah Books, 2004), 113.

This Week's Scripture

I am my lover's and my lover is mine.

Song of Solomon 6:3 MSG

This Week's Application

- ° Individually, write down your answers to the following questions:

  - How can you create a safe atmosphere in your bedroom and communicate value to each other in your sexual expression?

  - Are there areas you need to safeguard to better protect your intimacy? If so, what are they? (For example, the shows you're watching, the things you're reading, the protocols you maintain concerning friendships with the opposite sex.)

- ° Talk about how you can pursue sexual intimacy. Share what brings you pleasure physically. Talk about the things that bring joy, excitement, and a giggle in the bedroom.

- ° Determine ways you can foster mutual connection and pleasure together.

This Week's Prayer

Father, help us to protect our relationship by always remaining faithful in our thoughts. Inspire us to pursue intimacy and provide a place of belonging in our bedroom. Enable us to provide pleasure, comfort, and connection exclusively to each other. Energize us to always look forward to our intimate time of connection, just as you intended.

REMEMBER ...
Nothing
IS IMPOSSIBLE
with God

Remember … Nothing Is Impossible with God

*D*uring an extended time of prayer, God asked us, *Is anything too difficult for me? Is anything impossible for me? Is there anything I withhold from those who love me?* Each time we sincerely answered, "No, Lord. Nothing's impossible for you. And according to your Word, you withhold nothing from those who love you."

God interrupted. *You live limited to your own thinking. You trust in your abilities, not my capabilities.*

Taken aback, we responded, "What? We trust you, Lord. We always do what you call us to."

Instead of reprimanding us, God interrupted again, whispering a huge promise. We immediately realized He was right. His plan was bigger. We lived limited. We needed to trust Him even more.

How about you? Ever limit God or reduce His miracles to what you're capable of accomplishing? If so, stretch your faith and remember that the impossible becomes possible with God. Moses lifted his staff and God parted the Red Sea. Joshua blew trumpets and the walls of Jericho crumbled. David hurled some stones from a simple sling and Goliath fell. God always involves us in the miracle, but He never leaves us to accomplish it on our own. Nothing is too big for Him.

Today, invite God's limitless power to accomplish what He called you to do together.

This Week's Scripture

Now faith is confidence in what we hope for
and assurance about what we do not see.

HEBREWS 11:1

This Week's Application

○ Meditate on Hebrews 11:1 together.

○ Ask each other: In what ways do we live limited to our *abilities* rather than trust God's *capabilities*? In what ways do we need to surrender our limitations for God's limitless power?

○ Determine how you can welcome greater spiritual connection with each other and believe for God's purpose together.

This Week's Prayer

Father, we know the impossible becomes possible with you. Remove our doubts, fears, and any limited thinking. Fill us with greater expectation and faith.

Trust God
WITH YOUR
Outcome

Trust God
with Your Outcome

G. Campbell Morgan once wrote, "Waiting for God is not laziness. ... Waiting for God is not the abandonment of effort. Waiting for God means, first, activity under command; second, readiness for any new command that may come; third, the ability to do nothing until the command is given."

Yet, if you're anything like us, waiting is frustrating. We prefer action and immediate answers to God's promises. Can you relate? If so, you've probably learned, like us, that God doesn't always provide instantaneous results.

Noah waited nearly one hundred years before he witnessed God's fulfillment. Abraham believed God but didn't receive His promise until he was around one hundred years old. After Samuel anointed David as Israel's future king, David waited approximately fifteen more years before assuming the throne.

So why does God make us wait?

Because waiting produces maturity and humility. It teaches that God's agenda and timing trump ours. Waiting prepares us to walk in the promises God has given. Though it may not be our natural inclination, God desires us to create the habit of trusting Him with our outcome. How? By surrendering our timelines to His perfect timing.

In your marriage relationship, begin to recall God's promises for your marriage and look for ways to remind each other of God's promises even as you wait.

This Week's Scripture

The Lord is good to those whose hope is in him,
to the one who seeks him; it is good to wait quietly
for the salvation of the Lord.

Lamentations 3:25–26

This Week's Application

° As you talk together, ask each other: How is God calling us
to abandon our timeline and trust Him with our outcome?

° Consider how Lamentations 3:25–26 applies to your marriage. Write down a specific promise you are waiting for God
to fulfill.

° Discuss how you can align your marriage practically and
spiritually to welcome God's promise while you await His
fulfillment.

This Week's Prayer

*Father, forgive our impatience. Reassure us of your promises and
give us strength as we wait. We surrender our timeline and trust
you to fulfill all of your promises.*

LIVE
Like You
WERE DYING

Live Like You Were Dying

*S*everal years ago, country singer Tim McGraw recorded a song titled "Live Like You Were Dying." About the same time, an initial doctor's report gave an unfavorable outcome during an annual physical for Julie. In the end, the report turned out minor, nothing life threatening, but it changed our perspective on life.

Since then, we've met parents who sent their kids out but never saw them come home. We've experienced the loss of family members and watched others battle cancer. Each tragedy reminds us of life's brevity and causes us to evaluate how we want to live. Today, we choose to live like we're dying because we know that one day, unbeknown to us, we will breathe our last. Okay, we know—kinda heavy! Yet numbering our days builds wisdom.

Think about it. How would you live if you knew you were dying? How would you spend your days? What items on your to-do list would be less important and which aspects of your life would gain more significance? Where would you put your energy? What would you say to loved ones? Obviously, you can't negligently quit your job or abandon your day-to-day demands, but you can put an intentional plan of action together so you live for what matters most.

When we live life like we're dying, we embrace a powerful new way of thinking that invites a higher way of living in our marriage.

This Week's Scripture

Teach us to number our days,
that we may gain a heart of wisdom.

Psalm 90:12

This Week's Application

- Ask each other: What do we desire our future to look like? What practical steps can we take to begin to move toward it?

- Create a bucket list of three activities you want to endeavor to do as a couple. List three destinations you want to visit together.

- Identify the legacy you want to be remembered for as a couple, and determine ways you can begin to live that legacy every day. Have fun with this!

This Week's Prayer

Father, sometimes we get so busy with trivial matters and forget to express our love to each other. We forget to honor the most precious gift you've given us—life. Remind us to encourage each other to live life abundantly, to cherish every moment and seize every opportunity you grant us. Lord, prompt us to celebrate life together.

BUILD ON
Common
GROUND

Build on Common Ground

*C*ouples who determine to build on common ground and align their marriage to follow God's purpose are *not* easily divided. But how does a couple identify and build on common ground?

Over the years, we've trained sales agents in the principle of getting five yeses. Statistically, if the product is right for the client and they say yes five times, the agent makes the sale. Truthfully, this principle also works in marriage. You can build on common ground by asking each other simple questions you know you agree on. Look for questions you both will say yes to or respond to with a positive no. For example, you might ask:

- Do we want to live into God's purpose and experience a thriving marriage? Yes.
- Do we desire to enjoy life and fill our home with laughter? Yes.
- Do we want to fight? No.
- Do we want to live divided? No.
- Do we want to leave a legacy that demonstrates love, acceptance, and forgiveness? Yes.

Create new habits of looking for all the ways you agree with each other, rather than focusing on the things you don't completely see eye to eye on.

This Week's Scripture

I appeal to you, brothers and sisters, in the name of
our Lord Jesus Christ, that all of you agree with one another
in what you say and that there be no divisions among you,
but that you be perfectly united in mind and thought.

1 CORINTHIANS 1:10

This Week's Application

- Brainstorm and write down at least five declarative statements you agree on to build common ground in your marriage.
  You might write declarative statements like: We will discover
  and live into God's purpose; We will foster fun in our home;
  We will welcome each other's differences; We will suspend
  divisive conversations until we are better able to create an
  atmosphere of moving forward together; or We will demonstrate love, acceptance, and forgiveness to each other.

- Post these statements in places where you will see them
  regularly (like on the bathroom mirror, on kitchen cabinets,
  etc.).

This Week's Prayer

*Father, assist us to identify what we agree on. Allow us to know
how to move forward to build the future you desire for us as a couple. Thank you for helping us become more unified in our thoughts
as we build on common ground together.*

Establish
YOUR CORE
Values

Establish Your Core Values

*E*very successful business, thriving church, or growing organization focuses on key values to shape their culture and accomplish their initiatives. Yet when it comes to marriage, few couples ever consider establishing the core values they will live by for their family culture.

Obviously, no couple would intentionally object to establishing core family values; most just never consider it. Still, understanding and establishing core values empowers us, much like a business, to be more successful in shaping our family culture and accomplishing our initiatives.

Last week, you initiated the process of establishing greater unity in your marriage by identifying your five yeses and creating unified statements for common ground. Your core values go even deeper. Core values reveal why you do what you do, your beliefs, and the principles and standards by which you live. When a core value is violated, we often feel frustrated or angry. So becoming aware of our core values marks the first step toward honoring them, both personally and for our spouse.

A few of our primary core values are family, freedom, authenticity, celebration, and excellence. Each value inspires us to live purposefully, to explore possibilities, and to make room for creativity and time for reflection. We say no to opportunities that threaten the well-being of our family's legacy, no matter how good the opportunity appears. We provide margin in our schedule to ensure we aren't tied down to a lot of busyness. We strive to intentionally live the same way in public as we do in private.

This Week's Scripture

Finally, all of you, be like-minded,
be sympathetic, love one another,
be compassionate and humble.

1 Peter 3:8

This Week's Application

○ Identify your shared core values by answering the following with single-word responses:

  • We value _____ (list three to five things you appreciate or treasure in life).

  • We need _____ (list three to five things essential for your well-being as a couple).

  • We feel angst if _____ (list three things that inspire peace or unity) is taken away or is lacking in our life.

○ Brainstorm your core values and what those values mean to you as a couple.

○ Post these core values in places where you will see them often.

This Week's Prayer

Father, assist us to understand what makes each other tick so we can honor each other's values, and help us to identify the values we have in common so we can live into the purpose you desire for our marriage.

Envision
YOUR *Ideal*
MARRIAGE
AND
Live Into It

Envision Your Ideal Marriage and Live into It

*W*hat do you really want for your marriage?

As kids grow up, most of them envision what their marriage will look like. They meet the spouse of their dreams, buy their dream home, and then enjoy each other's company in their happily-ever-after dream world. What keeps that vision from becoming a reality? What stops couples from living into their dreams?

For us, our dreams got muddled by the day-to-day grind. Instead of dreaming, we focused on issues needing resolution. We justified feeling short-changed. We sabotaged our dreams by living me-focused instead of we-focused. We simply got entangled in the details of life, especially our difficulties, and eventually realized what we were doing wasn't working. We broke free of the monotony by asking: What do we really want? What does God desire? And how can we live our ideal vision?

Happy, thriving couples envision a hope-filled future. They work together toward a common goal or vision. They honor each other's core values. They don't get lost in the impossibilities of their immediate circumstances; they envision their ideal outcome and take small measurable steps to move toward it together. They wholeheartedly accept that God holds a common vision for them as a couple, and welcome His Spirit to show them how to live it.

This Week's Scripture

"For I know the plans I have for you," declares the LORD,
"plans to prosper you and not to harm you,
plans to give you hope and a future."

JEREMIAH 29:11

This Week's Application

○ Take a moment together to consider your ideal marriage. What does it look like? What does it feel like? For a moment, suspend all of the things keeping you from that ideal vision and embrace God's promise and purpose for your marriage.

○ With His vision in mind, consider where you are living, what you are doing, and how you are enjoying your time together. What things would you change, and what things would you keep the same?

○ This week, spend time sharing and capturing the hope you envision of your ideal marriage. Write it down. Add more details as you dream together.

This Week's Prayer

Father, breathe fresh life into our marriage. Empower us to see what you want us to become as a couple. We welcome your plans for us. As we set our intention to dream together, invade our minds with excitement for where you are taking us.

MANAGE
FOR WHAT
Is Most
IMPORTANT

Manage for What Is Most Important

Kids, careers, and a ton of other important details of life compete for our time and shout for our attention. How does a couple truly balance it all?

Lives of regret echo with belated whispers of, "I'll do that when ..." Or, "I'm gonna do that right after ..." But if we aren't careful, our best intentions get filled with other demands and postponed to another time and another day. Unless we safeguard what matters most, we live by the whim of what seems most urgent, and busyness robs us of our desired outcome.

Our friend Tammy Maltby says *busy* means "being under Satan's yoke." Truthfully, no one escapes busyness without intentionality. If we want to develop habits that welcome vibrant, thriving marriages, we need to slow our pace and manage for what is most important. In other words, we need to carefully choose our priorities with a specific end in mind. If we don't, we find ourselves ruled by our circumstances and never really live the life we want or God intended. When we prioritize what matters most, the other details of our life fall into place and help us to restore balance.

As a couple, what do you want to safeguard and manage for in your marriage? What life-giving activities fill your needs and direct you toward what matters most? What pursuits or interests that support God's vision for your marriage do you need to prioritize?

This Week's Scripture

But seek first his kingdom and his righteousness,
and all these things
will be given to you as well.

MATTHEW 6:33

This Week's Application

○ Consider what replenishes and inspires you to be more and grow together.

○ Make a list of what's most important for you as a couple, to live into God's purpose. Maybe it's dinner around the table as a family. Or maybe it's creating greater connection by guarding your date night or taking more walks together. Maybe it's making time to replenish together physically, emotionally, or spiritually.

○ Once you create your list, schedule time for these activities in your calendar. Include them in your daily, weekly, or monthly activities. Appropriate the right amount of time for them and then defend them ferociously. Manage for them!

This Week's Prayer

Father, motivate us to prioritize and manage for the things that are most important. Show us how to honor you, and each other, by what we do daily.

MANAGE
Against
THINGS THAT
Sabotage

Manage Against Things That Sabotage

*W*hat keeps you from moving forward as a couple? What steals your energy or sabotages your time for connection with each other?

We frequently hear couples say, "We just don't have enough time." Yet time hasn't changed. We all share the same allotted twenty-four hours in each day. The real question is, how will we spend it? When we say we don't have enough time, what we're really saying is we need to prioritize what matters most and manage against the things that sabotage us.

What keeps you from growing together as a couple? What sabotages the achievements of your dreams or purpose? What threatens your time for dreaming together or connecting spiritually, emotionally, and physically?

Last week, you identified activities you wanted to manage for and prioritize into your schedule. This week, create the habit of removing the distractions or hindrances that sabotage your intentions. For example, do you busy your life by pursuing approval from others and unintentionally sabotage your own relationship's well-being? If saying yes seems your natural inclination and you find yourself involved in unwanted activities, consider practicing saying no for a while or responding with, "I need to check our schedule and get back to you."

In order to optimize and safeguard your priorities while fully enjoying quality time together, recognize what you need to manage against and fiercely safeguard against them.

This Week's Scripture

Be very careful, then, how you live—
not as unwise but as wise, making the most
of every opportunity, because the days are evil.

EPHESIANS 5:15–16

This Week's Application

- ° Identify your greatest time-wasters as a couple, and consider how you will minimize them.

- ° Discuss which activities keep you from enjoying more quality time together as a couple, and determine how you can remove them from your life.

- ° Focus on becoming united in your decisions and activities. What are some ways you can do this?

This Week's Prayer

Father, embolden us to put away the things that sabotage your purpose for us. Inspire us to enjoy our marriage, and each other, as we fight for our relationship and vision together.

Don't Settle
**FOR WHAT'S
GOOD ...**
Live for
WHAT'S *Great*

Don't Settle for What's Good ... Live for What's Great

*W*e all know the value of healthy compromise. As a couple, we need to cooperate and work together. But we should never compromise God's purpose. Too often, convenience sabotages living God's purpose. We make concessions, yielding to settle for what's good rather than inching forward to grab hold of God's best.

In Genesis 25, we read the story of Jacob and Esau. In essence, Jacob's got an awesome stew brewing. Esau, returning home from a hunt, says, "Quick, let me have some of that red stew! I'm famished!" Jacob replies, "First sell me your birthright." Jacob makes Esau sell him his birthright for a bowl of soup, and Esau's impatience and insatiable hunger for immediate gratification cost him his future.

Seems crazy, eh? Who gives up their promise for something as small as a bowl of soup?

Maybe the greater question is, will we sacrifice God's favor for immediate relief? Will we give up pursuing His purpose for our marriage, for our own immediate pleasure? Will we succumb to the status quo and get lured away from God's best, to pursue things like wealth, recognition, or a life of comfort?

Author Jim Collins points out, "Good is the enemy of great."* How can you align your marriage to actively pursue God's specific design? Have you compromised living His purpose by settling for something good, rather than living for what's great?

---

* Jim Collins, *Good to Great: Why Some Companies Make the Leap ... and Others Don't* (New York: HarperCollins Publishers Inc., 2001), 1.

This Week's Scripture

The wisdom of the prudent is to give thought to their ways, but the folly of fools is deception.

PROVERBS 14:8

This Week's Application

○ Over the last several weeks you've identified priorities you'd like to honor in your relationship. Are there areas in which you find yourself subtly selling out? In what areas have you become complacent or have negotiated your future for an immediate payoff?

○ When you think of God's perfect vision for your marriage, what areas have you stopped pursuing, or in what ways have you compromised His purpose? Reclaim His best. Talk about your future. Celebrate your growth. Remember to devote your time and energy to the things that matter the most.

○ Determine small steps of obedience you can take each day this week that will offer long-term payoffs for your future. Get them on the calendar if needed. Pray together and commit to pursue God's purpose as a couple.

This Week's Prayer

Father, inspire us to live in complete integrity. Cause us to recognize any compromises keeping us from living your perfect vision for our marriage. Empower us to encourage each other to embrace all you created us to do as a couple. In Jesus' name, amen.

DETERMINE
YOUR
Non-Negotiables

Determine Your Non-Negotiables

*E*ver hear the phrase "Never say never"? Or how about "Never use the words *never* or *always*"? Though overtures of accusation like "You never" or "You always" tend to exaggerate and escalate conversations, using words like *never* and *always* can help us define healthy boundaries for our relationship.

For example, think about the following statements. We will *never* lie. We will *never* steal. We will *never* cheat. Or how about the word *always* in the following statements. We will *always* love each other. We will *always* demonstrate respect. We will *always* choose to believe the best about each other and openly communicate that belief.

Determining our non-negotiables provides security in our marriage and helps us plan to win. As we create new habits to grow as a couple and live out God's purpose for our marriage, we need to declare what we will *never* compromise, no matter what. To sustain our marriage purpose, we need to clearly define what we will *always* protect.

What are the non-negotiables in your marriage? As a couple, what will you *never* compromise? And what will you *always* pursue and protect?

Zig Ziglar once said, "You were born to win, but to be a winner, you must plan to win, and expect to win."* Zig understood the importance of *never* compromising God's purpose and *always* pursuing it in such a way as to win. The apostle Paul put it another way in 1 Corinthians.

---

* Zig Ziglar, quoted at https://www.ziglar.com/quotes/you-were-born-to-win-but-to-be-a-winner/ (accessed August 8, 2017).

This Week's Scripture

Do you not know that in a race all the runners run,
but only one gets the prize?
Run in such a way as to get the prize.

1 CORINTHIANS 9:24

This Week's Application

○ Together, on a sheet of paper, brainstorm and write down the non-negotiables concerning your careers, family, and faith. Finish this statement: "We will never _____." On a separate page, complete this statement: "We will always _____." Include every aspect of your relationship—physical, intellectual, emotional, and spiritual.

○ Make your non-negotiables list a matter of prayer, and use it to speak words of affirmation over each other. For example: I will always make time for you. I will always put you above my career. I will never speak badly about you to others. And then live in such a way as to honor your list.

This Week's Prayer

Father, cause us to compromise and work toward a common vision but to never compromise living as one toward your purpose. May we never concede for what's good but always pursue your best, together.

DON'T LIVE
Resigned…
PURSUE GOD'S
Design

Don't Live Resigned ...
Pursue God's Design

*O*ur weekend was set. We dove into (a couple we'll refer to as) Harry and Sally's marriage retreat with great excitement. We prepared charts, outlined vision sheets, and felt prepared spiritually to facilitate growth. We opened their private couple's retreat with a typical question to stir conversation: "By the time we conclude our time together, what do you want to see happen?"

We asked primary objectives. We asked secondary questions to appeal to every life domain. The more we asked, the more we realized Harry and Sally seemed content to simply bide their time together. They reduced their relationship to convenience and cohabitation. When we probed deeper, we realized they hadn't experienced any major upsets. Neither had been unfaithful. No abuse occurred. Instead, a gradual fade reduced them to living resigned to an almost catatonic-like indifference to each other. They seemed comfortable shrugging away whatever came their way, impassively and withdrawn.

Helen Keller once said, "The most pathetic person in the world is someone who has sight but no vision." One thing is for certain, God never intended for us to live our marriage resigned. He desires for you to pursue His design and live life abundantly together. He longs for us to live inspired, to dream about our marriage purpose, and to pursue His design as a couple.

This Week's Scripture

The thief comes only to steal and kill and destroy;
I have come that they may have life, and have it to the full.

JOHN 10:10

This Week's Application

- Answer these questions:

  - As a couple, what inspires you?

  - What fills you with passion?

  - Together, who do you most care about?

- Each day this week, consider your answers to these questions. Determine ways you can use these answers to avoid resignation in your marriage.

- Grab your calendar and schedule time to specifically pursue these things together. Which things will you pursue first and why?

This Week's Prayer

Father, inspire us to pursue your design for our marriage and to never settle for less. We want to enjoy our marriage to its fullest. Show us how to best do that and honor each other.

Determine
SMALL
Measurable
STEPS

Determine Small Measurable Steps

A few years back, a couple of our close relatives visited us in our new Florida home. Being adventurous, they decided to take the scenic route. What they didn't account for was the wear and tear they'd experience physically during their journey. By the time they arrived, they were exhausted. Their joints hurt. Their muscles felt stiff and sore. Each time we suggested an activity, they politely declined. Truthfully, they could barely get up off the couch much less walk the beach. In sheer exhaustion, they decided to go back home.

As we waved goodbye, we said hello to a new future. Their struggle inspired us to make changes in our health. That day, we made decisions to join a gym, hire a trainer, and change the foods we ate. The changes weren't easy, but we knew what our future looked like if we didn't make them. We decided to radically pursue healthy living.

We disciplined ourselves to go to the gym, setting a minimum requirement of working out three times a week. We hired a trainer to keep us accountable, and avoided old staples in our diet by intentionally not purchasing potatoes, pizza, or pasta. Each small measurable step provided us with accountability to secure our desired result. Here's the good news: what once took a lot of discipline, we now enjoy as everyday habits.

So how about you and your desire to grow together as a couple? What disciplines can you apply to your daily efforts to secure your success?

This Week's Scripture

Let us not become weary in doing good,
for at the proper time we will reap a harvest
if we do not give up.

GALATIANS 6:9

This Week's Application

° For each of the following areas of your relationship, consider one way you can take a small, measurable step toward growth: physical fitness, emotional connection, sexual intimacy, financial unity, and family well-being.

° Once you've listed some of the small measurable steps, decide how you'll implement them together.

° At the end of the week, come back together and celebrate your areas of growth.

This Week's Prayer

Father, Scripture says if we commit our way to you, that you will direct our steps. Grant us wisdom to know which steps will produce the most life and move us to grow together as a couple.

SOW
Generously

Sow Generously

*I*t doesn't take a degree in botany to know that if you plant green bean seeds, you'll reap green beans. If you plant corn, a tomato plant won't magically pop out of the ground. The application remains the same for our marriage. We reap what we sow. The question arises: What seeds are you planting today that you'll harvest tomorrow?

In Galatians, the apostle Paul writes, "Do not be deceived: God cannot be mocked. Whatever a man sows, he will reap in return. The one who sows to please the flesh, from the flesh will reap destruction, but the one who sows to please the Spirit, from the Spirit will reap eternal life" (Galatians 6:7–8 BSB). Your commitment to reading this book demonstrates your desire to cultivate new habits of thought to grow your relationship. Your commitment will reap a harvest. So don't ever give up. Remember, what you feed grows and what you starve dies.

Last week, you specifically committed to determine and then implement small measurable steps in a variety of relationship areas. Diligently tend to and care for each seed you've planted. This week, concentrate specifically on your spiritual walk together. After all, as the apostle Paul pointed out, when we sow to please the Spirit, from the Spirit we reap eternal life. Our spiritual oneness impacts every area of our marriage. When we invest in our spiritual growth together, we reap life, wisdom, direction, and unity as a couple.

This Week's Scripture

Whoever sows sparingly will also reap sparingly,
and whoever sows generously will also reap generously.

2 CORINTHIANS 9:6

This Week's Application

○ Take a few moments to share one or two things God has been teaching you individually throughout this devotional.

○ Ask each other a few spiritual questions. For example: What about this week's Scripture stands out to you? How does this Scripture apply specifically to your life?

○ Grab your calendar and schedule two activities together to plant some intentional seeds for spiritual growth. How can you sow generously to reap huge spiritual rewards?

This Week's Prayer

Father, inspire us to plant seeds that unite us spiritually. Spur us to develop the habit of talking freely together and sharing what you are teaching. Quicken us to always provide each other space to share thoughts without judgment. We want to keep you first in our relationship. Show us ways we can do that so we reap the best harvest possible.

SCHEDULE TIME FOR
Reflection

Schedule Time for Reflection

*O*ur friend Scott Fay, who is vice president of the John Maxwell Team, writes, "Too many people just accept their lives rather than lead their lives."[*] If we want to lead our life and grow together in our marriage, we need to schedule time for reflection.

Several years ago, we realized that we spent a lot of time ministering to others. We advised couples to vacation together but rarely vacationed. We encouraged them to steal away from their day-to-day routine but maintained a packed schedule in our own marriage.

Our negligence resulted in a lot of busy activity. We kept saying yes to more and more. Each activity seemed important, worthy of our time, and even noble. But as we busied our lives helping others, we neglected our own need for personal retreat and time for reflection. Because we lacked time to reflect, we couldn't accurately discern what we needed to say yes to from what we needed to say no to. We felt stressed out and maxed out. It was time for our own personal retreat!

We quickly cleared an entire week's schedule and made time for reflection. We spent the first couple of days detoxing from life's busyness. We slept in. We laid in the sun. We ate at our favorite restaurants. Around day three, we analyzed where we were, where we were going, and what we needed to do to get there. We envisioned our future and spent time dreaming together. By the week's end, we held a clear plan of action of what to say yes to and what to say no to. Today, we intentionally protect our time for reflection, knowing how much it helps us protect our own relationship.

---

[*] Scott M. Fay, *Discover Your Sweet Spot* (New York: Morgan James Publishing, 2014), 14.

This Week's Scripture

Then, because so many people were coming
and going that they did not even have a chance to eat,
he said to them, "Come with me by yourselves
to a quiet place and get some rest."

Mark 6:31

This Week's Application

○ As a couple, is it time for a personal retreat? Take time now to find a time when you can get away for a week, a weekend, or even a night.

○ Schedule a time in the near future for regular personal reflection together.

○ During your times of reflection, talk about where you are, where you've come from, how much you've grown, and where you are heading.

This Week's Prayer

Father, as we serve others, remind us to always take time for each other to reflect and seek you together. Fill our thoughts with your thoughts. And help us to get away to a quiet place to rest, to discern what you think is best for our relationship.

Celebrate
YOUR *Progress*

Celebrate Your Progress

*A*ll of our children walked by the age of nine months old. We cheered each step. We celebrated every time they successfully put one foot in front of the other. Did they topple to the ground? Of course. Did we ever think, *Oh no. They're never going to get this*? Of course not. We understood their progress involved a process. Over time, they would learn balance. Their leg muscles would strengthen. Eventually, they would not only walk but would also run.

Growing together and living God's purpose for our marriage requires a process too. As we embrace the process (by introducing healthy habits of serving each other and putting each other's needs first), we learn how to thrive together. Will we stumble and even fall a time or two? Of course. But that doesn't mean we are doomed to failure. Eventually, we strengthen the right muscles by implementing the right habits. Our progress always involves a process.

Lao Tzu wrote, "A journey of a thousand miles begins with a single step."* So don't get worried if implementing new habits takes a little more time or intentionality than you first expected; instead, celebrate your progress. Eventually, you won't just walk; you will run!

---

* "A journey of a thousand miles begins with a single step," *Wikipedia*, https:// en.wikipedia.org/wiki/A_journey_of_a_thousand_miles_begins_with_a_single _step (accessed August 8, 2017).

This Week's Scripture

Those who hope in the LORD will renew their strength.
They will soar on wings like eagles; they will run and not
grow weary, they will walk and not be faint.

ISAIAH 40:31

This Week's Application

° Buildings aren't built overnight, and plants don't produce a harvest the morning after planting. Reflect on and celebrate how you've grown as a couple, even since you first began reading this devotional. Pray together, thanking God for your areas of growth.

° Each day, speak affirmation of the ways you appreciate your spouse. Celebrate together in some way.

° Write down your answers to these sentences individually, and then share your answers together: One of the ways I think we've grown the most is _____. I love that we implemented _____ in our marriage.

This Week's Prayer

Father, thank you that we are developing an increased hunger to learn and grow together. Energize us to celebrate our growth. Reveal new ways for us to honor each other, to laugh, and to celebrate our progress. Enable us to see how much we are growing and becoming who you intend for us to be.

Enjoy Every
MOMENT ...
Embrace
THE PROCESS

Enjoy Every Moment ...
Embrace the Process

*W*e hate to admit it, but sometimes we get wrapped up in the details of life. We get frustrated by our day-to-day struggles and forget to enjoy the journey. How about you? Ever get so future-minded that you fail to enjoy the moment? Ever get frustrated waiting for your breakthrough?

Several years ago, God taught us a powerful life lesson and called us to a new habit of living. Julie was about seven months pregnant, and it was one of the hottest summers we'd experienced in a while. She felt worn out from all the sleepless nights, her swollenness, and her stretched-out belly. She frequently said, "I'm so ready to be done with all of this!" Amid her frustrations, God interrupted her thoughts with His: *This will be the last time you experience pregnancy. Soak in every kick. Enjoy every moment. Embrace the process.*

His thoughts impacted both of us powerfully. We realized that we often failed to enjoy the simple moments of life—not just in pregnancy, but in many aspects.

God wants each of us and every married couple to choose life every day. Choose to enjoy every moment. Choose to embrace the process and celebrate your journey together daily.

This Week's Scripture

Choose life, so that you and your children
may live and that you may love the LORD your God,
listen to his voice, and hold fast to him.

DEUTERONOMY 30:19–20

This Week's Application

- No matter what your facing, God is with you. As a father, He desires for you to celebrate the gifts He's given. Each day this week, express one thing you're thankful for and one way you appreciate your spouse.

- Talk together about what is going well. Where have you made progress within your process? How can you appreciate the current moment?

- Determine ways that you can choose to laugh, love, and live life to its fullest. Journal how God is calling you to embrace His process.

This Week's Prayer

Father, remind us to patiently embrace the journey we are on together. Teach us to capture and enjoy the moments in each day. Assist us in cultivating the habit of an attitude of gratitude.

INSTEAD OF *Doing,* PRACTICE *Being*

Instead of Doing, Practice Being

*E*ver get distracted *doing* for God, or substitute your intimacy *with* Him in an exchange of activity *for* Him?

Sometimes we pick up weights God never intended us to carry. Sometimes we preoccupy ourselves with busyness and strain beneath the weight of "accomplishment." Can you relate? Does your ambition to do great things for God ever distract you from the joy of a loving relationship with Him?

As you pursue living more purpose-focused and embrace a unified vision as a couple, remember that above all, God desires your love. He desires a relationship with you. He desires for your *doing* to flow out of your *being*. He designed you with specific gifts and passions, and wants you to experience the joy of operating in those gifts.

So instead of succumbing to busy activities of *doing* for God, make every effort to *be* with God. When we pursue Him, our relationship inspires us and reveals how we can best offer our gifts back to Him as an expression of our love, devotion, and gratitude.

This Week's Scripture

"Martha, Martha," the Lord replied, "you are worried and upset about many things. But only one thing is necessary. Mary has chosen the good portion, and it will not be taken away from her."

Luke 10:42 BSB

This Week's Application

- Discuss whether each of you tends to be a Martha or a Mary. What are the pros and cons of each type of personality?

- Answer the following question: How can we better pursue a relationship with God and practice being for Him, instead of falling prey to the weight of doing for Him?

- What are some practical steps you can take when you feel pressed to do even though God just wants you to be with Him?

This Week's Prayer

Father, show us how to serve you best and in such a way that we aren't striving or busying our lives with hectic activities. Inspire us to serve you and fully enjoy using our gifts for your purposes.

STARVE
the Lies ...
FEED
the Truth

Starve the Lies ...
Feed the Truth

*Y*ears ago, the enemy taunted us with feelings of inferiority: *You're no-names from a no-name little town, and you are divorcees!* Honestly, we wanted to refute him. We wanted to contradict his accusations. We wanted to claim Scriptures to repudiate his indictments. Instead, we realized he was right—but only in part.

Isn't that how the enemy accuses? As the father of lies, he whispers half-truths laced with lies in an attempt to discourage and confuse us. In marriage, he whispers accusations against our spouse like: "He never helps with the housework." Or, "If she would say thank you more, then I wouldn't mind giving her a hand." When we feed his lies, we find reason to justify them and intensify the lies.

God desires us to live above the enemy's accusations by creating new habits of thought that welcome who He says we are as a couple. God desires us to starve the lies and feed the truth.

How? Simple. When the enemy laces his lies by whispering half-truths filled with accusation, agree with him. But don't stop there. Remind him (and each other) of the full truth of who God declares you to be. Encourage each other with thoughts or Scriptures to support truths like: "Our differences make us stronger." And, "God destined us for a purpose together."

This Week's Scripture

"You will know the truth,
and the truth will set you free."

John 8:32

This Week's Application

- ○ Remember, what you feed grows and what you starve dies. Take inventory of your thoughts. What thoughts are you feeding, individually and as a couple?

- ○ Spend time reminding each other of and being encouraged by God's promises. What is He speaking about you? What has He promised to you through Scripture? What does His Word declare about you as a couple?

- ○ Turn those promises into prayers and declare them over your marriage.

This Week's Prayer

Father, enable us to replace half-truths with the full truth of who you declare us to be. Set us free from discouragement and fear. Inspire us to pursue you, and align our marriage to be all it can be in you.

LIFT THE LID ...
Remember
GOD'S *Promise*

Lift the Lid …
Remember God's Promise

*W*orking in corporate America exposed us to inspiring thoughts from motivational writers and speakers all across the world. Somewhere along our journey, we heard a powerful illustration concerning a flea trainer who conditioned fleas to remain trapped inside an uncovered glass. Articles, YouTube videos, and speakers tell how, in the beginning, the flea jumps up only to hit the top of the lid. Eventually, the flea only jumps as high as the lid. The trainer then removes the lid, but the flea stays trapped even though the lid no longer exists.

We're not sure who caught fleas or figured out how to condition them to stay trapped—or what in the world possessed them to conjure up the idea—but one thing is for certain: every day, couples are conditioned by their own limiting beliefs. We've certainly hit our head on the proverbial lid of life, felt frustrated by our inability to jump free, and believed we were trapped.

Throughout marriage, every couple encounters barriers or lids. Your lid may be a doubt of your abilities. It may be past mistakes or failures. Or it may be cruel words or past pains. At times, you may feel as though you've jumped, time after time, only to hit your head on those confining lids. Today you may find yourself conditioned—still jumping but not with as much effort as before. If so, it's time for new conditioning.

How do you jump to reclaim the freedom God designed for you as a couple? Lift the lid by remembering God's promises, and recondition your mind to believe He will do what He says He will do.

This Week's Scripture

The one who calls you is faithful,
and he will do it.

1 Thessalonians 5:24

This Week's Application

- Scriptures say, "If you believe, you will receive whatever you ask for in prayer" (Matthew 21:22), and "If you have faith as small as a mustard seed, you can say to this mountain, 'Move from here to there,' and it will be moved" (Matthew 17:20). Discuss together what limitations you need to let go of or beliefs that are holding you back as a couple.

- Choose two things you will ask God for, and believe God for them.

- Each day this week, pray the prayer below together. Include in your prayer the specifics of what you are believing God to do in your marriage.

This Week's Prayer

Father, spur us on to believe for more and to welcome your promises. Help us to lift the lid and reclaim all you created us to be. We want to make a bigger impact as a couple.

Don't Mistake
GOD'S SILENCE
AS GOD'S
ABSENCE

Don't Mistake God's Silence as God's Absence

*E*ver get discouraged by the in-between times of life—like the time between hearing God's promise and waiting for Him to fulfill it? Ever ask questions like: "God, didn't you promise us that …"; "Didn't you say …"; or "Why is all of this happening? Where are you?" If so, you're not alone.

When we stepped out to follow God, we felt as if we walked out of a dream into a nightmare. Nothing made sense. During that season, God taught us an incredible truth. Today when we face adversity and struggles, we remind ourselves of that truth: Don't mistake God's silence as God's absence.

God always has a reason for the season. The things we perceive as good and the things we perceive as bad are simply the circumstances God uses to prepare us and position us for His promise.

In 1 Samuel, we read how Samuel anoints David as Israel's future king. But then, according to Scripture, David went back to tending sheep. What? Why? Later, God reveals skills David learned as he tended the sheep. In the wilderness, he learned how to kill the bear and the lion—the very skill that brought down Goliath, the feat that ultimately positioned David in the palace.

The same holds true for our marriage. What we consider "wasted years" actually prepares us to receive God's promise.

This Week's Scripture

"Be strong and courageous.
Do not be afraid or terrified because of them,
for the LORD your God goes with you;
he will never leave you nor forsake you."

DEUTERONOMY 31:6

This Week's Application

- ○ Think back over your life, both individually and as a couple. How has God used the in-between time to prepare you for something you would later face?

- ○ In every season of life, whether mountain top or valley low, setting aside time to replenish ourselves is vital. What helps you feel rested, inspired, or rejuvenated?

- ○ Together, schedule time to participate in activities that renew you physically, intellectually, emotionally, and spiritually. What things will you do first?

This Week's Prayer

Father, thank you that you are for us. Show us ways to recharge as a couple. Refresh us and fill us with strength, boldness, and laughter. Comfort us with your presence. Reminds us that you see us, hear us, and are near. Give us wisdom and clarity to know what steps to take next.

Align
YOUR ACTIONS
TO FOLLOW
God's Vision

Align Your Actions
to Follow God's Vision

*I*n our book *Two Are Better Than One* we wrote, "Our thoughts become our actions, our actions become our habits, our habits become our character, and our character defines who we are. Who we are determines how we do everything."*

You are on a powerful journey of creating new habits to a higher way of living as a couple. As you align your actions to follow His vision, remember that God is not bound by time or space. He sees your past, present, and future simultaneously; thus, when He whispered His promises to you in the past, He already saw them in their fulfillment.

He holds a plan and future for the two of you together. And He desires to communicate His plans and purpose for your marriage. So, what is God saying? What promises is He giving to you as a couple?

As you quiet yourselves together this week, share the direction you feel God leading you. Remind each other of God's promises and His faithfulness despite positive or negative circumstances. Consider ways you can boldly hold fast to God's promises and better align your life and marriage to follow Him.

After all, faith isn't conjuring up some noble notion and saying, "Here we go, God. Now bless." Faith simply hears God's voice and aligns to follow Him no matter what.

This Week's Scripture

* Greg and Julie Gorman, *Two Are Better Than One: God Has a Purpose for Your Marriage* (Racine, WI: BroadStreet Publishing Group, 2016), 64.

"I will not leave you until I have done
what I have promised you."

GENESIS 28:15

This Week's Application

○ Revisit the vision you shared together (concerning your ideal marriage) from week sixteen. Are there thoughts you need to shift? Are there actions you need to reinstate? What habits do you need to recommit to, in order to optimize your efforts and best live your ideal marriage? Are there areas of your life or character that need to be realigned in your marriage?

○ Write down some of the promises God has given you as a couple (or take them from week forty) and how He has brought any of them to pass in time. Each day this week read those promises to each other. When waiting for promises becomes frustrating, use these as reminders of His faithfulness.

○ List three practical ways you will commit to align your life to follow God's vision.

This Week's Prayer

Father, we put our trust in you. Thank you for never leaving us. We are listening to you. Thank you for your promises and for what is to come. Thank you in advance for leading us as a couple.

RELEASE
the Outcome

Release the Outcome

*E*ver feel stuck between surrender and action? Though surrender and action are necessary, sometimes they seem to compete with each other. The art of surrender and pursuing God's purpose resides in our understanding; God is God, and we are not. He won't always fit into the nice little neat box we try to fit Him in; He's much bigger. If we can ever fully explain God, we've made Him too small. So even when we don't understand God's actions, we can always trust His character. After all, He isn't just the essence of love; He *is* love.

Over a three-year span of time, God posed us with the same question: *Will you serve me here? If this is all it is, if you never fully experience the promises I've given, will you serve me right where you are, no matter what?* Each time, we answered with a resounding, "Yes, Lord! If this is all it is, we will serve you here." Until one day, at our absolute lowest, for the first time ever, we replied with a condition: we needed to know He still loved us and that He was near.

After giving our condition, God awakened Julie with this thought: *Faith isn't contingent on the outcome of your circumstances. Faith resides in the unshakable confidence of who I am and my good intent toward you.* In that moment, God reminded us that His intent toward us was good, regardless of what we saw at that time. Our circumstances didn't negate His love. And He called us to release our outcome to Him.

This Week's Scripture

And we know that in all things
God works for the good of those who love him,
who have been called according to his purpose.

Romans 8:28

This Week's Application

° Discuss a few ways that you, as a couple, can practice surrender and release your outcome to God, while maintaining
  a steady walk toward His promise.

° Ask each other: How can I best encourage you this week?
  What one thing are you believing God for that I can pray with
  you about? Then pray for each other.

° List some scriptural promises that will help you keep faith
  during times when you're not seeing God's plan—or when
  His plan isn't what you'd hoped for.

This Week's Prayer

*Father, thank you for being our strong tower in all seasons. We
stop now to acknowledge that we trust you. Help us to discern how
we can actively pursue you and believe for the best, while always
releasing the outcome to you.*

DO THE
Unexpected

Do the Unexpected

*L*et's face it, following God doesn't always make sense in the natural.

Can you imagine bystanders looking at Gideon, speculating, "You're going to reduce your army of how many thousands to just three hundred men? And God told you to do it?" Or how about David throwing off all conventional methods of battle and running full force, with just a sling and five stones, to slay the feared Goliath? Yet David never shrank from the bear or lion *nor* did he cower at Goliath. Then when Saul sought his life, David bravely spared Saul's life, determining not to raise a hand against God's anointed. David trusted God to defend his life and lived above his circumstances.

Then there's Abraham, who bravely put Isaac on the altar, trusting in God's character and His ability; he reckoned God could raise Isaac from the dead. He knew God's promise existed through Isaac and trusted Him to fulfill that promise. Or how about when Joshua and Caleb surveyed the land? Can you imagine their report? "Giants? Sure, there are giants! But you should see the size of those grapes!"

Bravery looks past conventional wisdom, past consequences and costs, and simply listens for the still small voice asking, "What has God said?"

This Week's Scripture

"As the heavens are higher than the earth,
so are my ways higher than your ways
and my thoughts than your thoughts."

Isaiah 55:9

This Week's Application

- ° Pursuing God's purpose requires listening for God's voice and trusting His wisdom. Take a moment to share your thoughts together: What's the craziest thing God ever asked you do? What's the most personal way He's spoken to you? Share your answers with each other.

- ° Each day this week, look for opportunities to consult God (through His Word or in prayer) and listen for His direction. What is He saying to you?

- ° Come together each night and discuss a way God surprised you. Have fun tapping into God's sense of humor.

This Week's Prayer

Father, speak to us clearly. Direct us. Give us the strength to obey. Fill us with faith to live bravely for you. Remind us to appreciate that your wisdom is higher than ours. Inspire us to laugh together with you. We love you, Lord.

MANAGE
for
MARGIN

Manage for Margin

*W*ork. Groceries. Football and swim practice. Day-to-day activities hold the potential to distract us from our purpose. It's all the little "Don't forget we have to …" and the "On your way, could you just…" that creep in to steal our time. If we aren't careful, we find ourselves running frantically from one thing to another, until the items on our to-do list become obligations rather than celebrations. We start to stress as timelines and deadlines get pressed, crunching our want-tos with our have-tos.

What's a couple to do? Articles peppered across the Internet suggest that chronic stress leads to disease. But how do we change the way we live?

As with every habit of living into God's higher way of living for our marriage, our victory begins in our mind-set. Changing the way we live means changing the way we think. When life gets busy, recognize it and reprioritize. Align your actions and your calendar with what matters most. Recognize and talk about the season of life you're in as a couple, and empower each other to say no to activities without guilt. Remember, "good is the enemy of great."*

Every quarter, we reprioritize our schedule. We schedule our projects, deadlines, speaking engagements, and conferences. We insert our kid's activities, special days, and family trips. We block out days for reflection, rest, and connection, and include buffer times on all of our deadlines. As we manage for margin, we reduce our stress and position our lives to celebrate each and every day.

---

* Jim Collins, *Good to Great: Why Some Companies Make the Leap … and Others Don't* (New York: HarperCollins Publishers Inc., 2001), 1.

This Week's Scripture

Trust in the LORD with all your heart
and lean not on your own understanding;
in all your ways submit to him,
and he will make your paths straight.

PROVERBS 3:5–6

This Week's Application

○ Together, consider your current schedule. As you fill it this week and next, consistently ask each other: Will this activity help or hinder our desired result as a couple?

○ Guard against time-wasters by frequently asking each other: What's our desired outcome for our marriage? What is God's intention for us?

○ Plan for your future. Let your answers guide you to remove unwanted distractions and to set your attention on God's intention. Make a list of some distractions you need to eliminate, and then eliminate a few of them in your schedule this week.

This Week's Prayer

Father, we want to love you first and celebrate life every day. Cause us to safeguard our time and honor you in it. Quicken us to better recognize what we need to say yes to and what we need to say no to, in order to build healthy margin for our marriage.

REPLENISH
Together

Replenish Together

I can't do this anymore! I hate our life. We never have time for us." Rash words spoken in a moment's flare cause couples to feel wounded and defeated. Eventually, dissension escalates. And as stressors mount, so do the walls between us.

Lack of replenishment in any marriage leaves couples depleted. So if you find yourself feeling short-fused, ready to explode, or (at a minimum) less than your best, more than likely you've forgotten to replenish.

After all, we can't give what we don't possess. If we are destitute, we can't provide for others. The best relationships make room for renewal and replenishment individually and together. True rest begins in the mind. Replenishment isn't just implementing a structured, organized plan; it includes positioning our hearts with a right attitude and renewing our mind.

Think about it. Ever schedule a date night, but instead of discovering each other, you replay the details of the day, consumed by looming tasks or deadlines in your mind? Or how about this: You're on vacation, but the wind and the waves can't relieve the steam of the pressure cooker you feel yourself in. Just how do we renew our mind? How do we replenish together with our spouse?

Jesus provides the solution for burnout: "Come away. Abide in me. And find rest!"

This Week's Scripture

Remain in me, as I also remain in you.
No branch can bear fruit by itself; it must remain in the vine.
Neither can you bear fruit unless you remain in me.

JOHN 15:4

This Week's Application

○ This week, brainstorm and list activities that renew you physically, emotionally, intellectually, and spiritually. This list shouldn't be a have-to list; it's a get-to list. Here are a few suggestions to get you started: take walks together, read a book together, listen to a podcast or sermon, or get a couple's massage.

○ Once you have your list, commit to doing those activities daily, weekly, or monthly. Put them on your schedule.

○ Pray with each other daily this week, even if it's only for a few minutes. Even when life gets busy, the renewal that comes from being in God's presence will help when you're between replenishment activities.

This Week's Prayer

Father, replenish our strength—physically, emotionally, intellectually, and spiritually. Fill our thoughts with your thoughts, and assist us to create better habits to live your purpose. Remind us to renew ourselves together!

Wait Patiently
AS YOU
Seize Your
PROMISE

Wait Patiently as You Seize Your Promise

*E*ver wonder why God makes us wait after He whispers a big promise? If you're anything like us, we despise waiting. If we aren't fifteen minutes early, we're running late. Sometimes we try to confine God's promises for our marriage to our timeline. Can you relate?

If so, remind each other of this powerful truth: God loves us enough to cause us to wait. Waiting refines our motives, removes impurities, and builds faith in what matters most. Our accomplishments aren't what matter most, and our end destination of fulfilled dreams aren't what matter most. What matters most is our journey of building a living, loving relationship with God together. Waiting actually prepares us to receive our long-awaited promise.

In Exodus 23:27–30, God shares how He wouldn't drive away all of Israel's enemies in a single year because the land would become desolate and the wild animals too numerous for them. Instead, He says, "Little by little I will drive them out before you, until you have increased enough to take possession of the land" (v. 30).

God didn't give His people the full promise of His blessing until they were prepared to manage, enjoy, and fully handle the possession of the promise. We can apply this truth to our marriage. In our journey toward embracing God's purpose as a couple and experiencing His promise, we encounter the process.

This Week's Scripture

Little by little I will drive them out before you, until you have increased enough to take possession of the land.

EXODUS 23:30

This Week's Application

° Consider some ways you can encourage each other to rest confidently in God's love and enjoy every season of life. Discuss three things you can celebrate together.

° As you wait patiently, share the things you are thankful for as a couple, and any lessons God has taught you lately. What is He pointing out to you individually and as a couple?

° Discuss how you want to grow and become all God created you to be.

This Week's Prayer

Father, your timing is perfect. We trust you with our present and our future. Remind us to remain strong for each other and to embrace the process leading to the fulfillment of your promise. Help us to encourage each other as we move forward.

Fight For (NOT WITH) Your Spouse

Fight for (Not with) Your Spouse

*I*n their book *The Seven Conflicts*, Tim and Joy Down write, "Each of us is born with an instinctive 'me first' attitude. But in marriage, each husband and wife has to cultivate a 'we first' mentality—and each needs to know that his or her partner shares that value."*

Several years ago, we faced huge decisions and even bigger battles. We moved three times and lived in three separate states all within an eleven-month period. No one knew of our previous success and no one cared. We were estranged from friends and stricken financially, and our faith felt assaulted. Everything we believed in seemed challenged.

Thankfully, our adversity caused an uncompromising unity. We sought to ensure each other's dreams would come true. Greg tirelessly worked two jobs to allow Julie to write and minister. Julie fasted and prayed for Greg and constantly offered encouragement and belief in his worth. Together we fought against the lies of how the other didn't measure up. Though we struggled, neither of us caved to giving up on our pursuit of living God's purpose. We didn't get it right every day, but with intentionality, we created predetermined habits of choosing life and choosing to believe the best about each other. As we did, we grew together and experienced breakthrough.

---

* Tim and Joy Downs, *The Seven Conflicts: Resolving the Most Common Disagreements in Marriage* (Chicago: Moody Publishers, 2003), 62.

This Week's Scripture

I appeal to you, brothers and sisters, in the name of
our Lord Jesus Christ, that all of you agree with one another
in what you say and that there be no divisions among you,
but that you be perfectly united in mind and thought.

1 Corinthians 1:10

This Week's Application

- Change any me-first thoughts to we-first thoughts by reflecting on the following: Have we allowed any comparisons, judgments, or scoreboards in our marriage?

- This week, determine ways to express your love for your spouse. List ways you will defend them and do a better job of making them your partner.

- Whenever you are tempted to fight *with* each other instead of *for* each other, remember this week's Scripture. If you need to, post it where you will see it often.

This Week's Prayer

Father, we thank you for each other. Cause us to always fight for—not with—each other. What you've called us to is too important for us to waste time fighting over little offenses. Bless my spouse this week. Give my spouse strength. Fill my spouse with wisdom, power, and laughter every day.

Dare to
DREAM
Together

Dare to Dream Together

*A*t one time, the four-minute mile seemed impossible. And then Roger Bannister proved that wrong and ran it in 3 minutes 59.4 seconds. Today, what once seemed unattainable serves as the standard for all professional middle-distance runners.

As a couple, how do you need to dream together? What steps can you take to encourage each other to press on? How can the resistance you're facing actually make you stronger together? As couples, God invites us to dream together. Our combined belief powerfully impacts our outcome. So, what keeps us from dreaming?

Ask a healthy six-year-old child what they want to be when they grow up, and listen to their responses. Typically, their responses seem unlimited. They dream impossible dreams, believing anything is possible. We all begin with big dreams, but then those dreams encounter obstacles like "No," "You can't," or "You'll never …"

Truly, negative circumstances can condition and impact our results. But conditioning works both ways. Resistance conditions us and makes us stronger. If we condition our bodies physically and practice running against resistance, we condition our muscles and strengthen our endurance.

Likewise, Scripture encourages us to make ourselves new in the attitude of our minds (Ephesians 4:23)—to not conform to the patterns of the world, but to renew our minds. When we do that, we test and approve God's perfect will (Romans 12:2). When we dream together and ask Him to perfect His purpose in our relationship, He grants us our desires!

This Week's Scripture

"If two of you on earth agree about anything they ask for, it will
be done for them by my Father in heaven."

Matthew 18:19

This Week's Application

o   This week, pull out your vision from week twenty-eight. How
    can you expand your vision? What needs to be added?

o   Together, discuss what promise you think God is whispering
    that you need to believe for together.

o   Write out your week twenty-eight vision afresh. Then, as Mat-
    thew 18:19 encourages, ask God to fulfill His promises for
    your marriage.

This Week's Prayer

*Father, inspire us to dream together, to believe you for your prom-
ises, and to faithfully follow where you lead. Empower us to fulfill
your purpose for our marriage.*

Live
LIKE A
TOURIST

Live Like a Tourist

*O*kay. We have a confession to make. We live about a mile from the beach and a couple of hours from Disney World, and Alligator Alley is even closer. But there was a time when we went many weeks without visiting the beach. It took seven years for us to visit a local wildlife preserve. And we felt stuck in a rut of eating at the same restaurants week in and week out.

So when our dear friends Scott and Katherine shared their motto to "live like a tourist," we probed for more details. They revealed their philosophy: "We ask ourselves, 'If we visited our area as a tourist, what would we do? What would we see? And how would we spend our time?'"

As with everything in life, we are always looking for ways to develop new ways of thinking, to embrace God's higher way of living. We were all in! Since then, their questions have shaped our date nights, our adventures with the kids, and our visits to the beach.

Living like a tourist added variety, discovery, and lots of laughter to our marriage. So how about it? What local attractions would you visit as a tourist in your area? How would you enjoy your surroundings? How can you live like a tourist?

This Week's Scripture

Great are the works of the Lord;
they are pondered by all who delight in them.

PSALM 111:2

This Week's Application

○ Choose three to five local attractions, sites to see, places to visit, and fun things to do, then add them to your calendar.

○ The next time you decide to go out to eat, pick a restaurant where you've never eaten before.

○ Answer this question: How can we better welcome variety and live like tourists right where we live? Think through this together.

This Week's Prayer

Father, thank you for the beauty of this world. Remind us to discover and delight in your works, right where we live. Spur us on to be mindful of all the blessings surrounding us every day.

CHANGE YOUR *How* TO *Who*

Change Your *How* to *Who*

S everal years ago, God whispered a huge promise to us. At first it seemed exciting. Our minds filled with endless possibilities. But it didn't take long for doubt to creep in. Real questions of *how* rampaged our exhilaration. Our mind shifted from *wow* to *how*.

In the midst of our struggle, we realized we'd shifted from celebrating God's promise to solving problems. The more we focused on the problems and the obstacles, the more the promise seemed impossible. Amid our problem-solving mode, God interjected His thoughts: *Change your* how *to* who.

Mary the mother of Jesus understood this when the angel appeared to her as a young virgin and told her of the promise to come. Mary didn't get lost in all the details. Oh, she did ask her own *how* question when she said, "How will this be … since I am a virgin?" (Luke 1:34). But Mary didn't linger in the *how* for long. With a little encouragement from an angel, she quickly moved beyond her own human limitations and looked to God's ability.

As you consider God's promise for your marriage, it may seem impossible. You may question how—just like us and just like Mary. Today, consider the *hows* in your marriage that need to be changed to *who*.

This Week's Scripture

For no word from God will ever fail.

Luke 1:37

This Week's Application

- ° Ask each other: What limitations or impossibilities are between us and the complete joy of living God's purpose for our marriage?

- ° On your refrigerator, post one thing you will both pray about and believe God for this week. Send up a prayer each time you see it.

- ° At the end of each day, pray together for your needs and thank God that nothing is impossible for Him.

This Week's Prayer

Father, we pause to acknowledge that we are yours. Help us to know your intent toward us is good. You are the God of possibilities. Enable us to believe beyond our own capabilities and trust your abilities for more. Thank you for your promises.

About the Authors

Join Greg and Julie at
MarriedForAPurpose.com
to discover other valuable resources
for your life and marriage.

———————

For daily inspiration, follow them at
Facebook.com/marriedforapurpose.

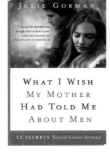

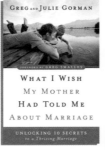

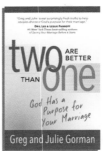